agents of S.L.A.M.

ONI PRESS

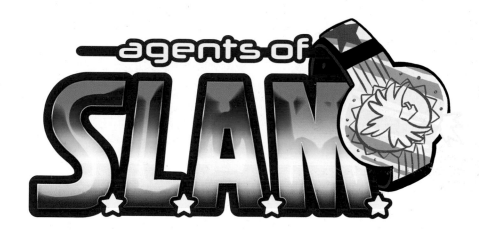

AN ONI PRESS PUBLICATION

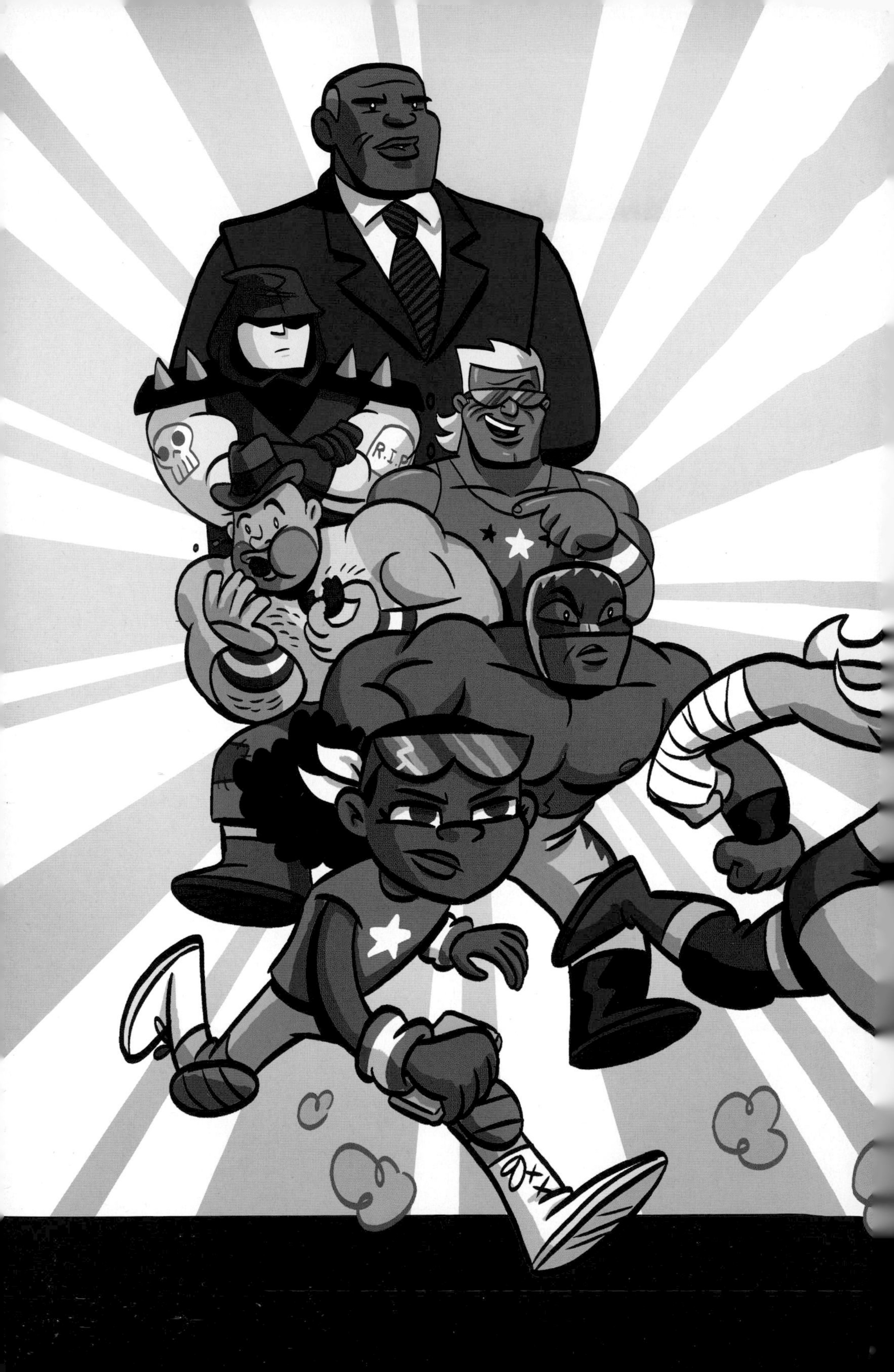
R.I.P

agents of S.L.A.M.

Created by

DAVE SCHEIDT & SCOOT MCMAHON

Writer   Writer/Artist

Colored by

HEIDI BLACK

Edited by
ANDREA COLVIN and GRACE SCHEIPETER

Designed by
SARAH ROCKWELL

Consulting Reader
JASMINE WALLS

PUBLISHED BY ONI-LION FORGE PUBLISHING GROUP, LLC.
James Lucas Jones, president & publisher • Charlie Chu, e.v.p. of creative
& business development • Steve Ellis, s.v.p. of games & operations
Alex Segura, s.v.p of marketing & sales • Michelle Nguyen, associate
publisher • Brad Rooks, director of operations • Amber O'Neill, special
projects manager • Margot Wood, director of marketing & sales • Katie
Sainz, marketing manager • Henry Barajas, sales manager • Tara Lehmann,
publicist • Holly Aitchison, consumer marketing manager • Troy Look,
director of design & production • Angie Knowles, production manager
Kate Z. Stone, senior graphic designer • Carey Hall, graphic designer
Sarah Rockwell, graphic designer • Hilary Thompson, graphic designer
Vincent Kukua, digital prepress technician • Chris Cerasi, managing
editor • Jasmine Amiri, senior editor • Shawna Gore, senior editor
Amanda Meadows, senior editor • Robert Meyers, senior editor, licensing
Desiree Rodriguez, editor • Grace Scheipeter, editor • Zack Soto, editor
Ben Eisner, game developer • Jung Lee, logistics coordinator • Kuian
Kellum, warehouse assistant • **Joe Nozemack, publisher emeritus**

ONIPRESS.COM

@DAVESCHEIDT
@SCOOTCOMICS
@ELECTRICABYSS

FIRST EDITION: APRIL 2022

ISBN: 978-1-63715-022-1
EISBN: 978-1-63715-031-3

LIBRARY OF CONGRESS CONTROL NUMBER: 2021942394

1 2 3 4 5 6 7 8 9 10
PRINTED IN CHINA.

★★★ CHAPTER
1

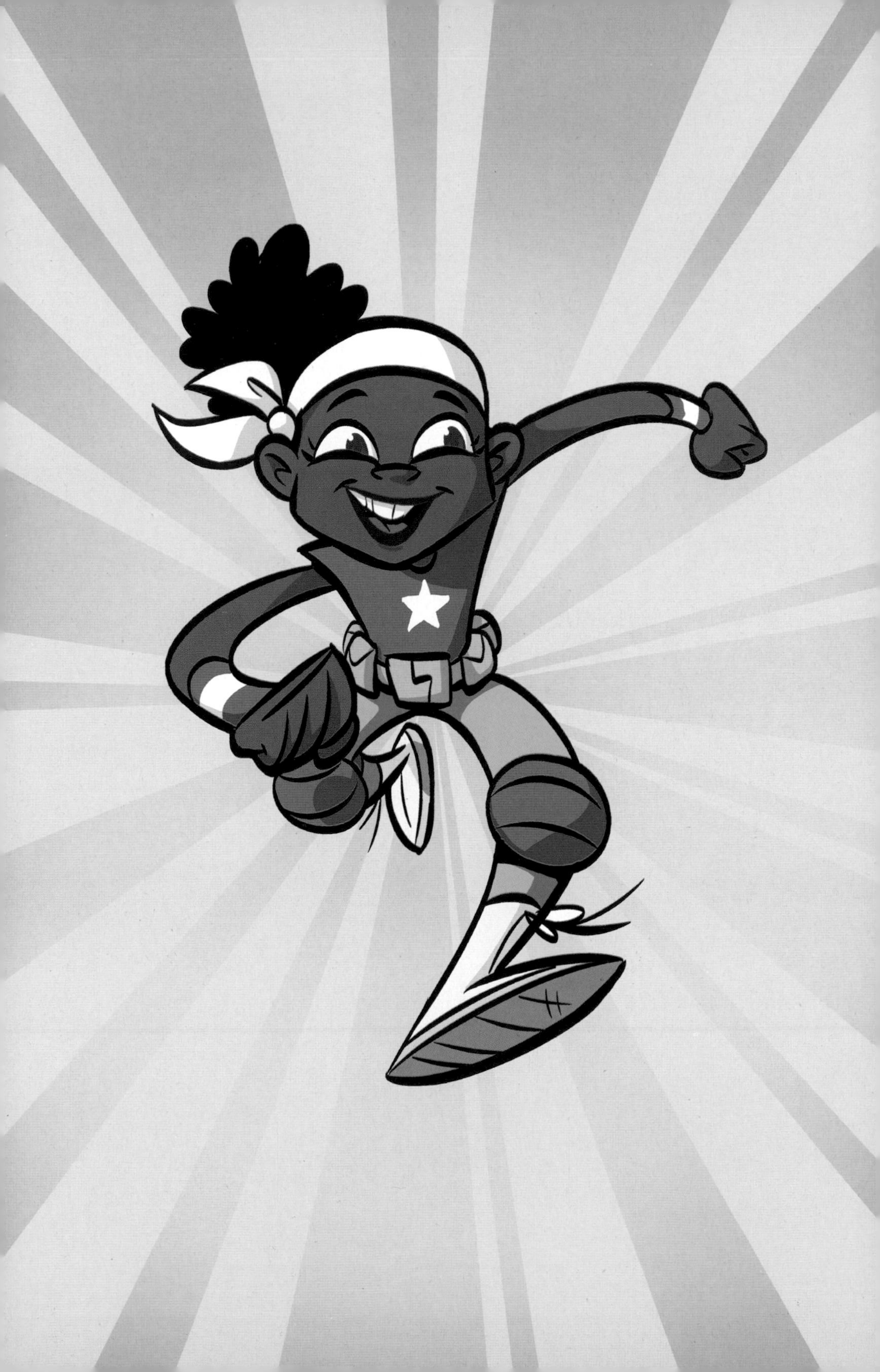

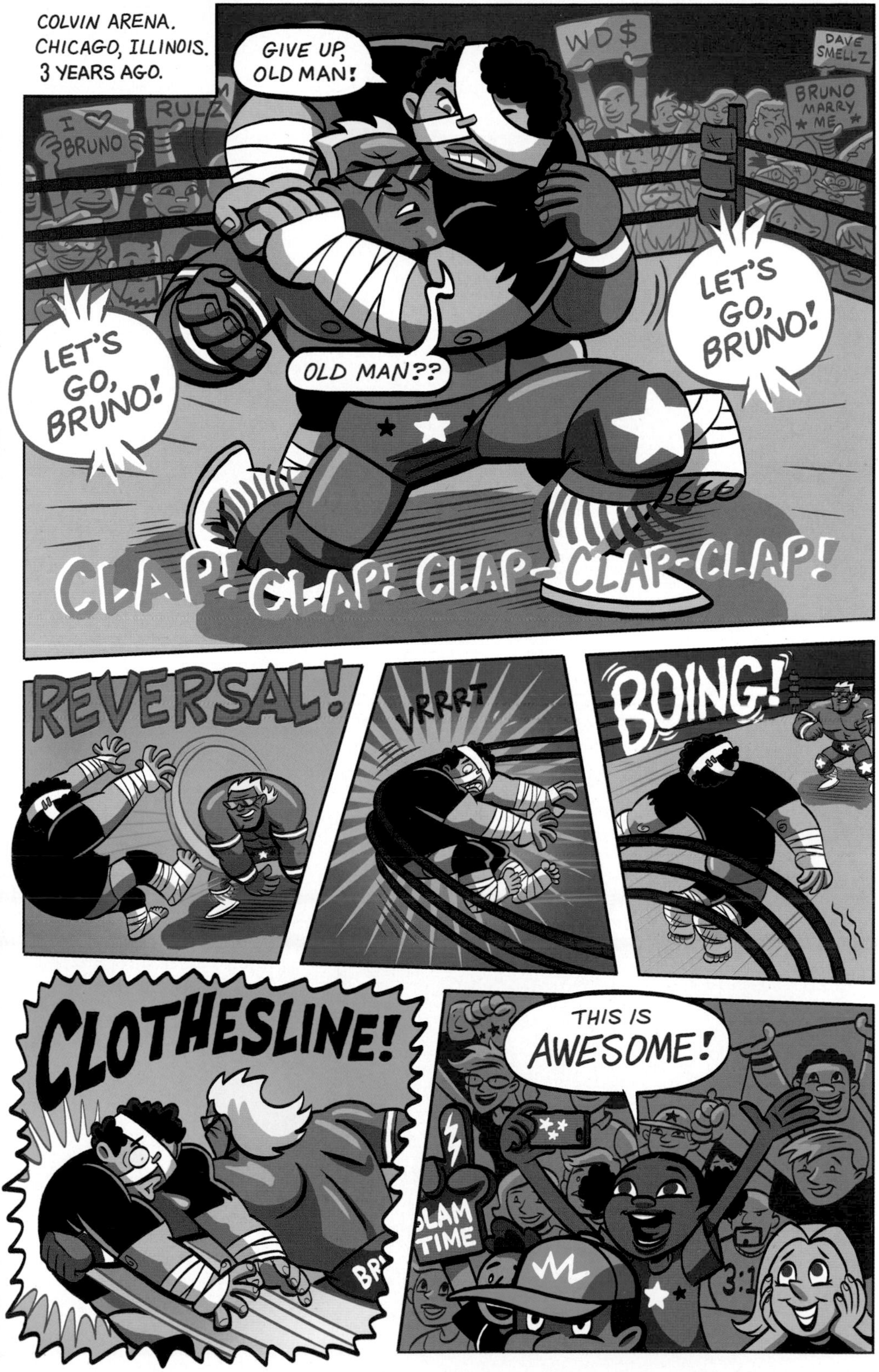
COLVIN ARENA.
CHICAGO, ILLINOIS.
3 YEARS AGO.
GIVE UP, OLD MAN!
WD$
DAVE SMELLZ
BRUNO MARRY ME
I ♥ BRUNO
RULZ
LET'S GO, BRUNO!
OLD MAN??
LET'S GO, BRUNO!
CLAP! CLAP! CLAP-CLAP-CLAP!
REVERSAL!
VRRRT
BOING!
CLOTHESLINE!
THIS IS AWESOME!
SLAM TIME

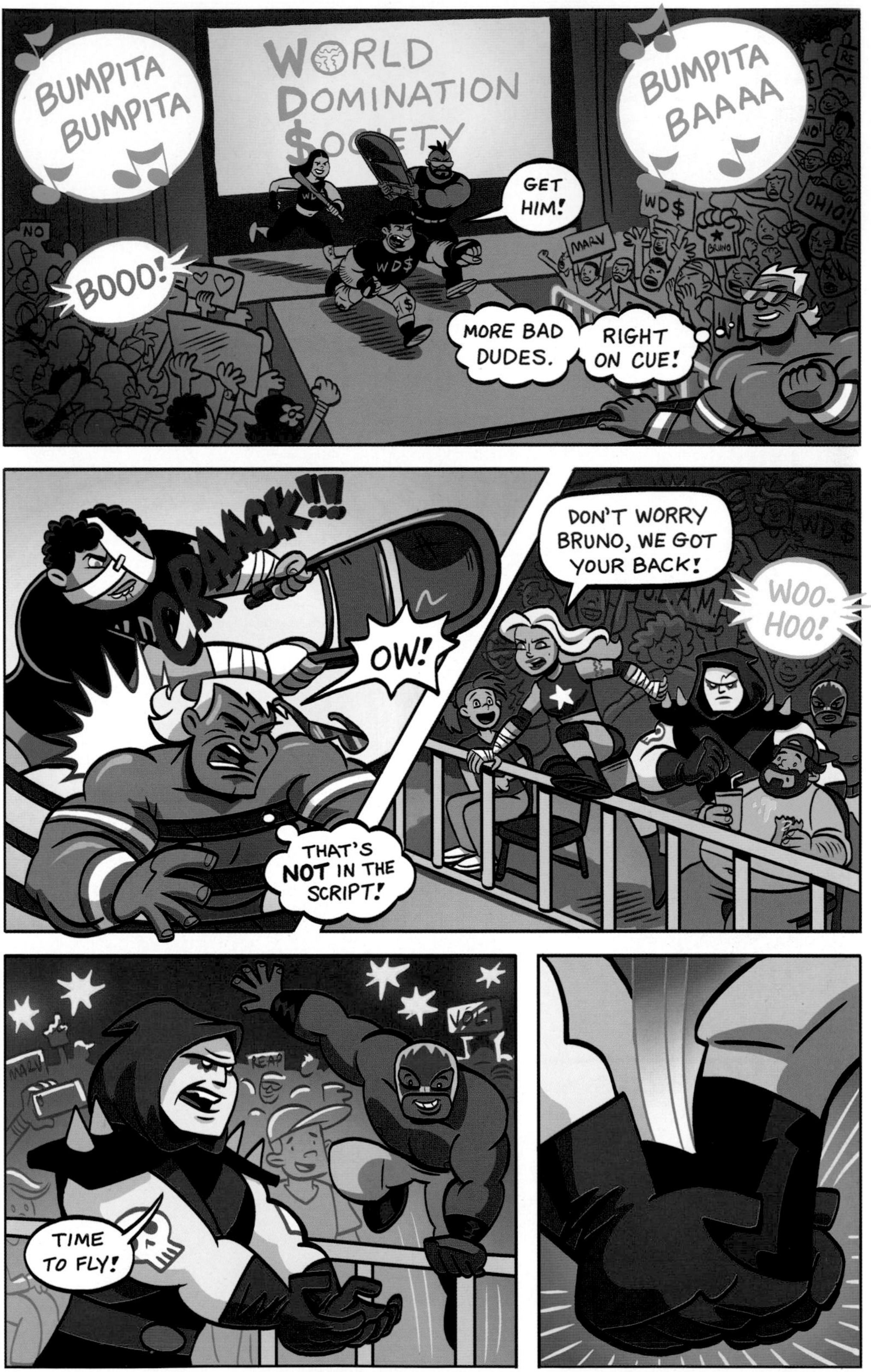
WORLD DOMINATION $OCIETY
BUMPITA BUMPITA
BUMPITA BAAAA
GET HIM!
BOOO!
MORE BAD DUDES.
RIGHT ON CUE!
CRAACK!!!
OW!
THAT'S NOT IN THE SCRIPT!
DON'T WORRY BRUNO, WE GOT YOUR BACK!
WOO-HOO!
TIME TO FLY!

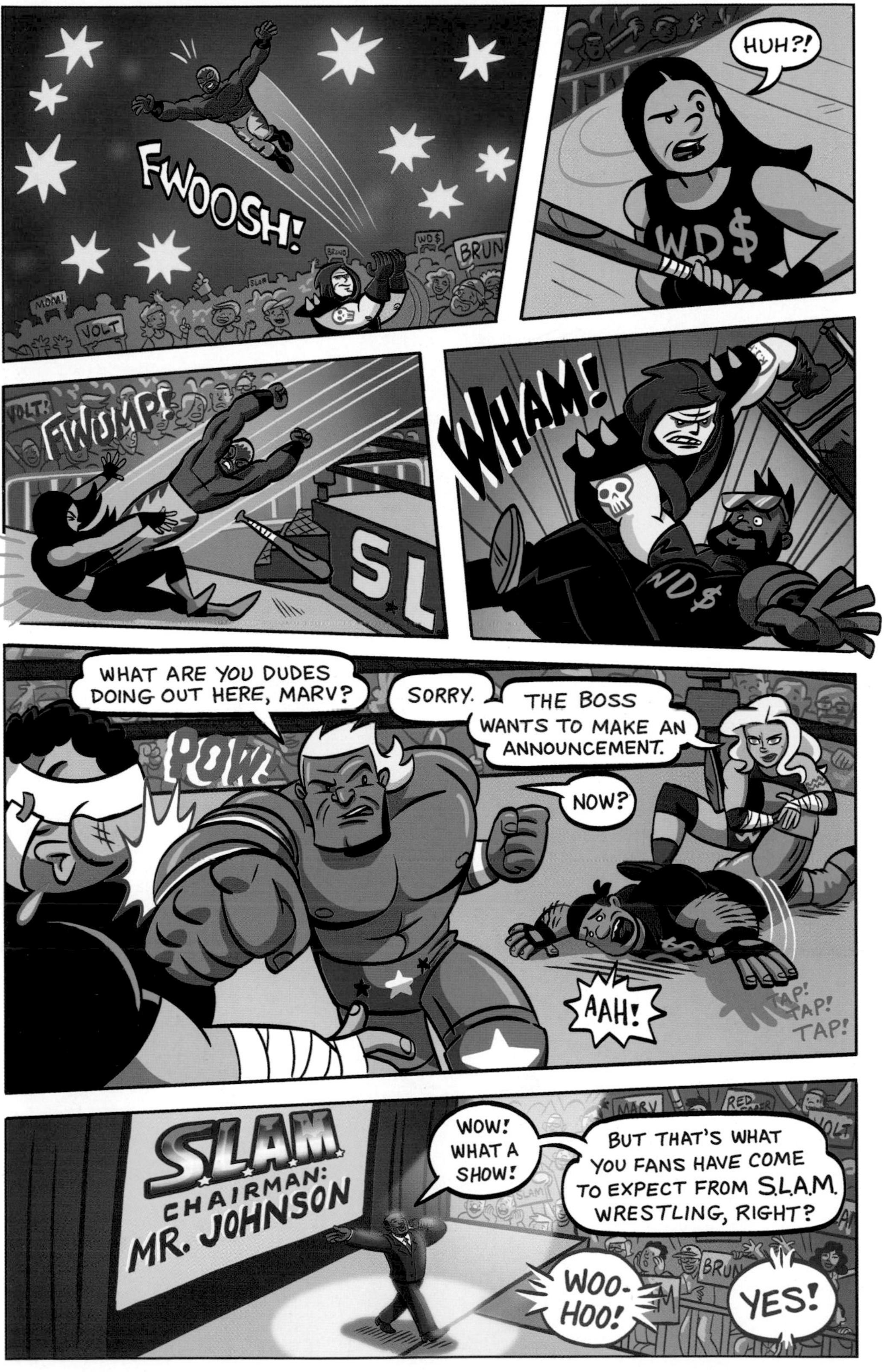
FWOOSH!
MOM!
VOLT
SLAM
WD$
BRUN
HUH?!
WD$
VOLT!
FWUMP!
SL
WHAM!
WD$
WHAT ARE YOU DUDES DOING OUT HERE, MARV?
POW!
SORRY.
THE BOSS WANTS TO MAKE AN ANNOUNCEMENT.
NOW?
AAH!
TAP! TAP! TAP!
S.L.A.M.
CHAIRMAN: MR. JOHNSON
WOW! WHAT A SHOW!
BUT THAT'S WHAT YOU FANS HAVE COME TO EXPECT FROM S.L.A.M. WRESTLING, RIGHT?
MARV
VOLT
WOO-HOO!
YES!

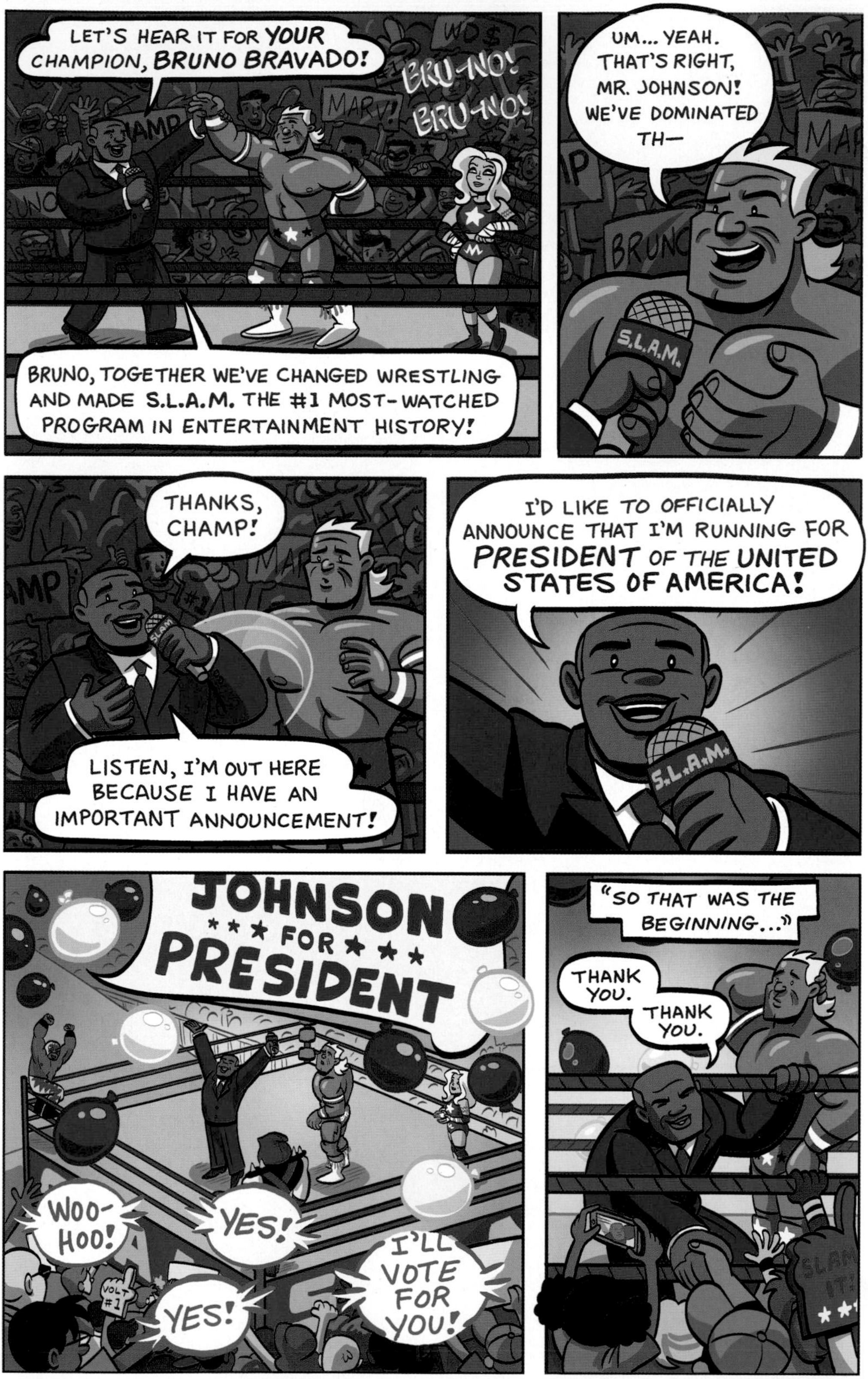
LET'S HEAR IT FOR YOUR CHAMPION, BRUNO BRAVADO!
BRU-NO! BRU-NO!
BRUNO, TOGETHER WE'VE CHANGED WRESTLING AND MADE S.L.A.M. THE #1 MOST-WATCHED PROGRAM IN ENTERTAINMENT HISTORY!
UM... YEAH. THAT'S RIGHT, MR. JOHNSON! WE'VE DOMINATED TH—
S.L.A.M.
THANKS, CHAMP!
LISTEN, I'M OUT HERE BECAUSE I HAVE AN IMPORTANT ANNOUNCEMENT!
I'D LIKE TO OFFICIALLY ANNOUNCE THAT I'M RUNNING FOR PRESIDENT OF THE UNITED STATES OF AMERICA!
S.L.A.M.
JOHNSON FOR PRESIDENT
WOO-HOO!
YES!
YES!
I'LL VOTE FOR YOU!
"SO THAT WAS THE BEGINNING..."
THANK YOU.
THANK YOU.

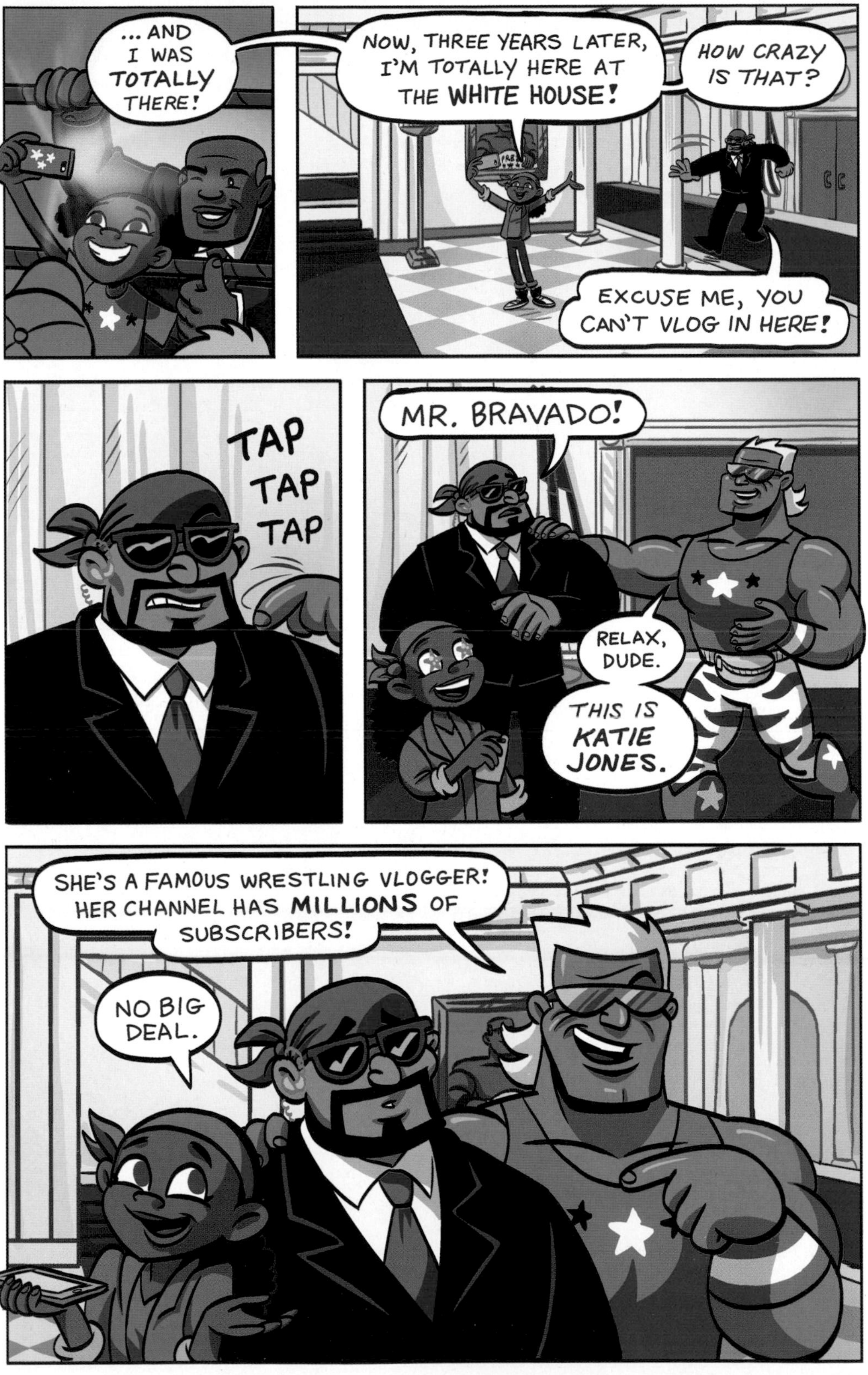
... AND I WAS TOTALLY THERE!
NOW, THREE YEARS LATER, I'M TOTALLY HERE AT THE WHITE HOUSE!
HOW CRAZY IS THAT?
EXCUSE ME, YOU CAN'T VLOG IN HERE!
TAP TAP TAP
MR. BRAVADO!
RELAX, DUDE.
THIS IS KATIE JONES.
SHE'S A FAMOUS WRESTLING VLOGGER! HER CHANNEL HAS MILLIONS OF SUBSCRIBERS!
NO BIG DEAL.

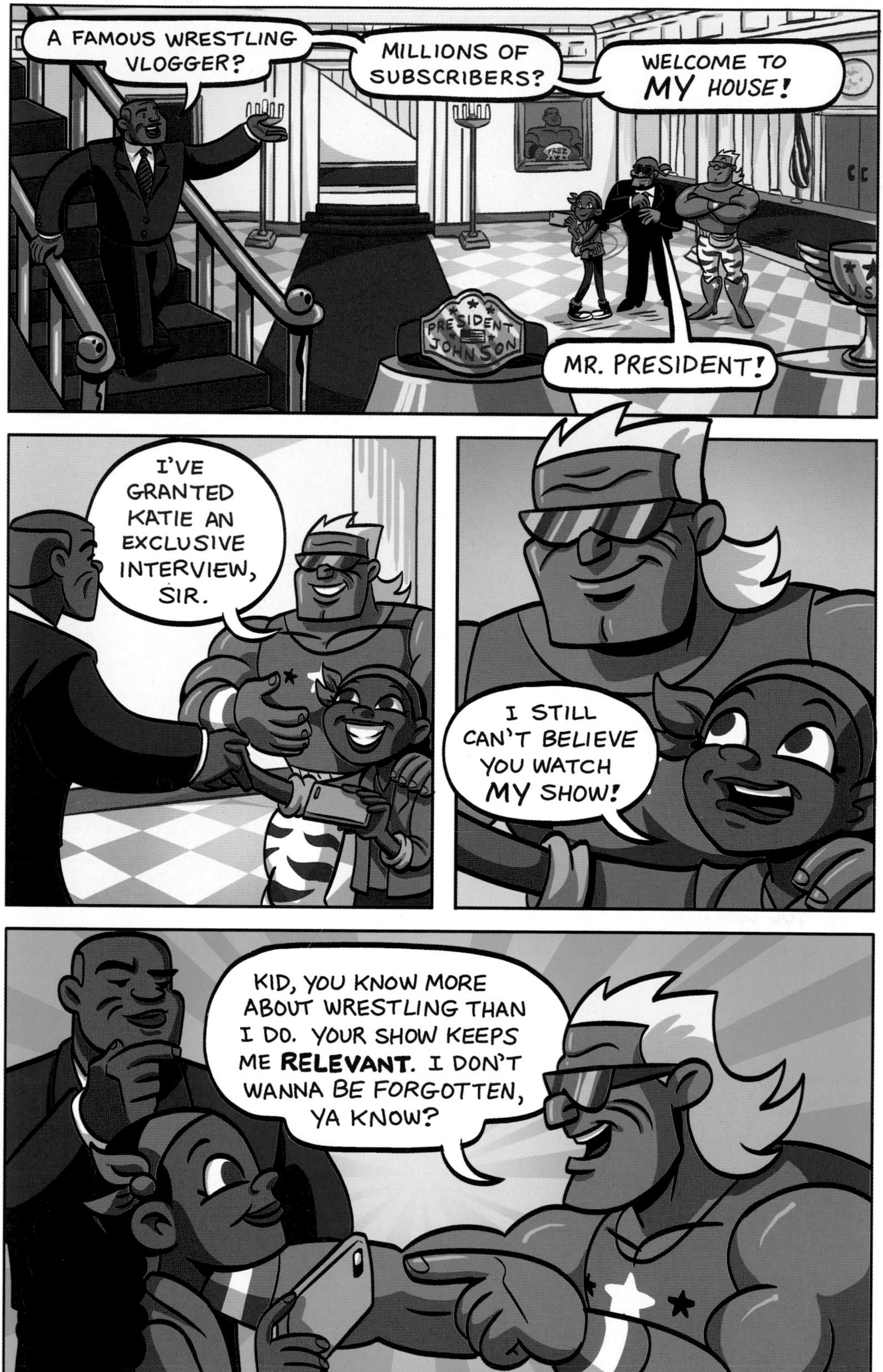
A FAMOUS WRESTLING VLOGGER?
MILLIONS OF SUBSCRIBERS?
WELCOME TO MY HOUSE!
MR. PRESIDENT!
PRESIDENT JOHNSON
I'VE GRANTED KATIE AN EXCLUSIVE INTERVIEW, SIR.
I STILL CAN'T BELIEVE YOU WATCH MY SHOW!
KID, YOU KNOW MORE ABOUT WRESTLING THAN I DO. YOUR SHOW KEEPS ME RELEVANT. I DON'T WANNA BE FORGOTTEN, YA KNOW?

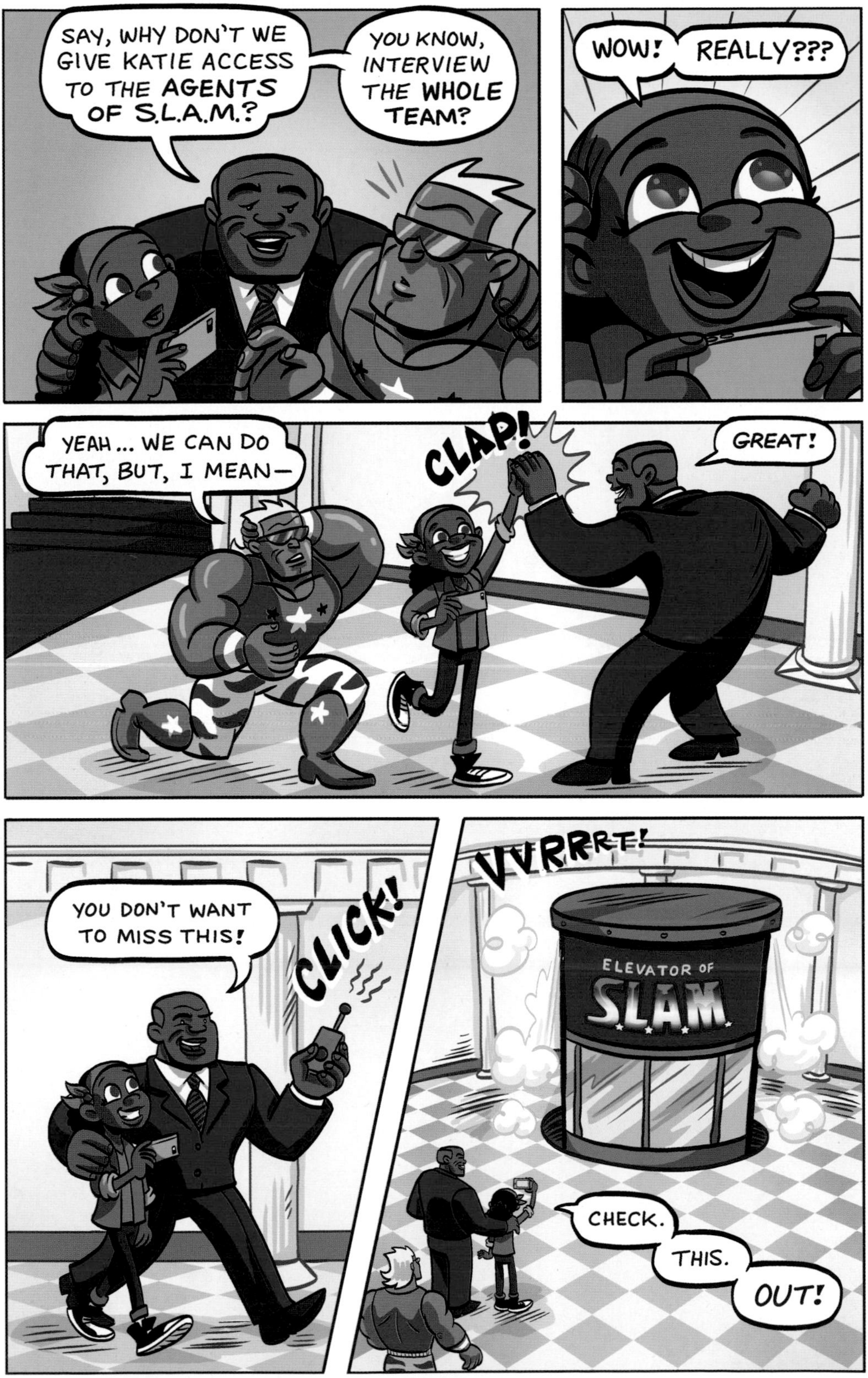
SAY, WHY DON'T WE GIVE KATIE ACCESS TO THE AGENTS OF S.L.A.M.?
YOU KNOW, INTERVIEW THE WHOLE TEAM?
WOW!
REALLY???
YEAH... WE CAN DO THAT, BUT, I MEAN—
CLAP!
GREAT!
YOU DON'T WANT TO MISS THIS!
CLICK!
VVRRRRT!
ELEVATOR OF SLAM
CHECK.
THIS.
OUT!

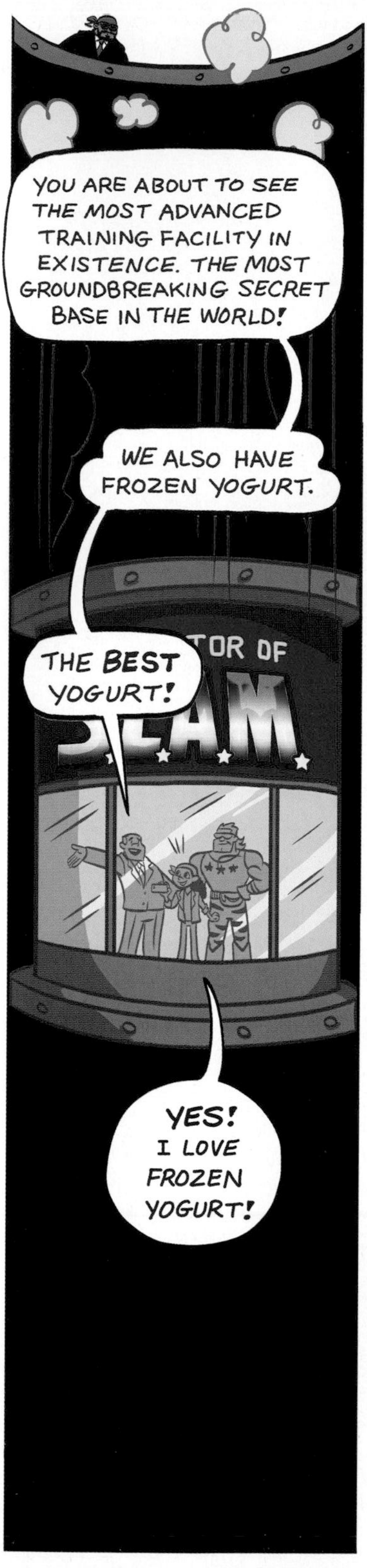
YOU ARE ABOUT TO SEE THE MOST ADVANCED TRAINING FACILITY IN EXISTENCE. THE MOST GROUNDBREAKING SECRET BASE IN THE WORLD!
WE ALSO HAVE FROZEN YOGURT.
THE BEST YOGURT!
YES! I LOVE FROZEN YOGURT!

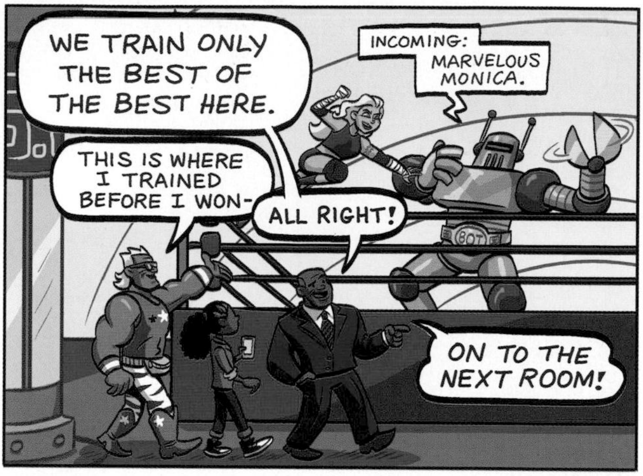
WE TRAIN ONLY THE BEST OF THE BEST HERE.
INCOMING: MARVELOUS MONICA.
THIS IS WHERE I TRAINED BEFORE I WON-
ALL RIGHT!
BOT
ON TO THE NEXT ROOM!

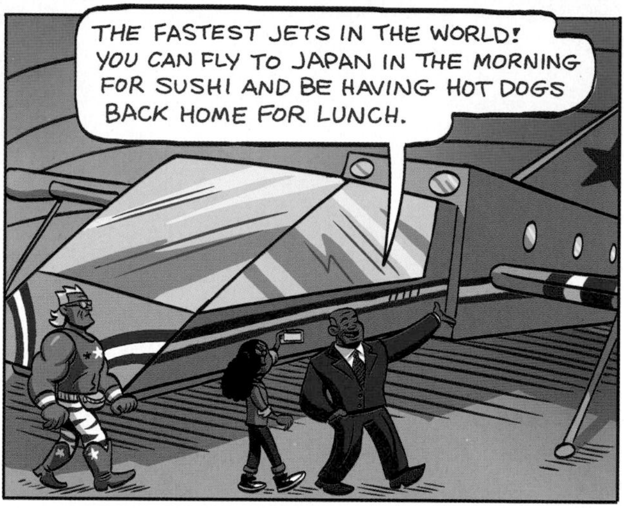
THE FASTEST JETS IN THE WORLD! YOU CAN FLY TO JAPAN IN THE MORNING FOR SUSHI AND BE HAVING HOT DOGS BACK HOME FOR LUNCH.

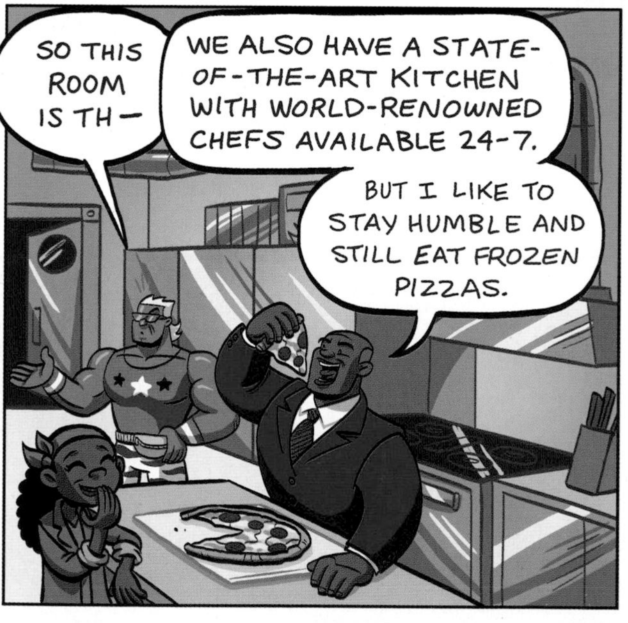
SO THIS ROOM IS TH—
WE ALSO HAVE A STATE-OF-THE-ART KITCHEN WITH WORLD-RENOWNED CHEFS AVAILABLE 24-7.
BUT I LIKE TO STAY HUMBLE AND STILL EAT FROZEN PIZZAS.

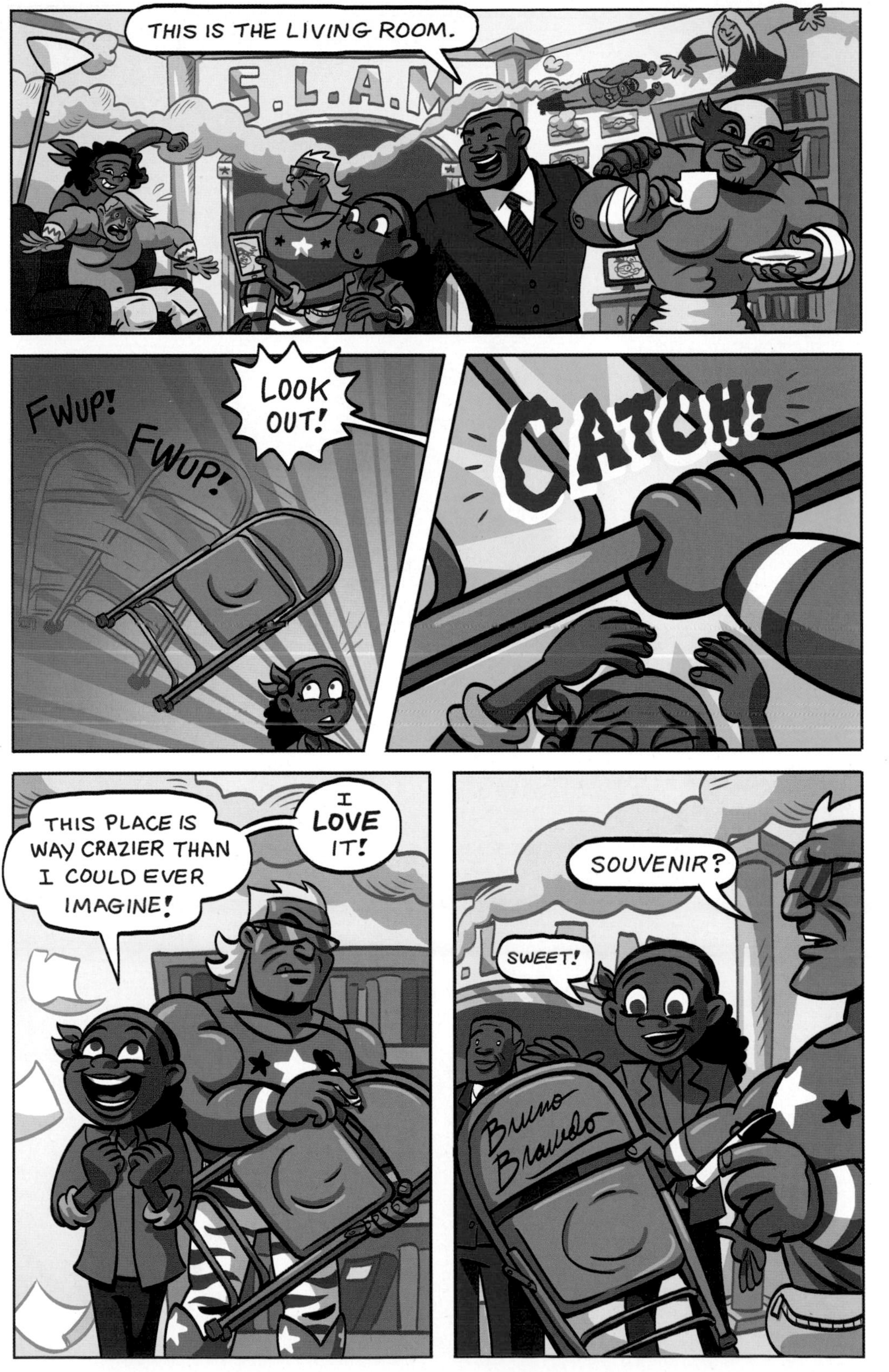
THIS IS THE LIVING ROOM.
S.L.A.M
FWUP!
FWUP!
LOOK OUT!
CATCH!
THIS PLACE IS WAY CRAZIER THAN I COULD EVER IMAGINE!
I LOVE IT!
SOUVENIR?
SWEET!
Bruno Bravado

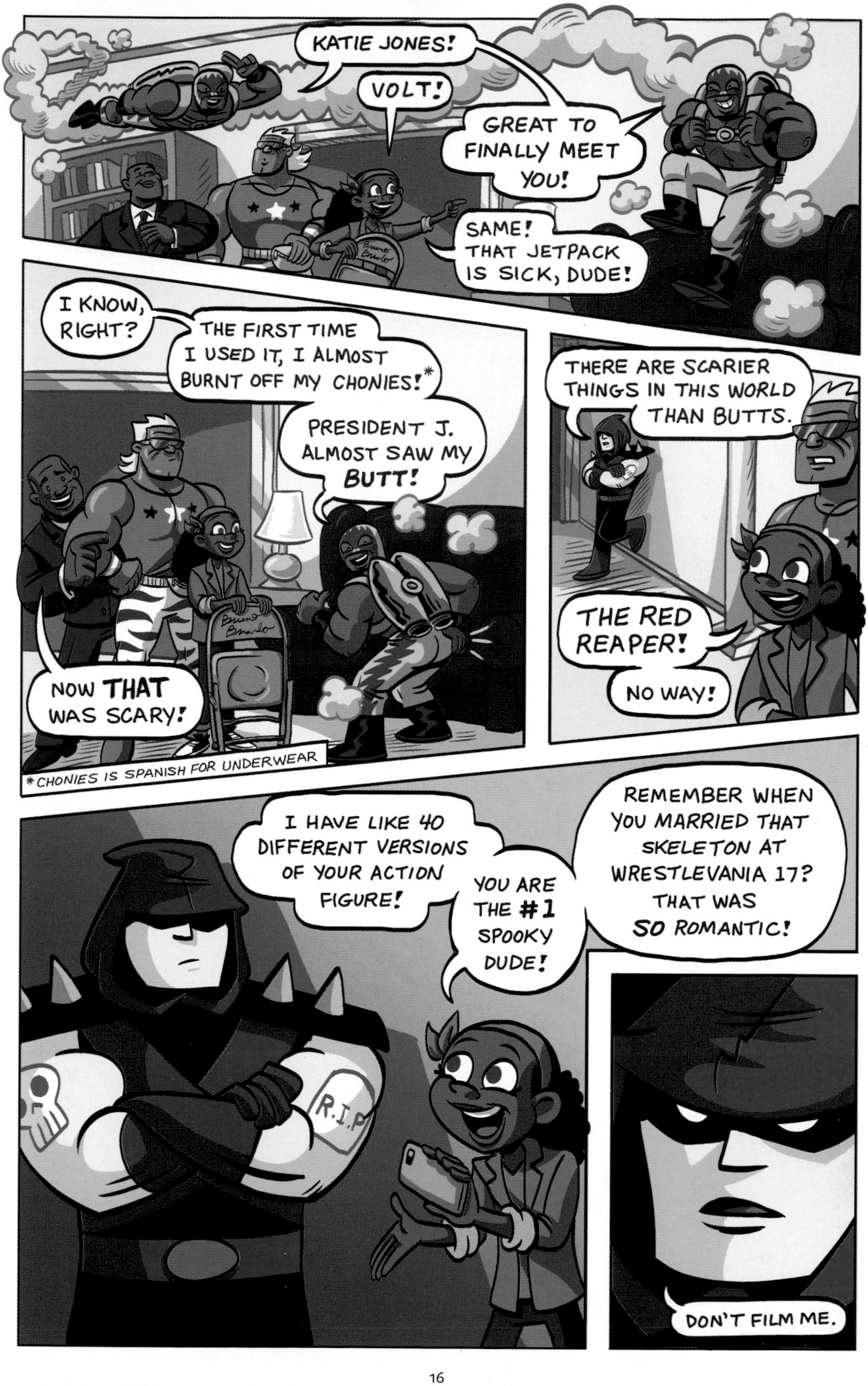
KATIE JONES!
VOLT!
GREAT TO FINALLY MEET YOU!
SAME! THAT JETPACK IS SICK, DUDE!
I KNOW, RIGHT?
THE FIRST TIME I USED IT, I ALMOST BURNT OFF MY CHONIES!*
PRESIDENT J. ALMOST SAW MY BUTT!
NOW THAT WAS SCARY!
*CHONIES IS SPANISH FOR UNDERWEAR
THERE ARE SCARIER THINGS IN THIS WORLD THAN BUTTS.
THE RED REAPER!
NO WAY!
I HAVE LIKE 40 DIFFERENT VERSIONS OF YOUR ACTION FIGURE!
YOU ARE THE #1 SPOOKY DUDE!
REMEMBER WHEN YOU MARRIED THAT SKELETON AT WRESTLEVANIA 17? THAT WAS SO ROMANTIC!
R.I.P
DON'T FILM ME.

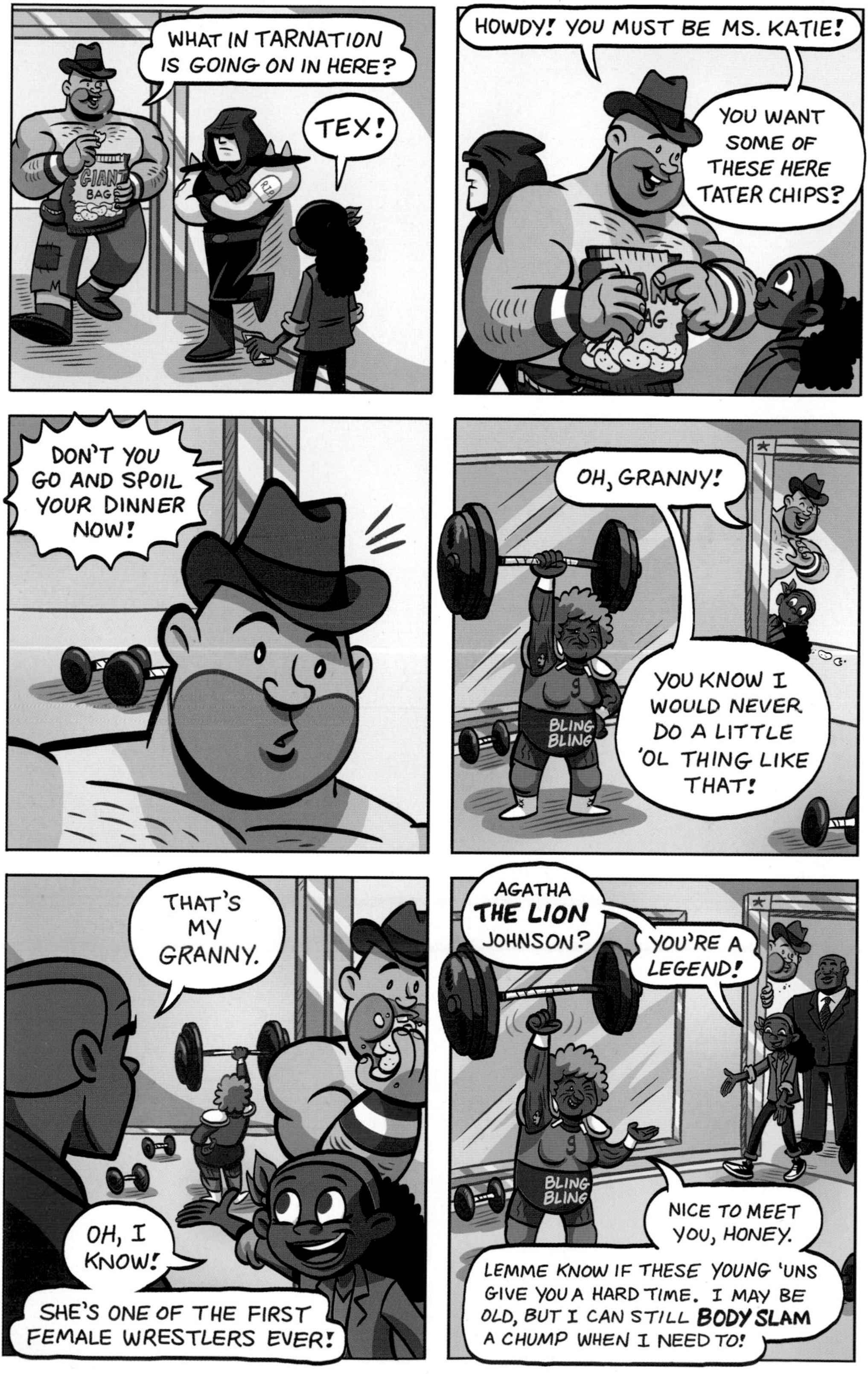
WHAT IN TARNATION IS GOING ON IN HERE?
TEX!
GIANT BAG
R.I.P.
HOWDY! YOU MUST BE MS. KATIE!
YOU WANT SOME OF THESE HERE TATER CHIPS?
DON'T YOU GO AND SPOIL YOUR DINNER NOW!
OH, GRANNY!
YOU KNOW I WOULD NEVER DO A LITTLE 'OL THING LIKE THAT!
BLING BLING
THAT'S MY GRANNY.
OH, I KNOW!
SHE'S ONE OF THE FIRST FEMALE WRESTLERS EVER!
AGATHA **THE LION** JOHNSON?
YOU'RE A LEGEND!
BLING BLING
NICE TO MEET YOU, HONEY.
LEMME KNOW IF THESE YOUNG 'UNS GIVE YOU A HARD TIME. I MAY BE OLD, BUT I CAN STILL **BODY SLAM** A CHUMP WHEN I NEED TO!

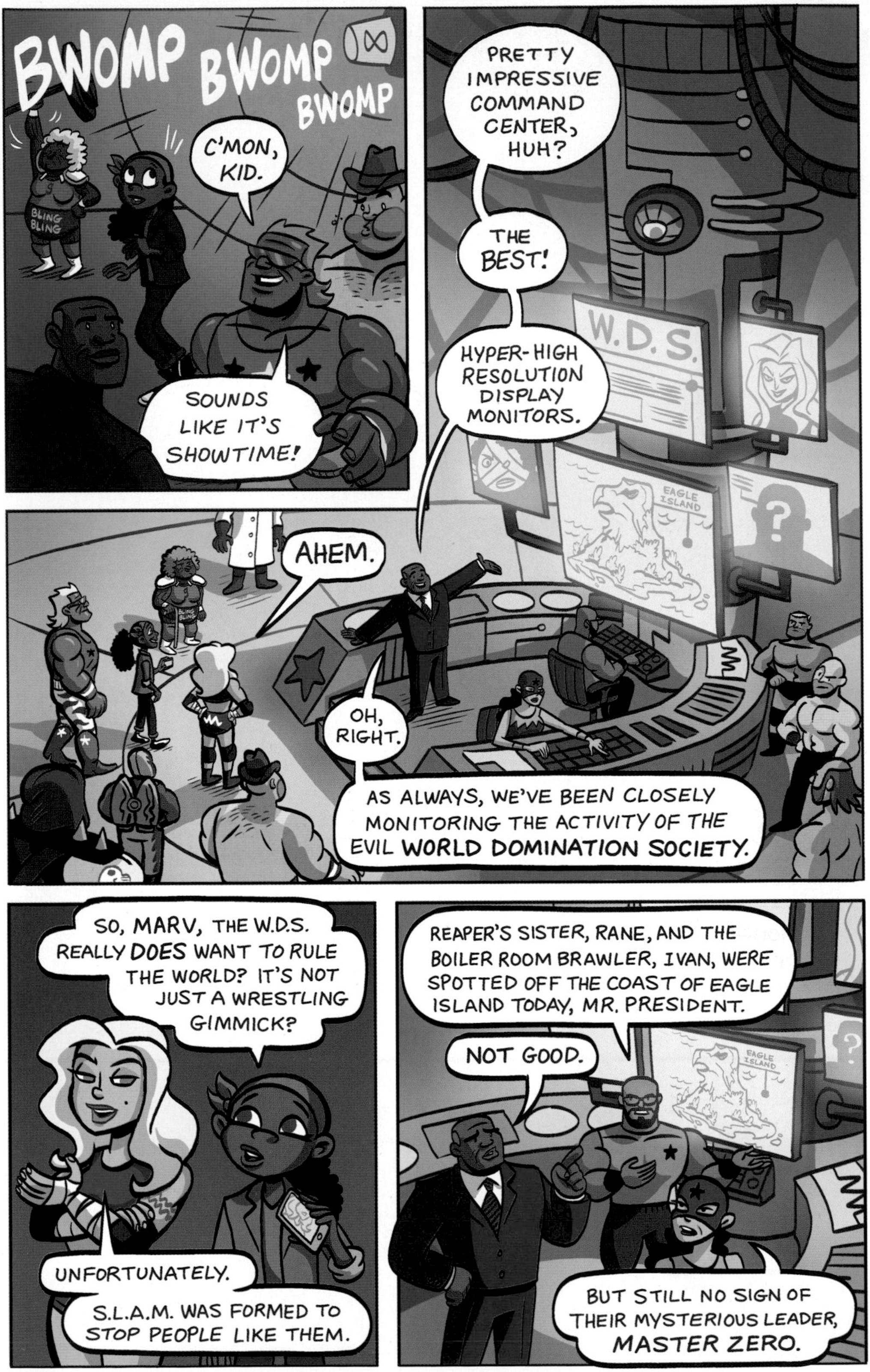

BWOMP BWOMP BWOMP
BLING BLING
C'MON, KID.
SOUNDS LIKE IT'S SHOWTIME!
PRETTY IMPRESSIVE COMMAND CENTER, HUH?
THE BEST!
HYPER-HIGH RESOLUTION DISPLAY MONITORS.
W.D.S.
EAGLE ISLAND
AHEM.
BLING BLING
OH, RIGHT.
AS ALWAYS, WE'VE BEEN CLOSELY MONITORING THE ACTIVITY OF THE EVIL WORLD DOMINATION SOCIETY.
SO, MARV, THE W.D.S. REALLY DOES WANT TO RULE THE WORLD? IT'S NOT JUST A WRESTLING GIMMICK?
UNFORTUNATELY.
S.L.A.M. WAS FORMED TO STOP PEOPLE LIKE THEM.
REAPER'S SISTER, RANE, AND THE BOILER ROOM BRAWLER, IVAN, WERE SPOTTED OFF THE COAST OF EAGLE ISLAND TODAY, MR. PRESIDENT.
NOT GOOD.
EAGLE ISLAND
BUT STILL NO SIGN OF THEIR MYSTERIOUS LEADER, MASTER ZERO.

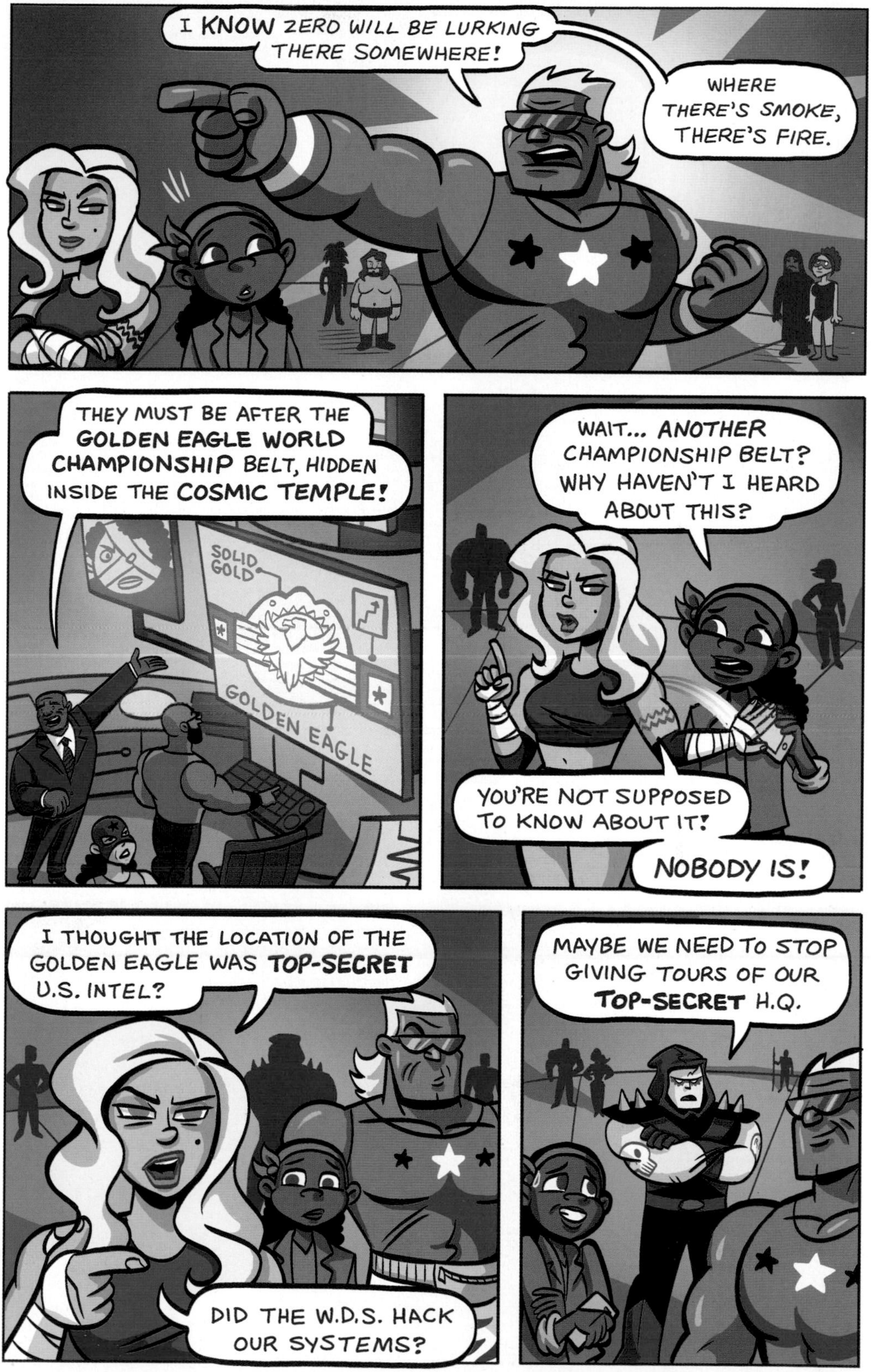
I KNOW ZERO WILL BE LURKING THERE SOMEWHERE!
WHERE THERE'S SMOKE, THERE'S FIRE.
THEY MUST BE AFTER THE GOLDEN EAGLE WORLD CHAMPIONSHIP BELT, HIDDEN INSIDE THE COSMIC TEMPLE!
SOLID GOLD
GOLDEN EAGLE
WAIT... ANOTHER CHAMPIONSHIP BELT? WHY HAVEN'T I HEARD ABOUT THIS?
YOU'RE NOT SUPPOSED TO KNOW ABOUT IT!
NOBODY IS!
I THOUGHT THE LOCATION OF THE GOLDEN EAGLE WAS TOP-SECRET U.S. INTEL?
DID THE W.D.S. HACK OUR SYSTEMS?
MAYBE WE NEED TO STOP GIVING TOURS OF OUR TOP-SECRET H.Q.

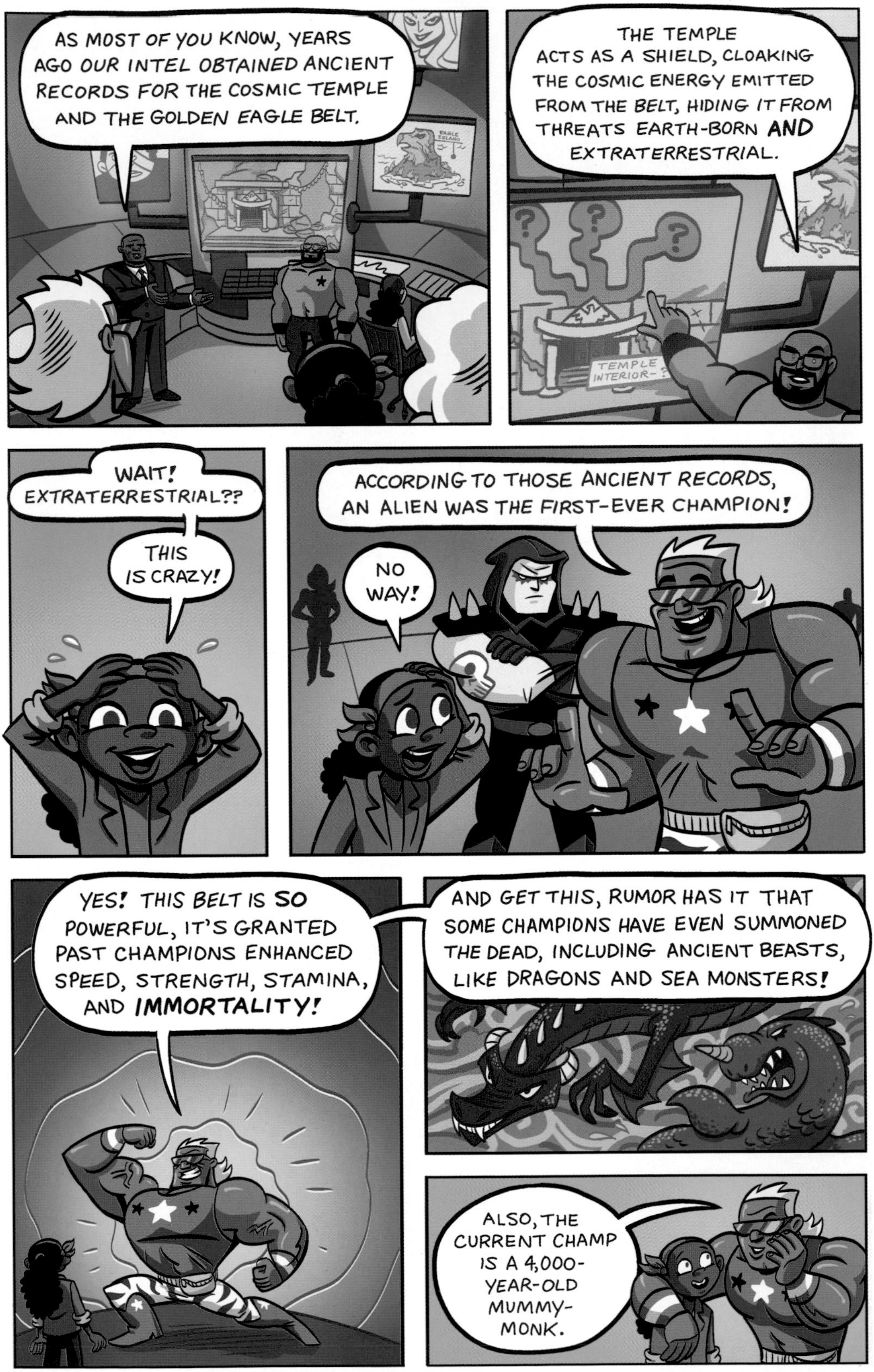
AS MOST OF YOU KNOW, YEARS AGO OUR INTEL OBTAINED ANCIENT RECORDS FOR THE COSMIC TEMPLE AND THE GOLDEN EAGLE BELT.
EAGLE ISLAND
THE TEMPLE ACTS AS A SHIELD, CLOAKING THE COSMIC ENERGY EMITTED FROM THE BELT, HIDING IT FROM THREATS EARTH-BORN **AND** EXTRATERRESTRIAL.
TEMPLE INTERIOR-?
WAIT! EXTRATERRESTRIAL??
THIS IS CRAZY!
ACCORDING TO THOSE ANCIENT RECORDS, AN ALIEN WAS THE FIRST-EVER CHAMPION!
NO WAY!
YES! THIS BELT IS **SO** POWERFUL, IT'S GRANTED PAST CHAMPIONS ENHANCED SPEED, STRENGTH, STAMINA, AND **IMMORTALITY!**
AND GET THIS, RUMOR HAS IT THAT SOME CHAMPIONS HAVE EVEN SUMMONED THE DEAD, INCLUDING ANCIENT BEASTS, LIKE DRAGONS AND SEA MONSTERS!
ALSO, THE CURRENT CHAMP IS A 4,000-YEAR-OLD MUMMY-MONK.

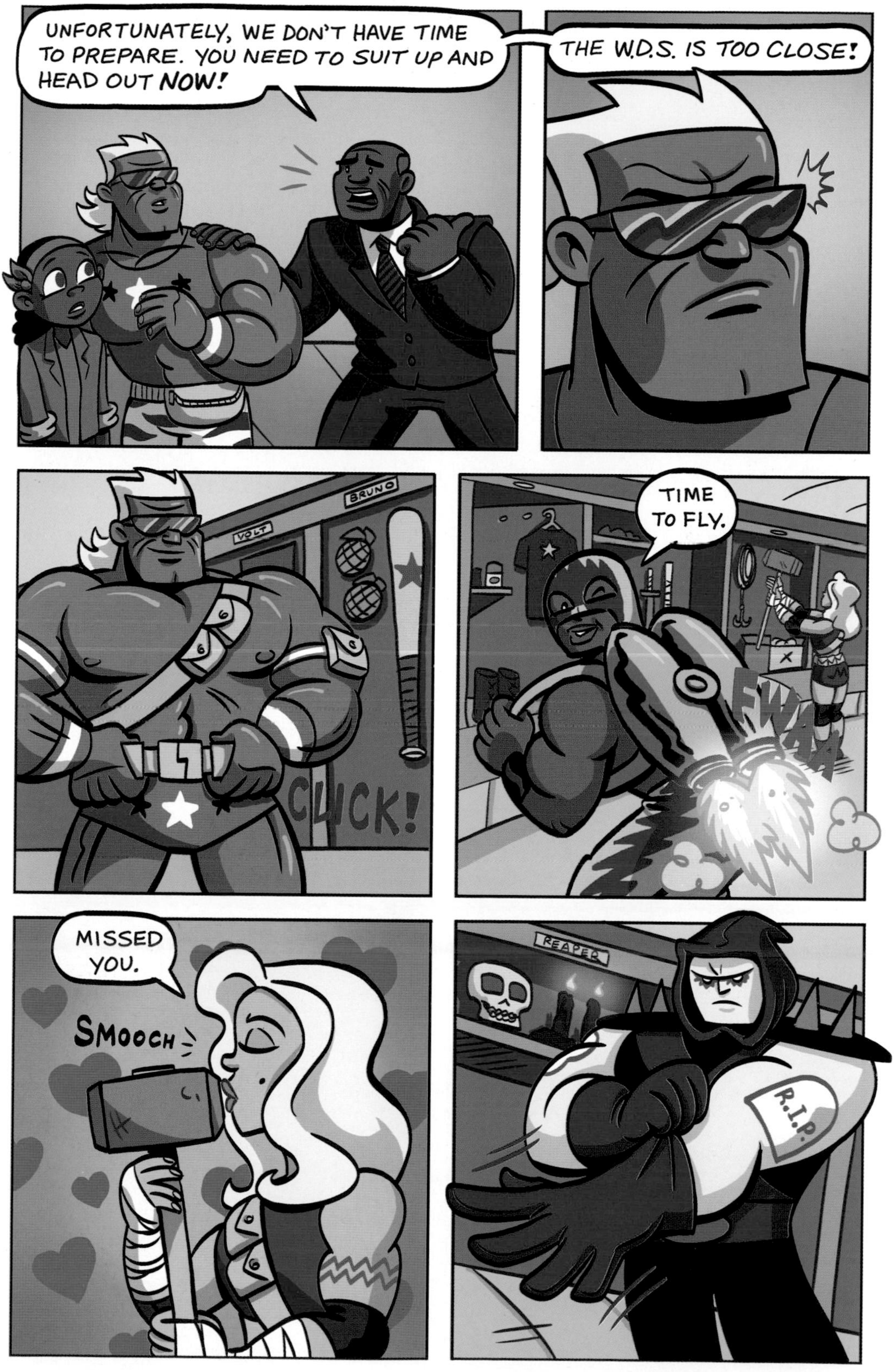
UNFORTUNATELY, WE DON'T HAVE TIME TO PREPARE. YOU NEED TO SUIT UP AND HEAD OUT NOW!
THE W.D.S. IS TOO CLOSE!
BRUNO
VOLT
CLICK!
TIME TO FLY.
FWAA
MISSED YOU.
SMOOCH
REAPER
R.I.P.

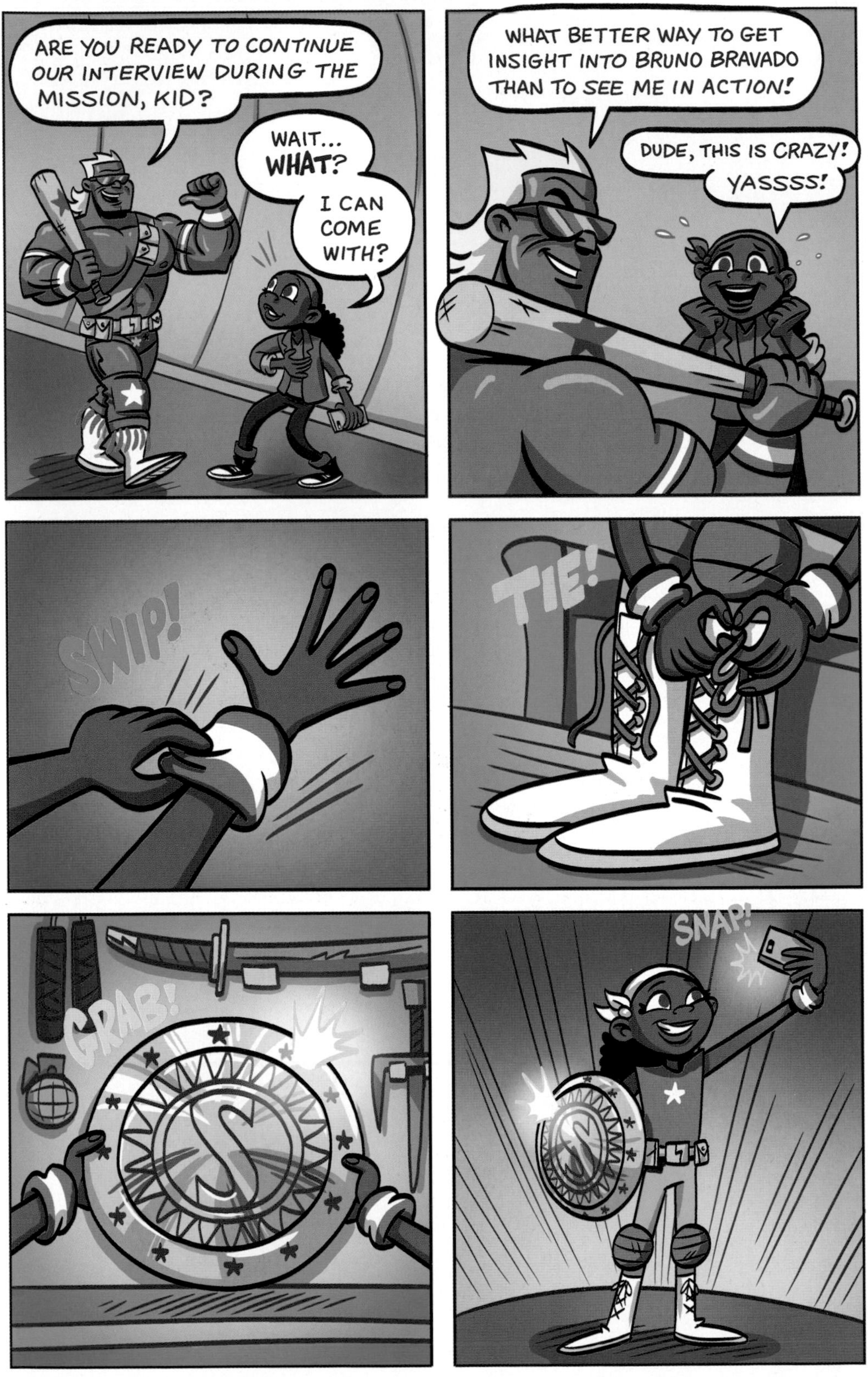
ARE YOU READY TO CONTINUE OUR INTERVIEW DURING THE MISSION, KID?
WAIT... WHAT?
I CAN COME WITH?
WHAT BETTER WAY TO GET INSIGHT INTO BRUNO BRAVADO THAN TO SEE ME IN ACTION!
DUDE, THIS IS CRAZY!
YASSSS!
SWIP!
TIE!
GRAB!
SNAP!

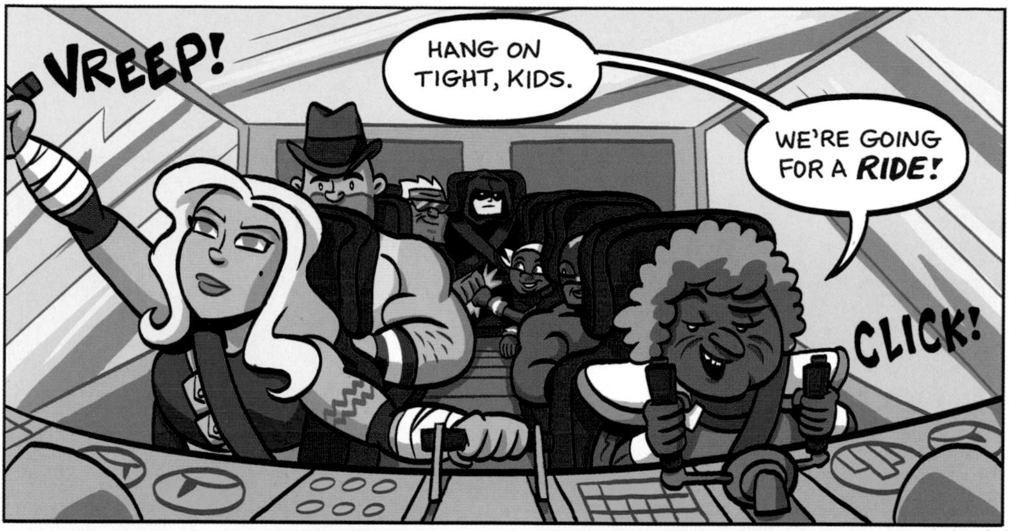
VREEP!
HANG ON TIGHT, KIDS.
WE'RE GOING FOR A RIDE!
CLICK!

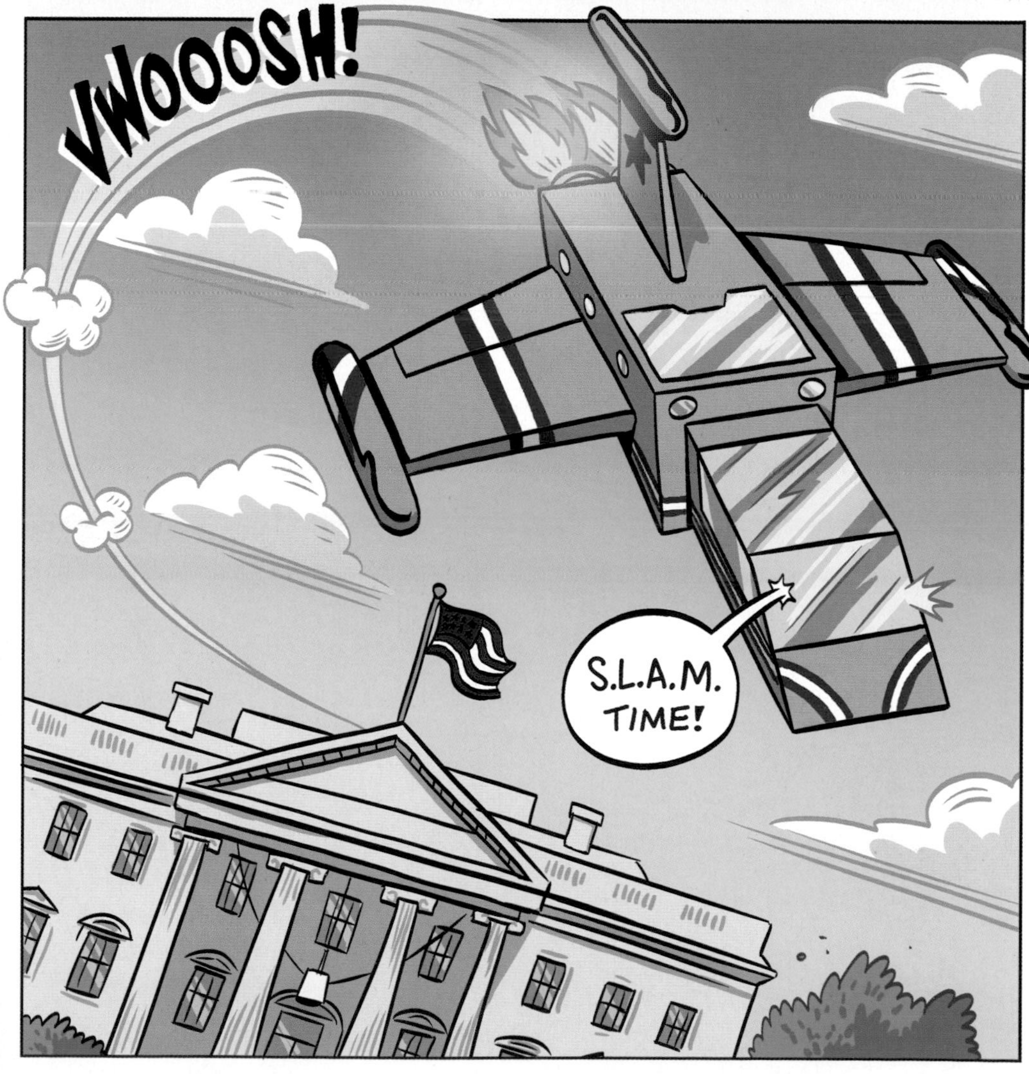
VWOOOSH!
S.L.A.M. TIME!

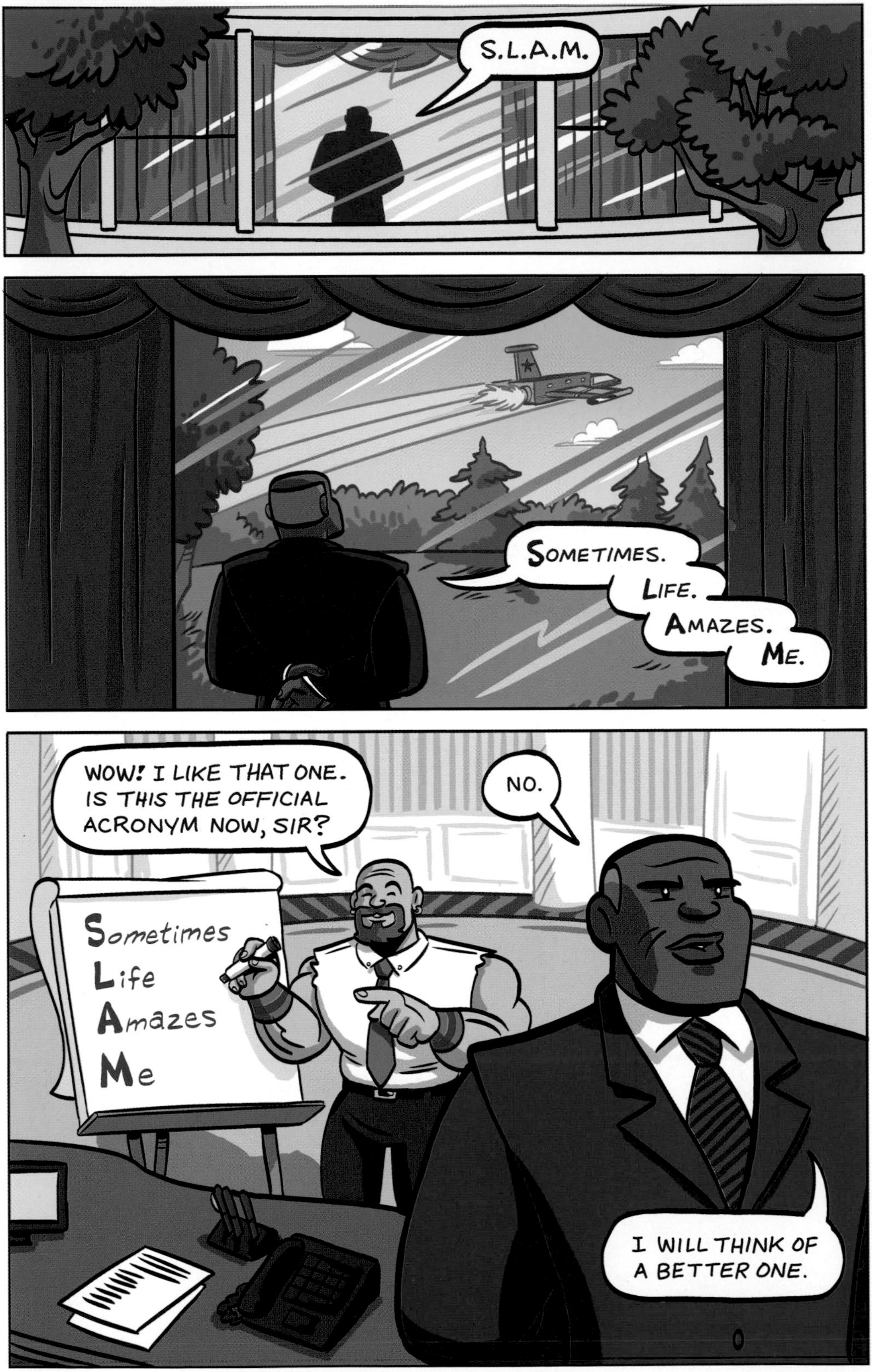
S.L.A.M.
SOMETIMES.
LIFE.
AMAZES.
ME.
WOW! I LIKE THAT ONE. IS THIS THE OFFICIAL ACRONYM NOW, SIR?
Sometimes
Life
Amazes
Me
NO.
I WILL THINK OF A BETTER ONE.

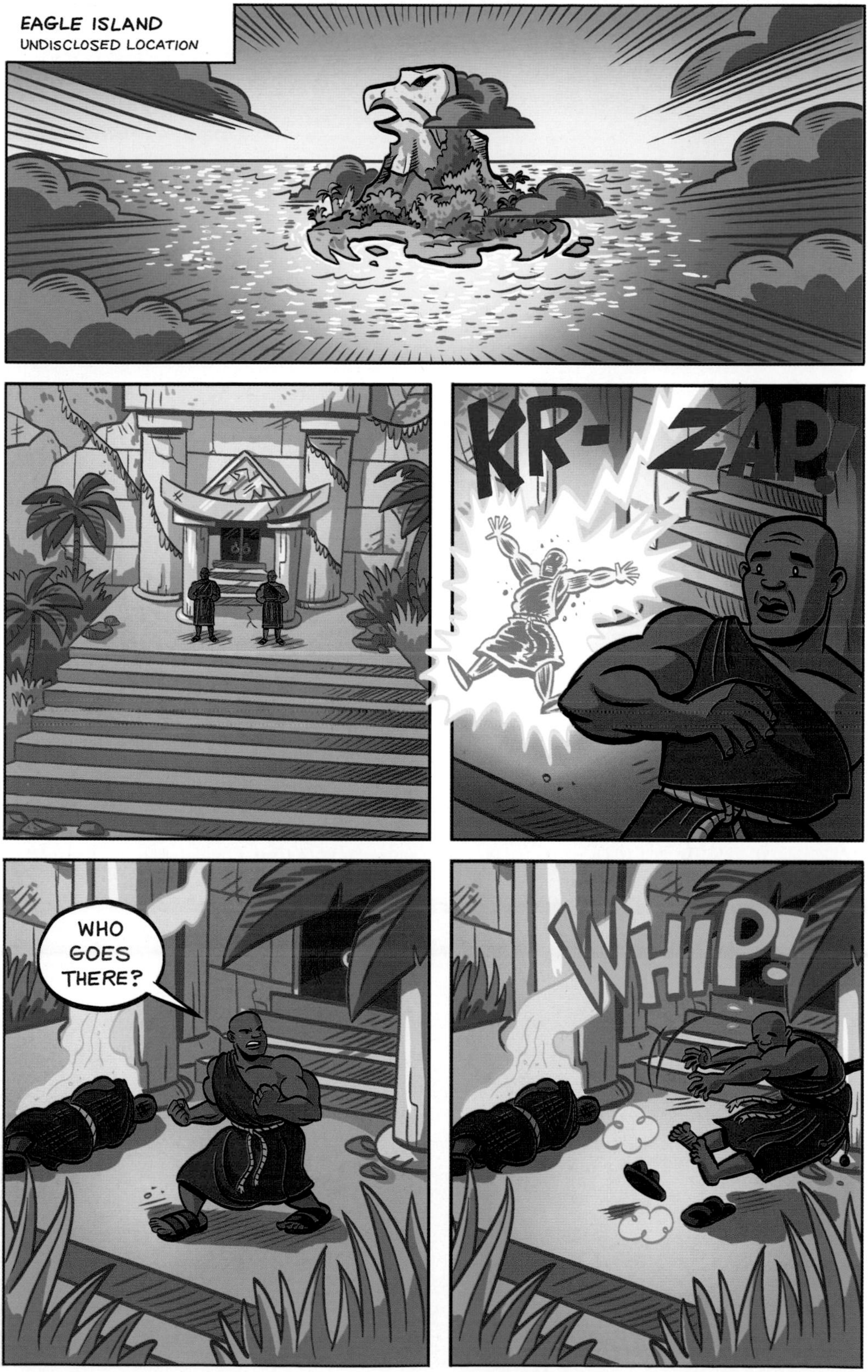
EAGLE ISLAND
UNDISCLOSED LOCATION
KR- ZAP!
WHO GOES THERE?
WHIP!

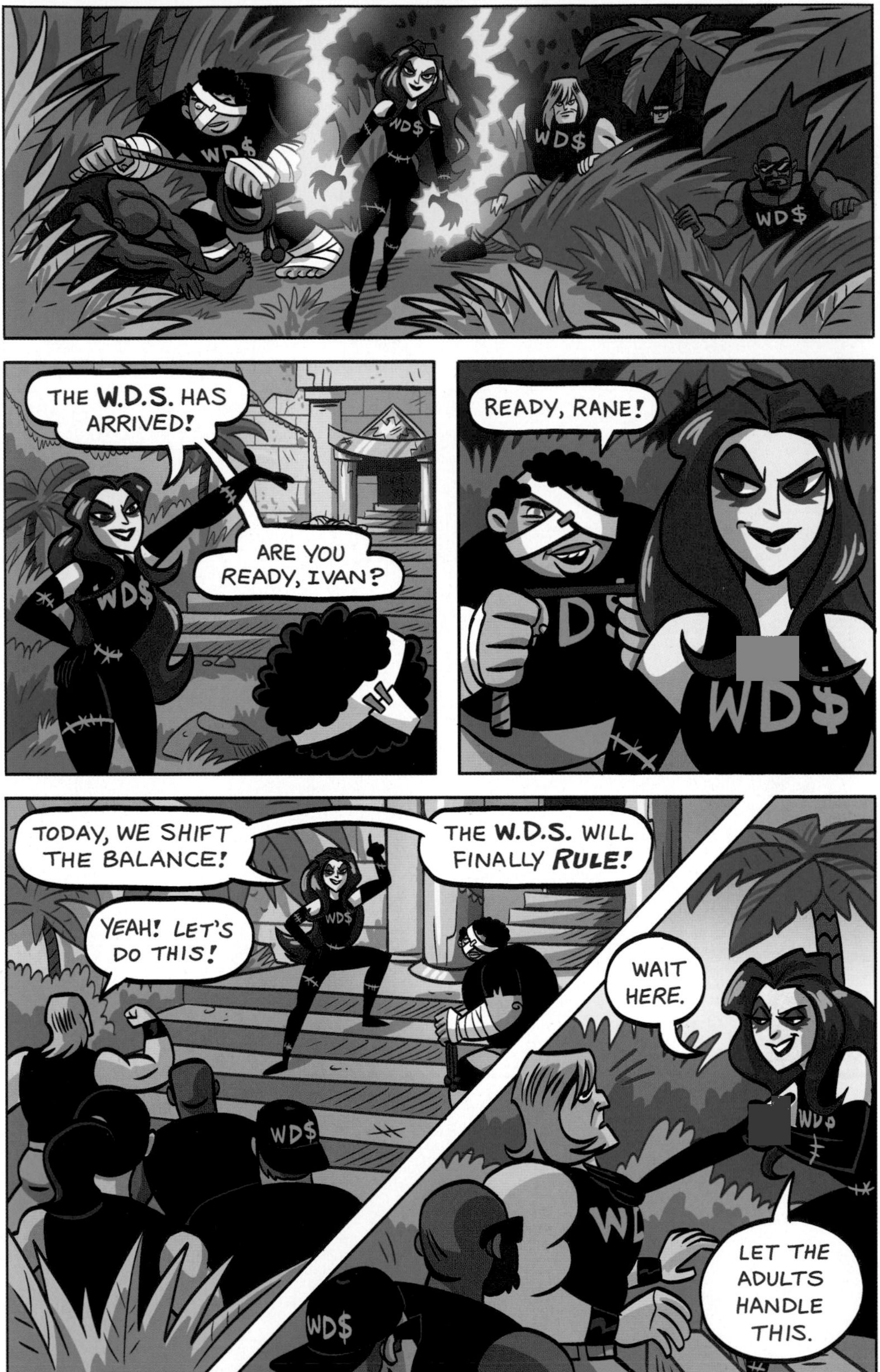
THE W.D.S. HAS ARRIVED!
ARE YOU READY, IVAN?
READY, RANE!
TODAY, WE SHIFT THE BALANCE!
THE W.D.S. WILL FINALLY RULE!
YEAH! LET'S DO THIS!
WAIT HERE.
LET THE ADULTS HANDLE THIS.

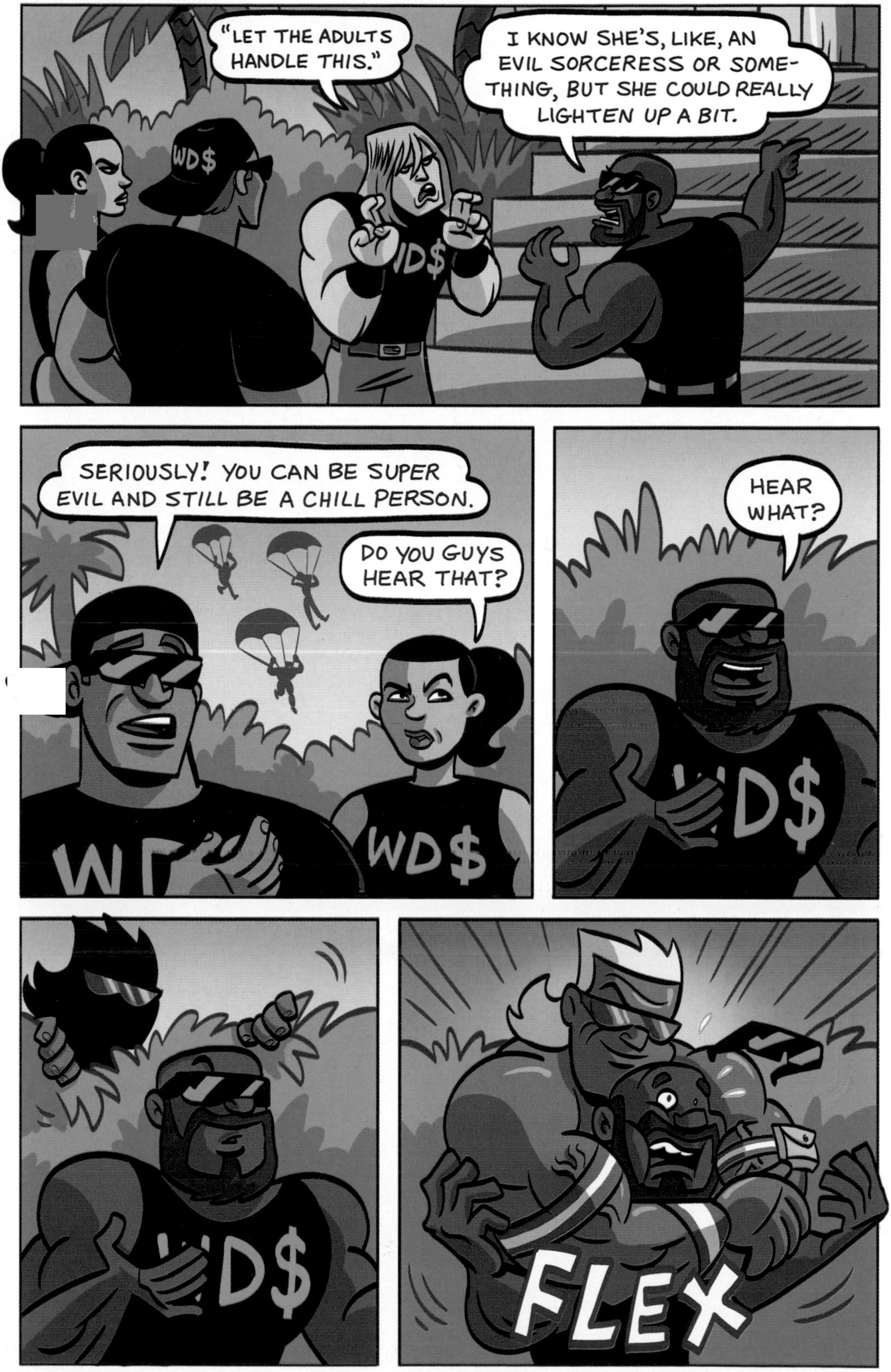
"LET THE ADULTS HANDLE THIS."
I KNOW SHE'S, LIKE, AN EVIL SORCERESS OR SOMETHING, BUT SHE COULD REALLY LIGHTEN UP A BIT.
SERIOUSLY! YOU CAN BE SUPER EVIL AND STILL BE A CHILL PERSON.
DO YOU GUYS HEAR THAT?
HEAR WHAT?
FLEX

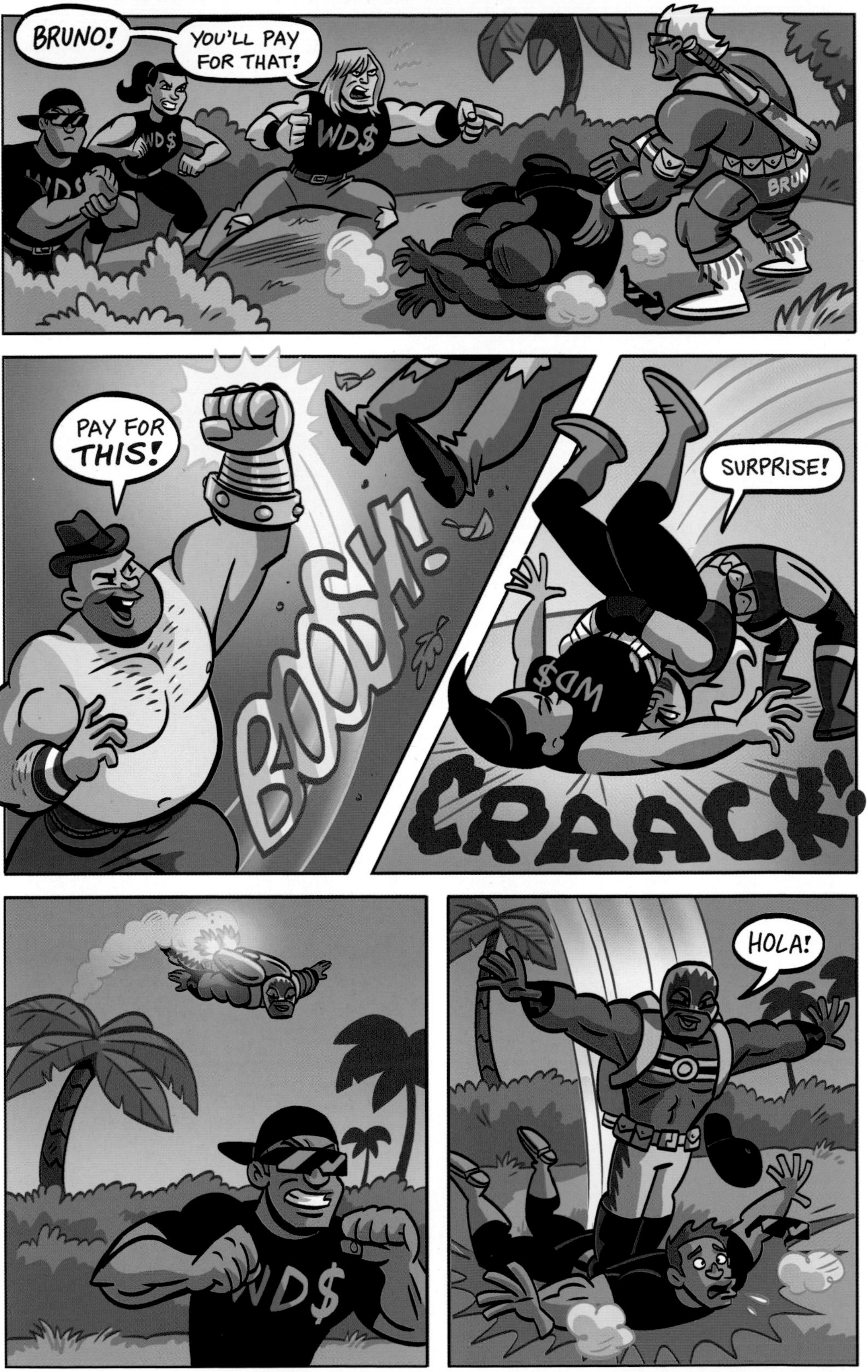
BRUNO!
YOU'LL PAY FOR THAT!
BRUN
WD$
PAY FOR THIS!
BOOSH!
SURPRISE!
CRAACK!
HOLA!

YOU USED THE **FEARSOME FLEX** BACK THERE! YOU HAVEN'T USED THAT MOVE IN YEARS!

YOU KNOW YOUR STUFF. YOU'D MAKE A GOOD TAG-TEAM PARTNER, KID!

BRUNO BRAVADO JUST TOLD ME I'D MAKE A GOOD TAG-TEAM PARTNER! GONNA DIE NOW!

LIVE

BRUNO INTERVIEW

ANYWAY, THIS FEELS TOO TOP SECRET... MAYBE I SHOULD STOP THE LIVESTREAM.

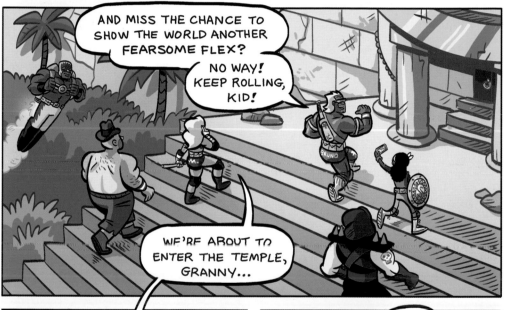

AND MISS THE CHANCE TO SHOW THE WORLD ANOTHER FEARSOME FLEX?

NO WAY! KEEP ROLLING, KID!

WE'RE ABOUT TO ENTER THE TEMPLE, GRANNY...

... KEEP AN EYE OUT FOR MORE W.D.S. GOONS.

ZZZ

WOO!

THIS IS IT! **SO** AWESOME!

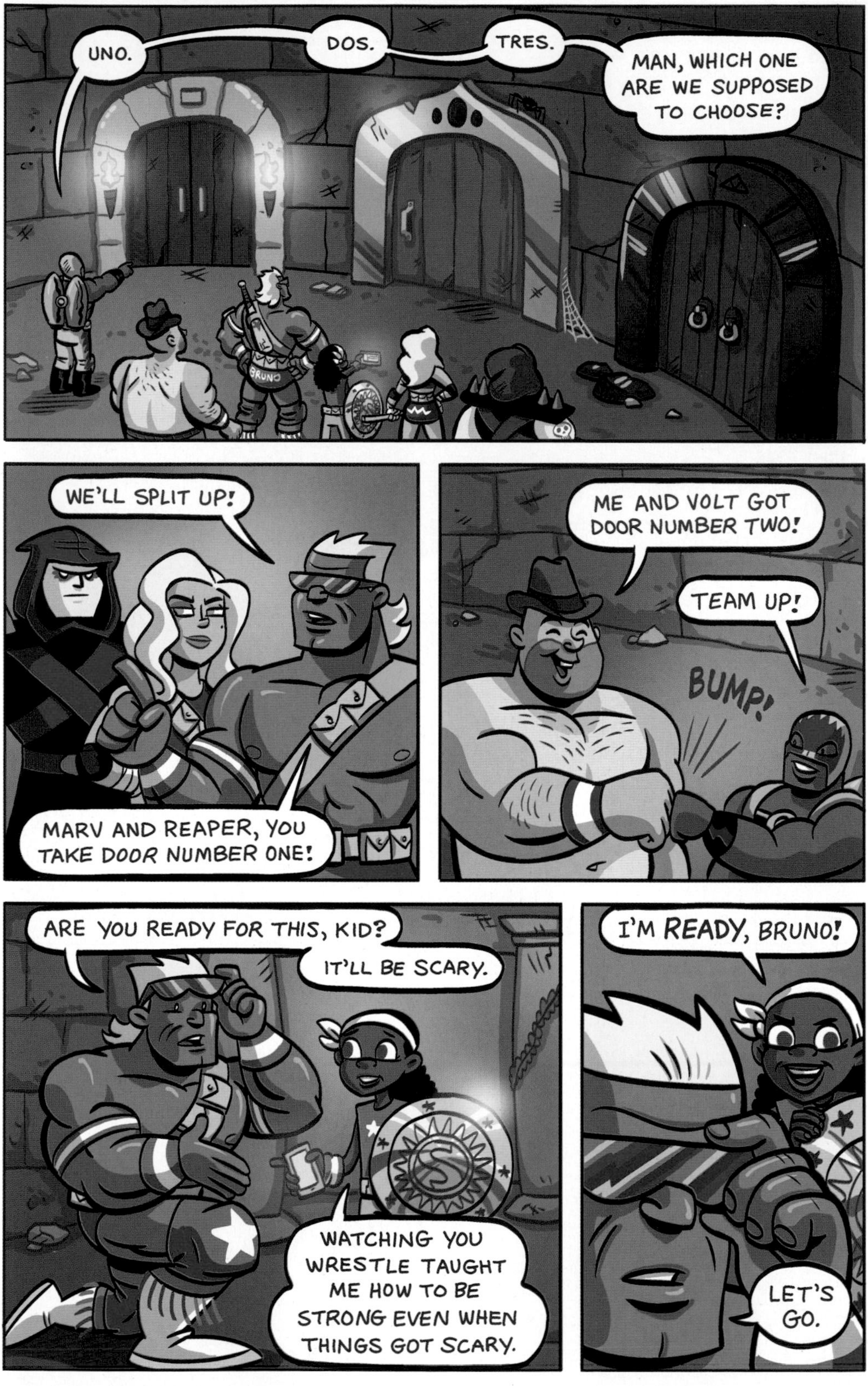
UNO.
DOS.
TRES.
MAN, WHICH ONE ARE WE SUPPOSED TO CHOOSE?
WE'LL SPLIT UP!
MARV AND REAPER, YOU TAKE DOOR NUMBER ONE!
ME AND VOLT GOT DOOR NUMBER TWO!
TEAM UP!
BUMP!
ARE YOU READY FOR THIS, KID?
IT'LL BE SCARY.
WATCHING YOU WRESTLE TAUGHT ME HOW TO BE STRONG EVEN WHEN THINGS GOT SCARY.
I'M READY, BRUNO!
LET'S GO.

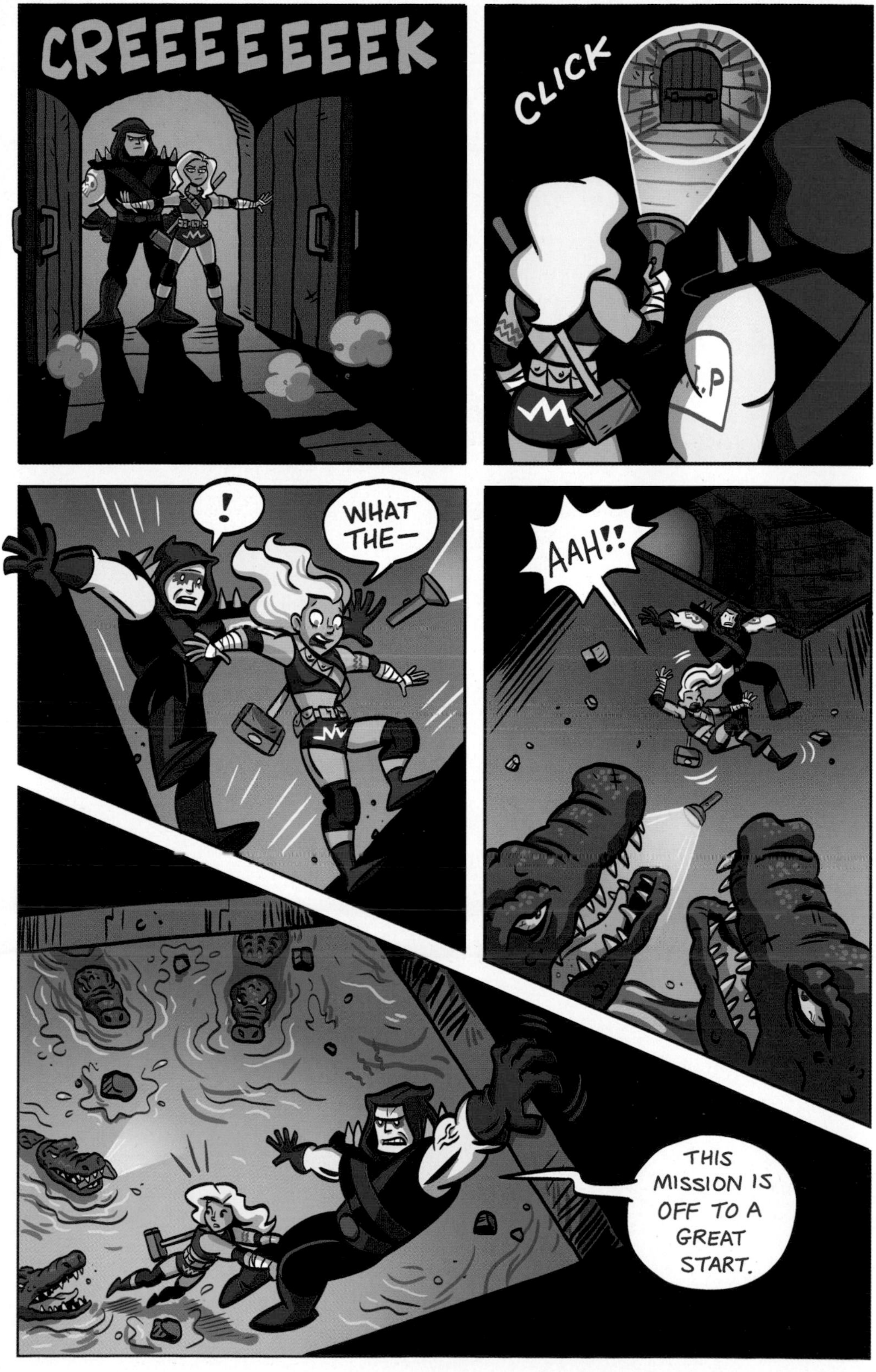
CREEEEEEEK
CLICK
R.I.P
!
WHAT THE—
AAH!!
THIS MISSION IS OFF TO A GREAT START.

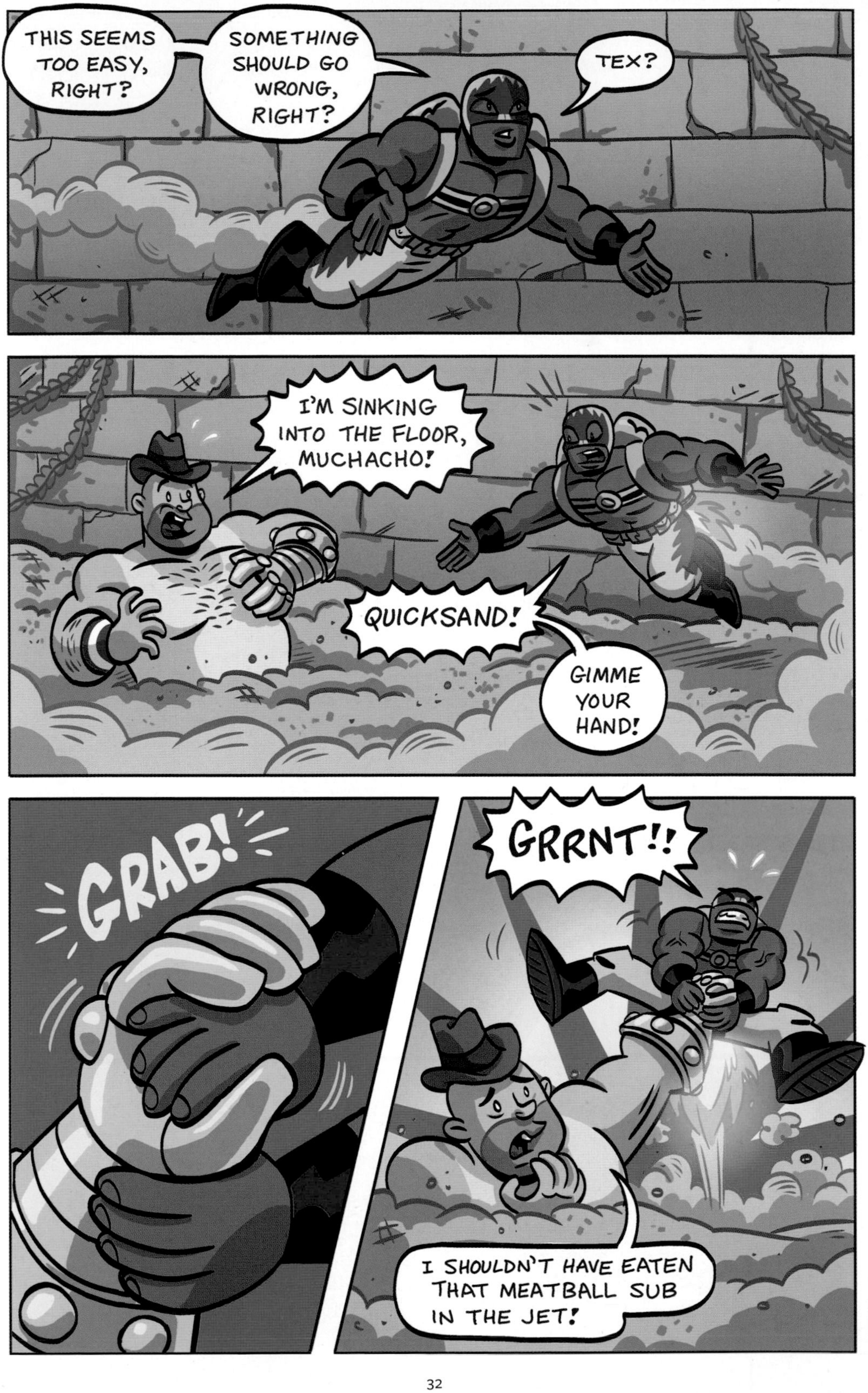
THIS SEEMS TOO EASY, RIGHT?
SOMETHING SHOULD GO WRONG, RIGHT?
TEX?
I'M SINKING INTO THE FLOOR, MUCHACHO!
QUICKSAND!
GIMME YOUR HAND!
GRAB!
GRRNT!!
I SHOULDN'T HAVE EATEN THAT MEATBALL SUB IN THE JET!

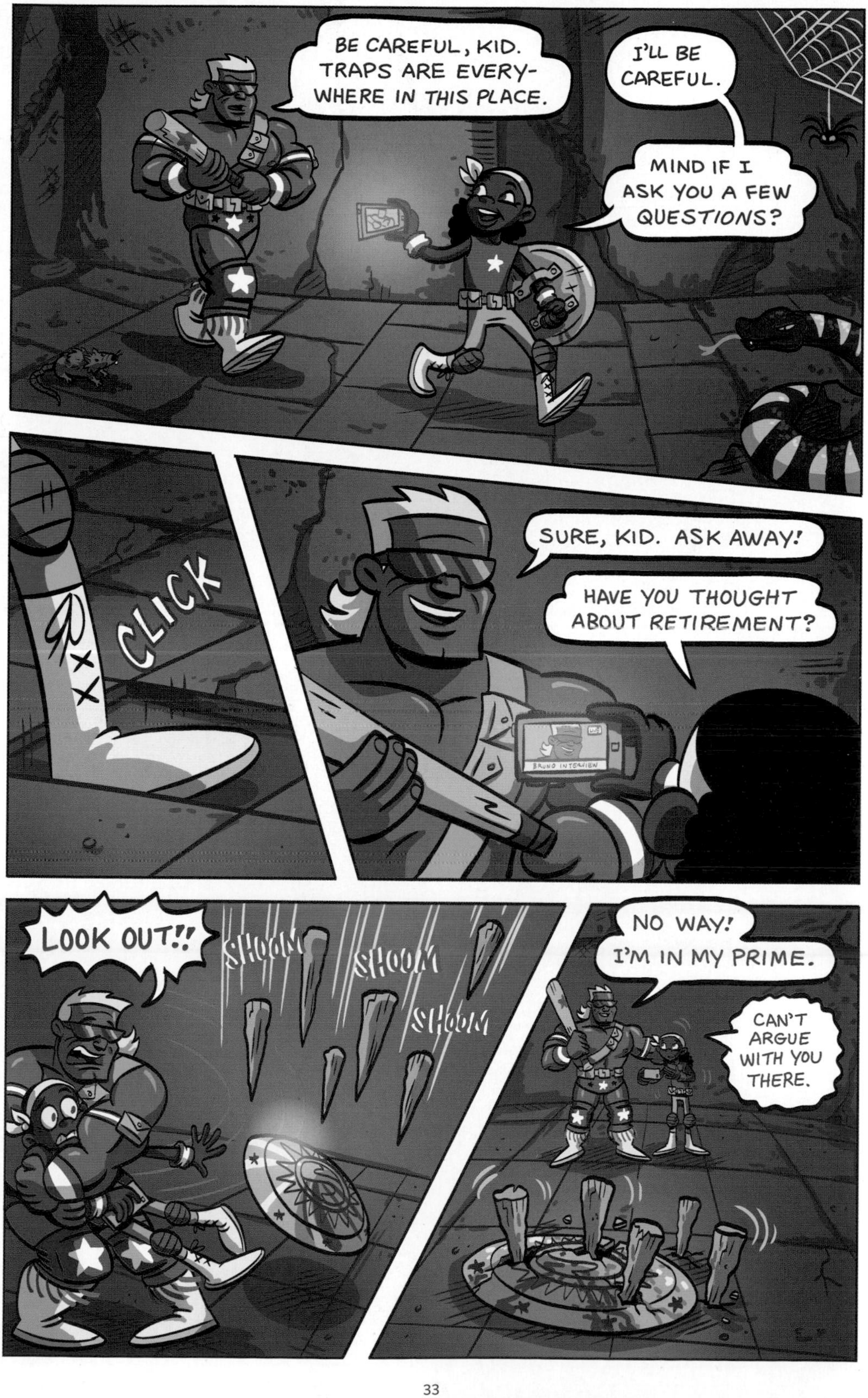
BE CAREFUL, KID. TRAPS ARE EVERY-WHERE IN THIS PLACE.
I'LL BE CAREFUL.
MIND IF I ASK YOU A FEW QUESTIONS?
CLICK
SURE, KID. ASK AWAY!
HAVE YOU THOUGHT ABOUT RETIREMENT?
LOOK OUT!!
SHOOM
SHOOM
SHOOM
NO WAY! I'M IN MY PRIME.
CAN'T ARGUE WITH YOU THERE.

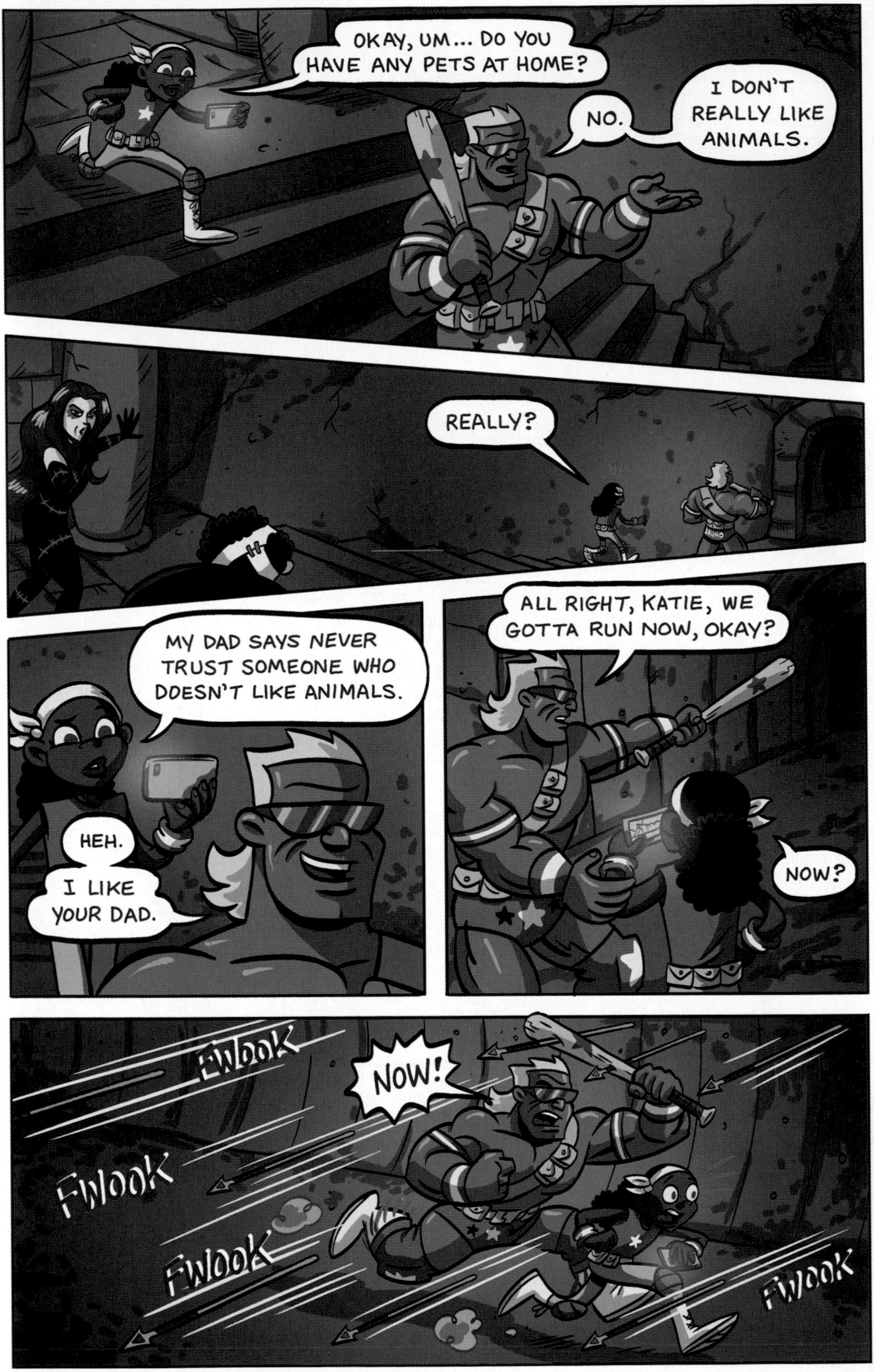

OKAY, UM... DO YOU HAVE ANY PETS AT HOME?
NO.
I DON'T REALLY LIKE ANIMALS.
REALLY?
MY DAD SAYS NEVER TRUST SOMEONE WHO DOESN'T LIKE ANIMALS.
HEH.
I LIKE YOUR DAD.
ALL RIGHT, KATIE, WE GOTTA RUN NOW, OKAY?
NOW?
FWOOK
NOW!
FWOOK
FWOOK
FWOOK

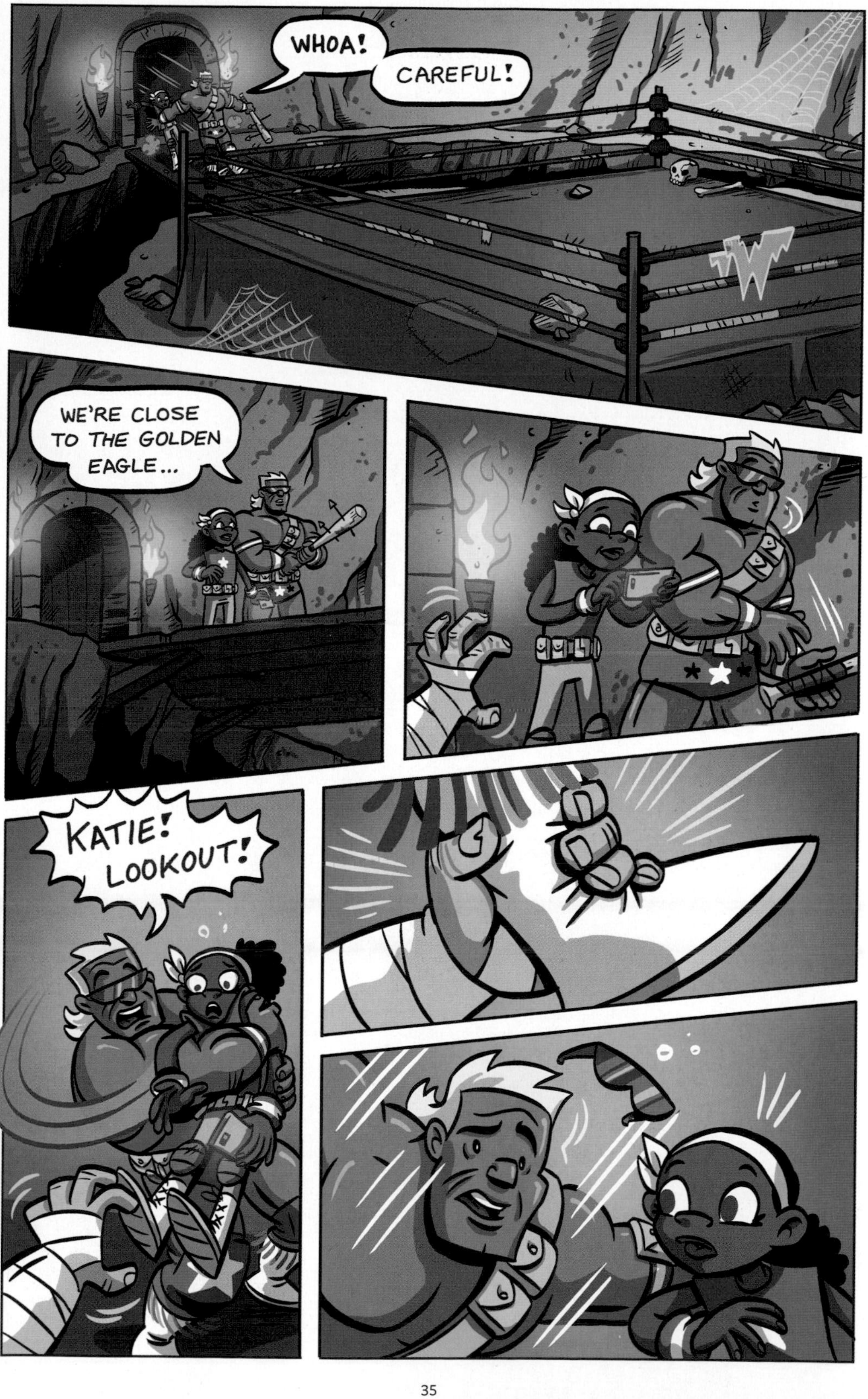
WHOA!
CAREFUL!
WE'RE CLOSE TO THE GOLDEN EAGLE...
KATIE! LOOKOUT!

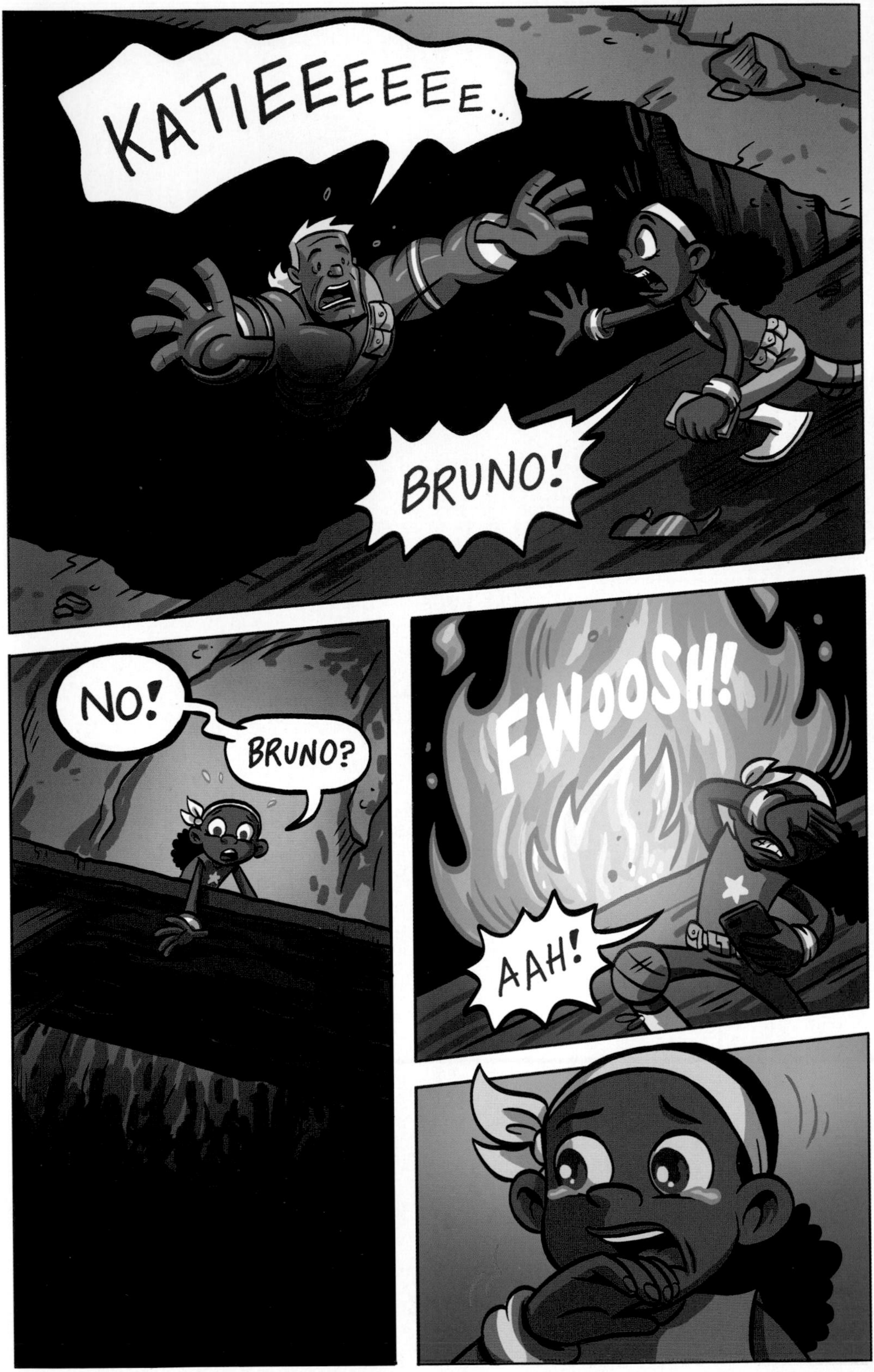
KATIEEEEEEE...
BRUNO!
NO!
BRUNO?
FWOOSH!
AAH!

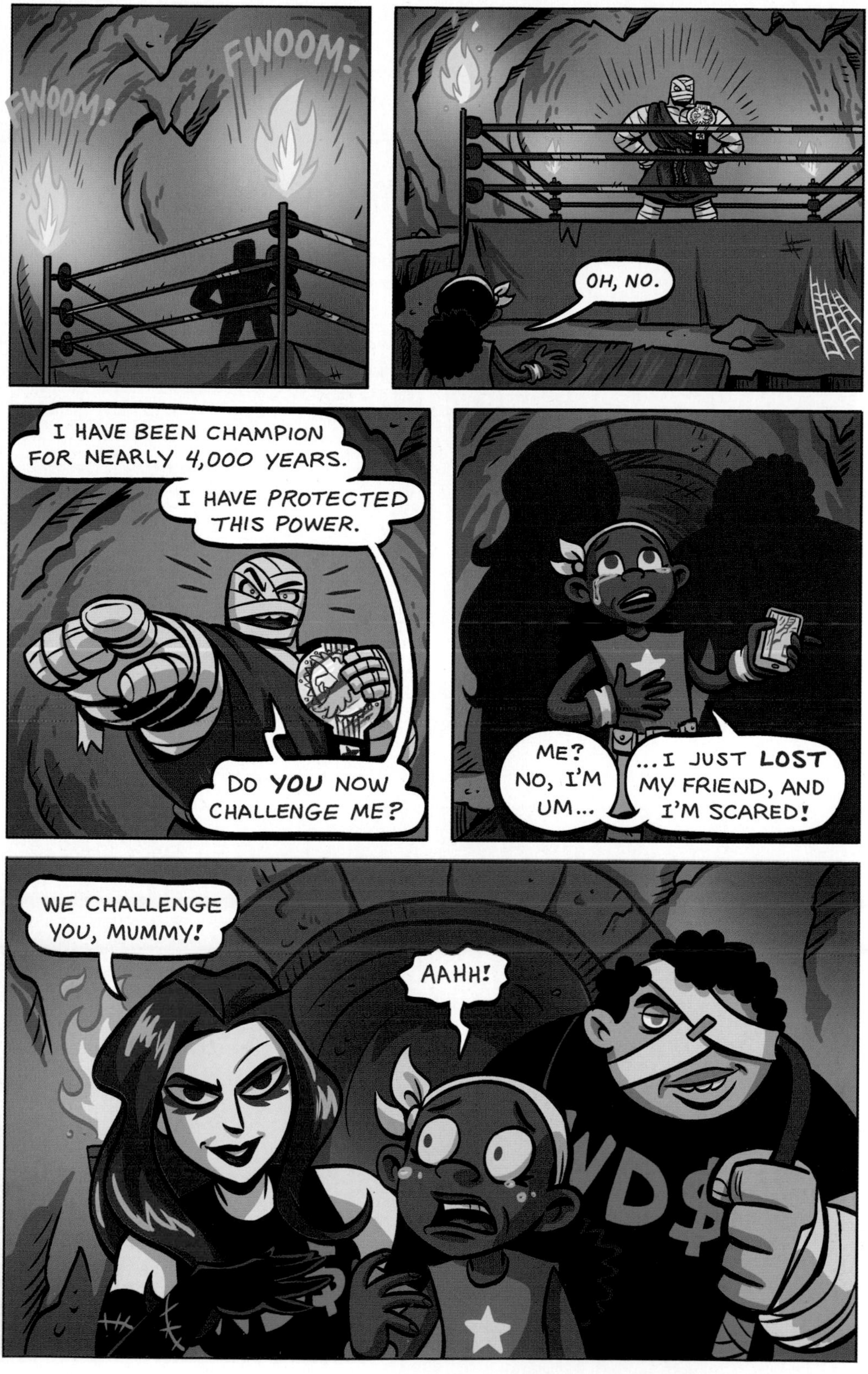
FWOOM!
FWOOM!
OH, NO.
I HAVE BEEN CHAMPION FOR NEARLY 4,000 YEARS.
I HAVE PROTECTED THIS POWER.
DO YOU NOW CHALLENGE ME?
ME? NO, I'M UM...
...I JUST LOST MY FRIEND, AND I'M SCARED!
WE CHALLENGE YOU, MUMMY!
AAHH!

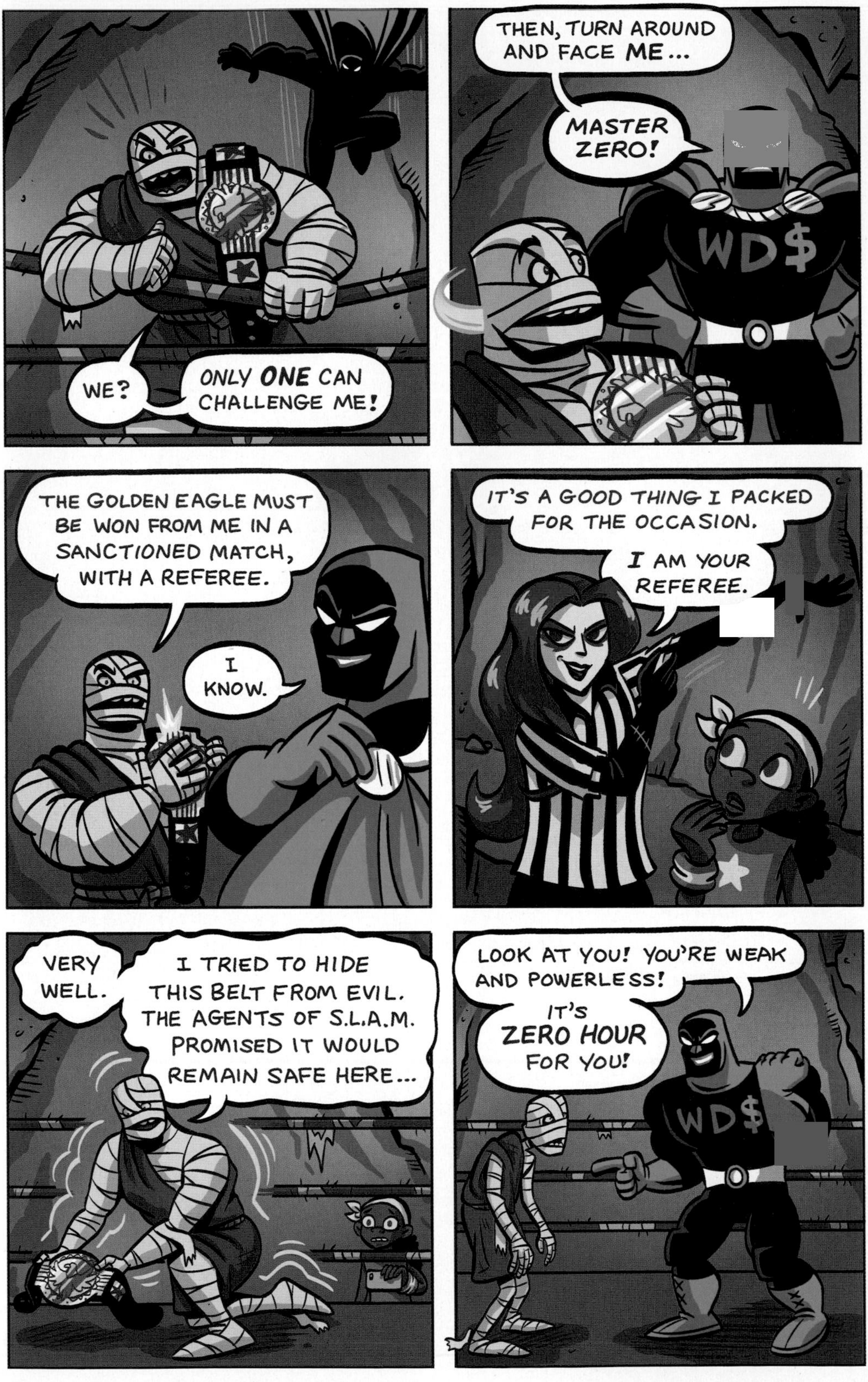
ONLY ONE CAN CHALLENGE ME!
WE?
THEN, TURN AROUND AND FACE ME...
MASTER ZERO!
THE GOLDEN EAGLE MUST BE WON FROM ME IN A SANCTIONED MATCH, WITH A REFEREE.
I KNOW.
IT'S A GOOD THING I PACKED FOR THE OCCASION.
I AM YOUR REFEREE.
VERY WELL.
I TRIED TO HIDE THIS BELT FROM EVIL. THE AGENTS OF S.L.A.M. PROMISED IT WOULD REMAIN SAFE HERE...
LOOK AT YOU! YOU'RE WEAK AND POWERLESS!
IT'S ZERO HOUR FOR YOU!

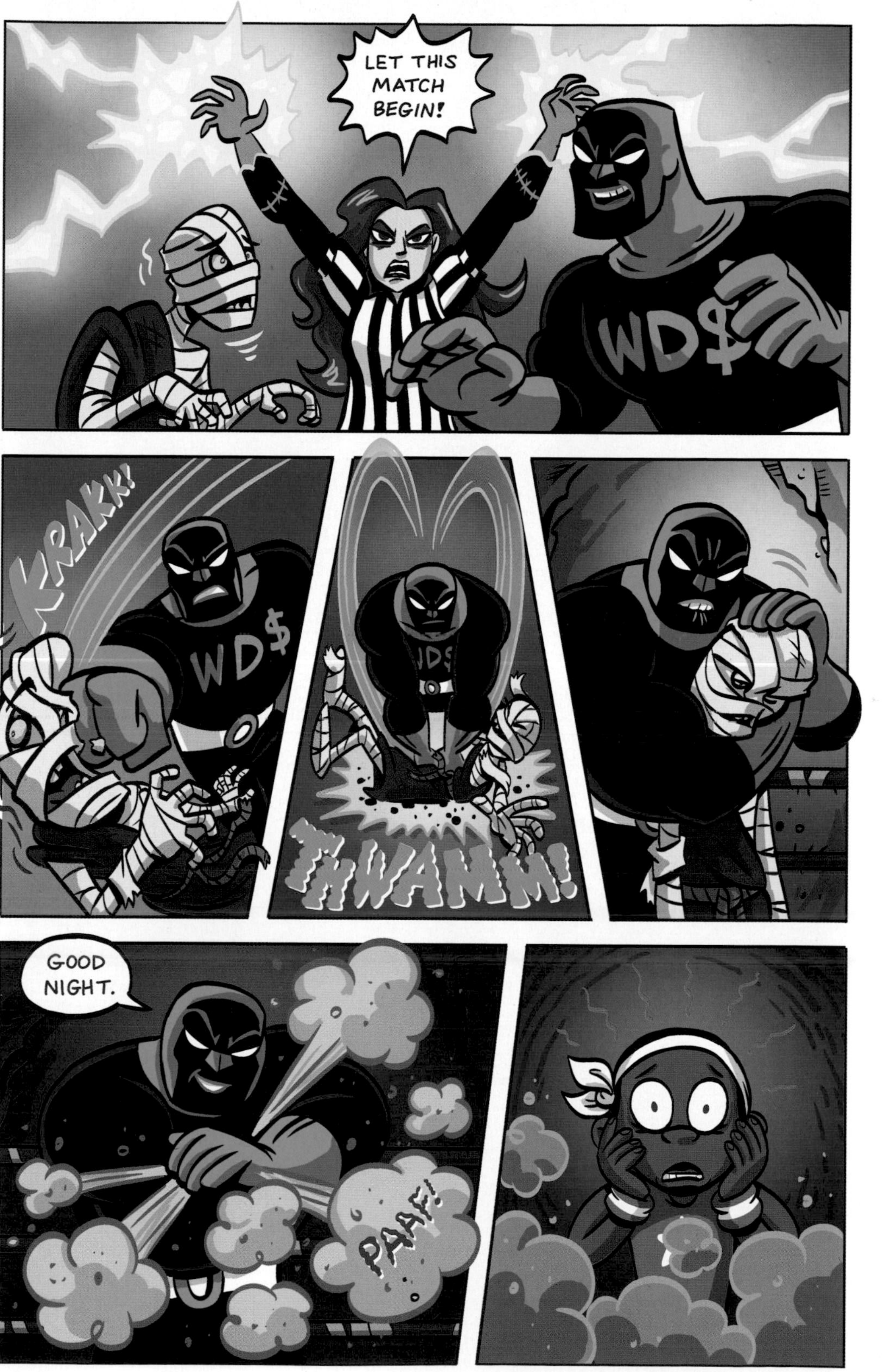
LET THIS MATCH BEGIN!
WD$
KRAKK!
WD$
WD$
THWAMM!
GOOD NIGHT.
PAAF!!

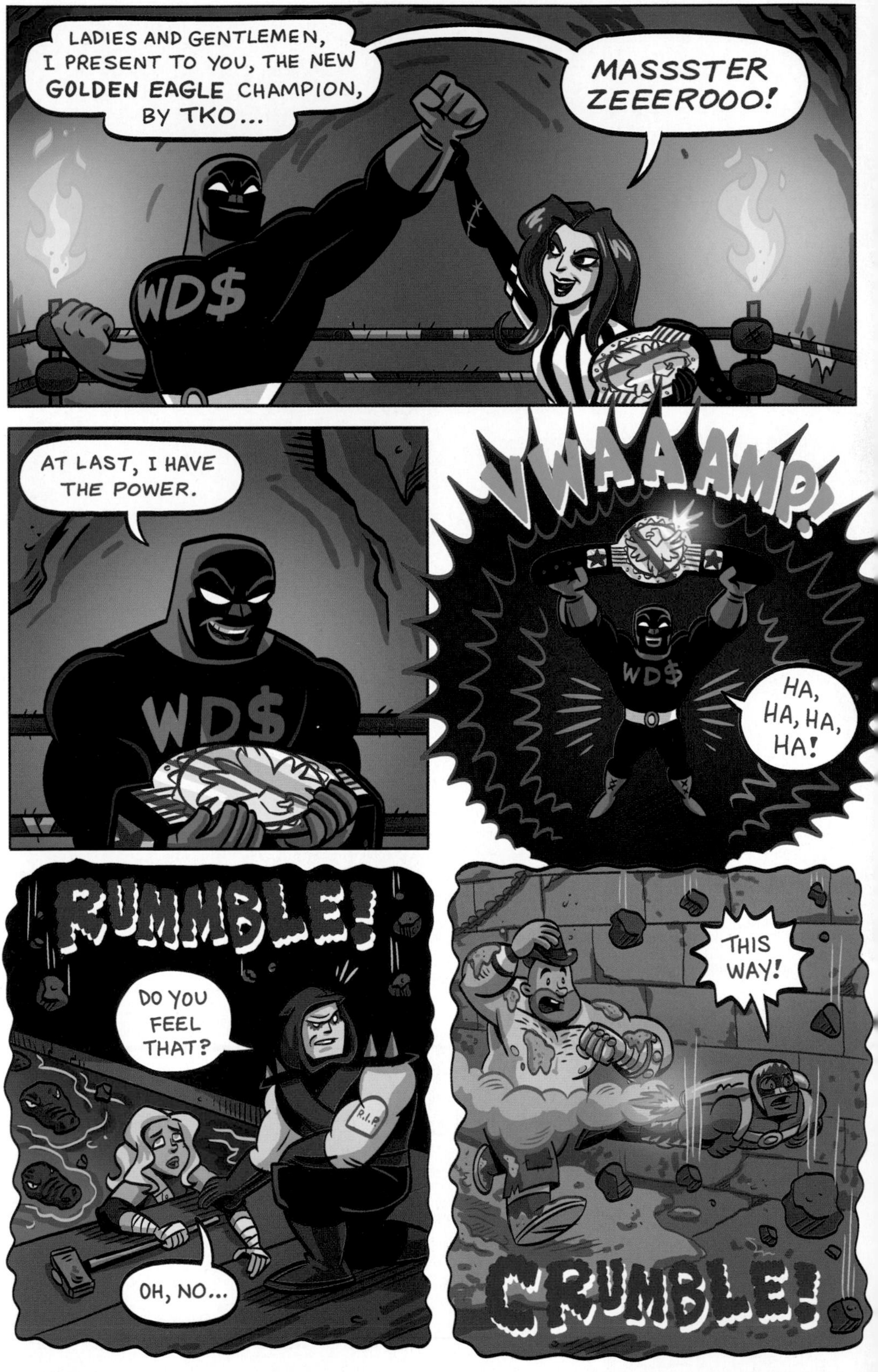
LADIES AND GENTLEMEN, I PRESENT TO YOU, THE NEW GOLDEN EAGLE CHAMPION, BY TKO...
MASSSTER ZEEEROOO!
WD$
AT LAST, I HAVE THE POWER.
WD$
VWAAAAMP!
WD$
HA, HA, HA, HA!
RUMMBLE!
DO YOU FEEL THAT?
R.I.P.
OH, NO...
THIS WAY!
CRUMBLE!

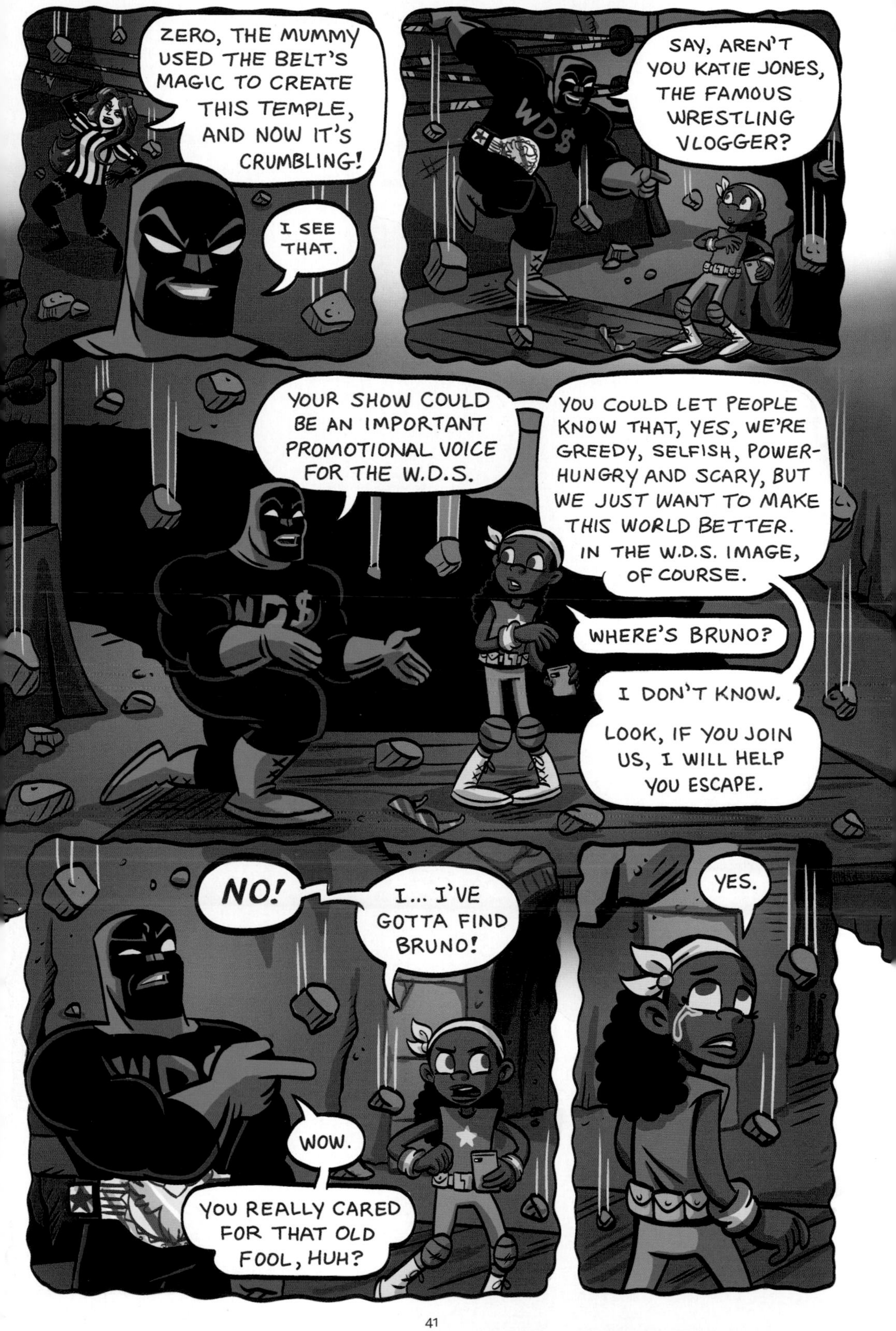
ZERO, THE MUMMY USED THE BELT'S MAGIC TO CREATE THIS TEMPLE, AND NOW IT'S CRUMBLING!
I SEE THAT.
SAY, AREN'T YOU KATIE JONES, THE FAMOUS WRESTLING VLOGGER?
YOUR SHOW COULD BE AN IMPORTANT PROMOTIONAL VOICE FOR THE W.D.S.
YOU COULD LET PEOPLE KNOW THAT, YES, WE'RE GREEDY, SELFISH, POWER-HUNGRY AND SCARY, BUT WE JUST WANT TO MAKE THIS WORLD BETTER.
IN THE W.D.S. IMAGE, OF COURSE.
WHERE'S BRUNO?
I DON'T KNOW.
LOOK, IF YOU JOIN US, I WILL HELP YOU ESCAPE.
NO!
I... I'VE GOTTA FIND BRUNO!
WOW.
YOU REALLY CARED FOR THAT OLD FOOL, HUH?
YES.

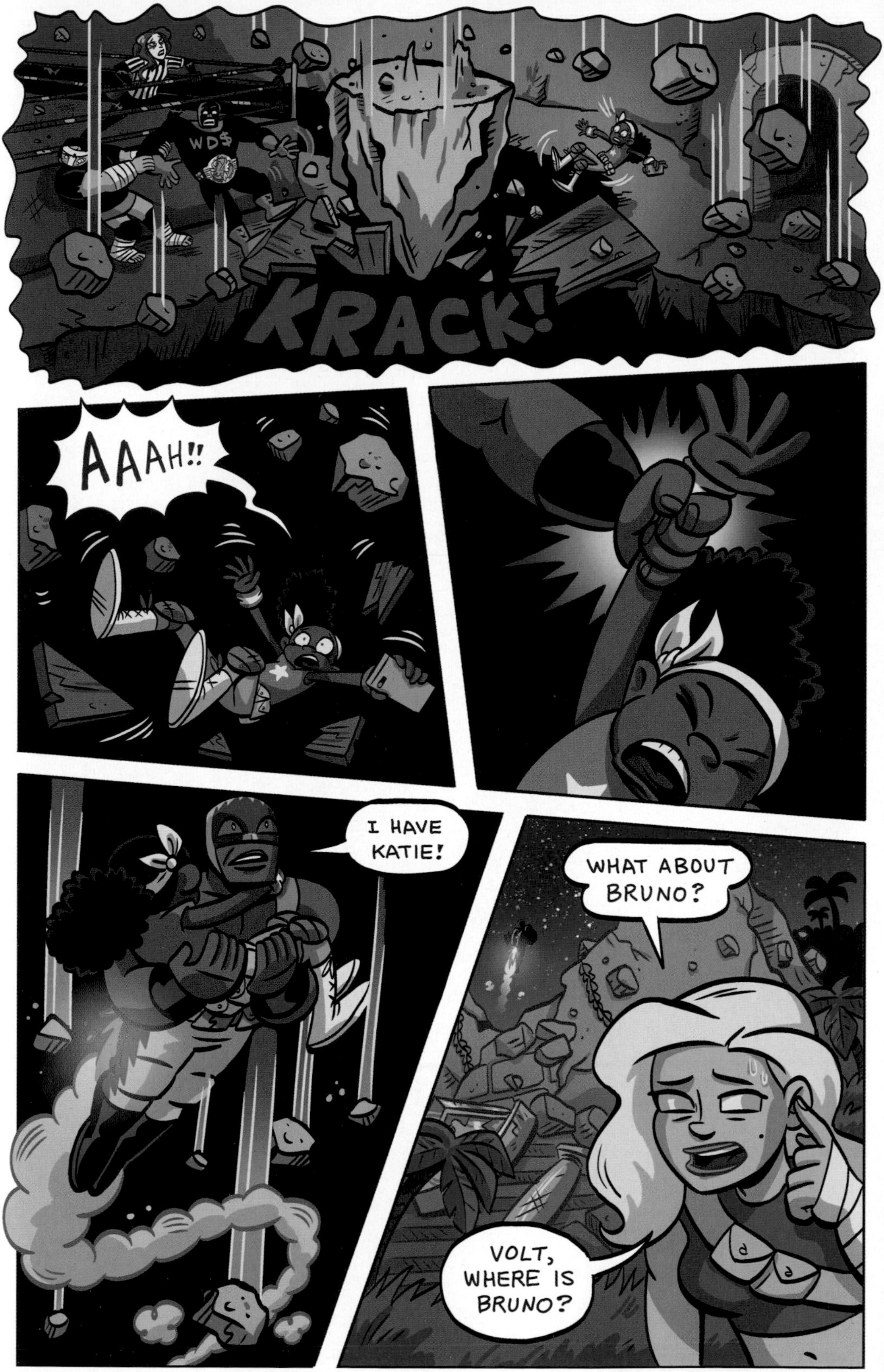
KRACK!
AAAH!!
I HAVE KATIE!
WHAT ABOUT BRUNO?
VOLT, WHERE IS BRUNO?

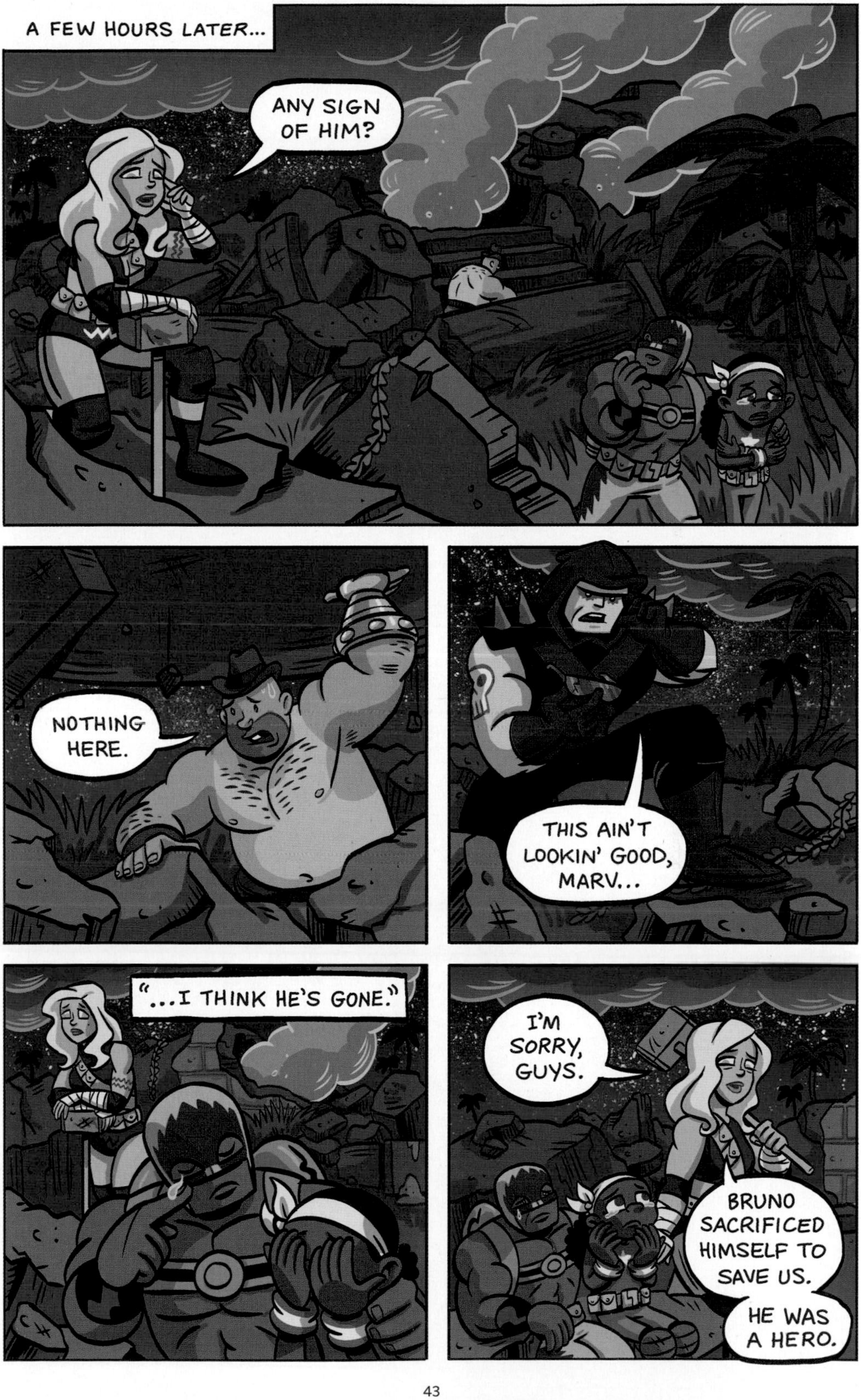
A FEW HOURS LATER...
ANY SIGN OF HIM?
NOTHING HERE.
THIS AIN'T LOOKIN' GOOD, MARV...
"...I THINK HE'S GONE."
I'M SORRY, GUYS.
BRUNO SACRIFICED HIMSELF TO SAVE US.
HE WAS A HERO.

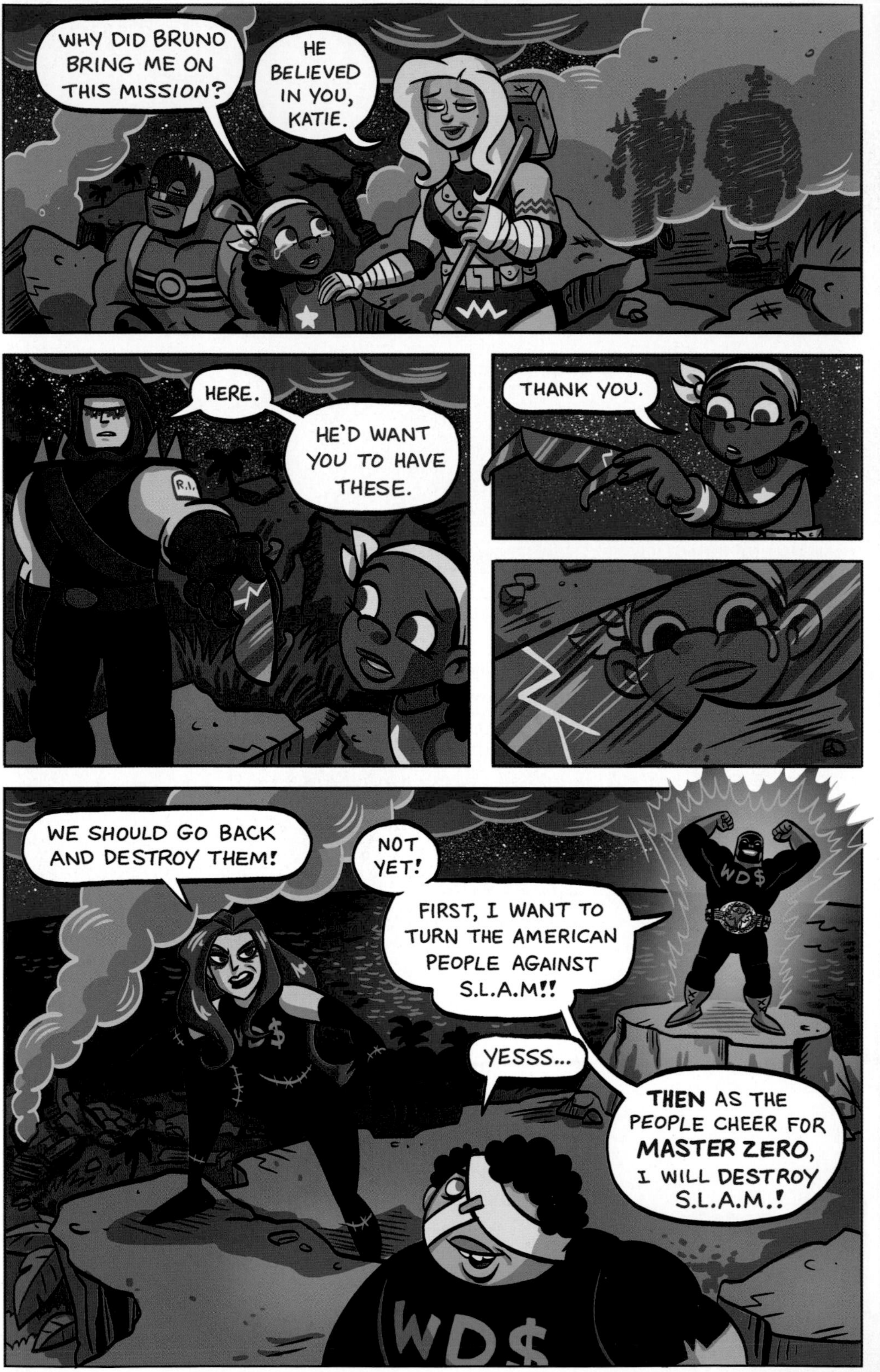
WHY DID BRUNO BRING ME ON THIS MISSION?
HE BELIEVED IN YOU, KATIE.
HERE.
HE'D WANT YOU TO HAVE THESE.
THANK YOU.
WE SHOULD GO BACK AND DESTROY THEM!
NOT YET!
FIRST, I WANT TO TURN THE AMERICAN PEOPLE AGAINST S.L.A.M!!
YESSS...
THEN AS THE PEOPLE CHEER FOR MASTER ZERO, I WILL DESTROY S.L.A.M.!
WD$
WD$
WD$

★★★ CHAPTER 2

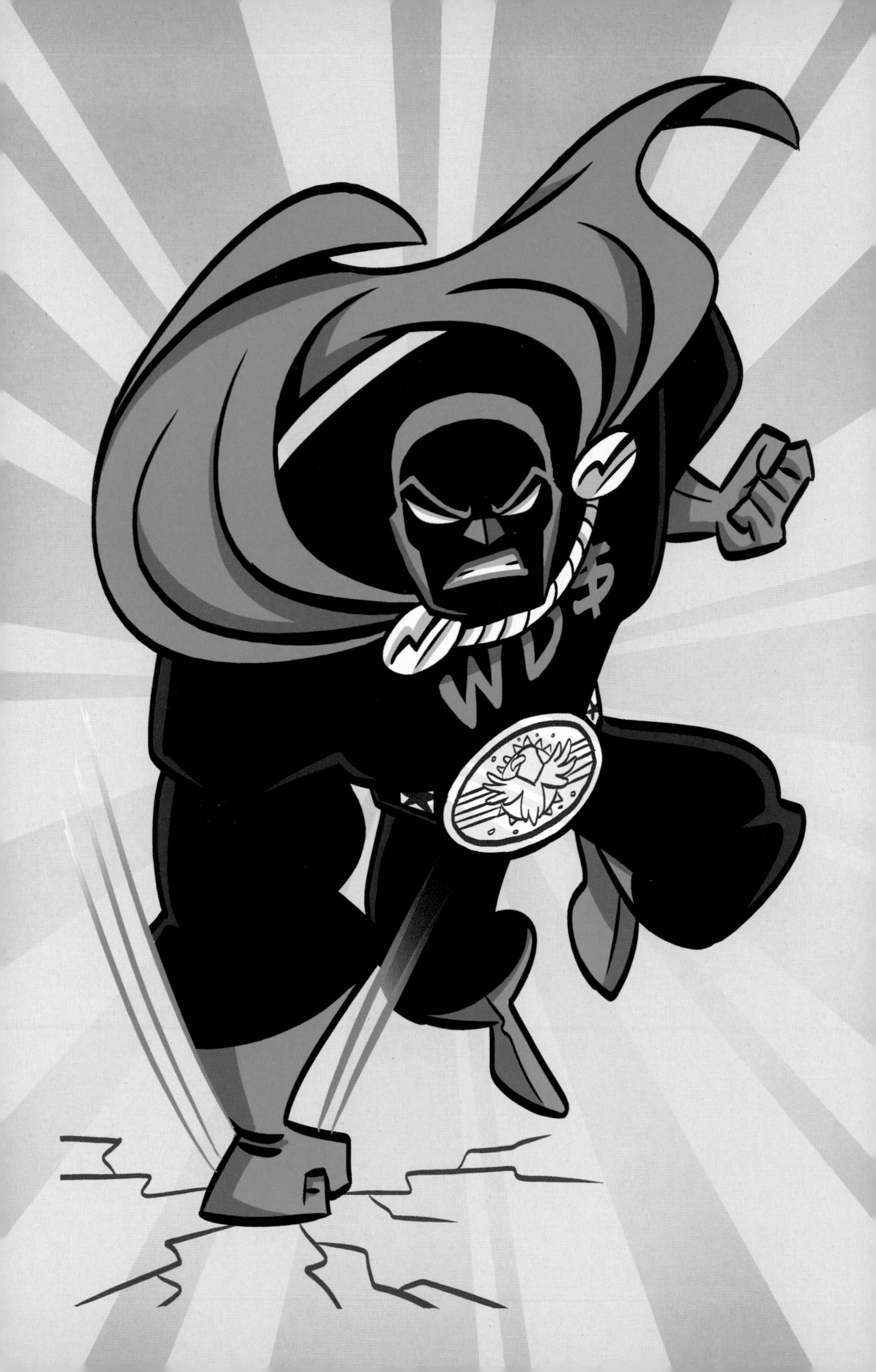
WD$

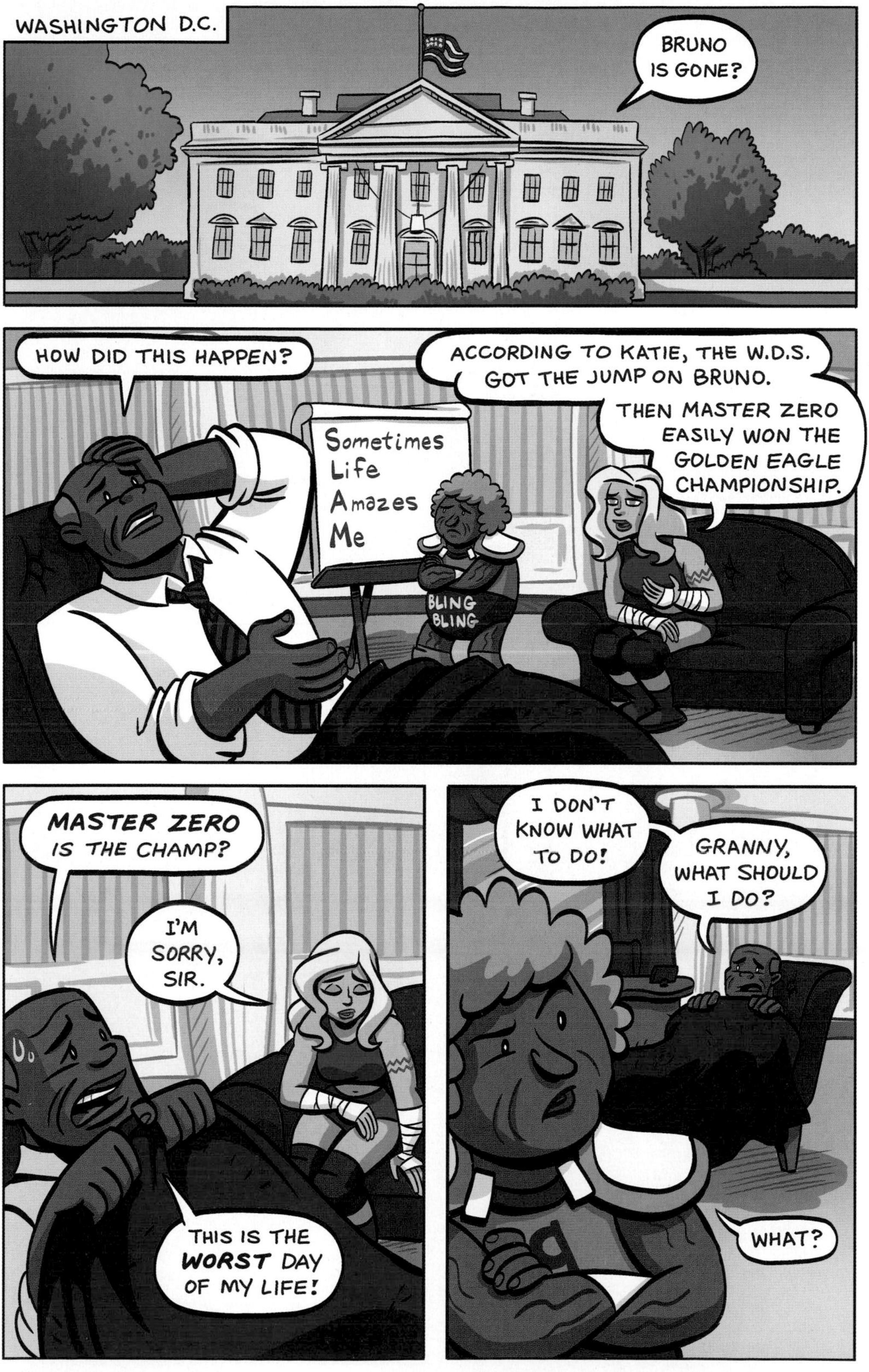
WASHINGTON D.C.
BRUNO IS GONE?
HOW DID THIS HAPPEN?
ACCORDING TO KATIE, THE W.D.S. GOT THE JUMP ON BRUNO.
THEN MASTER ZERO EASILY WON THE GOLDEN EAGLE CHAMPIONSHIP.
Sometimes Life Amazes Me
BLING BLING
MASTER ZERO IS THE CHAMP?
I'M SORRY, SIR.
THIS IS THE WORST DAY OF MY LIFE!
I DON'T KNOW WHAT TO DO!
GRANNY, WHAT SHOULD I DO?
WHAT?

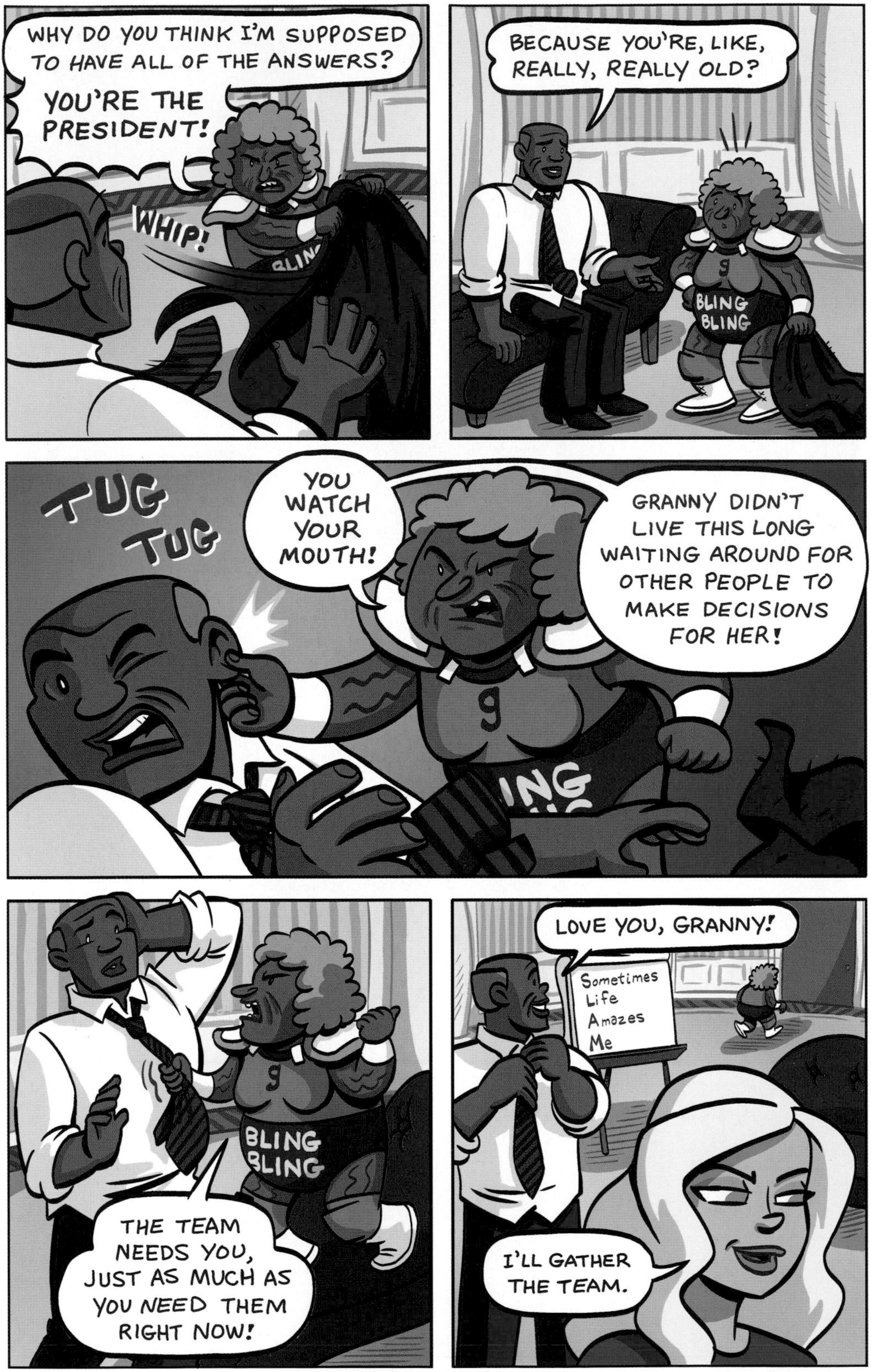
WHY DO YOU THINK I'M SUPPOSED TO HAVE ALL OF THE ANSWERS?
YOU'RE THE PRESIDENT!
WHIP!
BLING
BECAUSE YOU'RE, LIKE, REALLY, REALLY OLD?
BLING BLING
TUG TUG
YOU WATCH YOUR MOUTH!
GRANNY DIDN'T LIVE THIS LONG WAITING AROUND FOR OTHER PEOPLE TO MAKE DECISIONS FOR HER!
ING
BLING BLING
THE TEAM NEEDS YOU, JUST AS MUCH AS YOU NEED THEM RIGHT NOW!
LOVE YOU, GRANNY!
Sometimes Life Amazes Me
I'LL GATHER THE TEAM.

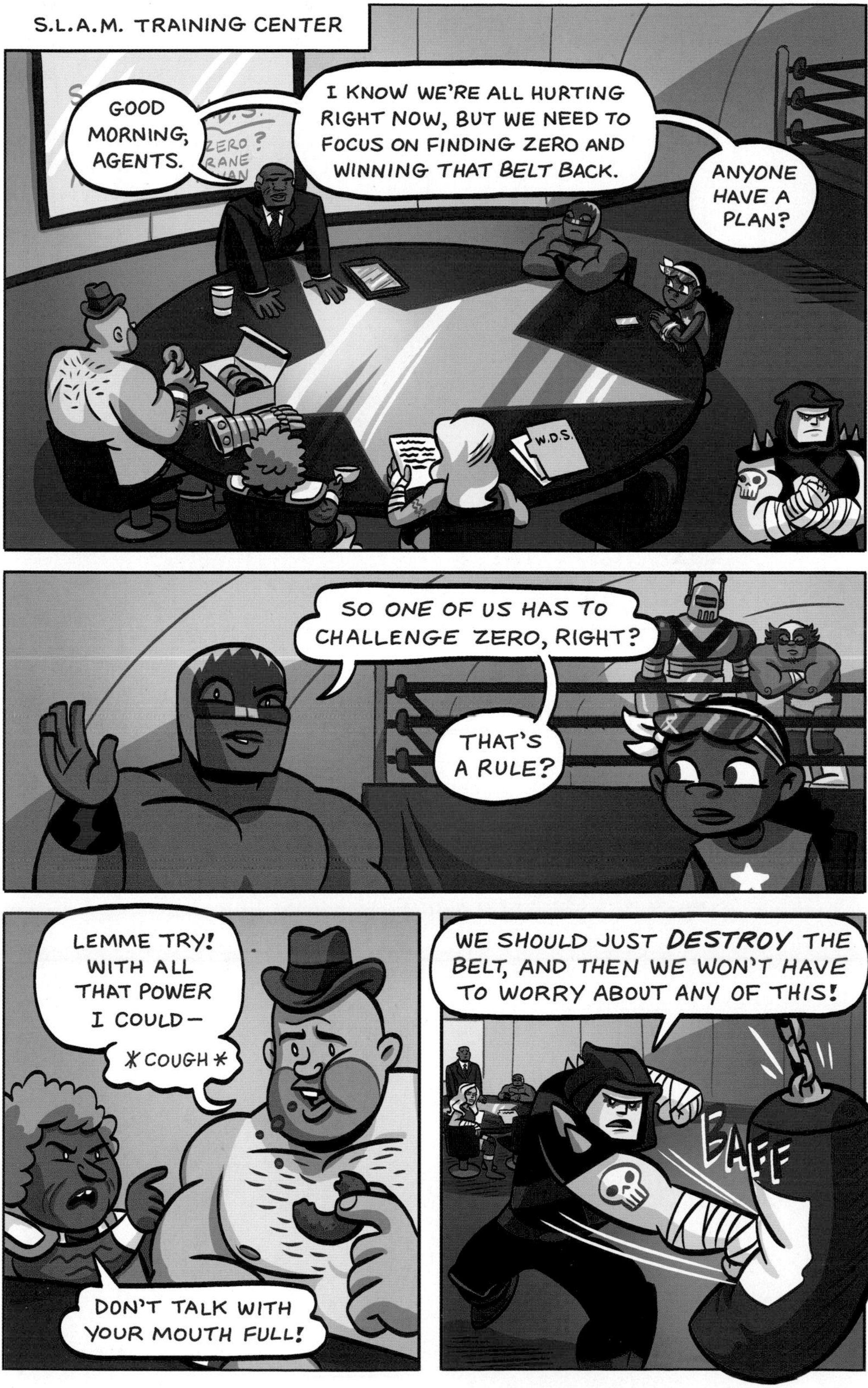
S.L.A.M. TRAINING CENTER
GOOD MORNING, AGENTS.
I KNOW WE'RE ALL HURTING RIGHT NOW, BUT WE NEED TO FOCUS ON FINDING ZERO AND WINNING THAT BELT BACK.
ANYONE HAVE A PLAN?
W.D.S.
SO ONE OF US HAS TO CHALLENGE ZERO, RIGHT?
THAT'S A RULE?
LEMME TRY! WITH ALL THAT POWER I COULD—
COUGH
DON'T TALK WITH YOUR MOUTH FULL!
WE SHOULD JUST DESTROY THE BELT, AND THEN WE WON'T HAVE TO WORRY ABOUT ANY OF THIS!
BAFF

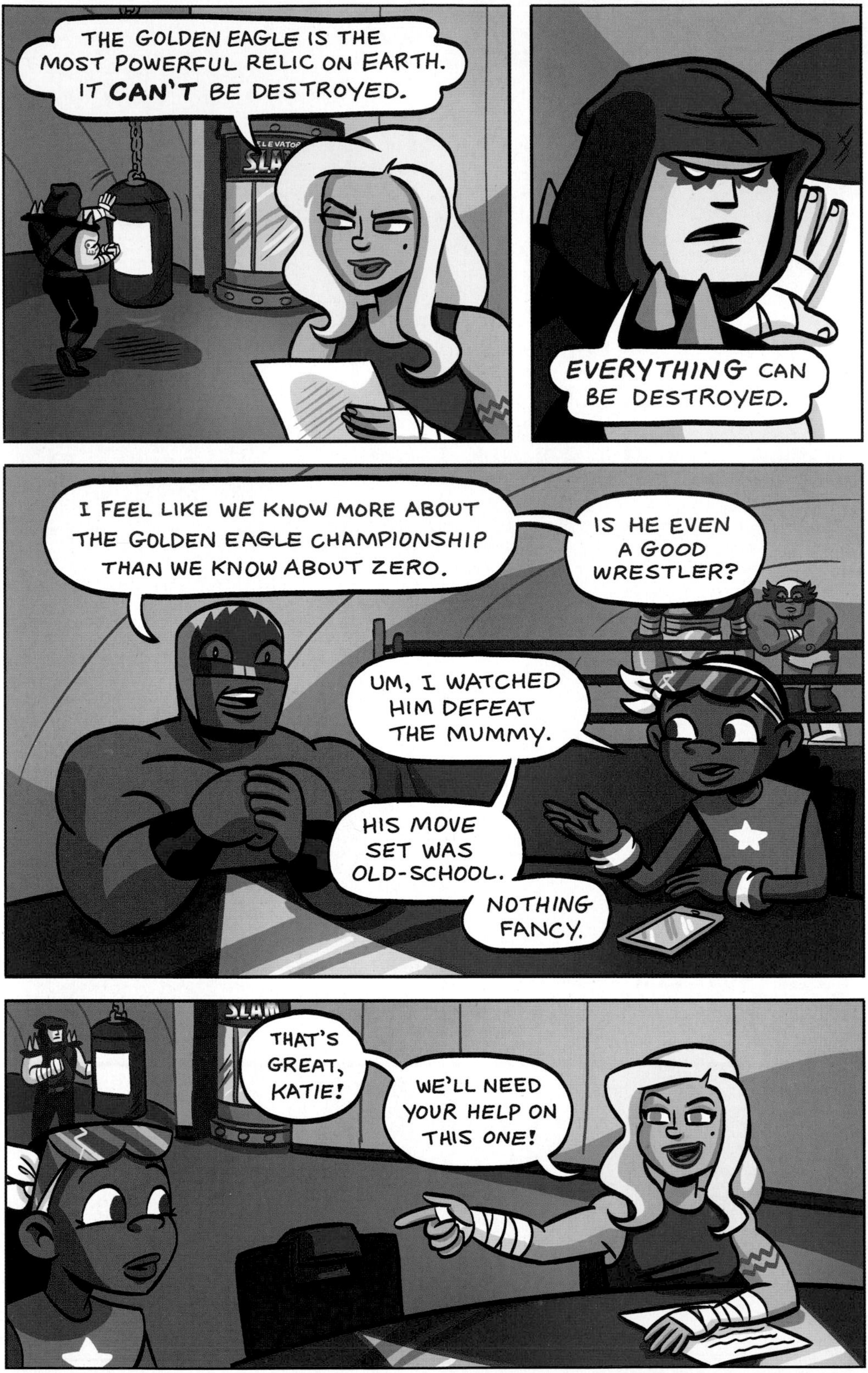
THE GOLDEN EAGLE IS THE MOST POWERFUL RELIC ON EARTH. IT **CAN'T** BE DESTROYED.
EVERYTHING CAN BE DESTROYED.
I FEEL LIKE WE KNOW MORE ABOUT THE GOLDEN EAGLE CHAMPIONSHIP THAN WE KNOW ABOUT ZERO.
IS HE EVEN A GOOD WRESTLER?
UM, I WATCHED HIM DEFEAT THE MUMMY.
HIS MOVE SET WAS OLD-SCHOOL.
NOTHING FANCY.
S.L.A.M
THAT'S GREAT, KATIE!
WE'LL NEED YOUR HELP ON THIS ONE!

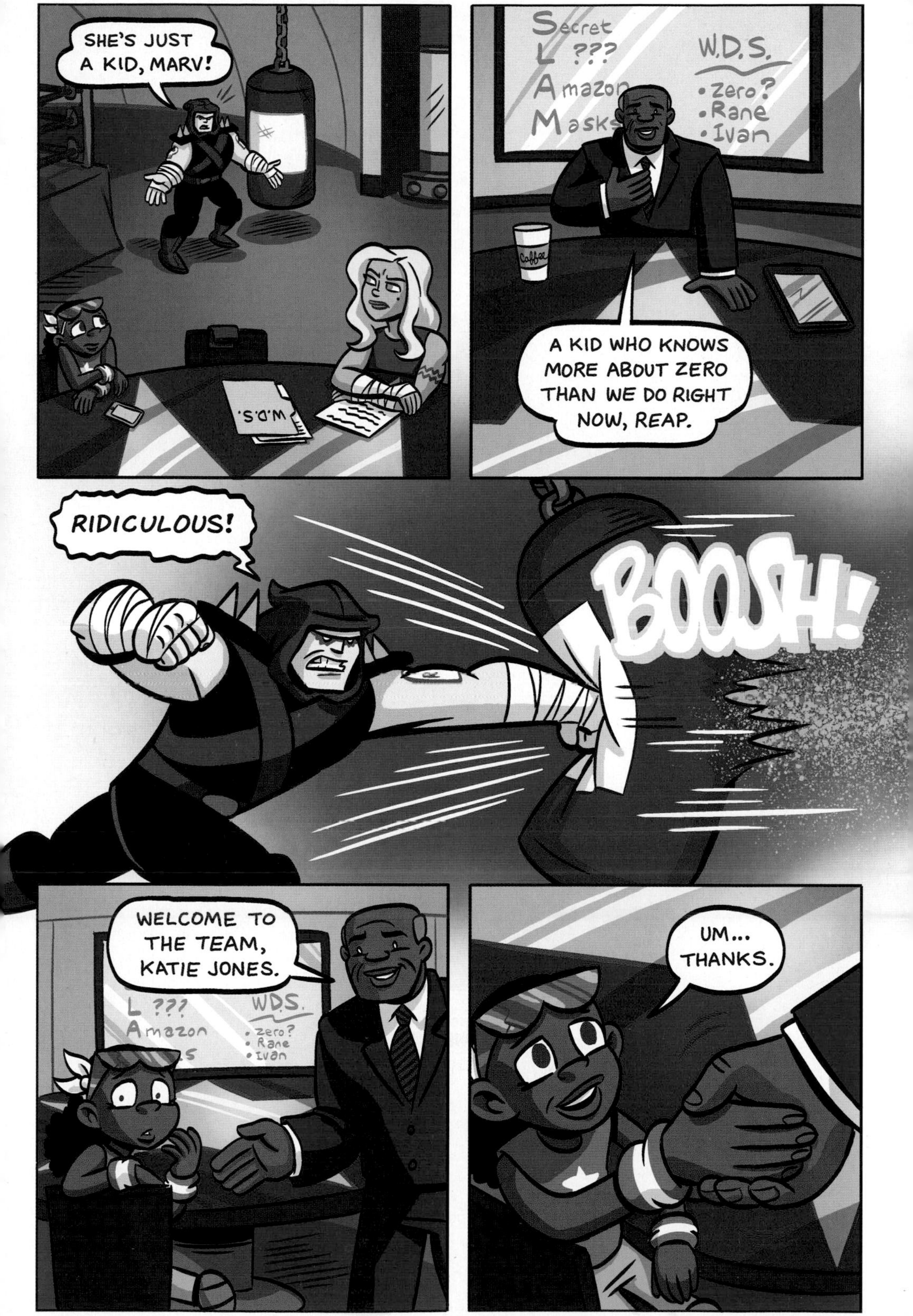
SHE'S JUST A KID, MARV!
W.D.S.
Secret
L ???
Amazon
Masks
W.D.S.
• Zero?
• Rane
• Ivan
Coffee
A KID WHO KNOWS MORE ABOUT ZERO THAN WE DO RIGHT NOW, REAP.
RIDICULOUS!
BOOSH!
WELCOME TO THE TEAM, KATIE JONES.
L ???
Amazon
W.D.S.
• Zero?
• Rane
• Ivan
UM... THANKS.

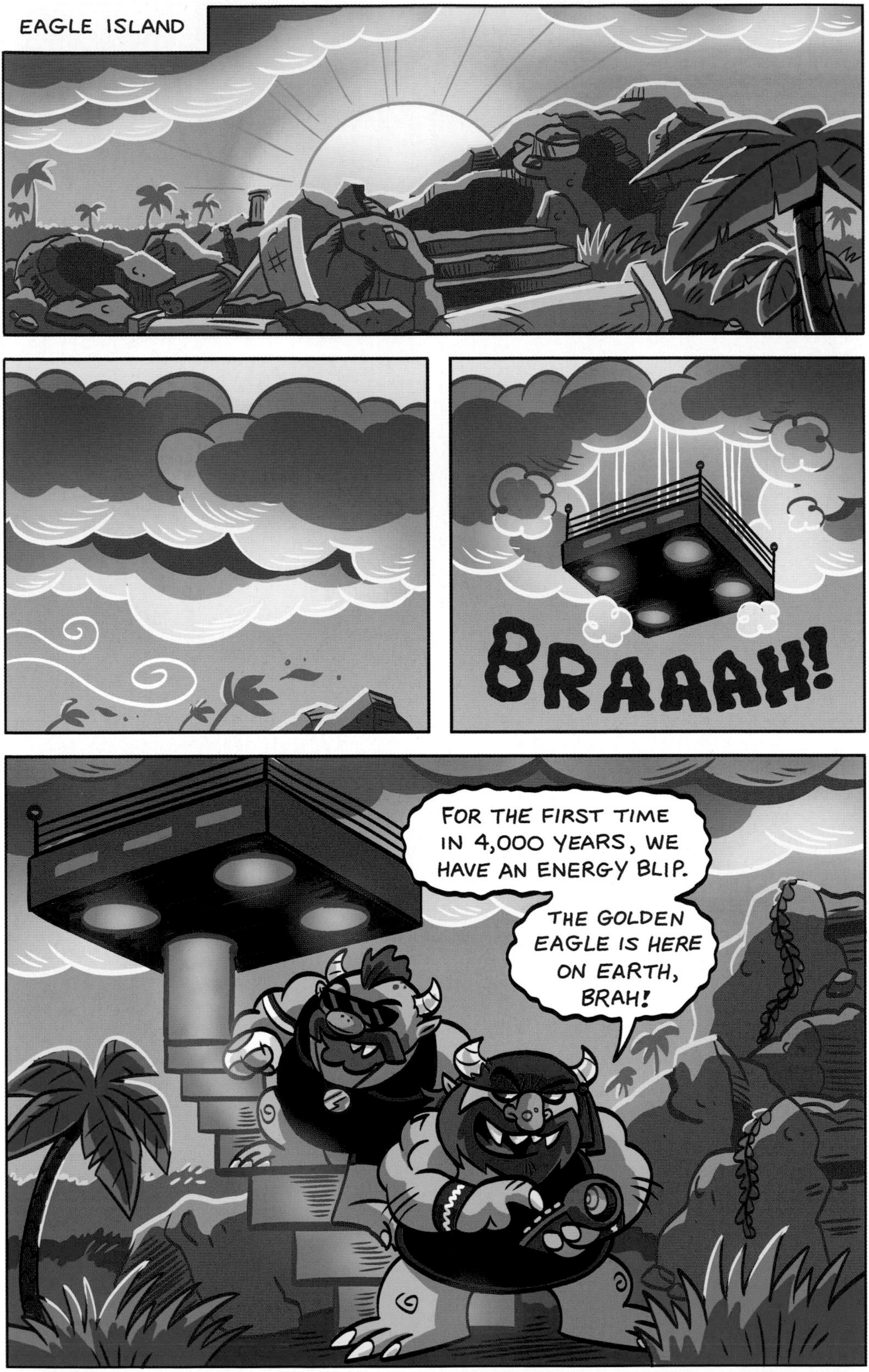
EAGLE ISLAND
BRAAAH!
FOR THE FIRST TIME IN 4,000 YEARS, WE HAVE AN ENERGY BLIP.
THE GOLDEN EAGLE IS HERE ON EARTH, BRAH!

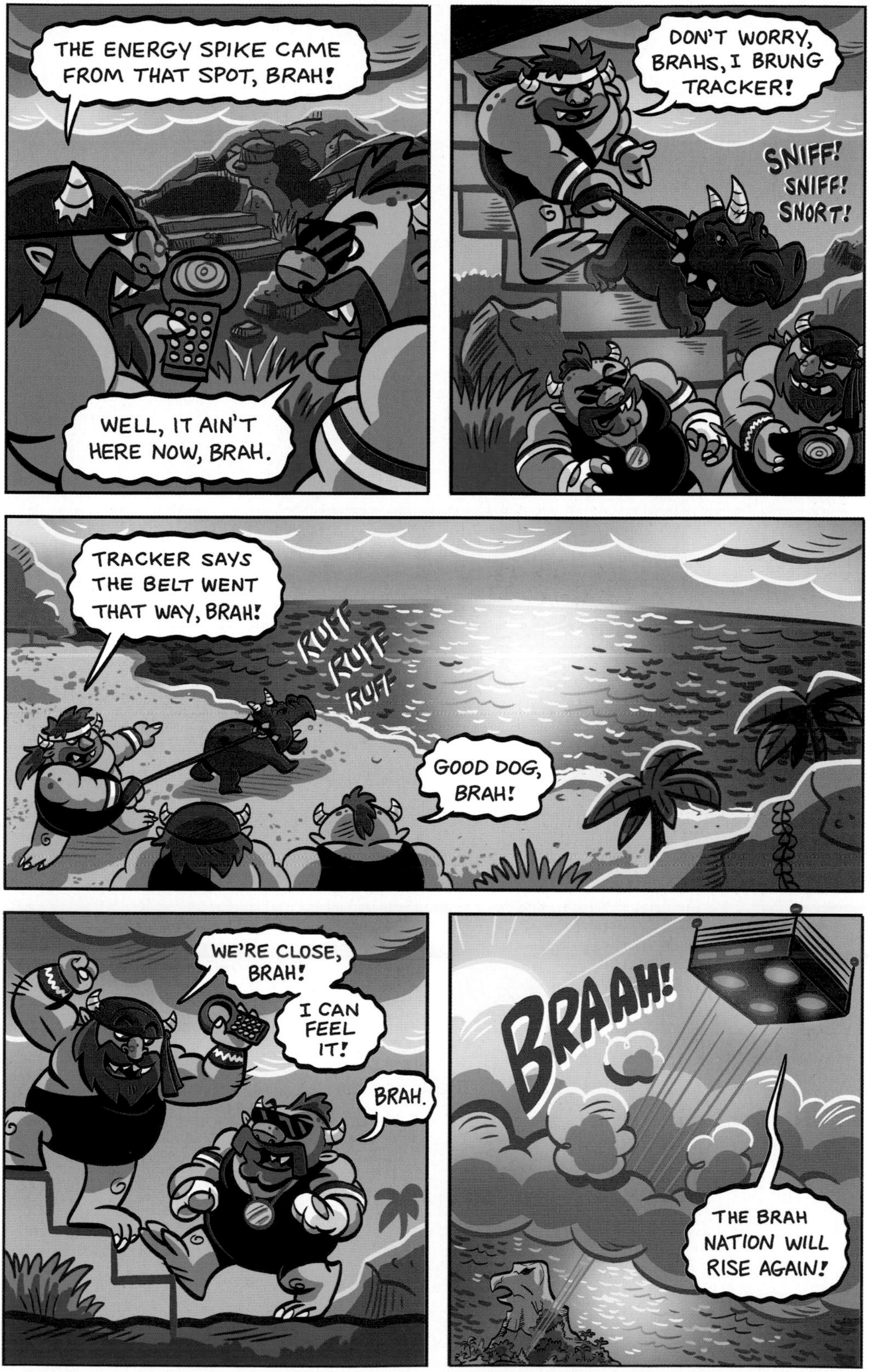
THE ENERGY SPIKE CAME FROM THAT SPOT, BRAH!
WELL, IT AIN'T HERE NOW, BRAH.
DON'T WORRY, BRAHS, I BRUNG TRACKER!
SNIFF! SNIFF! SNORT!
TRACKER SAYS THE BELT WENT THAT WAY, BRAH!
RUFF RUFF RUFF
GOOD DOG, BRAH!
WE'RE CLOSE, BRAH!
I CAN FEEL IT!
BRAH.
BRAAH!
THE BRAH NATION WILL RISE AGAIN!

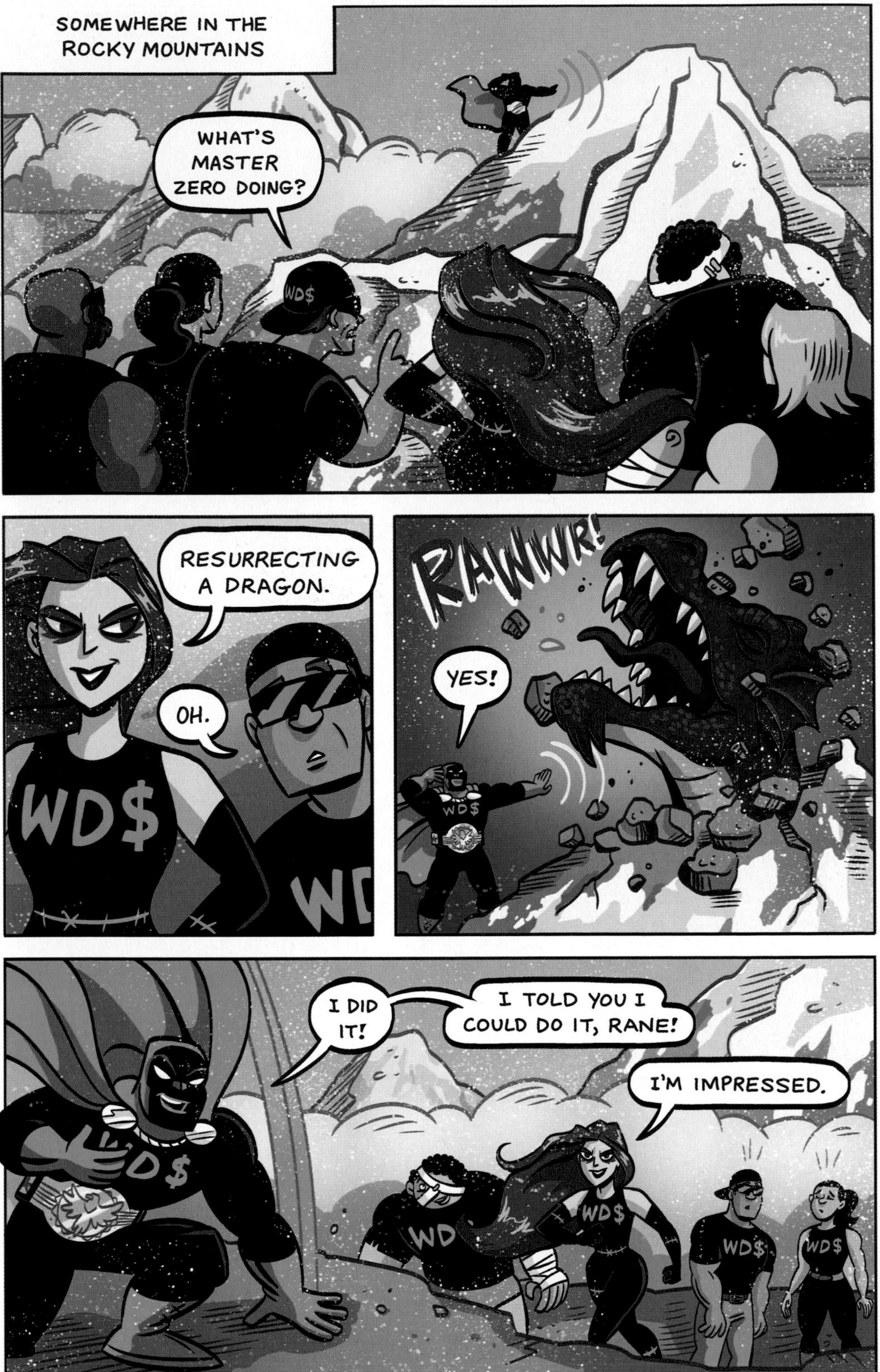
SOMEWHERE IN THE ROCKY MOUNTAINS
WHAT'S MASTER ZERO DOING?
RESURRECTING A DRAGON.
OH.
RAWWR!
YES!
I DID IT!
I TOLD YOU I COULD DO IT, RANE!
I'M IMPRESSED.

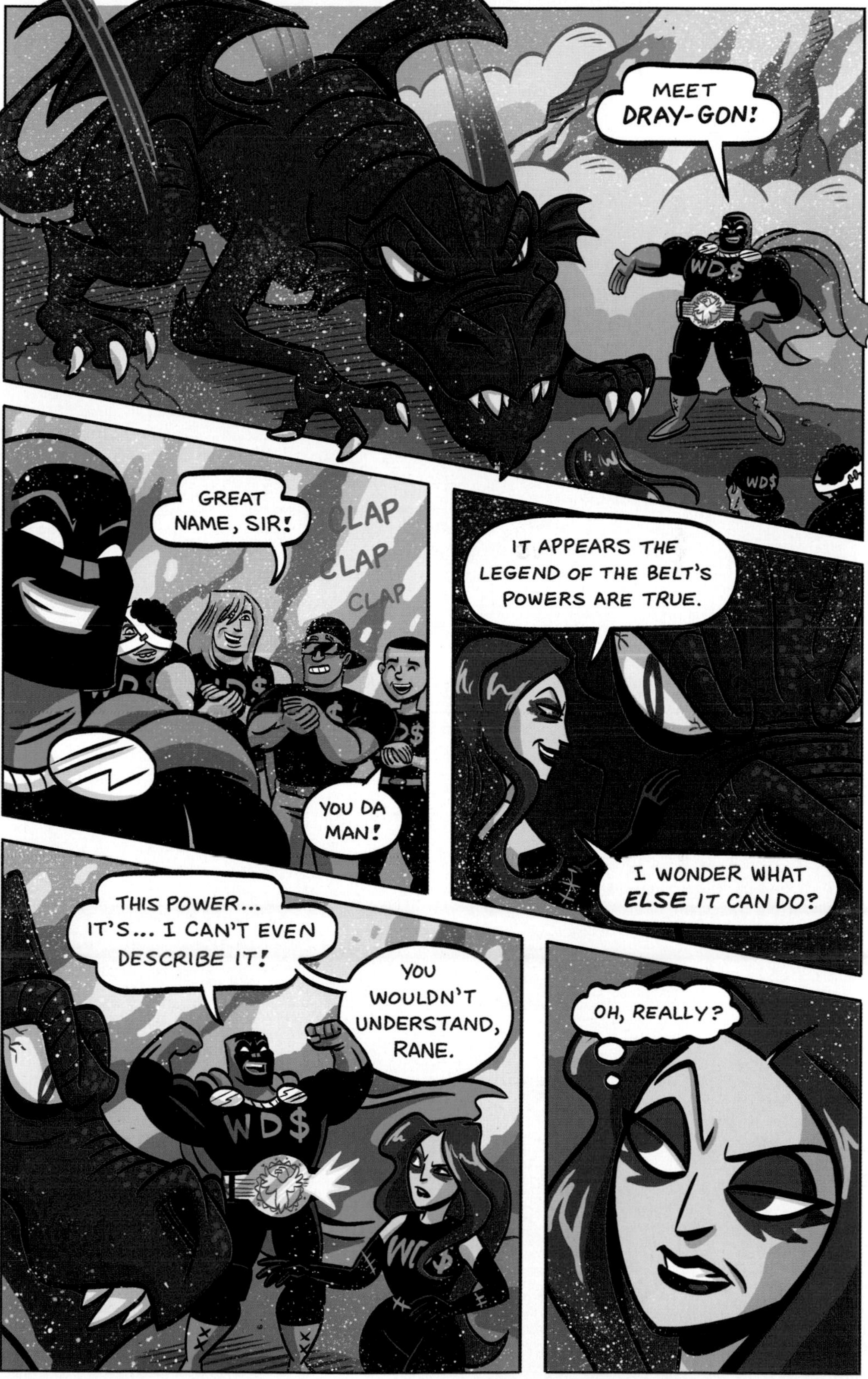
MEET DRAY-GON!
GREAT NAME, SIR!
CLAP CLAP CLAP
YOU DA MAN!
IT APPEARS THE LEGEND OF THE BELT'S POWERS ARE TRUE.
I WONDER WHAT ELSE IT CAN DO?
THIS POWER... IT'S... I CAN'T EVEN DESCRIBE IT!
YOU WOULDN'T UNDERSTAND, RANE.
OH, REALLY?

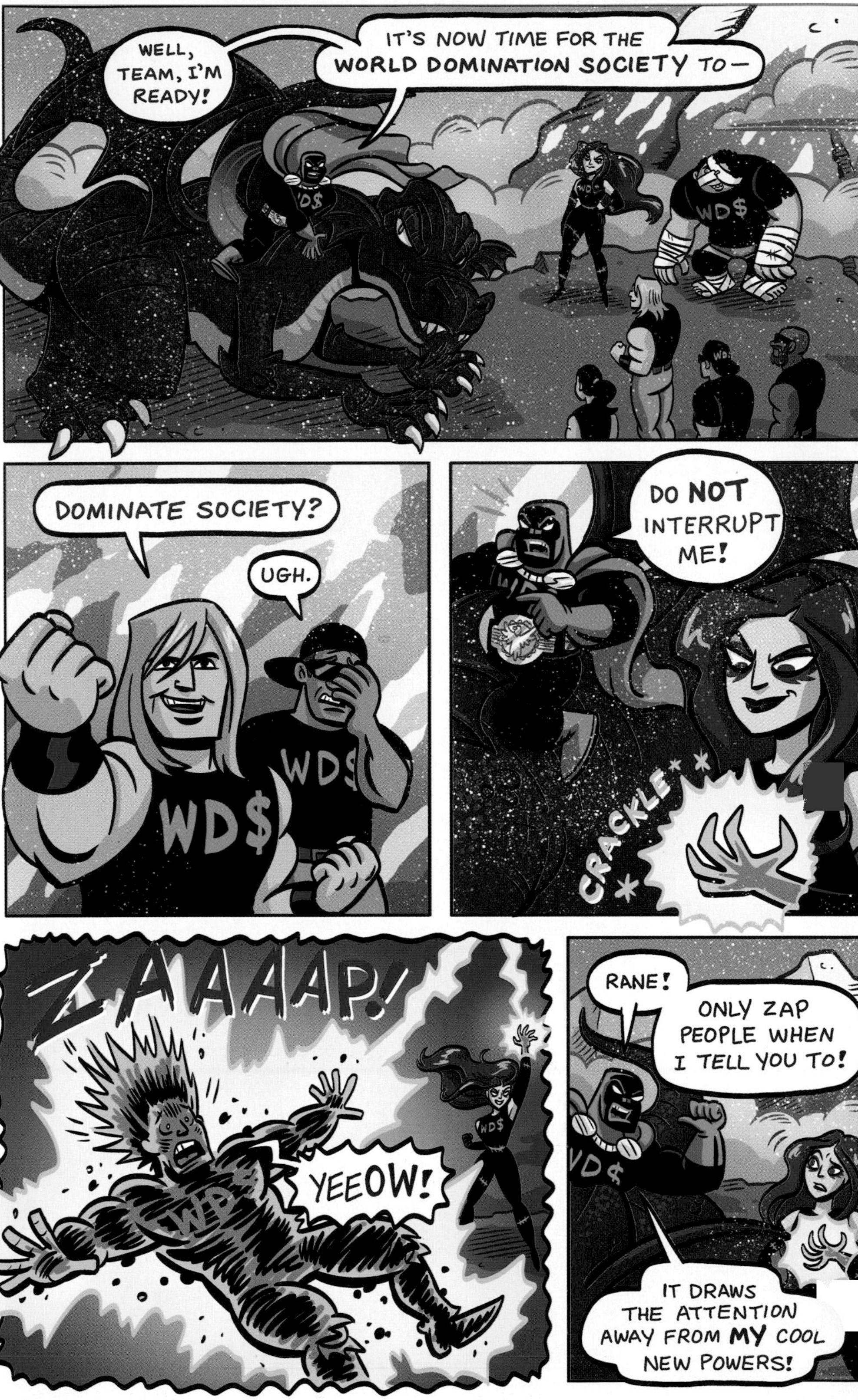
WELL, TEAM, I'M READY!
IT'S NOW TIME FOR THE WORLD DOMINATION SOCIETY TO—
WD$
DOMINATE SOCIETY?
UGH.
WD$
WD$
DO NOT INTERRUPT ME!
CRACKLE
ZAAAAP!
YEEOW!
WD$
RANE!
ONLY ZAP PEOPLE WHEN I TELL YOU TO!
IT DRAWS THE ATTENTION AWAY FROM MY COOL NEW POWERS!

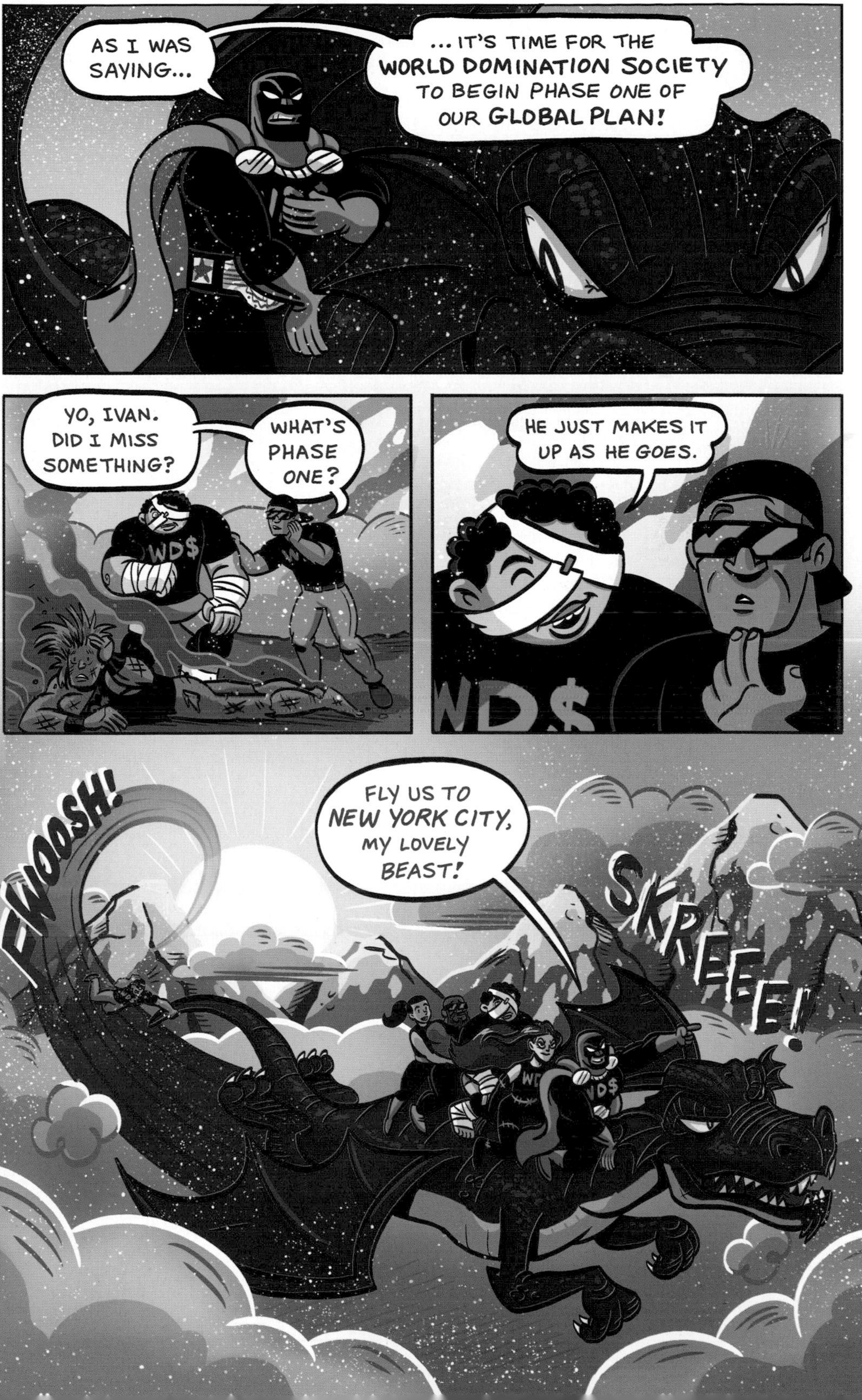
AS I WAS SAYING...
... IT'S TIME FOR THE WORLD DOMINATION SOCIETY TO BEGIN PHASE ONE OF OUR GLOBAL PLAN!
YO, IVAN. DID I MISS SOMETHING?
WHAT'S PHASE ONE?
WD$
HE JUST MAKES IT UP AS HE GOES.
WD$
FWOOSH!
FLY US TO NEW YORK CITY, MY LOVELY BEAST!
SKREEEE!
WD$

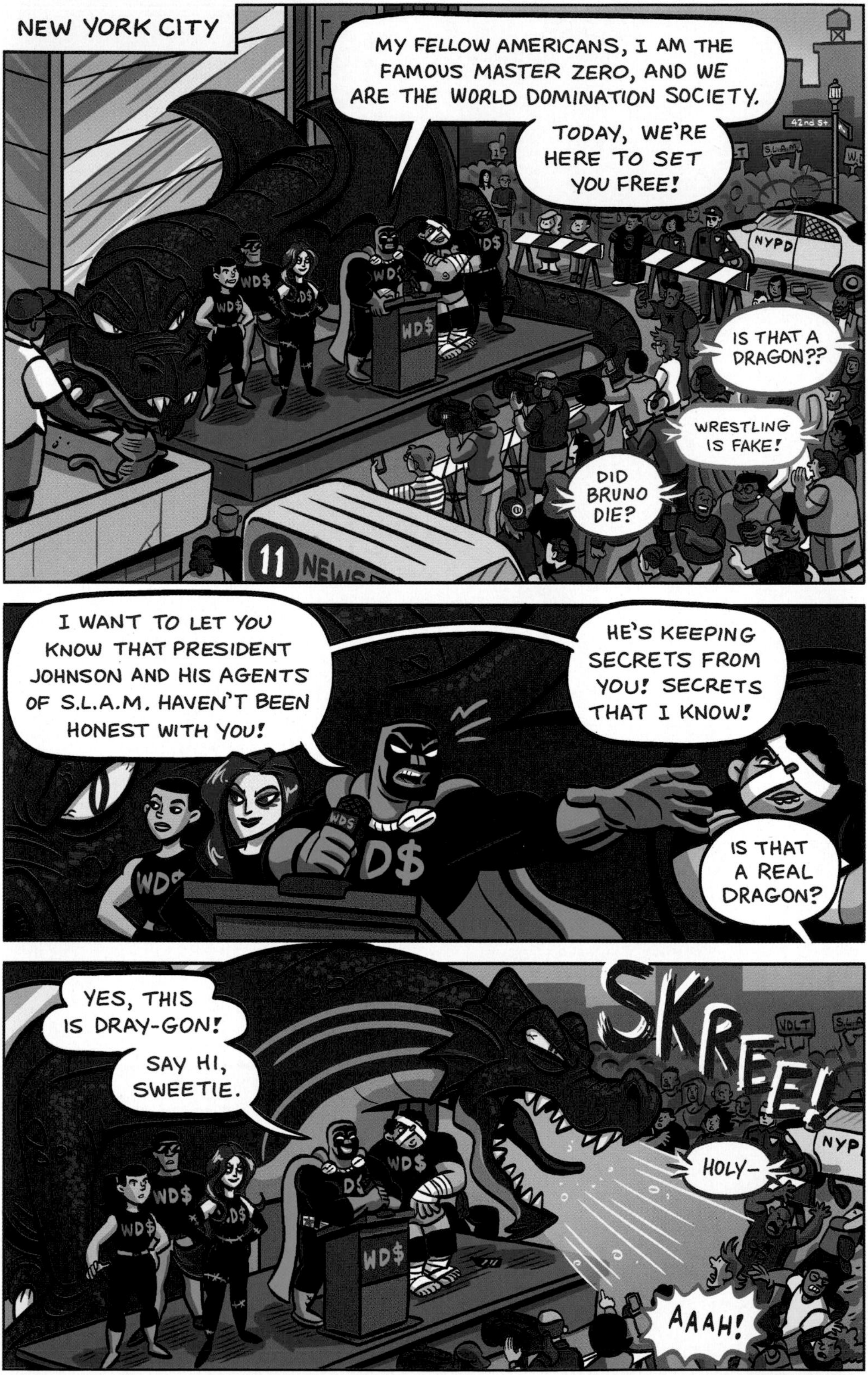
NEW YORK CITY
MY FELLOW AMERICANS, I AM THE FAMOUS MASTER ZERO, AND WE ARE THE WORLD DOMINATION SOCIETY.
TODAY, WE'RE HERE TO SET YOU FREE!
42nd St.
S.L.A.M.
NYPD
WD$
IS THAT A DRAGON??
WRESTLING IS FAKE!
DID BRUNO DIE?
11 NEWS
I WANT TO LET YOU KNOW THAT PRESIDENT JOHNSON AND HIS AGENTS OF S.L.A.M. HAVEN'T BEEN HONEST WITH YOU!
HE'S KEEPING SECRETS FROM YOU! SECRETS THAT I KNOW!
IS THAT A REAL DRAGON?
YES, THIS IS DRAY-GON!
SAY HI, SWEETIE.
SKREEE!
HOLY-
AAAH!

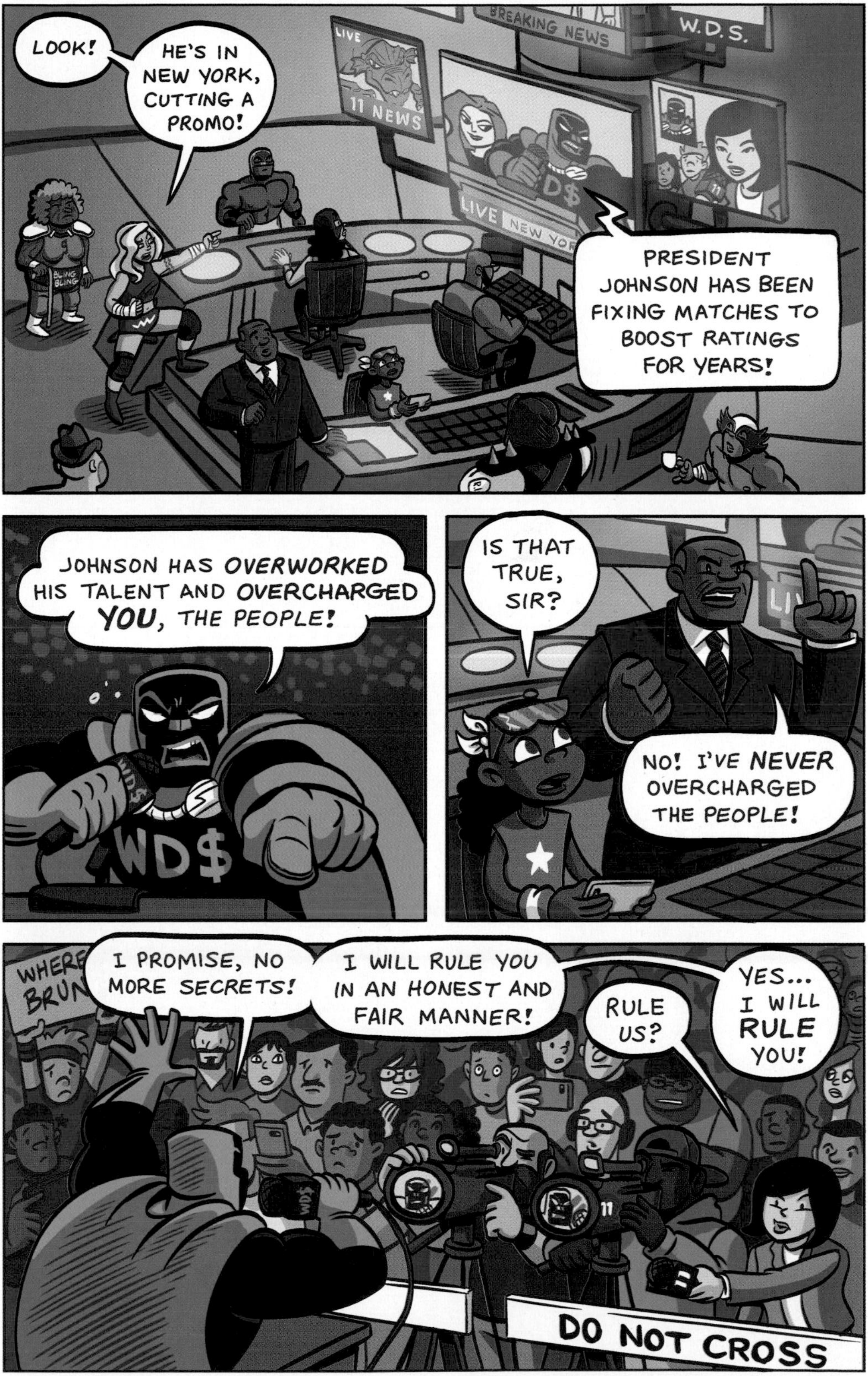
LOOK!
HE'S IN NEW YORK, CUTTING A PROMO!
BREAKING NEWS
W.D.S.
LIVE
11 NEWS
LIVE NEW YORK
PRESIDENT JOHNSON HAS BEEN FIXING MATCHES TO BOOST RATINGS FOR YEARS!
BLING BLING
JOHNSON HAS OVERWORKED HIS TALENT AND OVERCHARGED YOU, THE PEOPLE!
WD$
IS THAT TRUE, SIR?
NO! I'VE NEVER OVERCHARGED THE PEOPLE!
I PROMISE, NO MORE SECRETS!
I WILL RULE YOU IN AN HONEST AND FAIR MANNER!
RULE US?
YES... I WILL RULE YOU!
DO NOT CROSS

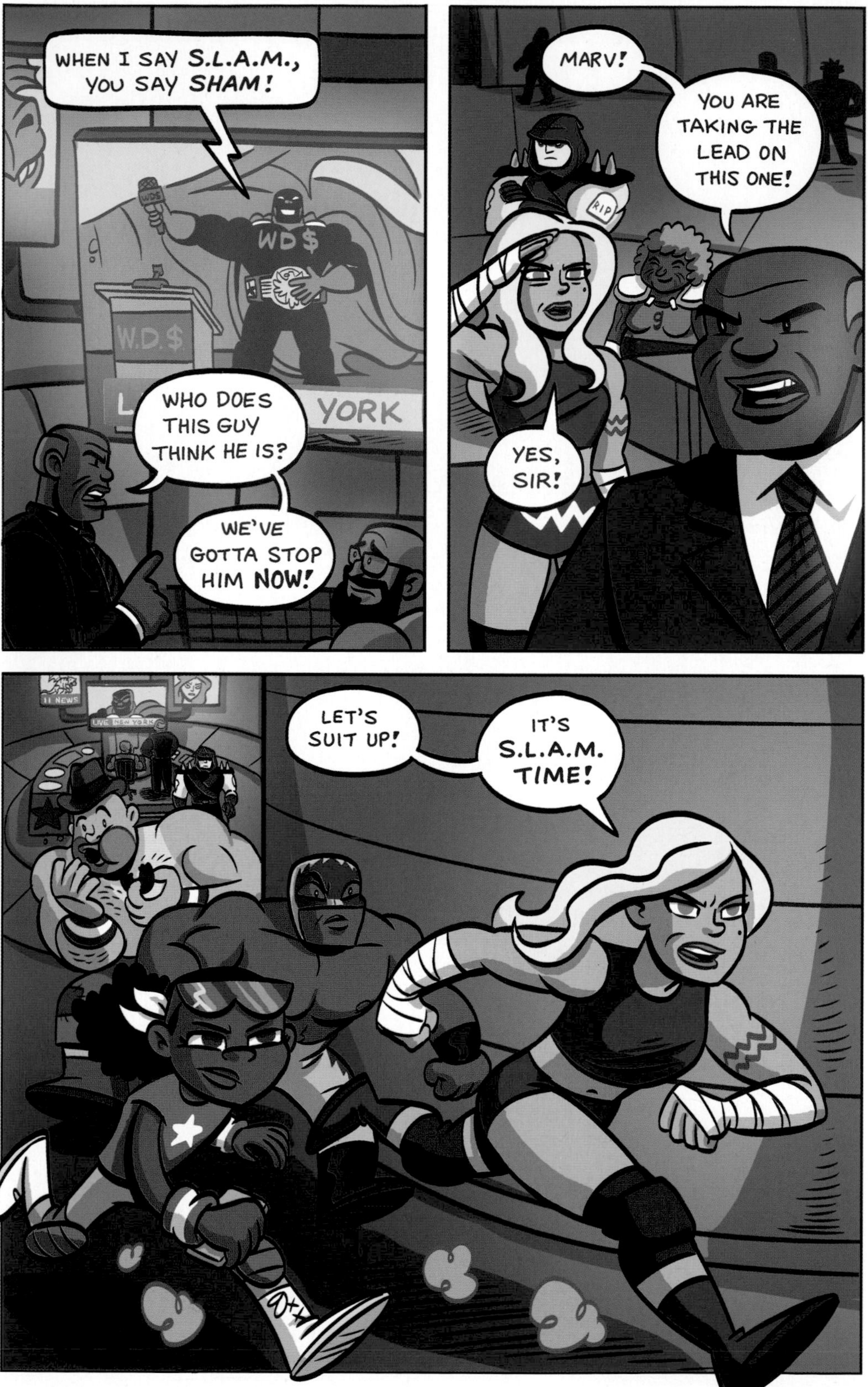
WHEN I SAY S.L.A.M., YOU SAY SHAM!
WDS
WD$
W.D.$
YORK
WHO DOES THIS GUY THINK HE IS?
WE'VE GOTTA STOP HIM NOW!
MARV!
YOU ARE TAKING THE LEAD ON THIS ONE!
RIP
YES, SIR!
11 NEWS
LIVE NEW YORK
LET'S SUIT UP!
IT'S S.L.A.M. TIME!

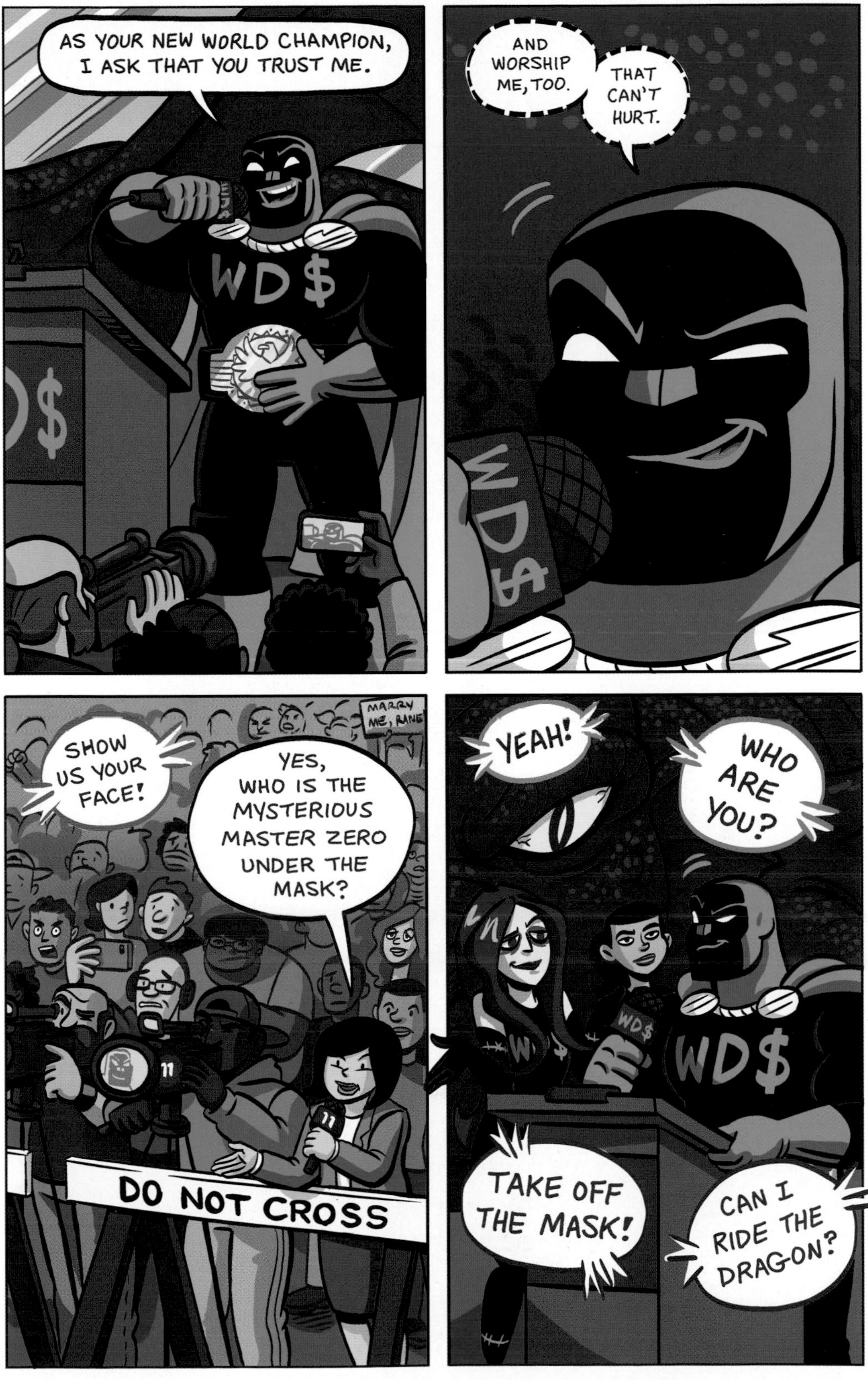

AS YOUR NEW WORLD CHAMPION, I ASK THAT YOU TRUST ME.
WD$
WD$
AND WORSHIP ME, TOO.
THAT CAN'T HURT.
WD$
MARRY ME, RANE
SHOW US YOUR FACE!
YES, WHO IS THE MYSTERIOUS MASTER ZERO UNDER THE MASK?
DO NOT CROSS
YEAH!
WHO ARE YOU?
WD$
WD$
TAKE OFF THE MASK!
CAN I RIDE THE DRAGON?

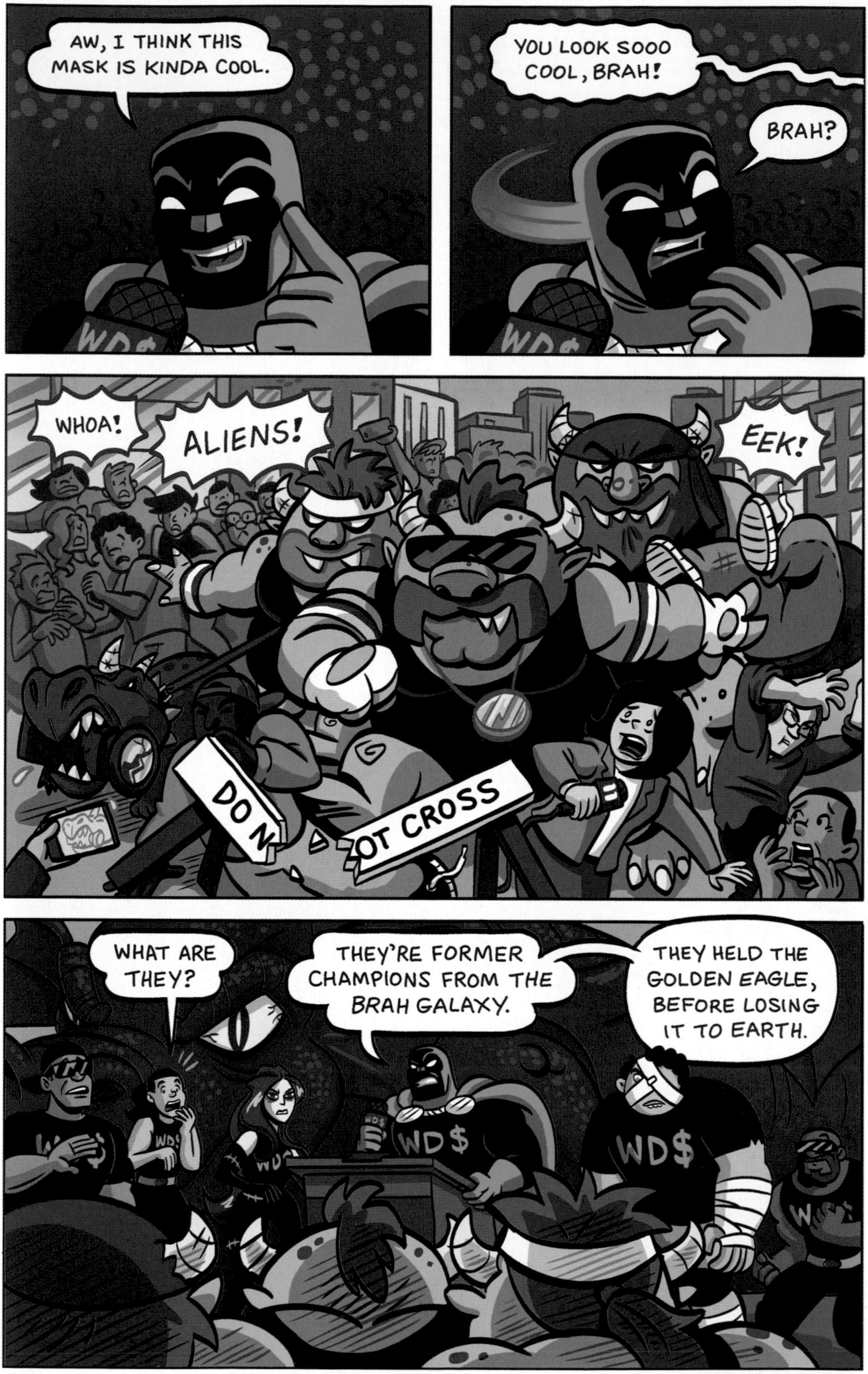
AW, I THINK THIS MASK IS KINDA COOL.
WD$
YOU LOOK SOOO COOL, BRAH!
BRAH?
WD$
WHOA!
ALIENS!
EEK!
DO N
OT CROSS
WHAT ARE THEY?
THEY'RE FORMER CHAMPIONS FROM THE BRAH GALAXY.
THEY HELD THE GOLDEN EAGLE, BEFORE LOSING IT TO EARTH.
WD$
WD$
WD$

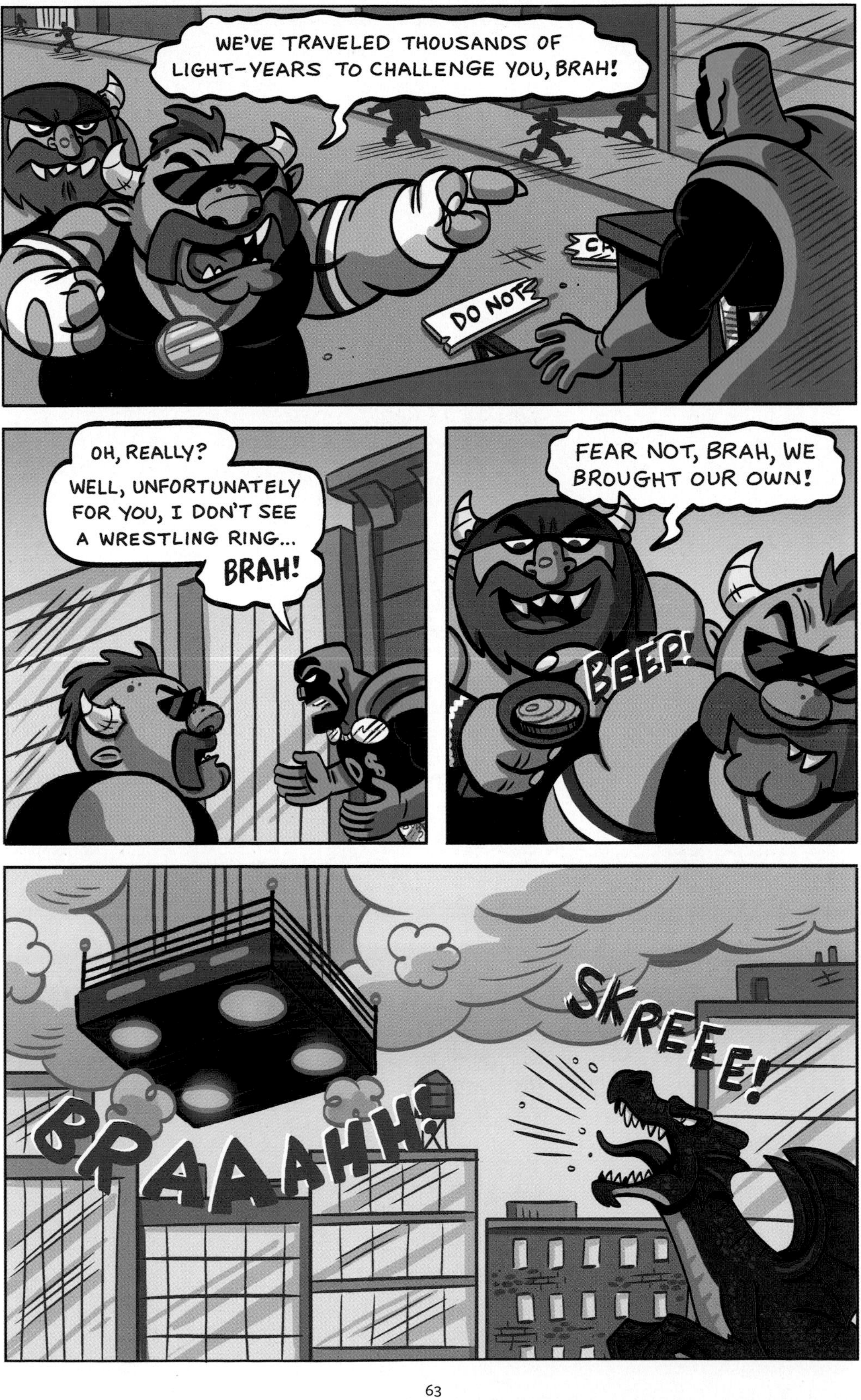

WE'VE TRAVELED THOUSANDS OF LIGHT-YEARS TO CHALLENGE YOU, BRAH!
DO NOT
OH, REALLY? WELL, UNFORTUNATELY FOR YOU, I DON'T SEE A WRESTLING RING... BRAH!
FEAR NOT, BRAH, WE BROUGHT OUR OWN!
BEEP!
BRAAAHH!
SKREEEE!

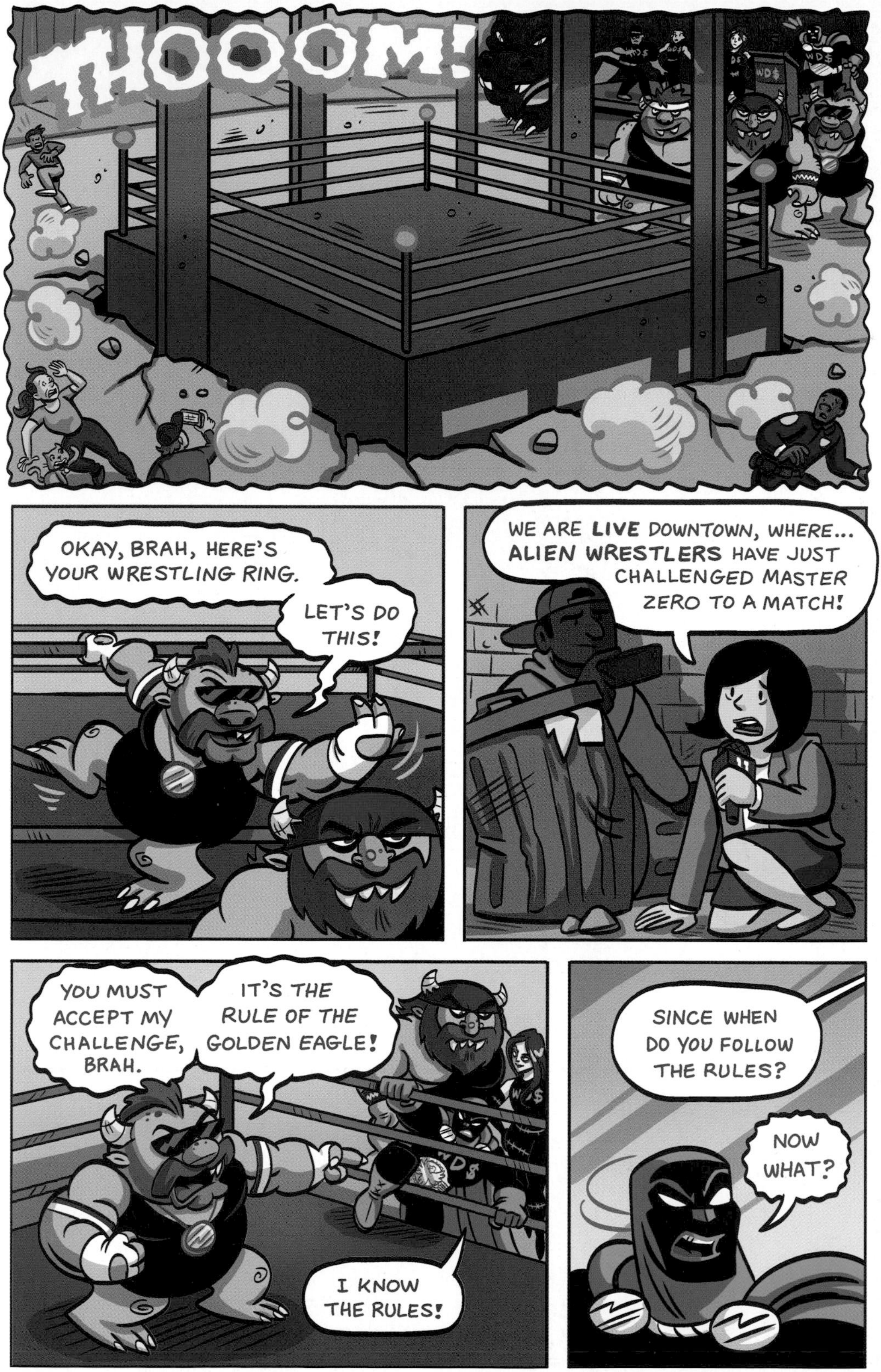
THOOOM!
WD$
OKAY, BRAH, HERE'S YOUR WRESTLING RING.
LET'S DO THIS!
WE ARE LIVE DOWNTOWN, WHERE... ALIEN WRESTLERS HAVE JUST CHALLENGED MASTER ZERO TO A MATCH!
YOU MUST ACCEPT MY CHALLENGE, BRAH.
IT'S THE RULE OF THE GOLDEN EAGLE!
I KNOW THE RULES!
SINCE WHEN DO YOU FOLLOW THE RULES?
NOW WHAT?

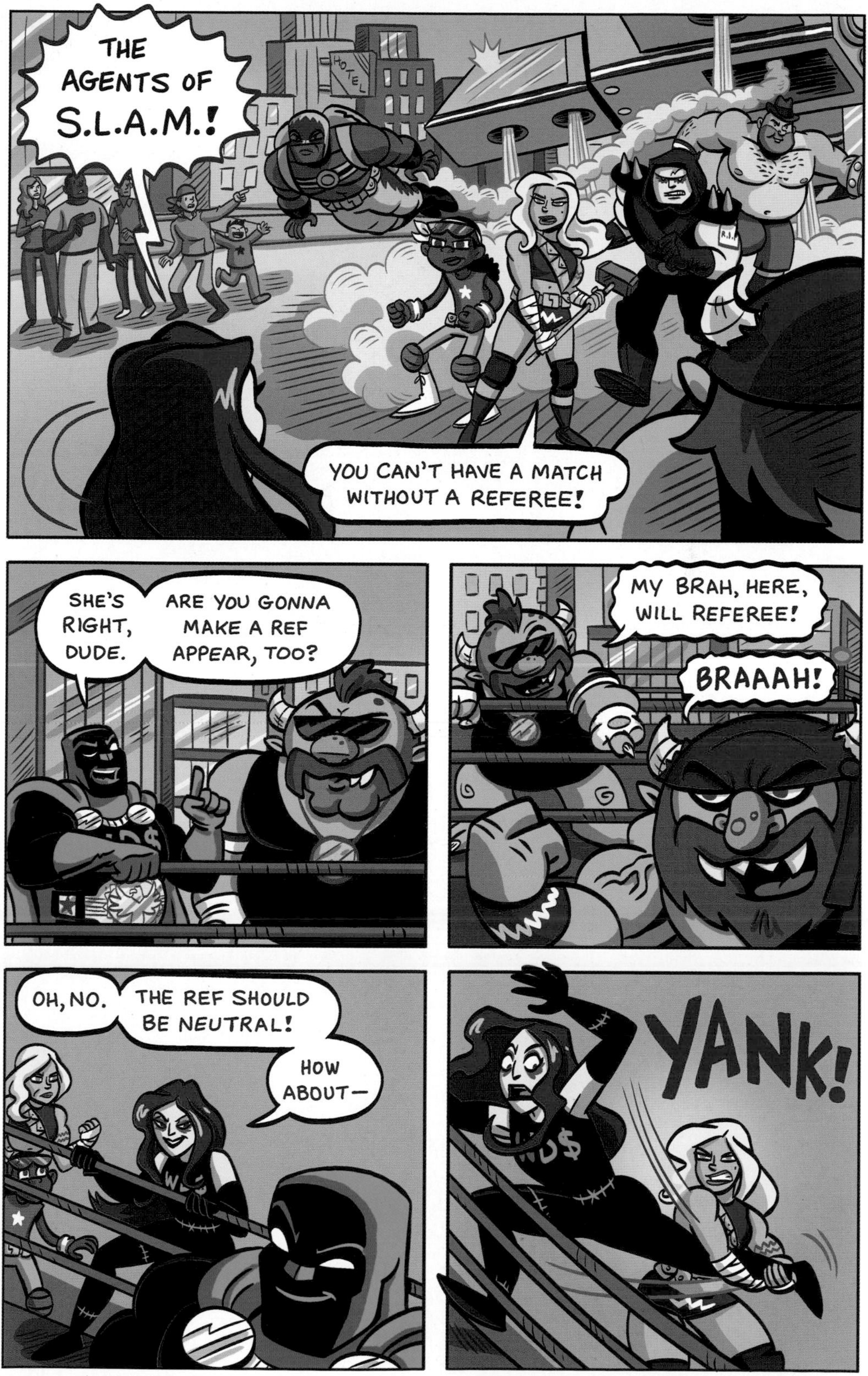
THE AGENTS OF S.L.A.M.!
YOU CAN'T HAVE A MATCH WITHOUT A REFEREE!
SHE'S RIGHT, DUDE.
ARE YOU GONNA MAKE A REF APPEAR, TOO?
MY BRAH, HERE, WILL REFEREE!
BRAAAH!
OH, NO.
THE REF SHOULD BE NEUTRAL!
HOW ABOUT—
YANK!

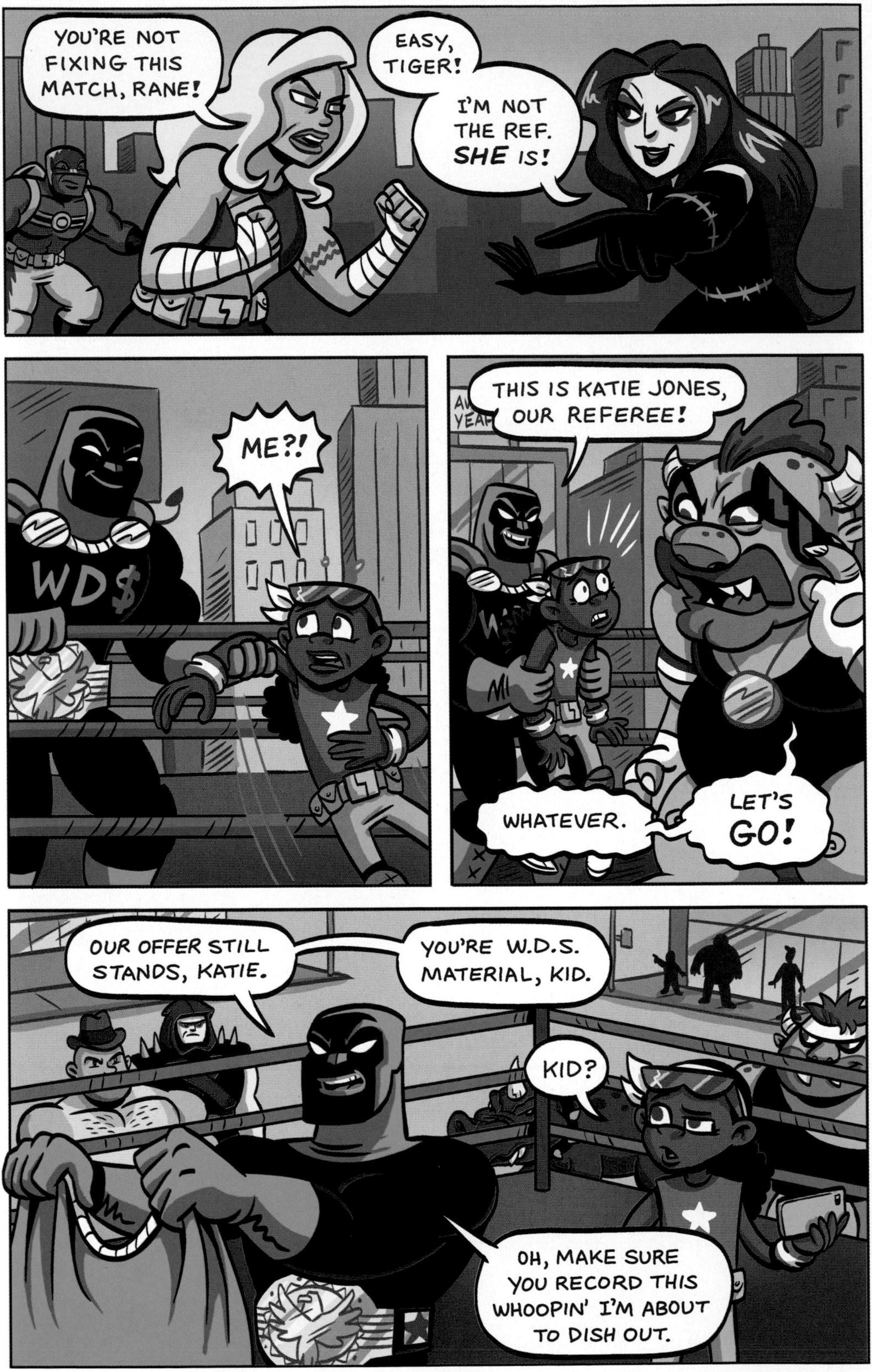
YOU'RE NOT FIXING THIS MATCH, RANE!
EASY, TIGER!
I'M NOT THE REF. SHE IS!
ME?!
THIS IS KATIE JONES, OUR REFEREE!
WHATEVER.
LET'S GO!
OUR OFFER STILL STANDS, KATIE.
YOU'RE W.D.S. MATERIAL, KID.
KID?
OH, MAKE SURE YOU RECORD THIS WHOOPIN' I'M ABOUT TO DISH OUT.

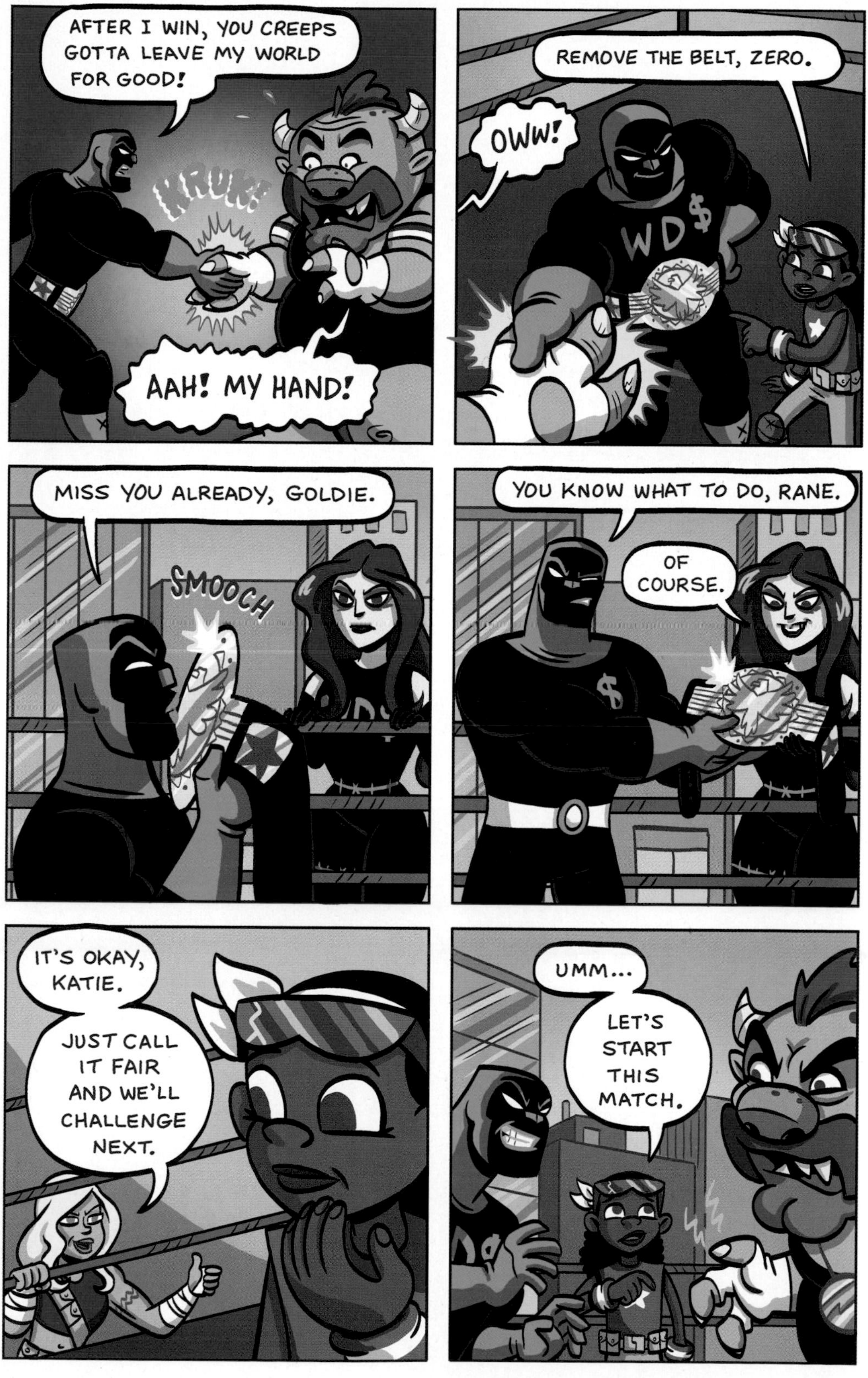
AFTER I WIN, YOU CREEPS GOTTA LEAVE MY WORLD FOR GOOD!
KRUK!
AAH! MY HAND!
REMOVE THE BELT, ZERO.
OWW!
WD$
MISS YOU ALREADY, GOLDIE.
SMOOCH
YOU KNOW WHAT TO DO, RANE.
OF COURSE.
IT'S OKAY, KATIE.
JUST CALL IT FAIR AND WE'LL CHALLENGE NEXT.
UMM...
LET'S START THIS MATCH.

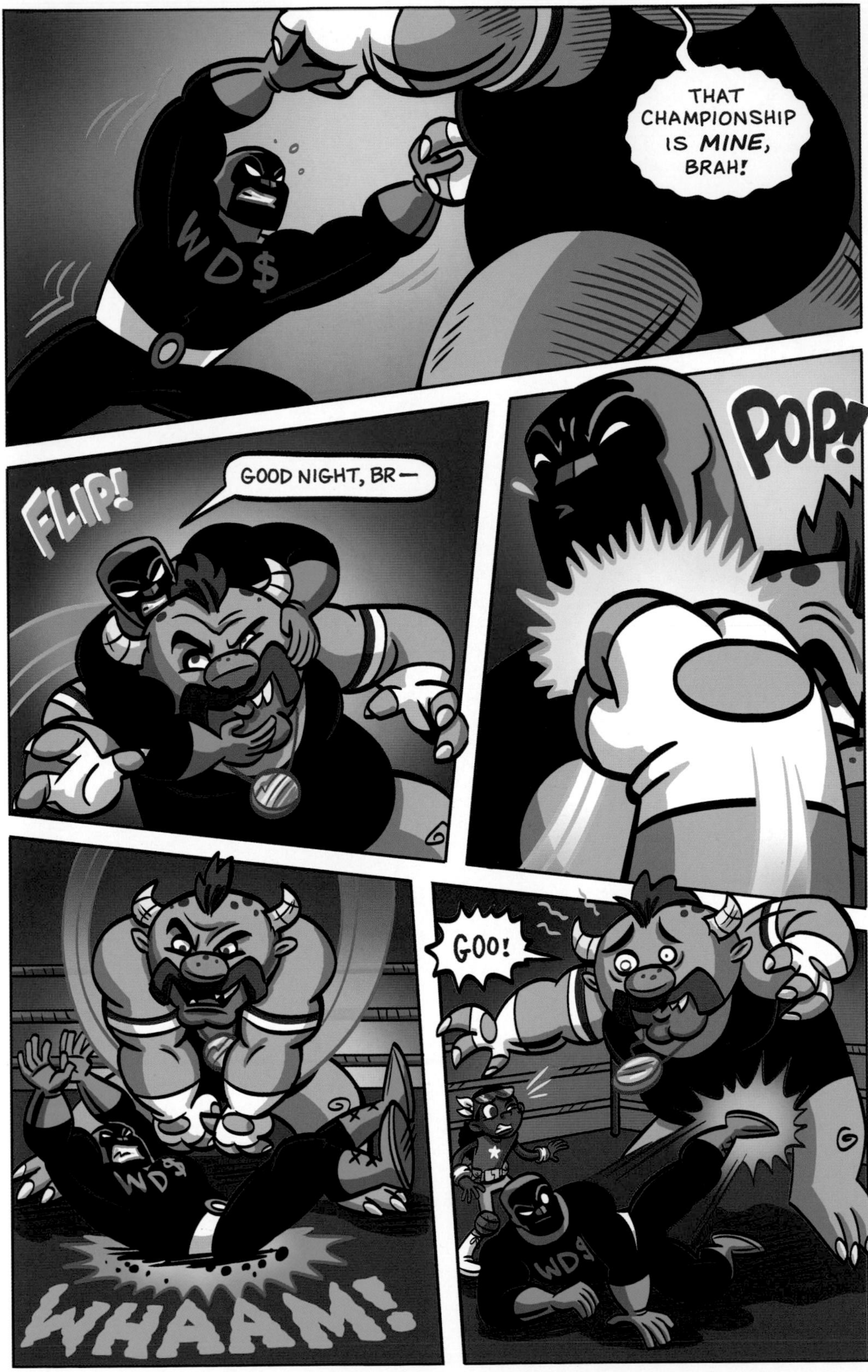
THAT CHAMPIONSHIP IS MINE, BRAH!
GOOD NIGHT, BR—
FLIP!
POP!
WHAM!
GOO!

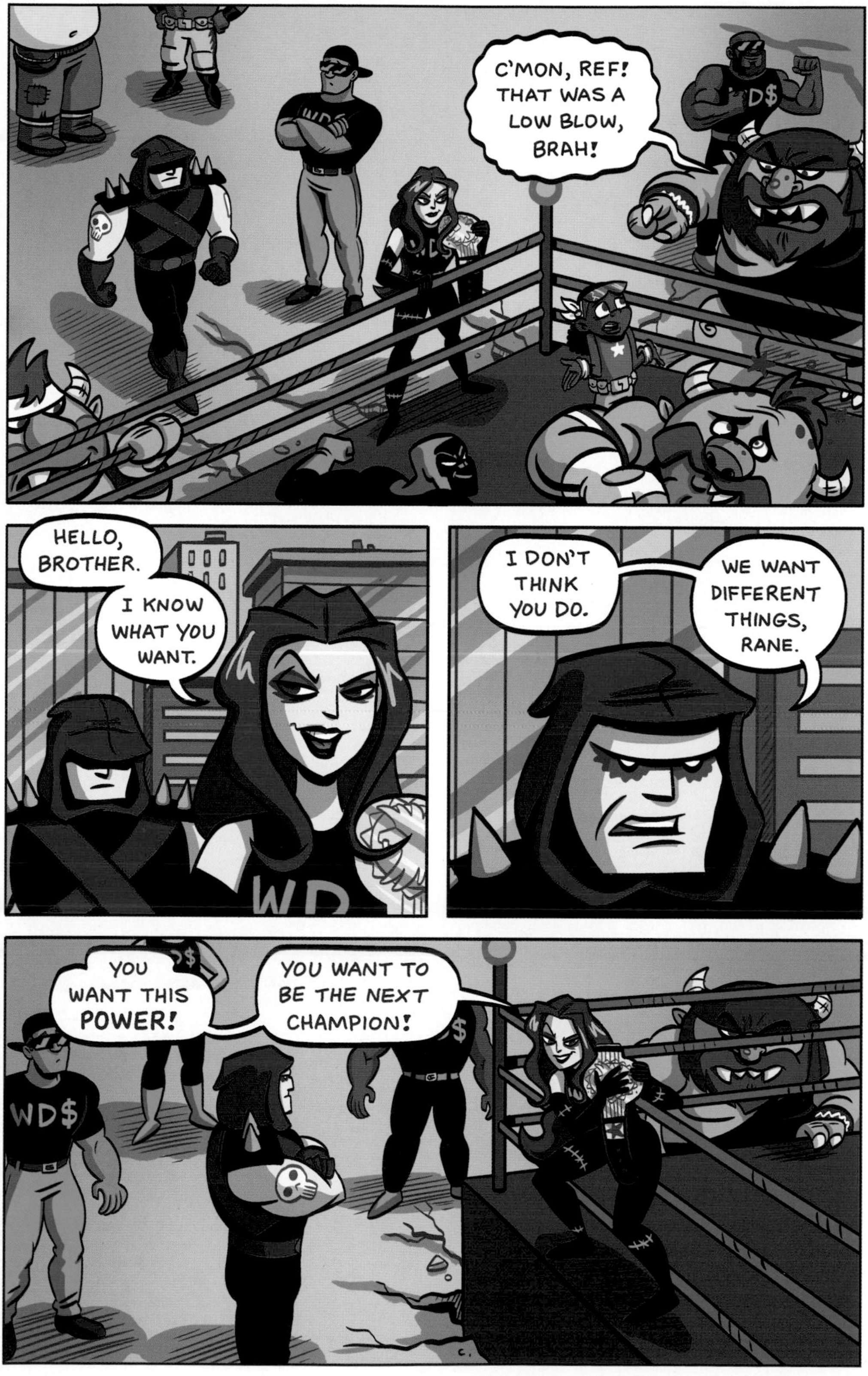
C'MON, REF! THAT WAS A LOW BLOW, BRAH!
HELLO, BROTHER.
I KNOW WHAT YOU WANT.
I DON'T THINK YOU DO.
WE WANT DIFFERENT THINGS, RANE.
YOU WANT THIS POWER!
YOU WANT TO BE THE NEXT CHAMPION!

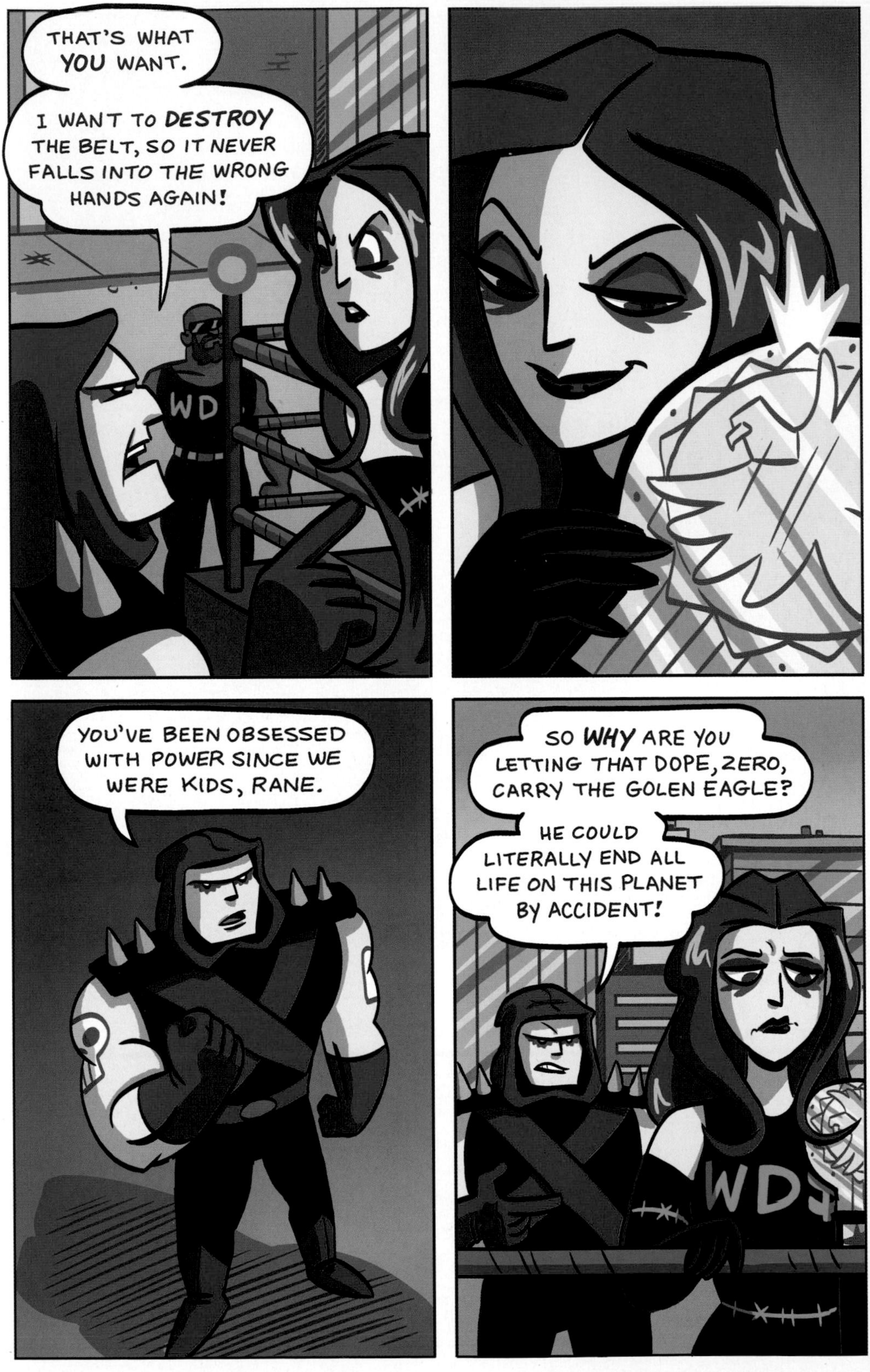
THAT'S WHAT YOU WANT.
I WANT TO DESTROY THE BELT, SO IT NEVER FALLS INTO THE WRONG HANDS AGAIN!
WD
YOU'VE BEEN OBSESSED WITH POWER SINCE WE WERE KIDS, RANE.
SO WHY ARE YOU LETTING THAT DOPE, ZERO, CARRY THE GOLEN EAGLE?
HE COULD LITERALLY END ALL LIFE ON THIS PLANET BY ACCIDENT!
WDJ

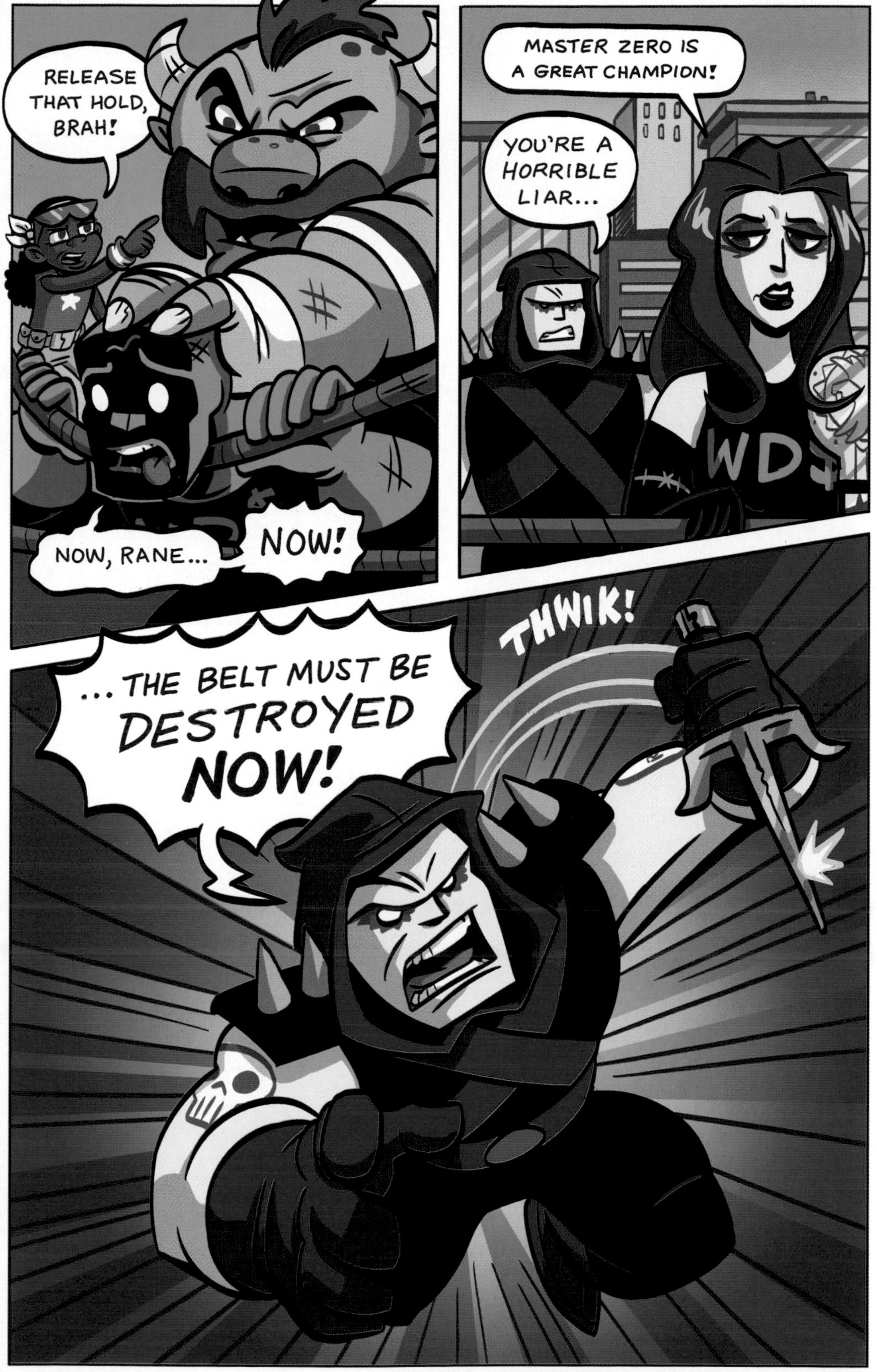
RELEASE THAT HOLD, BRAH!
NOW, RANE...
NOW!
MASTER ZERO IS A GREAT CHAMPION!
YOU'RE A HORRIBLE LIAR...
... THE BELT MUST BE DESTROYED NOW!
THWIK!

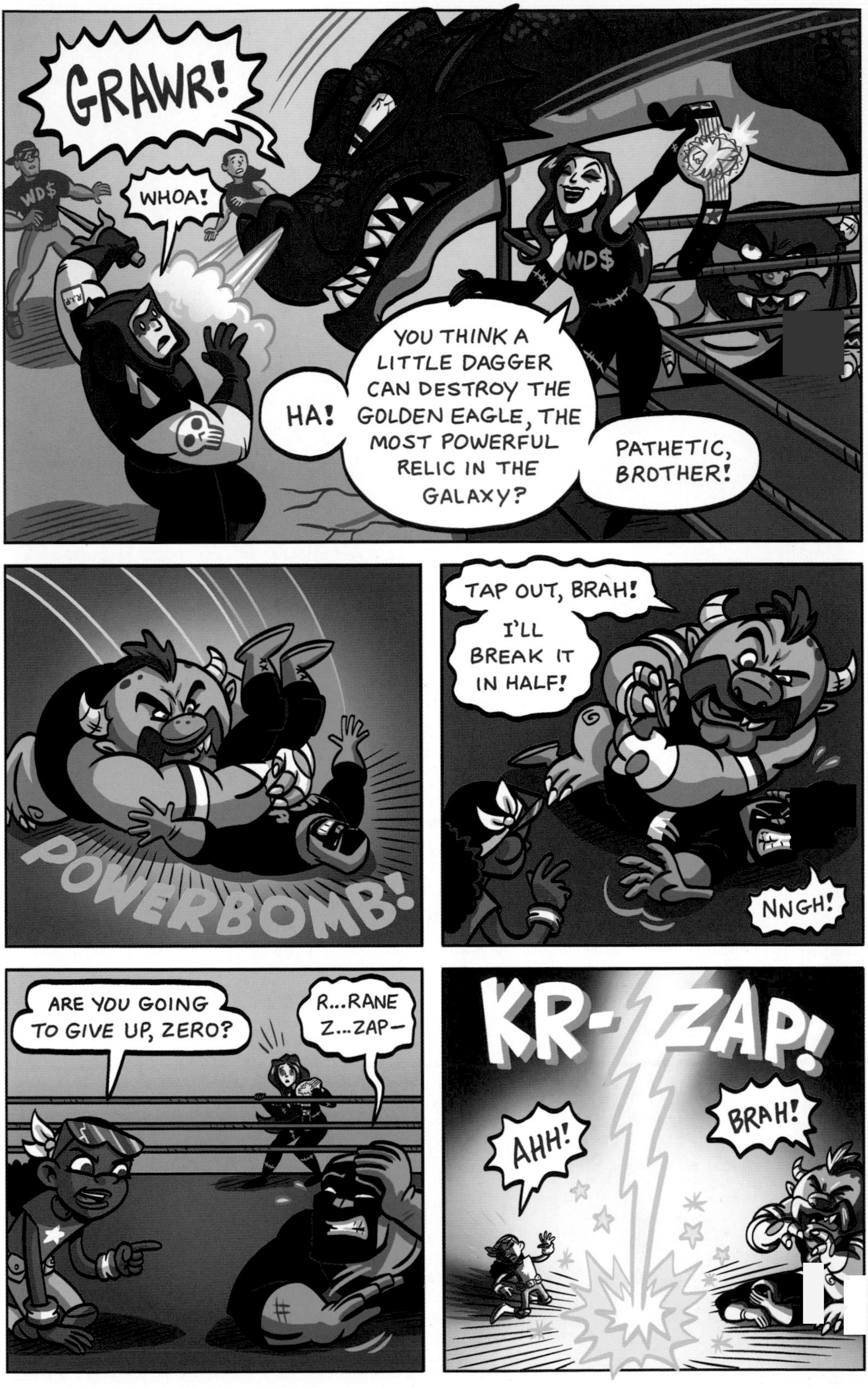
GRAWR!
WHOA!
WD$
R.I.P.
WD$
HA!
YOU THINK A LITTLE DAGGER CAN DESTROY THE GOLDEN EAGLE, THE MOST POWERFUL RELIC IN THE GALAXY?
PATHETIC, BROTHER!
POWERBOMB!
TAP OUT, BRAH!
I'LL BREAK IT IN HALF!
NNGH!
ARE YOU GOING TO GIVE UP, ZERO?
R...RANE Z...ZAP—
KR-ZAP!
AHH!
BRAH!

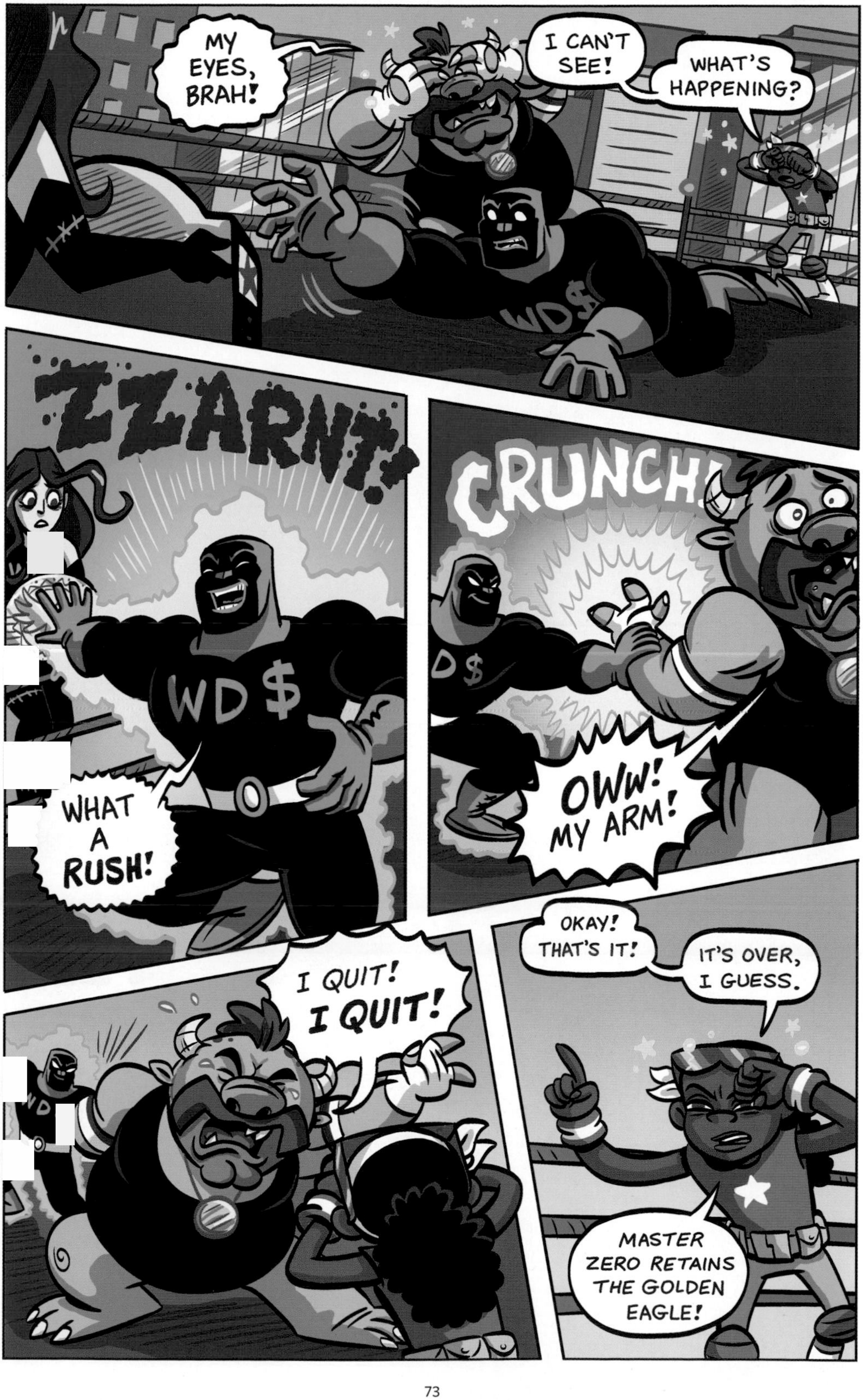
MY EYES, BRAH!
I CAN'T SEE!
WHAT'S HAPPENING?
ZZARNT!
WD$
WHAT A RUSH!
CRUNCH!
OWW! MY ARM!
I QUIT! I QUIT!
OKAY! THAT'S IT!
IT'S OVER, I GUESS.
MASTER ZERO RETAINS THE GOLDEN EAGLE!

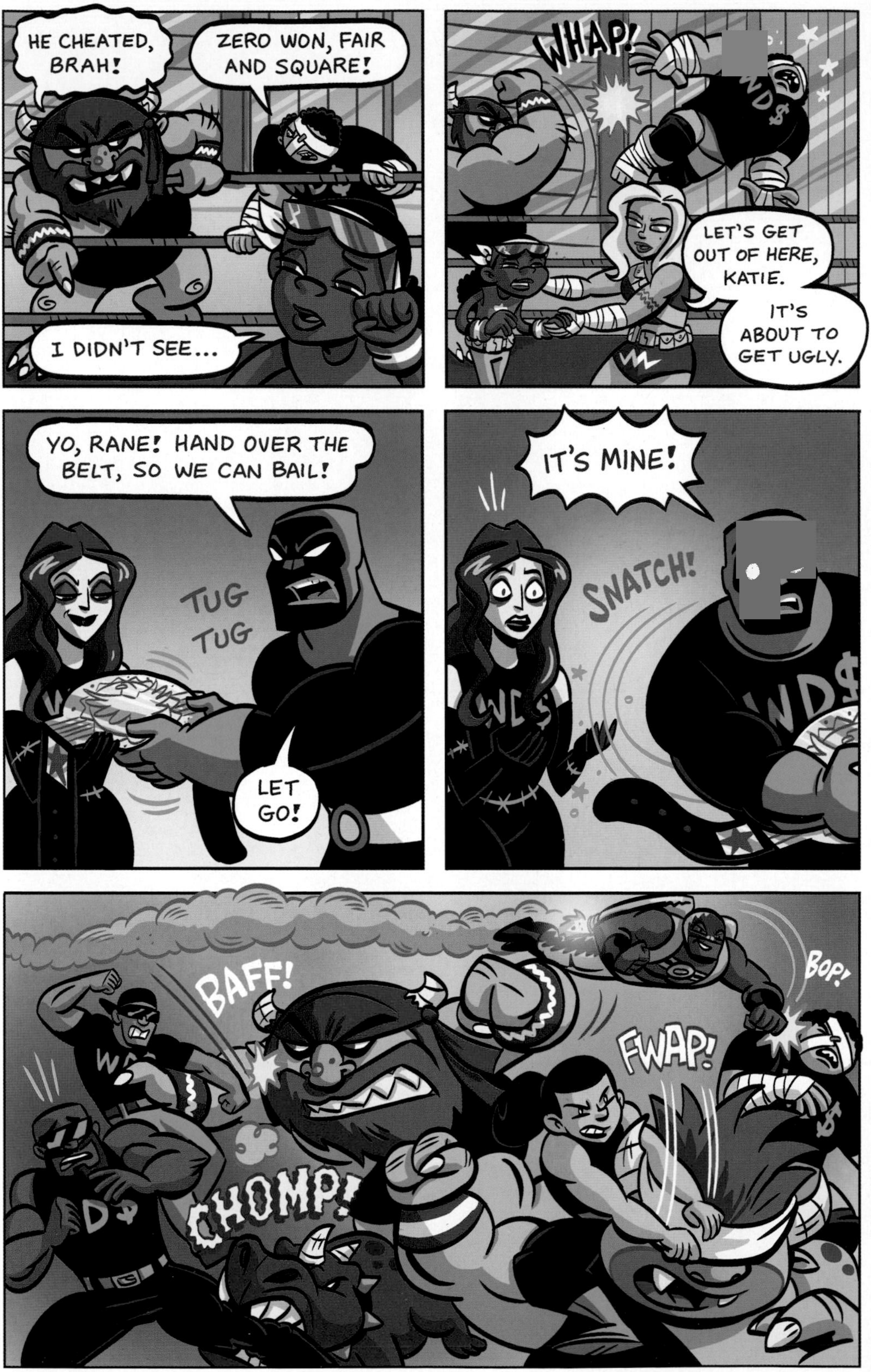
HE CHEATED, BRAH!
ZERO WON, FAIR AND SQUARE!
I DIDN'T SEE...
WHAP!
LET'S GET OUT OF HERE, KATIE.
IT'S ABOUT TO GET UGLY.
YO, RANE! HAND OVER THE BELT, SO WE CAN BAIL!
TUG TUG
LET GO!
IT'S MINE!
SNATCH!
BAFF!
BOP!
FWAP!
CHOMP!

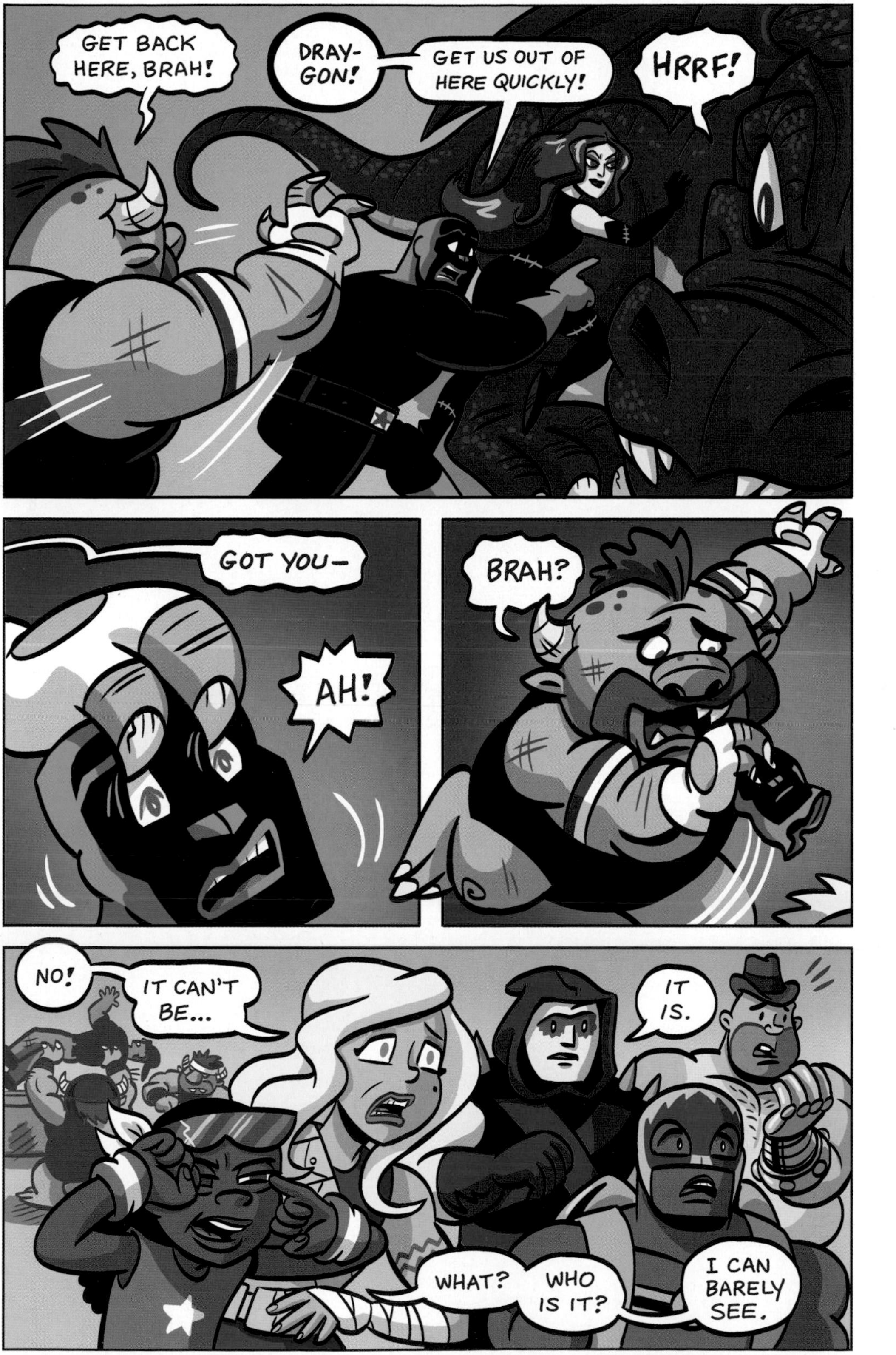
GET BACK HERE, BRAH!
DRAY-GON!
GET US OUT OF HERE QUICKLY!
HRRF!
GOT YOU–
AH!
BRAH?
NO!
IT CAN'T BE...
IT IS.
WHAT?
WHO IS IT?
I CAN BARELY SEE.

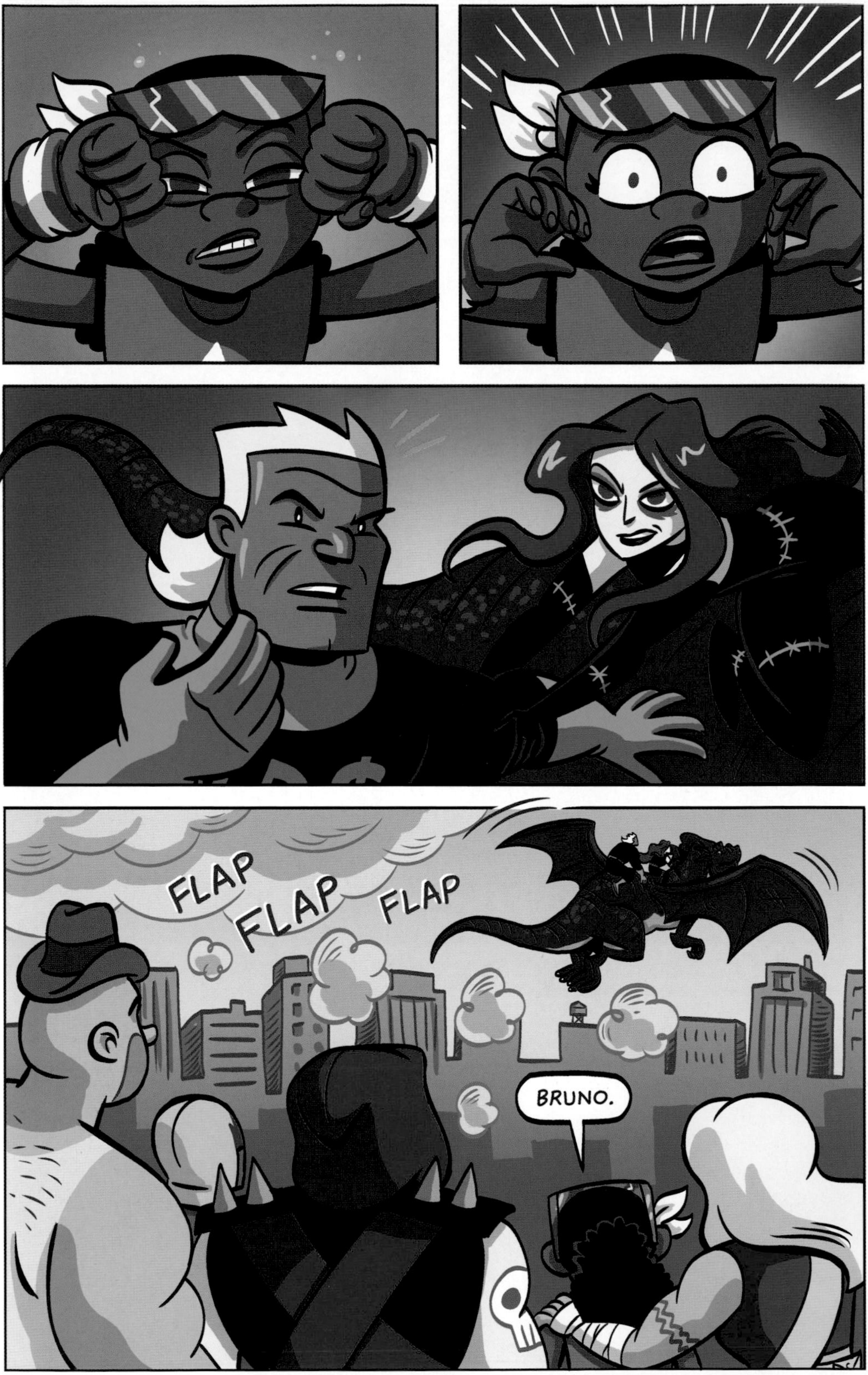
FLAP
FLAP
FLAP
BRUNO.

★ ★ ★

CHAPTER

3

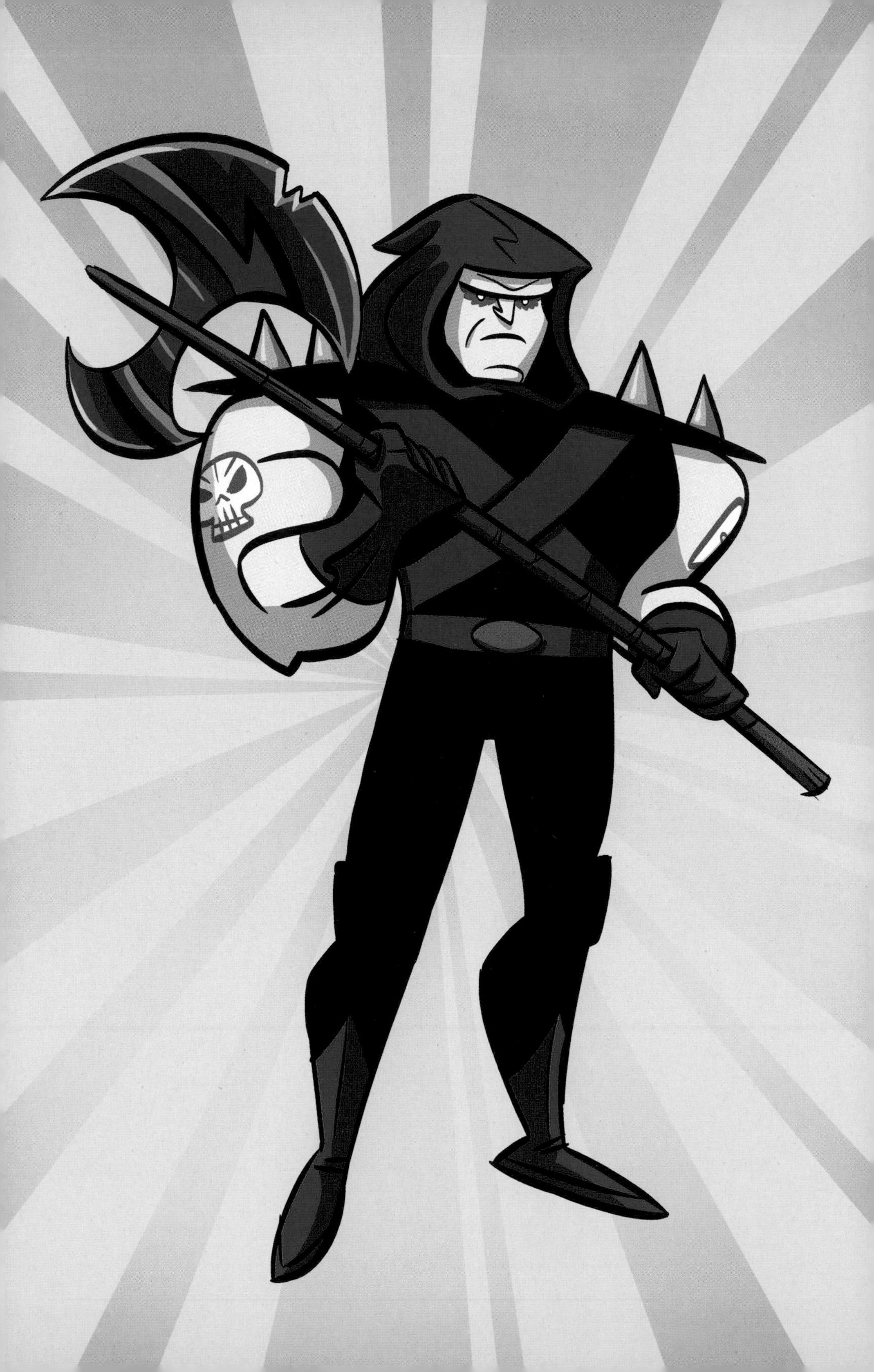

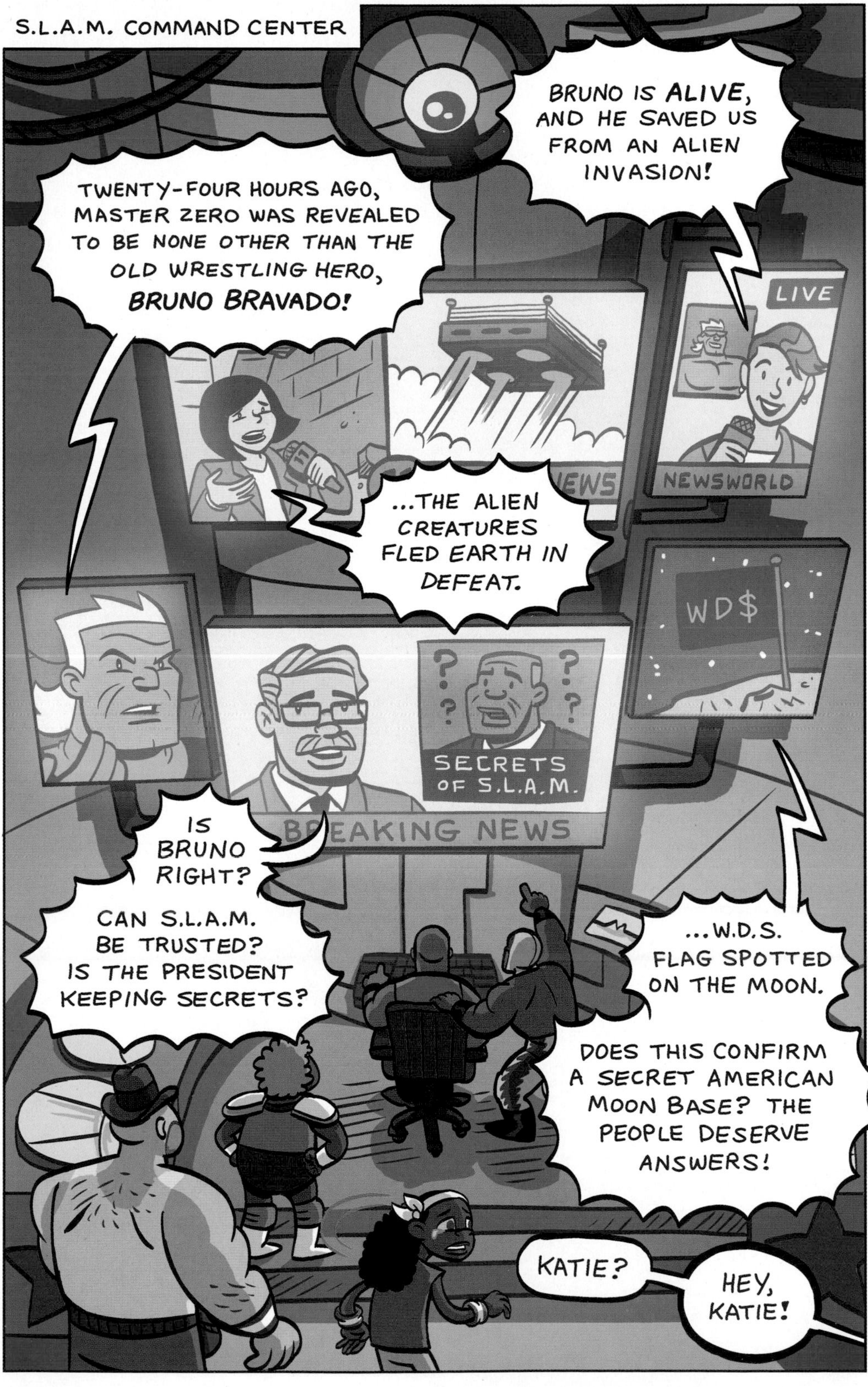
S.L.A.M. COMMAND CENTER
TWENTY-FOUR HOURS AGO, MASTER ZERO WAS REVEALED TO BE NONE OTHER THAN THE OLD WRESTLING HERO, BRUNO BRAVADO!
BRUNO IS ALIVE, AND HE SAVED US FROM AN ALIEN INVASION!
LIVE
NEWSWORLD
...THE ALIEN CREATURES FLED EARTH IN DEFEAT.
WD$
SECRETS OF S.L.A.M.
BREAKING NEWS
IS BRUNO RIGHT?
CAN S.L.A.M. BE TRUSTED? IS THE PRESIDENT KEEPING SECRETS?
...W.D.S. FLAG SPOTTED ON THE MOON.
DOES THIS CONFIRM A SECRET AMERICAN MOON BASE? THE PEOPLE DESERVE ANSWERS!
KATIE?
HEY, KATIE!

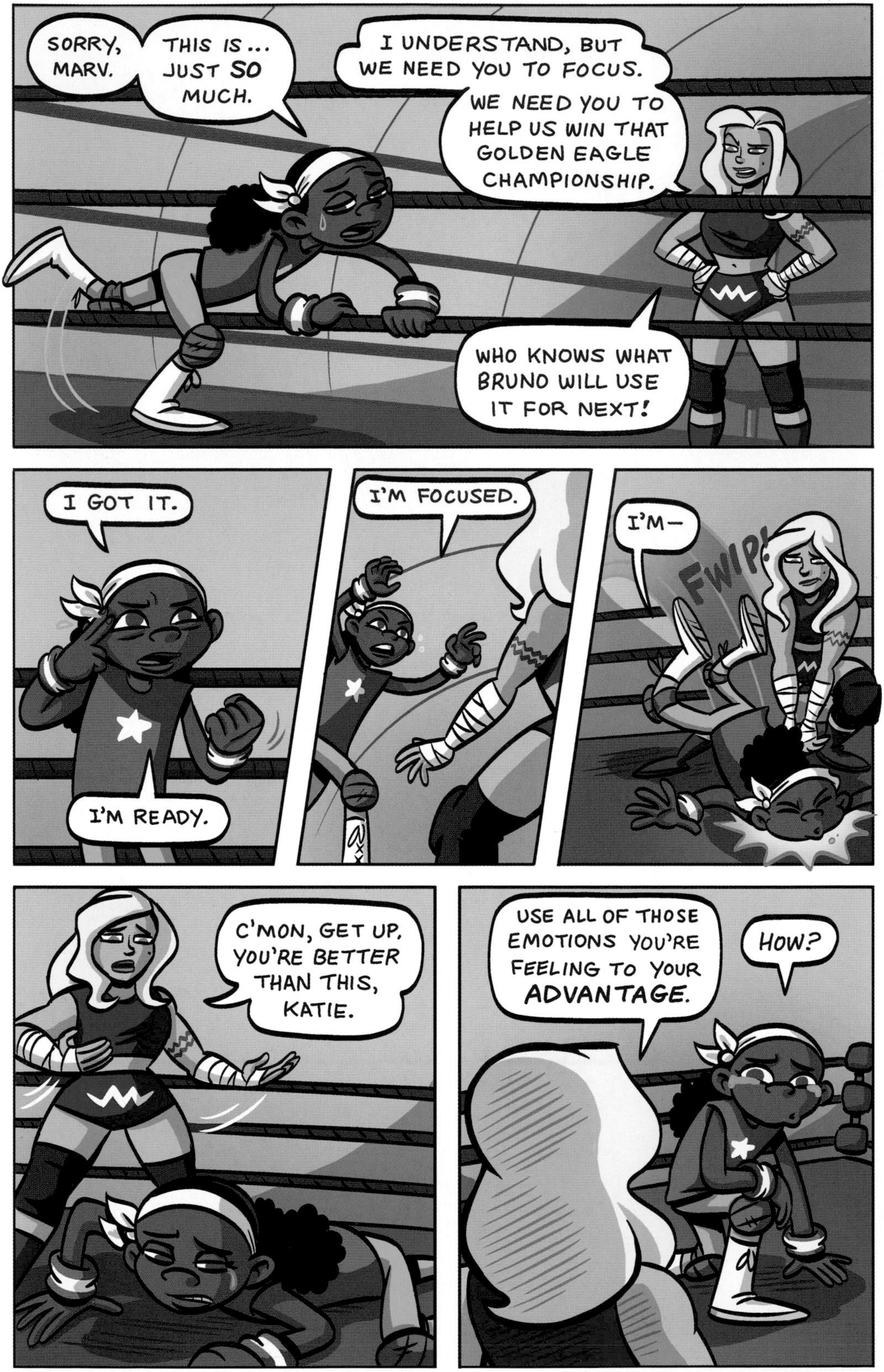
SORRY, MARV.
THIS IS... JUST SO MUCH.
I UNDERSTAND, BUT WE NEED YOU TO FOCUS.
WE NEED YOU TO HELP US WIN THAT GOLDEN EAGLE CHAMPIONSHIP.
WHO KNOWS WHAT BRUNO WILL USE IT FOR NEXT!
I GOT IT.
I'M READY.
I'M FOCUSED.
I'M—
FWIP!
C'MON, GET UP. YOU'RE BETTER THAN THIS, KATIE.
USE ALL OF THOSE EMOTIONS YOU'RE FEELING TO YOUR ADVANTAGE.
HOW?

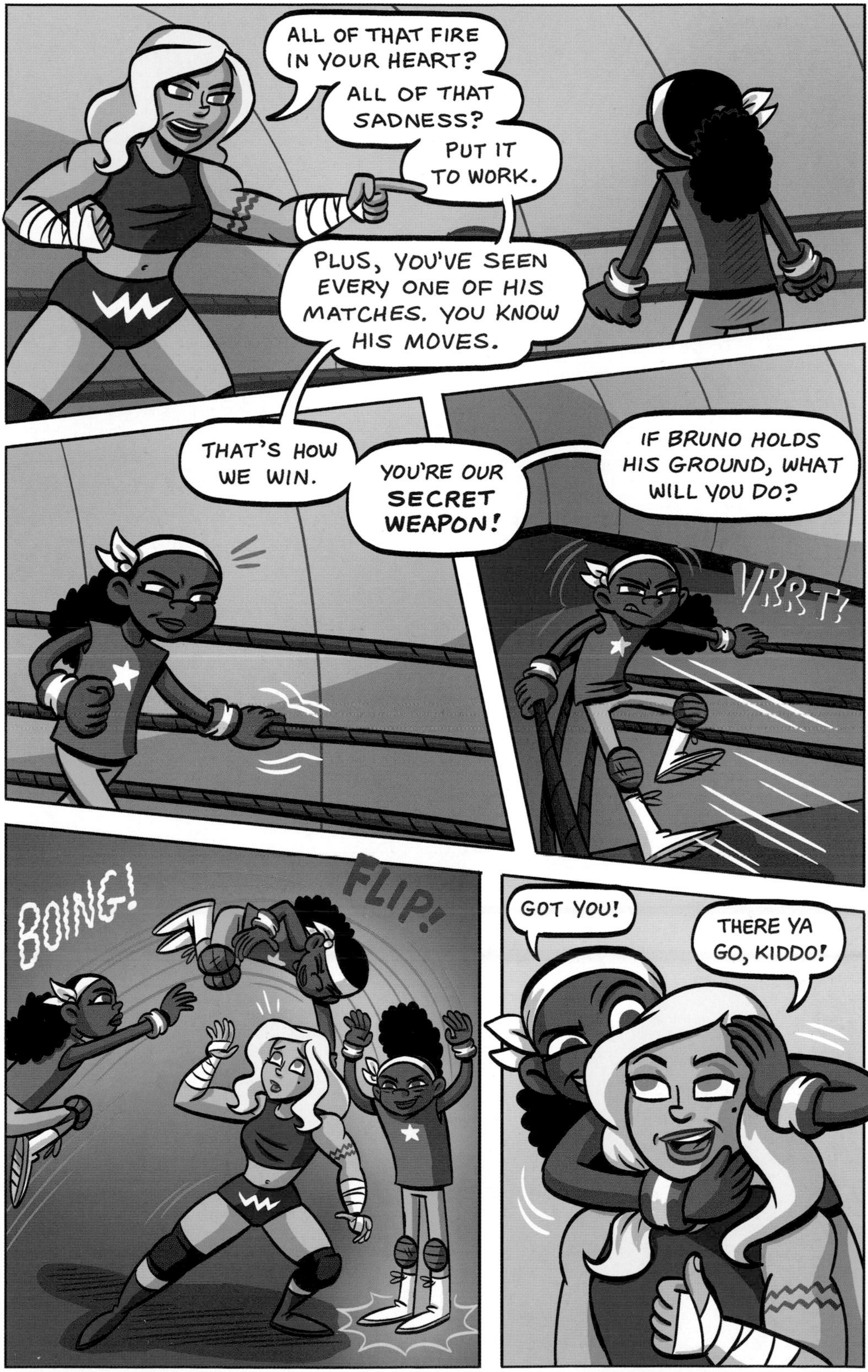
ALL OF THAT FIRE IN YOUR HEART?
ALL OF THAT SADNESS?
PUT IT TO WORK.
PLUS, YOU'VE SEEN EVERY ONE OF HIS MATCHES. YOU KNOW HIS MOVES.
THAT'S HOW WE WIN.
YOU'RE OUR SECRET WEAPON!
IF BRUNO HOLDS HIS GROUND, WHAT WILL YOU DO?
VRRT!
BOING!
FLIP!
GOT YOU!
THERE YA GO, KIDDO!

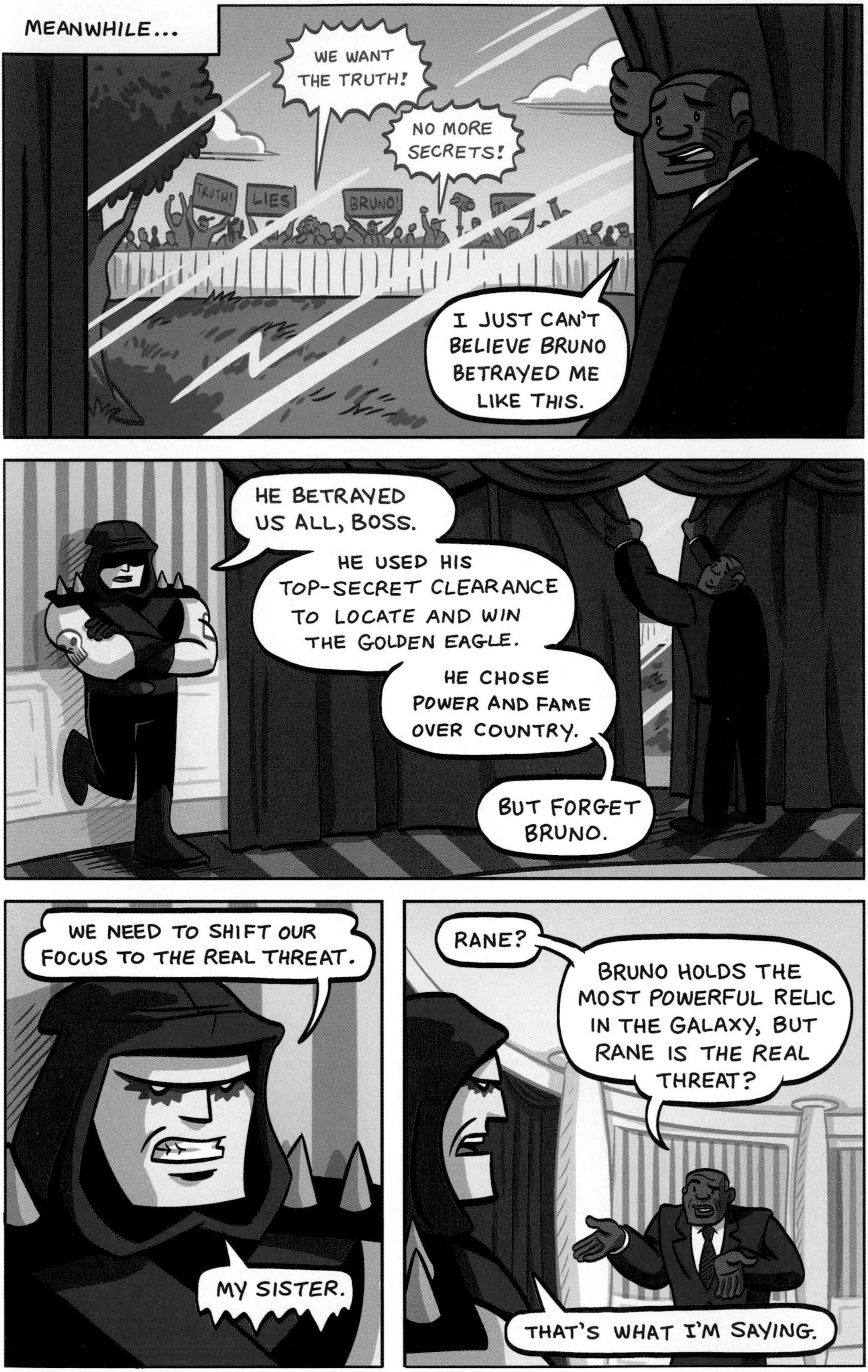
MEANWHILE...
WE WANT THE TRUTH!
NO MORE SECRETS!
TRUTH!
LIES
BRUNO!
I JUST CAN'T BELIEVE BRUNO BETRAYED ME LIKE THIS.
HE BETRAYED US ALL, BOSS.
HE USED HIS TOP-SECRET CLEARANCE TO LOCATE AND WIN THE GOLDEN EAGLE.
HE CHOSE POWER AND FAME OVER COUNTRY.
BUT FORGET BRUNO.
WE NEED TO SHIFT OUR FOCUS TO THE REAL THREAT.
MY SISTER.
RANE?
BRUNO HOLDS THE MOST POWERFUL RELIC IN THE GALAXY, BUT RANE IS THE REAL THREAT?
THAT'S WHAT I'M SAYING.

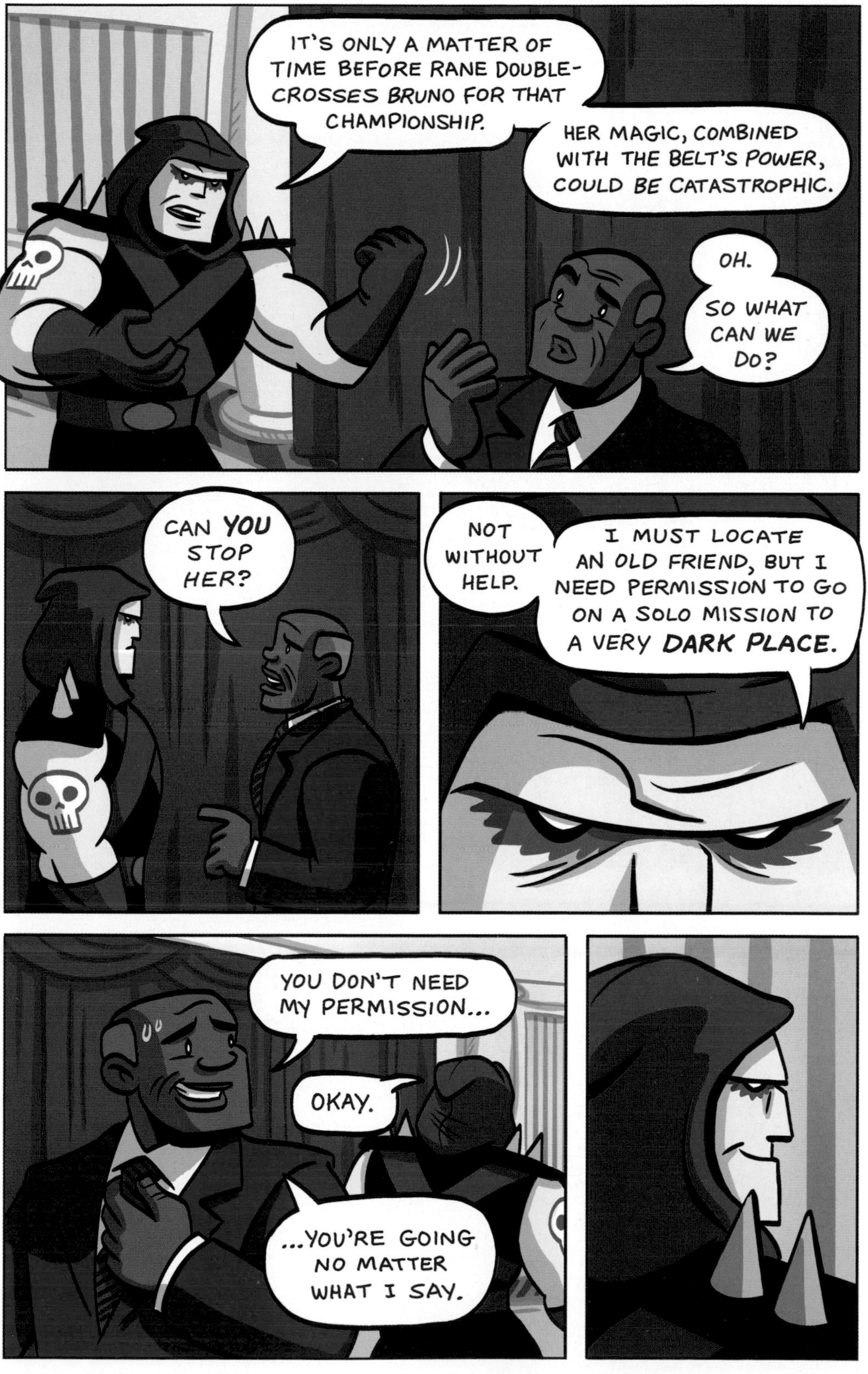
IT'S ONLY A MATTER OF TIME BEFORE RANE DOUBLE-CROSSES BRUNO FOR THAT CHAMPIONSHIP.
HER MAGIC, COMBINED WITH THE BELT'S POWER, COULD BE CATASTROPHIC.
OH.
SO WHAT CAN WE DO?
CAN YOU STOP HER?
NOT WITHOUT HELP.
I MUST LOCATE AN OLD FRIEND, BUT I NEED PERMISSION TO GO ON A SOLO MISSION TO A VERY DARK PLACE.
YOU DON'T NEED MY PERMISSION...
OKAY.
...YOU'RE GOING NO MATTER WHAT I SAY.

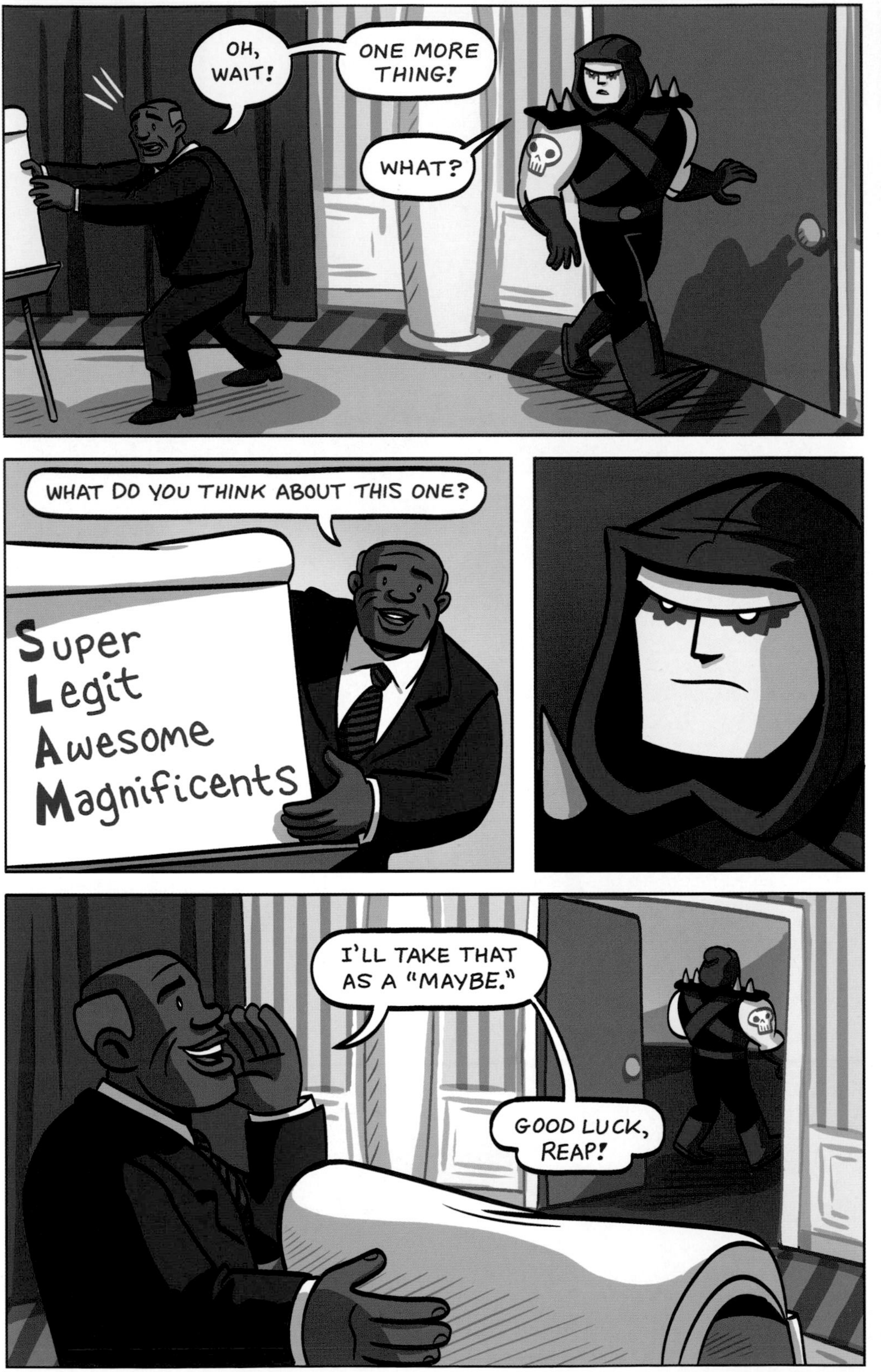
OH, WAIT!
ONE MORE THING!
WHAT?
WHAT DO YOU THINK ABOUT THIS ONE?
Super
Legit
Awesome
Magnificents
I'LL TAKE THAT AS A "MAYBE."
GOOD LUCK, REAP!

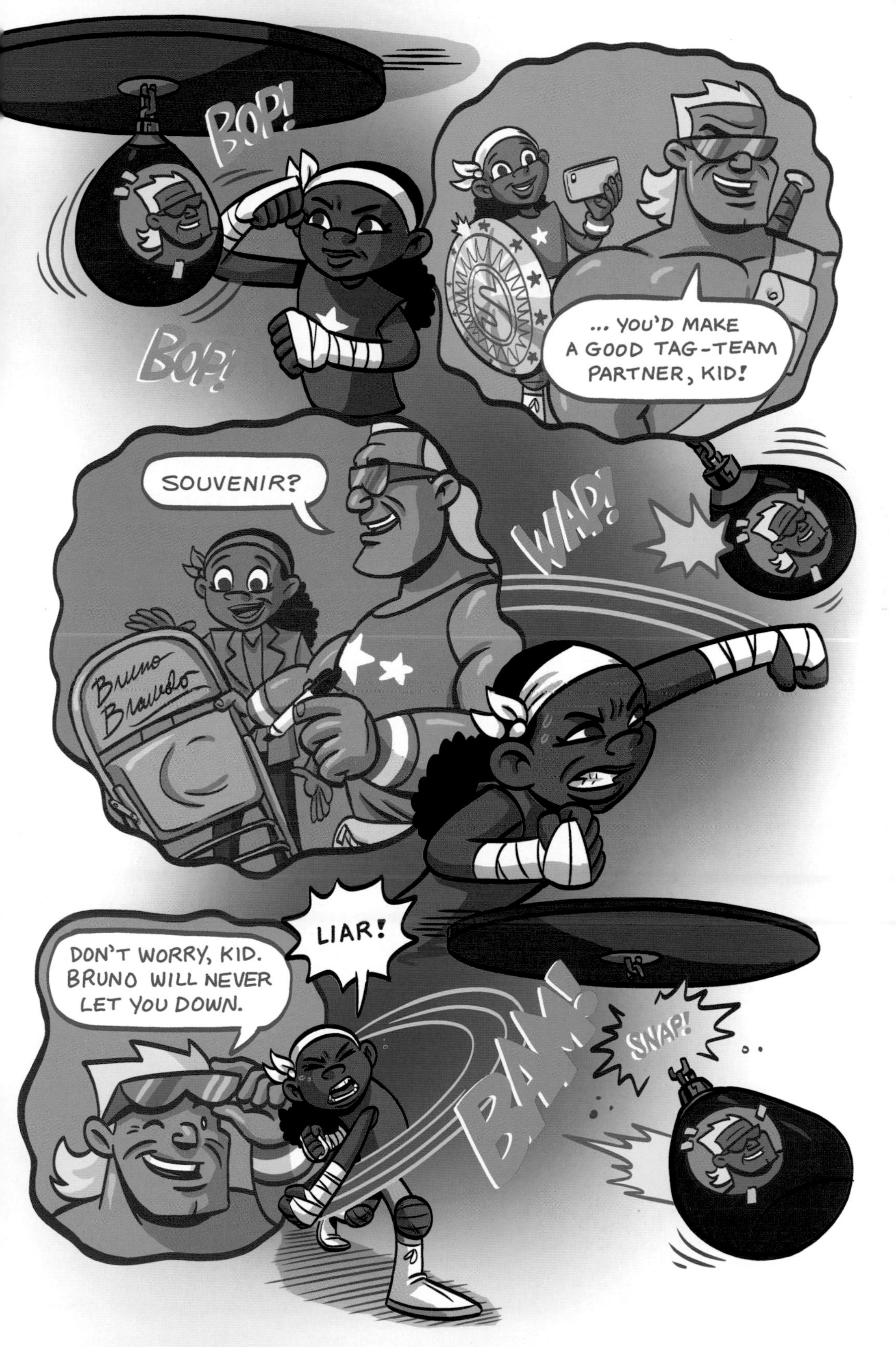
BOP!
BOP!
... YOU'D MAKE A GOOD TAG-TEAM PARTNER, KID!
SOUVENIR?
WAP!
Bruno Bravado
DON'T WORRY, KID. BRUNO WILL NEVER LET YOU DOWN.
LIAR!
BAM!
SNAP!
. .

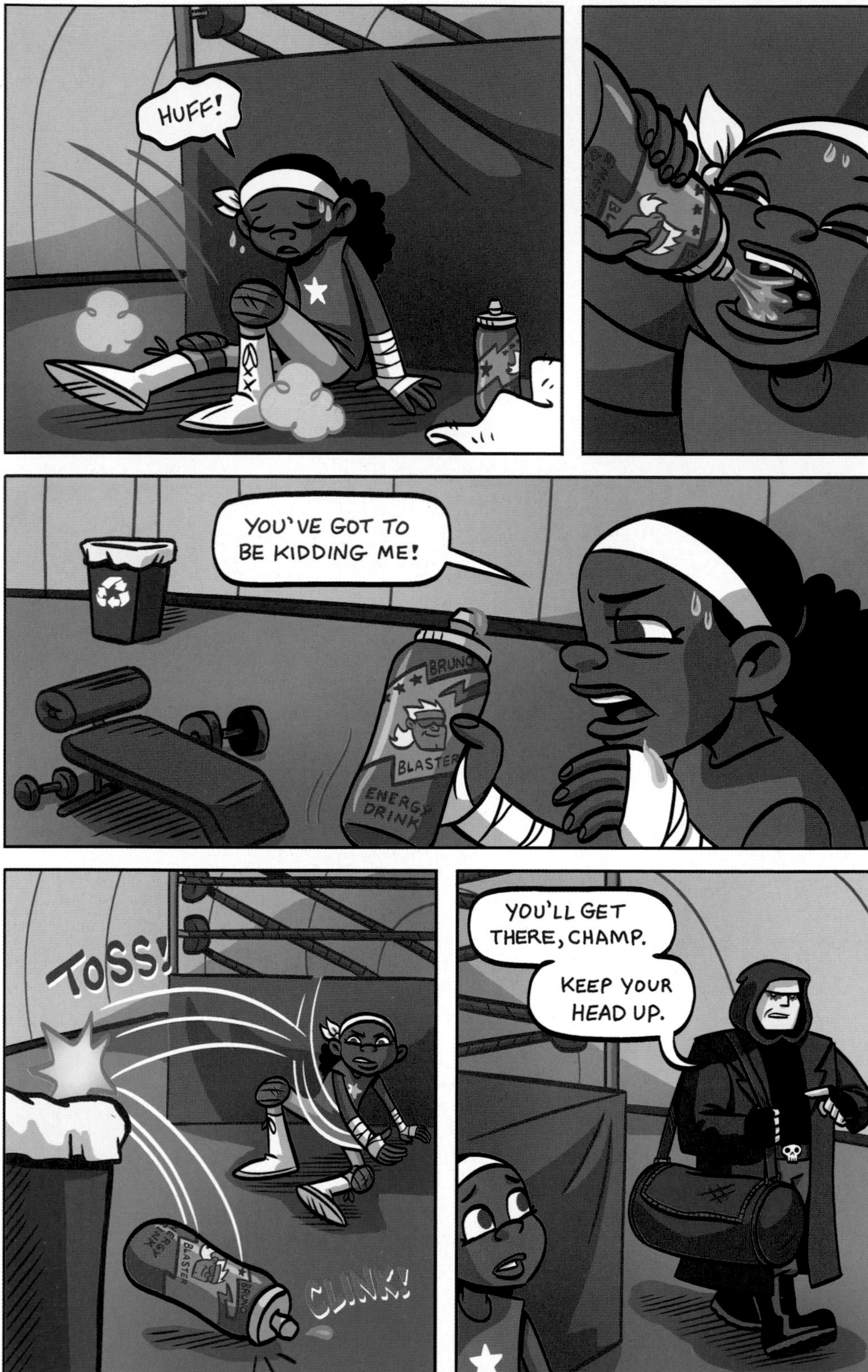
HUFF!
YOU'VE GOT TO BE KIDDING ME!
BRUNO
BLASTER
ENERGY DRINK
TOSS!
CLINK!
YOU'LL GET THERE, CHAMP.
KEEP YOUR HEAD UP.

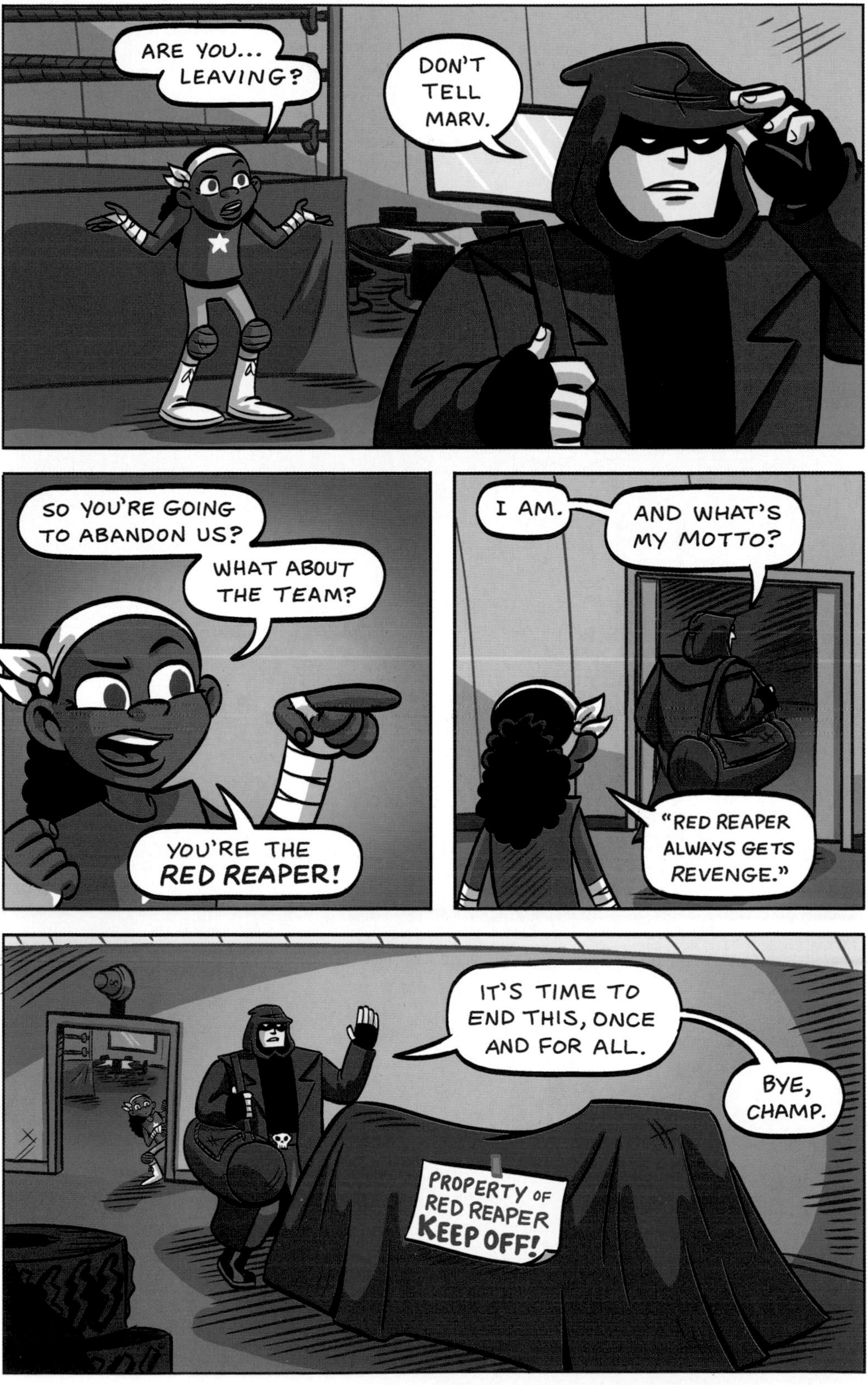
ARE YOU... LEAVING?
DON'T TELL MARV.
SO YOU'RE GOING TO ABANDON US?
WHAT ABOUT THE TEAM?
YOU'RE THE RED REAPER!
I AM.
AND WHAT'S MY MOTTO?
"RED REAPER ALWAYS GETS REVENGE."
IT'S TIME TO END THIS, ONCE AND FOR ALL.
BYE, CHAMP.
PROPERTY OF RED REAPER KEEP OFF!

THUD!

REV REV

VRRMM

SNATCH!

VRRRMMMMM

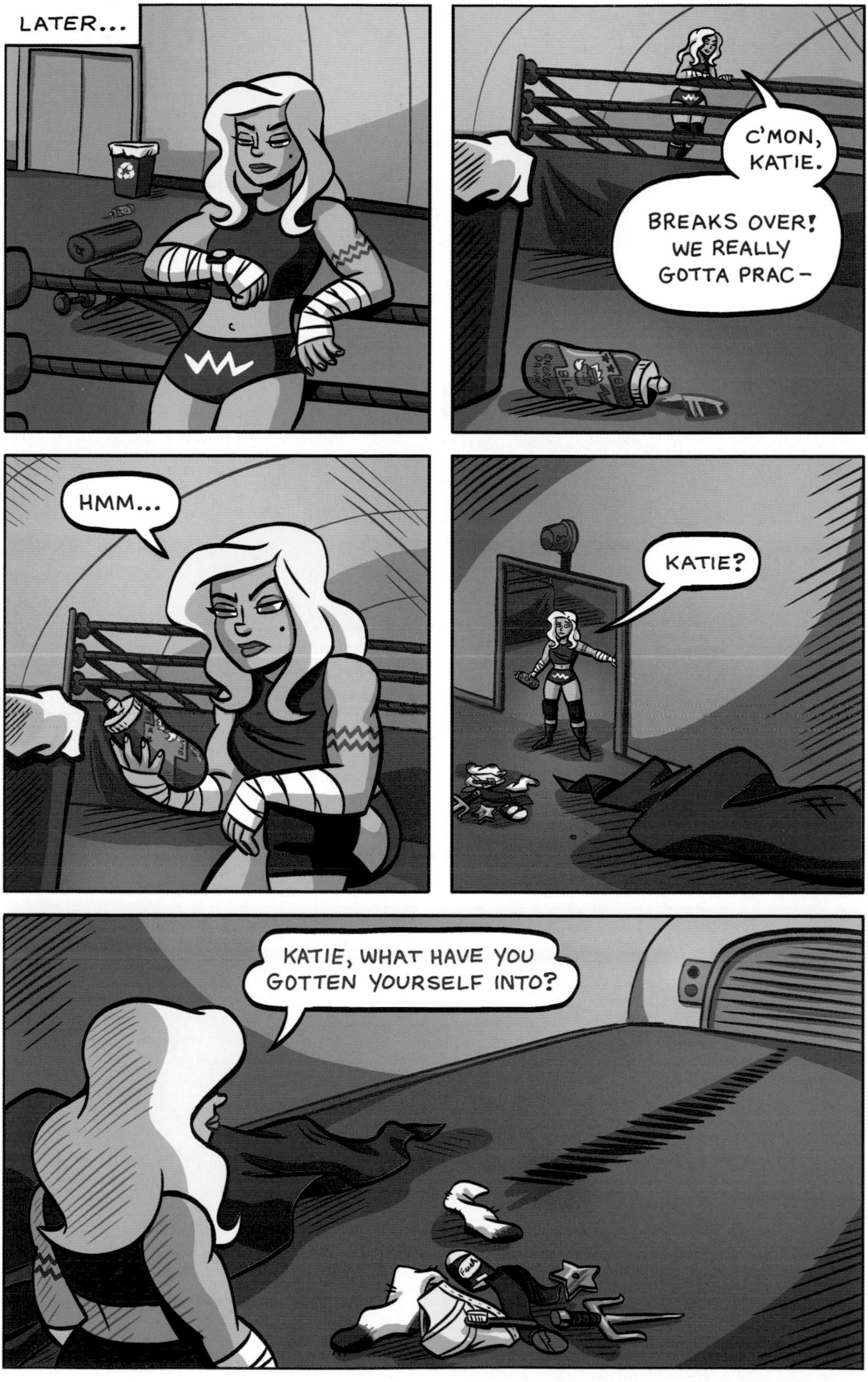
LATER...
C'MON, KATIE.
BREAKS OVER! WE REALLY GOTTA PRAC-
HMM...
KATIE?
KATIE, WHAT HAVE YOU GOTTEN YOURSELF INTO?

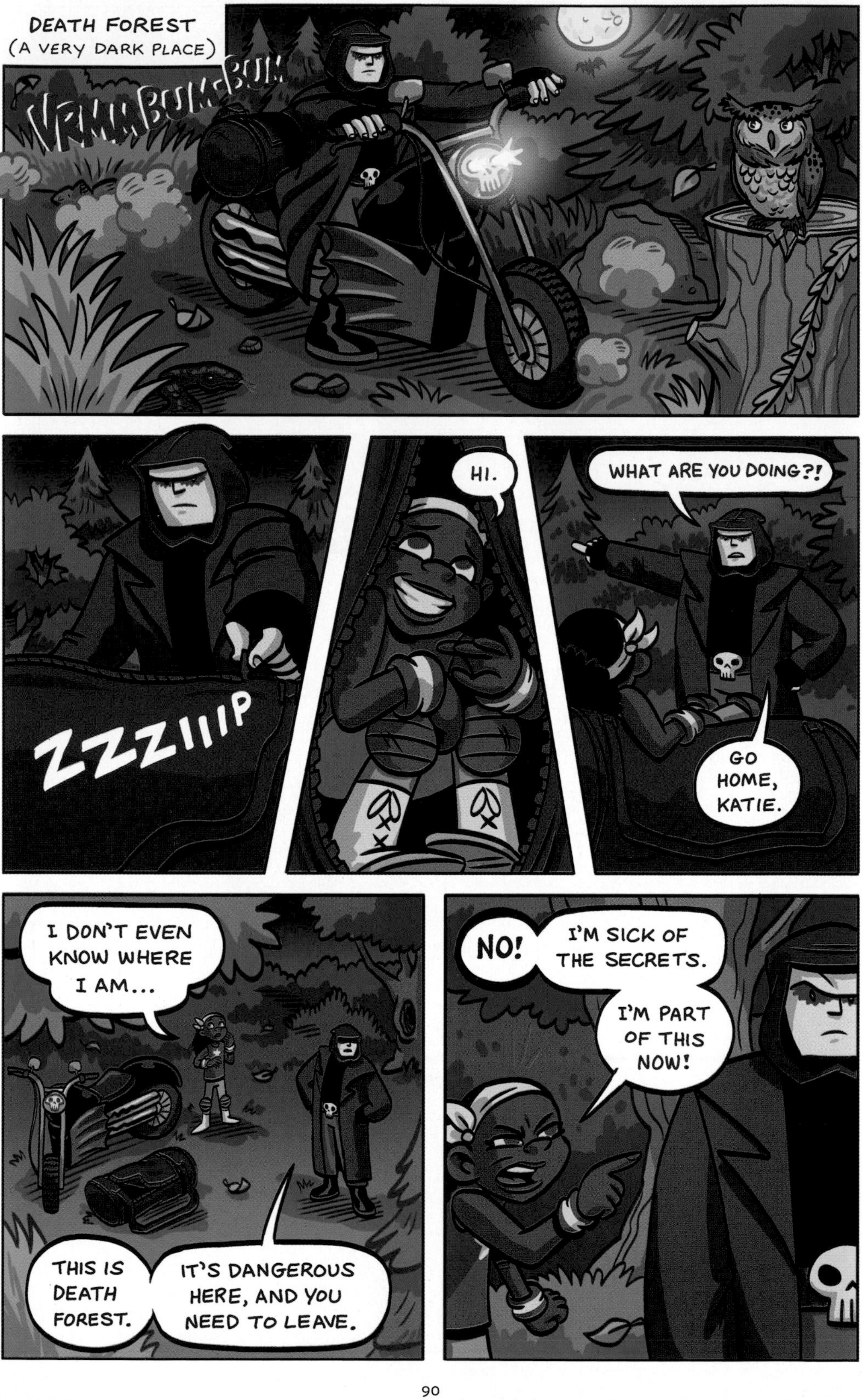
DEATH FOREST
(A VERY DARK PLACE)
VRMMBUM-BUM
ZZZIIIP
HI.
WHAT ARE YOU DOING?!
GO HOME, KATIE.
I DON'T EVEN KNOW WHERE I AM...
THIS IS DEATH FOREST.
IT'S DANGEROUS HERE, AND YOU NEED TO LEAVE.
NO!
I'M SICK OF THE SECRETS.
I'M PART OF THIS NOW!

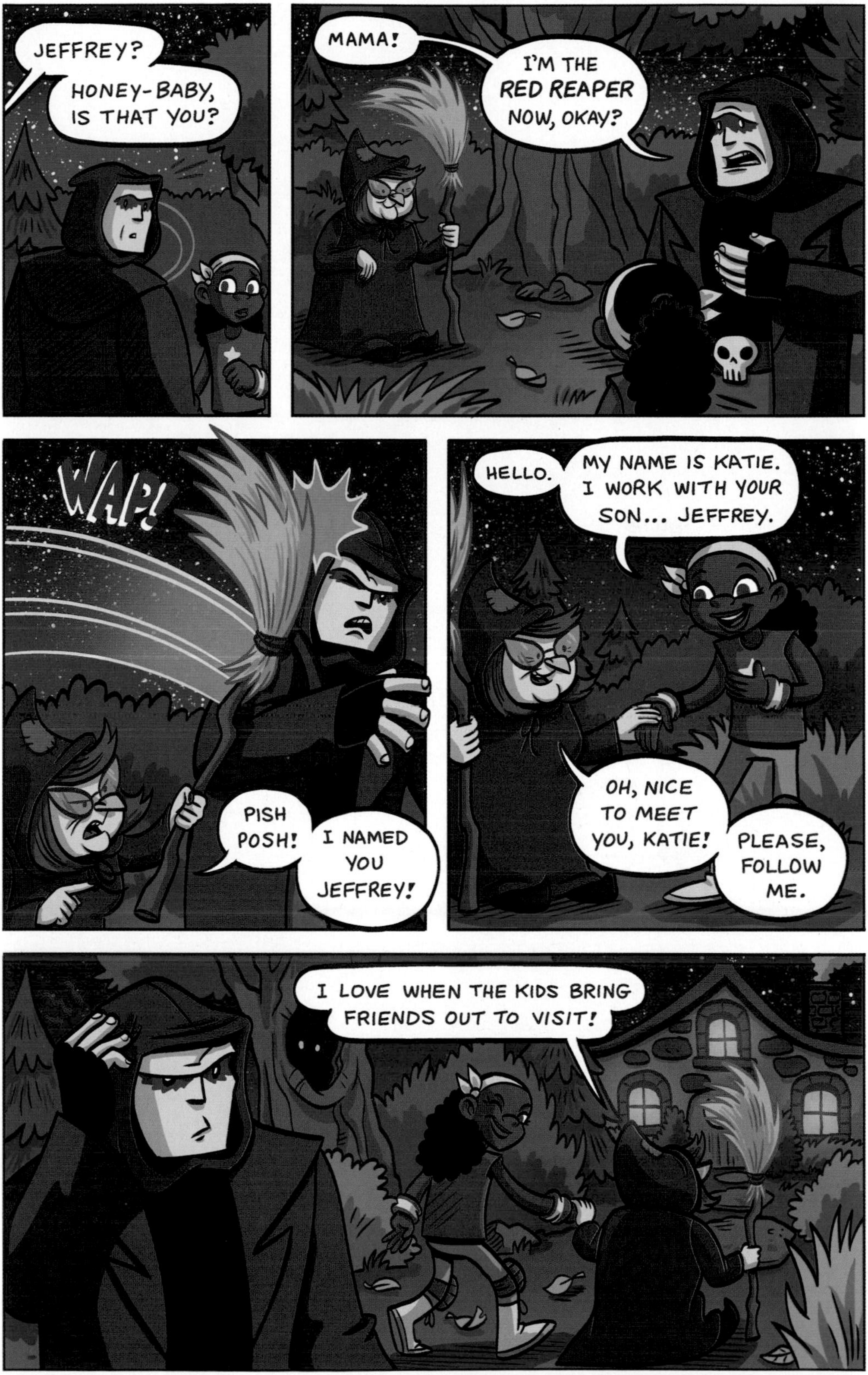
JEFFREY?
HONEY-BABY, IS THAT YOU?
MAMA!
I'M THE RED REAPER NOW, OKAY?
WAP!
PISH POSH!
I NAMED YOU JEFFREY!
HELLO.
MY NAME IS KATIE. I WORK WITH YOUR SON... JEFFREY.
OH, NICE TO MEET YOU, KATIE!
PLEASE, FOLLOW ME.
I LOVE WHEN THE KIDS BRING FRIENDS OUT TO VISIT!

WOW. THESE PHOTOS!

YOU KNOW THAT BRUNO BRAVADO WAS ALWAYS EVERYONE'S FAVORITE.

EVERYONE EXCEPT RANE.

SHE NEVER LIKED HIM.

YOU DO KNOW THAT RANE IS WORKING FOR BRUNO NOW, RIGHT?

HAVEN'T YOU SEEN THE NEWS?

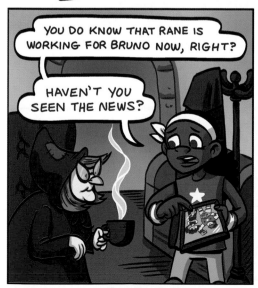

OH, SWEETIE.

IT'S ALL A SHOW.

A WORK.

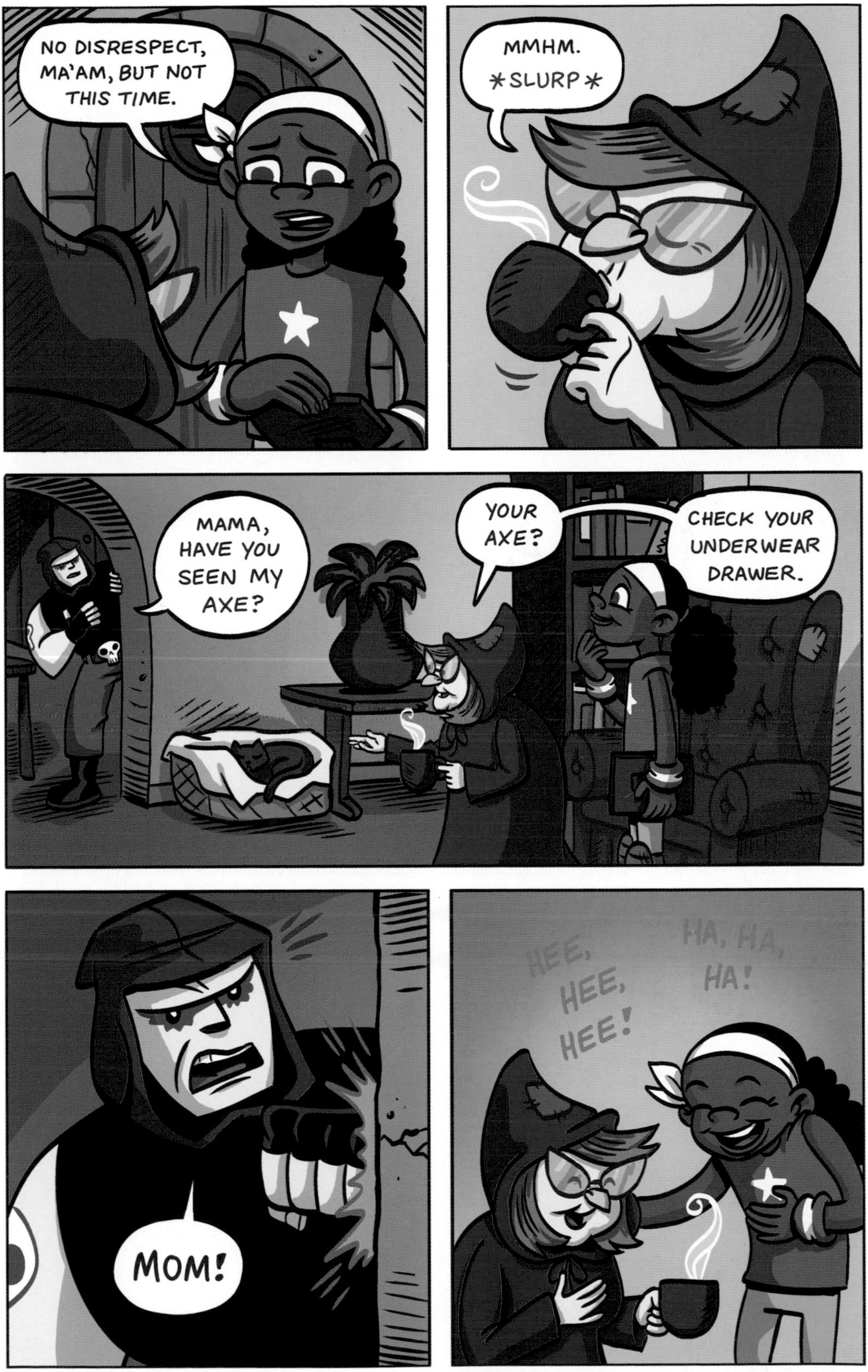
NO DISRESPECT, MA'AM, BUT NOT THIS TIME.
MMHM. *SLURP*
MAMA, HAVE YOU SEEN MY AXE?
YOUR AXE?
CHECK YOUR UNDERWEAR DRAWER.
MOM!
HEE, HEE, HEE!
HA, HA, HA!

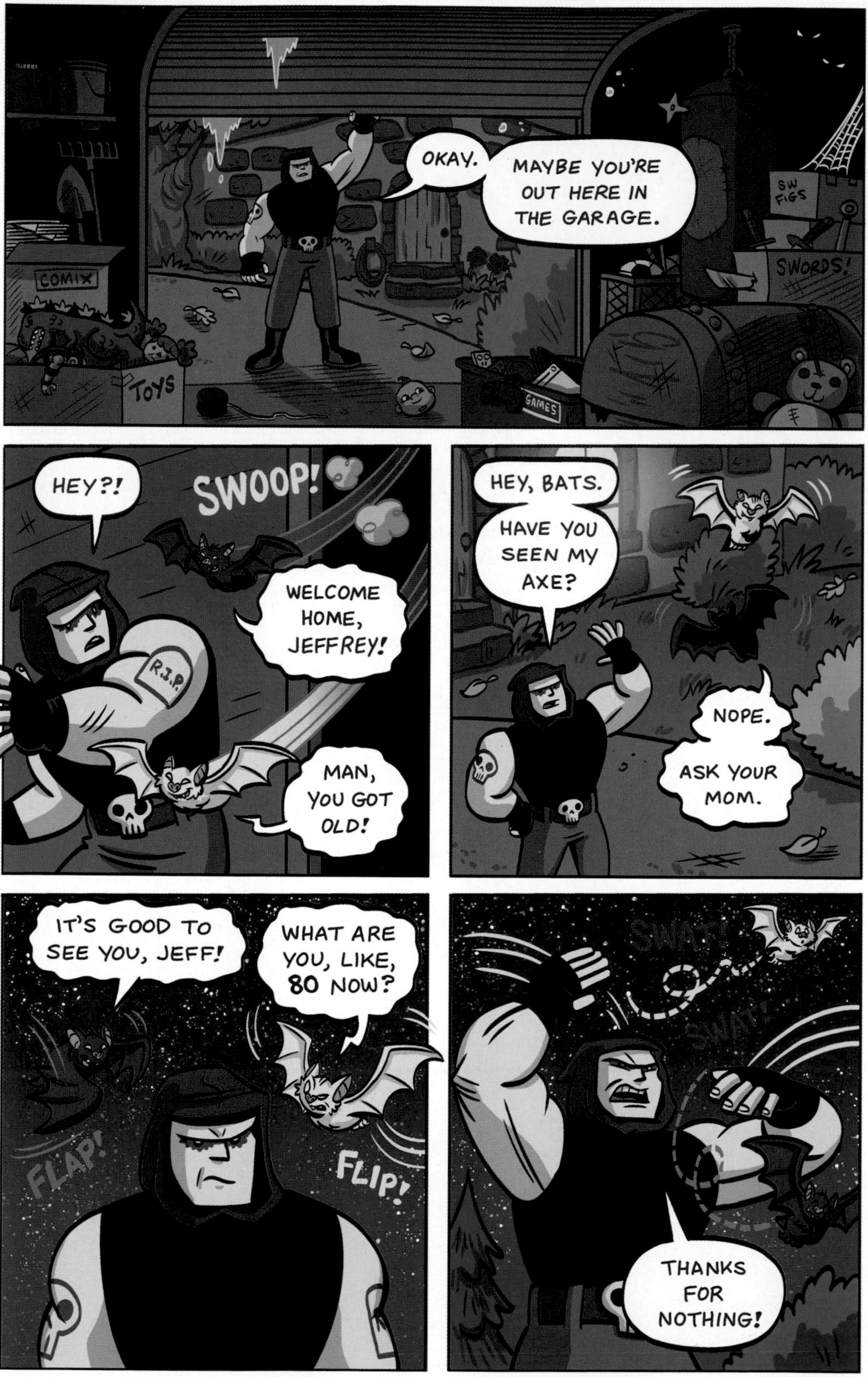

OKAY.
MAYBE YOU'RE OUT HERE IN THE GARAGE.
COMIX
TOYS
GAMES
SW FIGS
SWORDS!
HEY?!
SWOOP!
WELCOME HOME, JEFFREY!
R.I.P.
MAN, YOU GOT OLD!
HEY, BATS.
HAVE YOU SEEN MY AXE?
NOPE.
ASK YOUR MOM.
IT'S GOOD TO SEE YOU, JEFF!
WHAT ARE YOU, LIKE, 80 NOW?
FLAP!
FLIP!
SWAT!
SWAT!
THANKS FOR NOTHING!

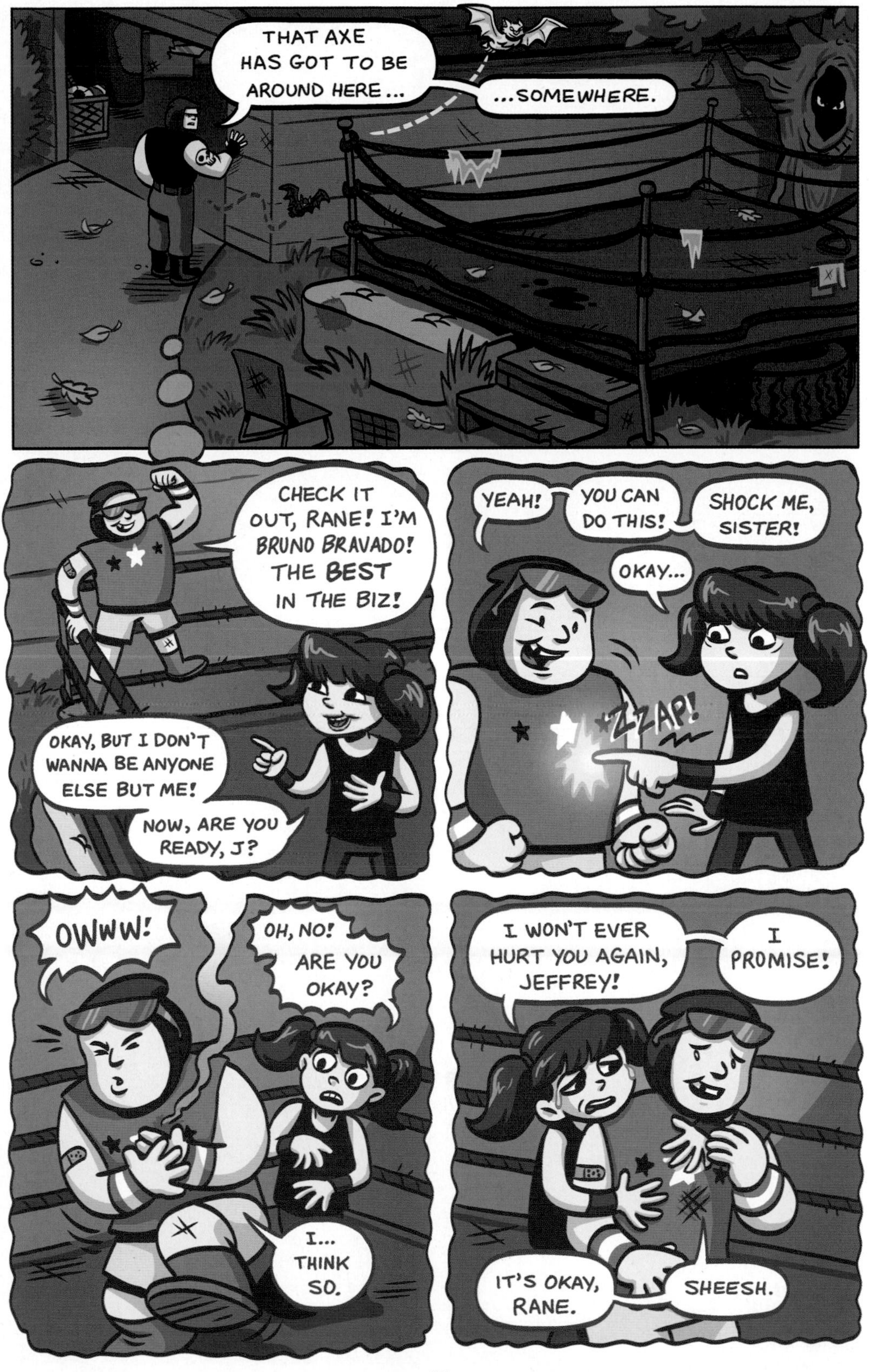
THAT AXE HAS GOT TO BE AROUND HERE...
...SOMEWHERE.
CHECK IT OUT, RANE! I'M BRUNO BRAVADO! THE BEST IN THE BIZ!
OKAY, BUT I DON'T WANNA BE ANYONE ELSE BUT ME!
NOW, ARE YOU READY, J?
YEAH!
YOU CAN DO THIS!
SHOCK ME, SISTER!
OKAY...
ZZAP!
OWWW!
OH, NO! ARE YOU OKAY?
I... THINK SO.
I WON'T EVER HURT YOU AGAIN, JEFFREY!
I PROMISE!
IT'S OKAY, RANE.
SHEESH.

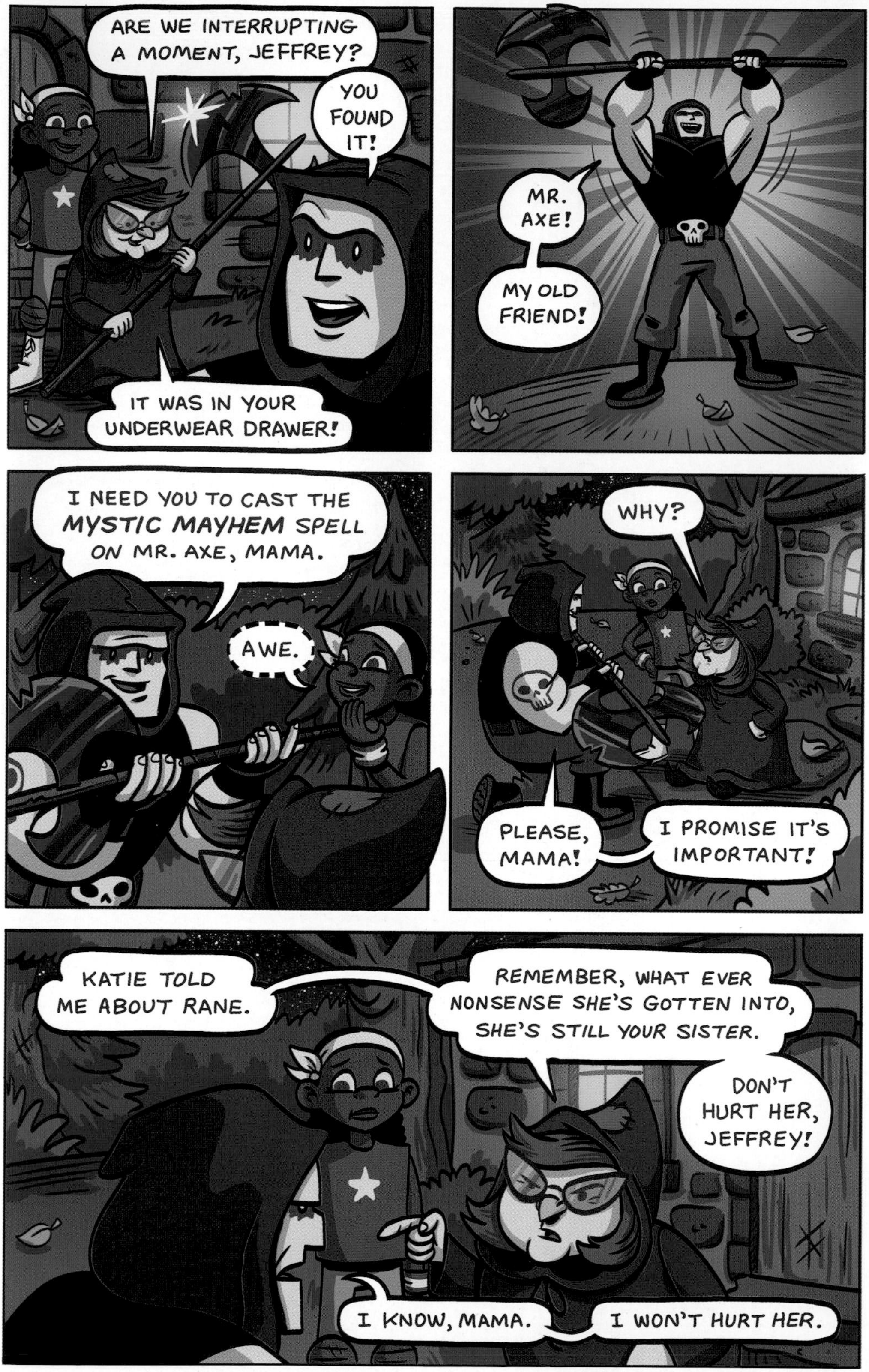
ARE WE INTERRUPTING A MOMENT, JEFFREY?
YOU FOUND IT!
IT WAS IN YOUR UNDERWEAR DRAWER!
MR. AXE!
MY OLD FRIEND!
I NEED YOU TO CAST THE MYSTIC MAYHEM SPELL ON MR. AXE, MAMA.
AWE.
WHY?
PLEASE, MAMA!
I PROMISE IT'S IMPORTANT!
KATIE TOLD ME ABOUT RANE.
REMEMBER, WHAT EVER NONSENSE SHE'S GOTTEN INTO, SHE'S STILL YOUR SISTER.
DON'T HURT HER, JEFFREY!
I KNOW, MAMA.
I WON'T HURT HER.

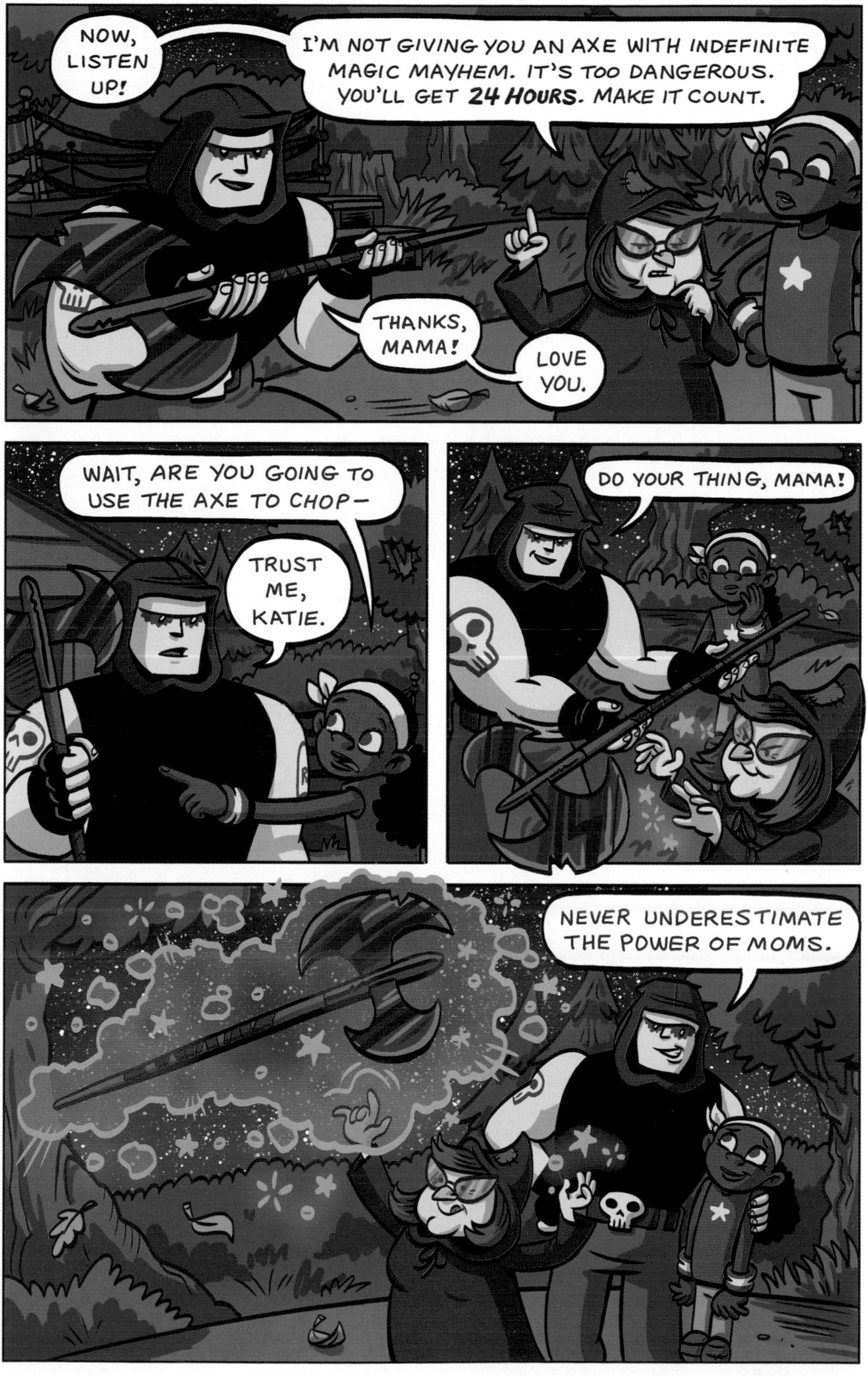
NOW, LISTEN UP!
I'M NOT GIVING YOU AN AXE WITH INDEFINITE MAGIC MAYHEM. IT'S TOO DANGEROUS. YOU'LL GET 24 HOURS. MAKE IT COUNT.
THANKS, MAMA!
LOVE YOU.
WAIT, ARE YOU GOING TO USE THE AXE TO CHOP—
TRUST ME, KATIE.
DO YOUR THING, MAMA!
NEVER UNDERESTIMATE THE POWER OF MOMS.

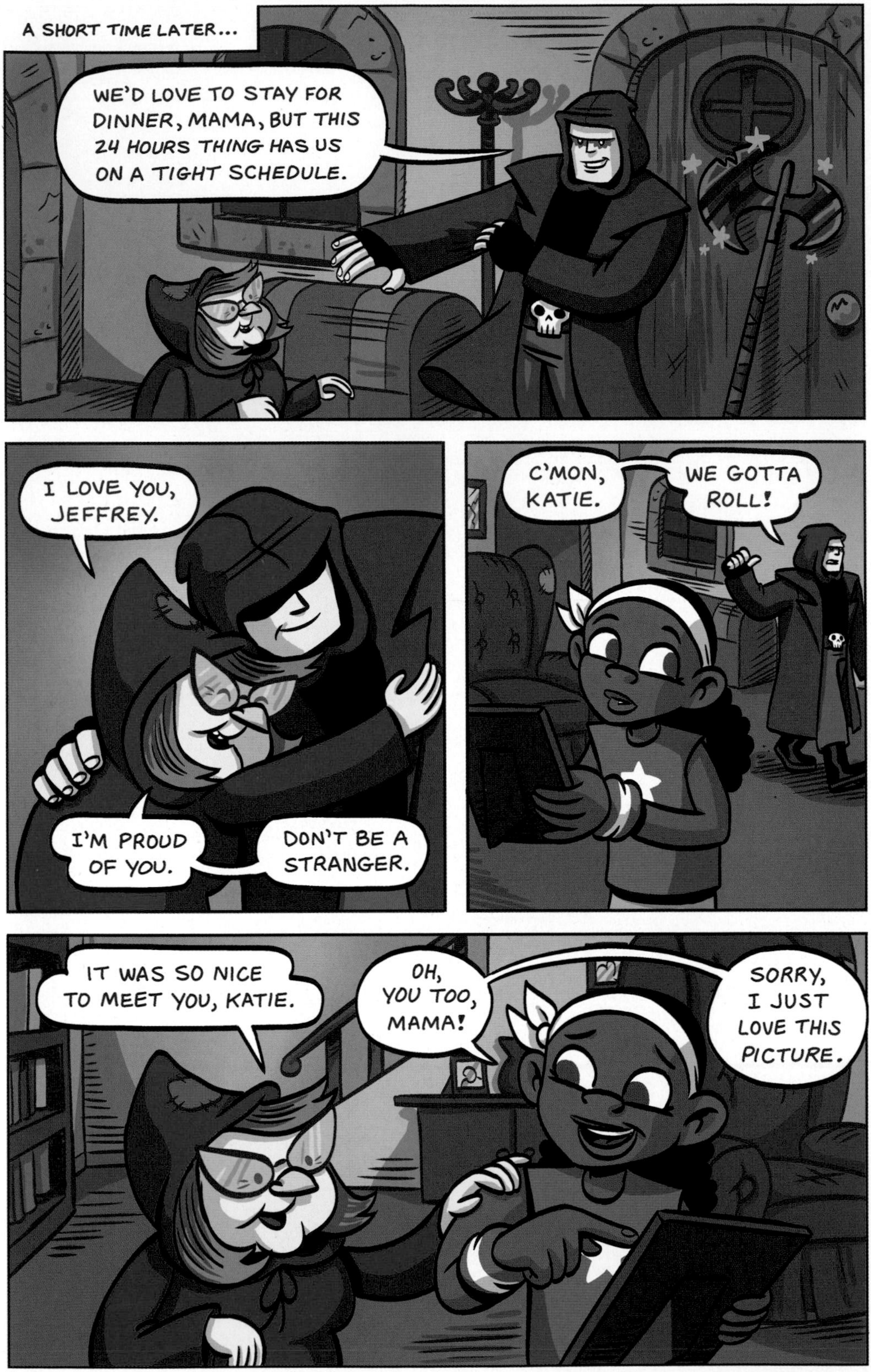
A SHORT TIME LATER...
WE'D LOVE TO STAY FOR DINNER, MAMA, BUT THIS 24 HOURS THING HAS US ON A TIGHT SCHEDULE.
I LOVE YOU, JEFFREY.
I'M PROUD OF YOU.
DON'T BE A STRANGER.
C'MON, KATIE.
WE GOTTA ROLL!
IT WAS SO NICE TO MEET YOU, KATIE.
OH, YOU TOO, MAMA!
SORRY, I JUST LOVE THIS PICTURE.

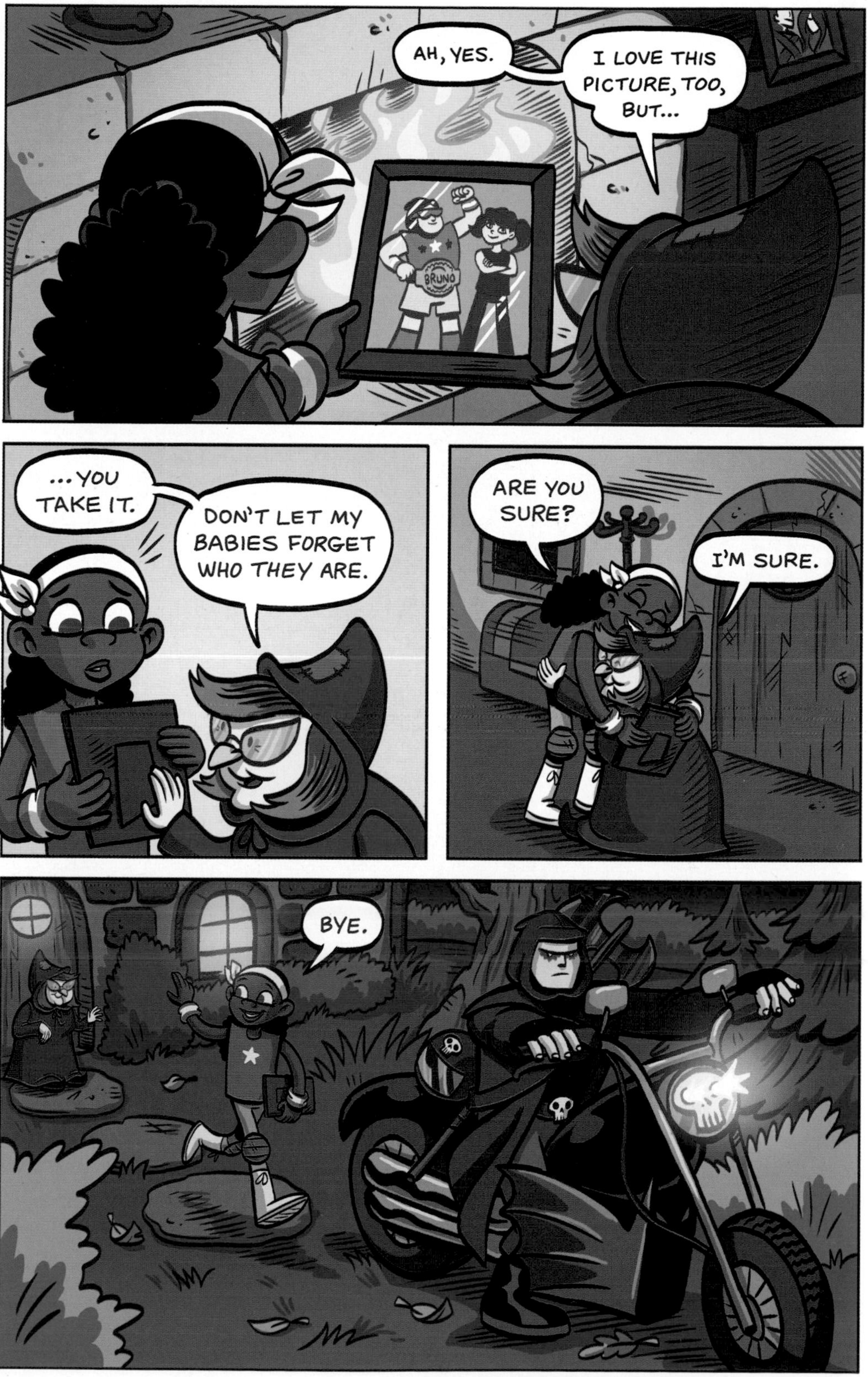
AH, YES.
I LOVE THIS PICTURE, TOO, BUT...
BRUNO
...YOU TAKE IT.
DON'T LET MY BABIES FORGET WHO THEY ARE.
ARE YOU SURE?
I'M SURE.
BYE.

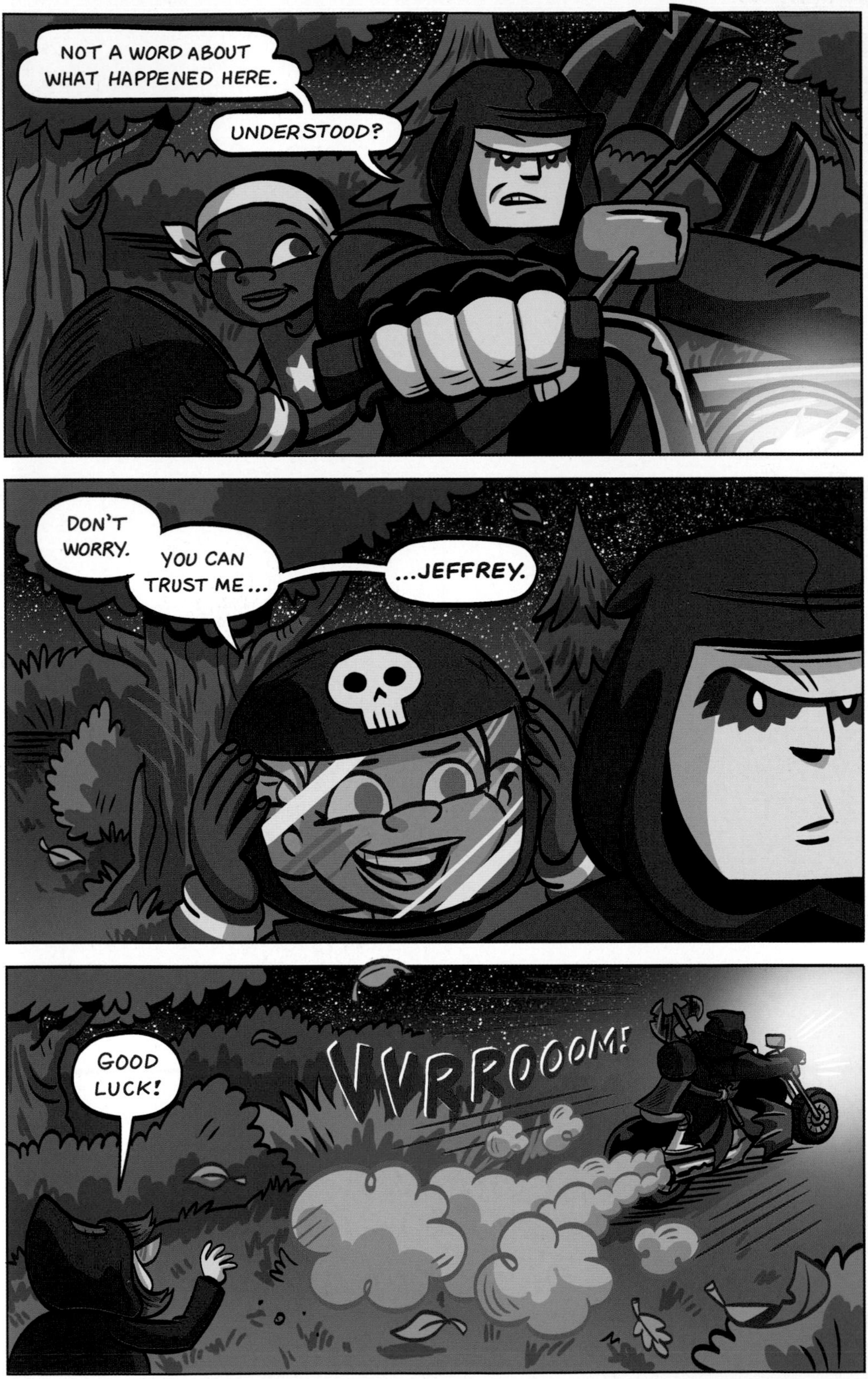
NOT A WORD ABOUT WHAT HAPPENED HERE.
UNDERSTOOD?
DON'T WORRY.
YOU CAN TRUST ME...
...JEFFREY.
GOOD LUCK!
VVRROOOM!

★ ★ ★

CHAPTER
4

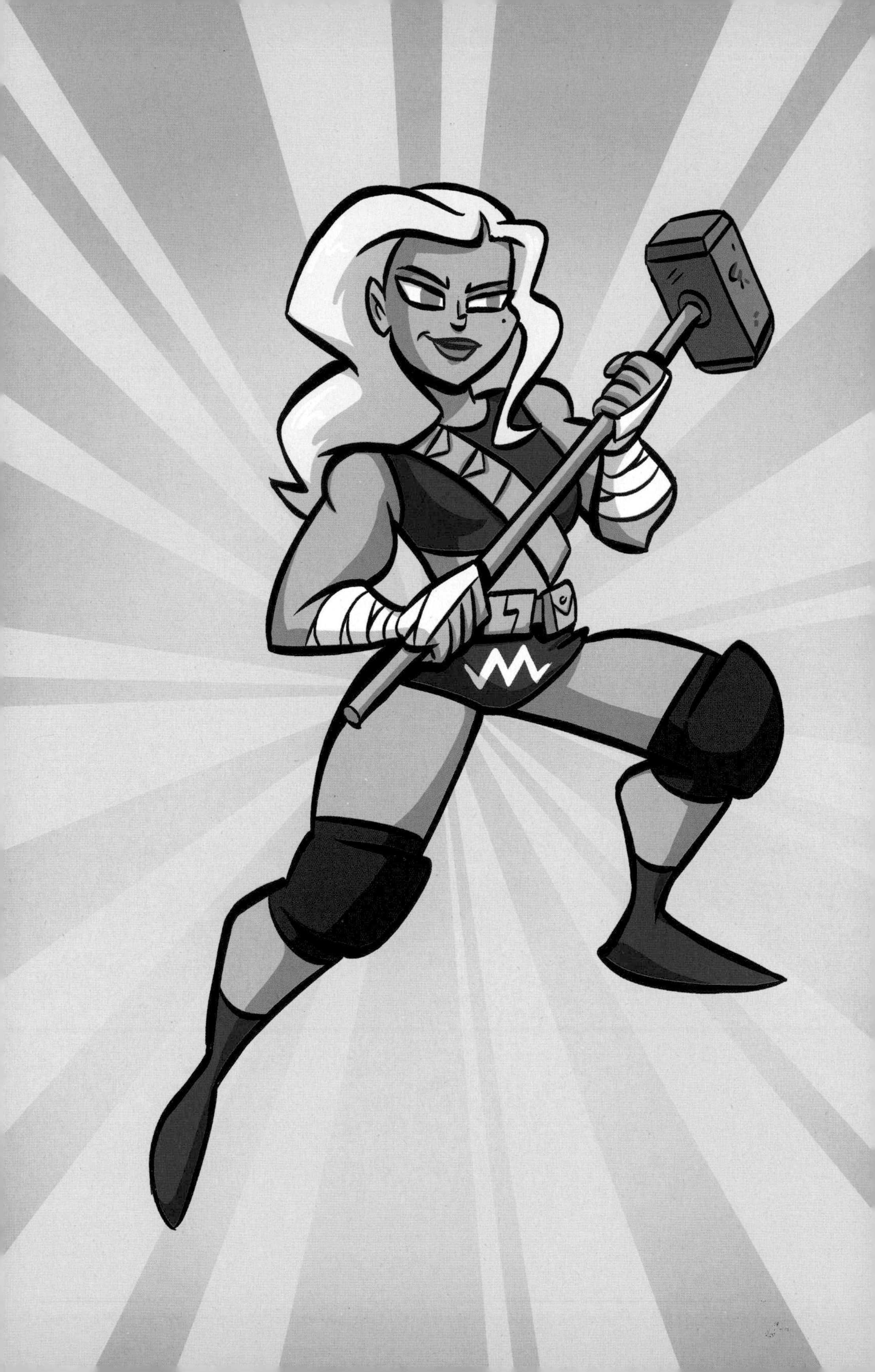

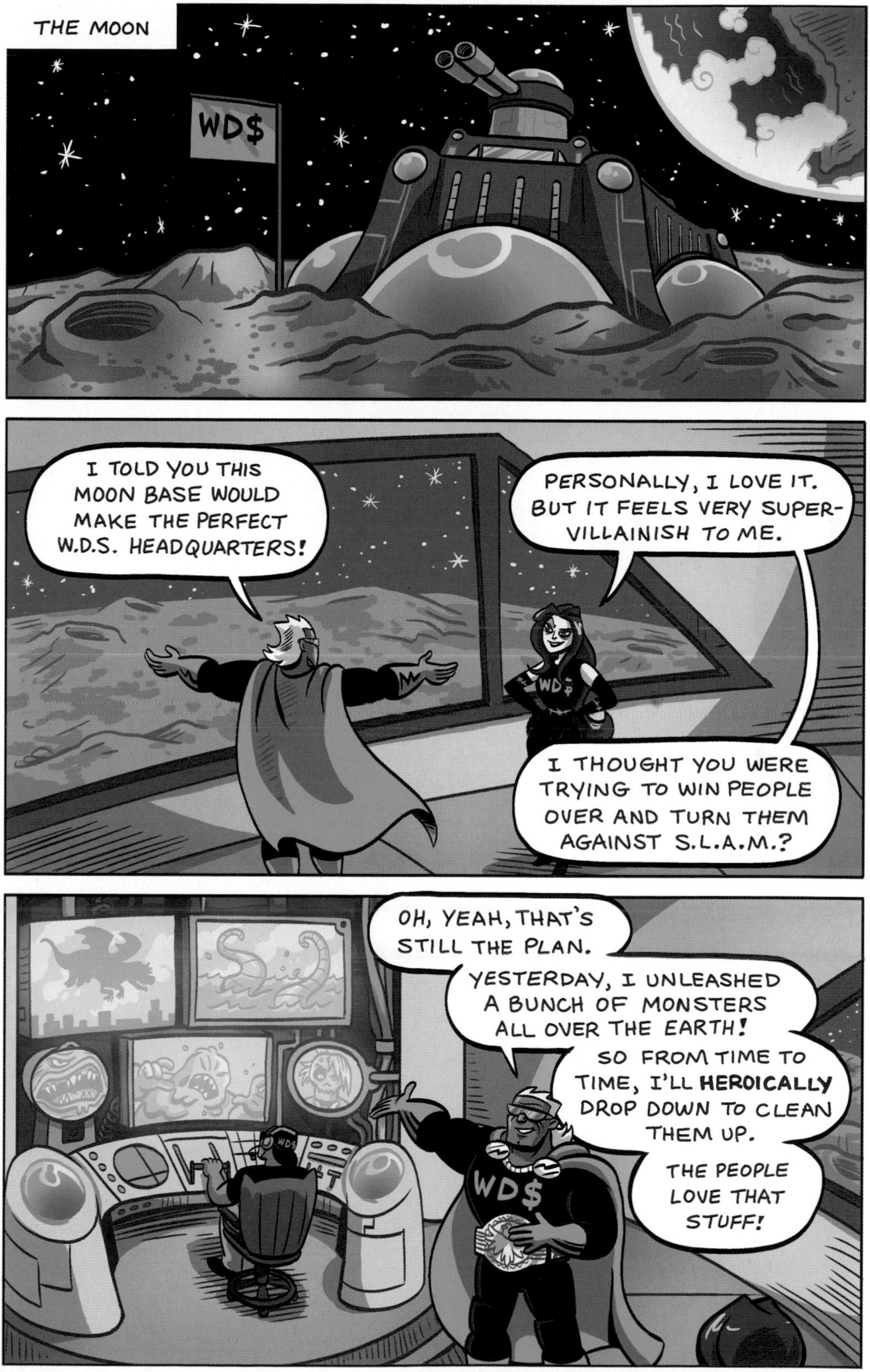
THE MOON
WD$
I TOLD YOU THIS MOON BASE WOULD MAKE THE PERFECT W.D.S. HEADQUARTERS!
PERSONALLY, I LOVE IT. BUT IT FEELS VERY SUPER-VILLAINISH TO ME.
I THOUGHT YOU WERE TRYING TO WIN PEOPLE OVER AND TURN THEM AGAINST S.L.A.M.?
OH, YEAH, THAT'S STILL THE PLAN.
YESTERDAY, I UNLEASHED A BUNCH OF MONSTERS ALL OVER THE EARTH!
SO FROM TIME TO TIME, I'LL **HEROICALLY** DROP DOWN TO CLEAN THEM UP.
THE PEOPLE LOVE THAT STUFF!
WD$

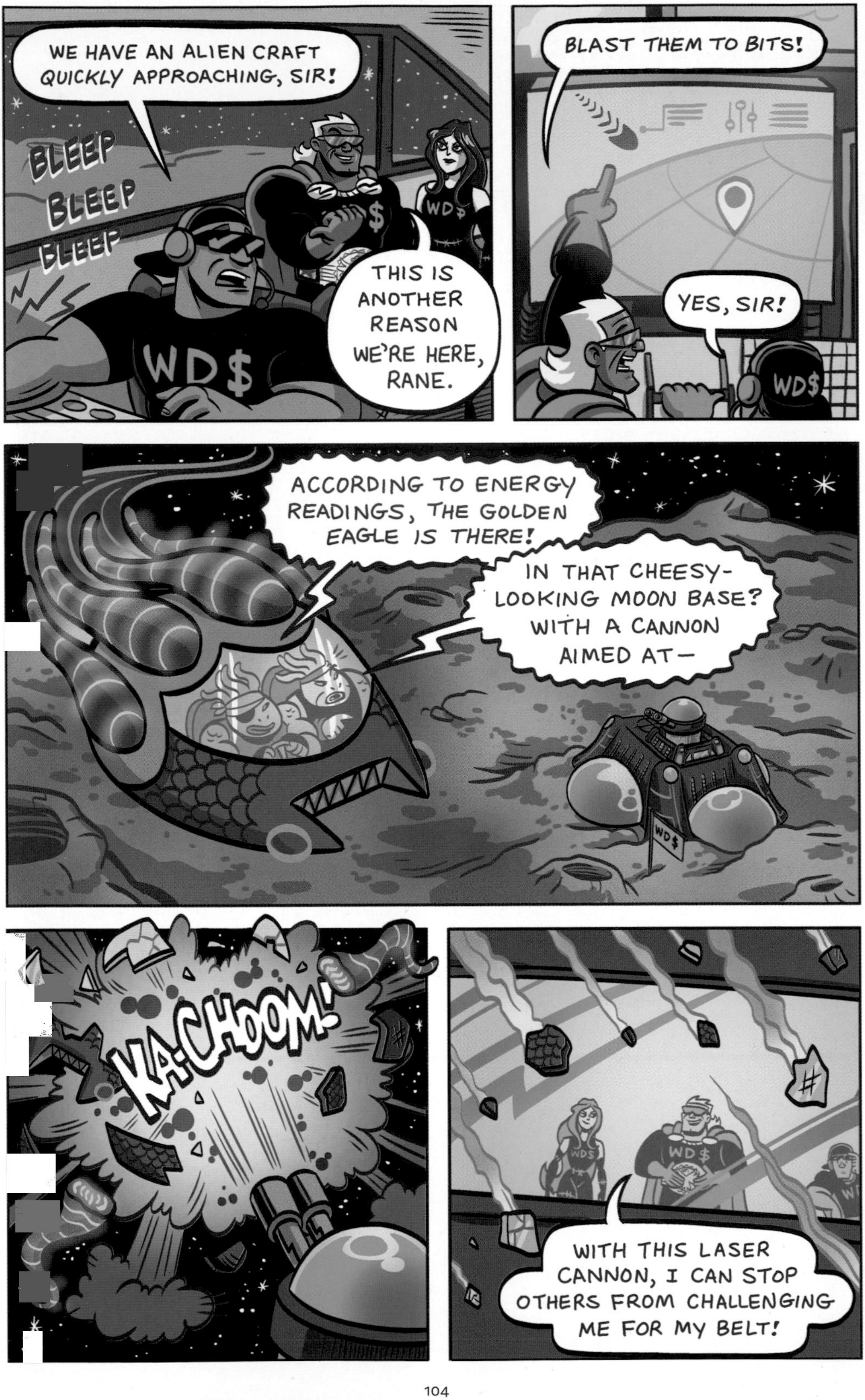
WE HAVE AN ALIEN CRAFT QUICKLY APPROACHING, SIR!
BLEEP BLEEP BLEEP
WD$
THIS IS ANOTHER REASON WE'RE HERE, RANE.
BLAST THEM TO BITS!
YES, SIR!
WD$
ACCORDING TO ENERGY READINGS, THE GOLDEN EAGLE IS THERE!
IN THAT CHEESY-LOOKING MOON BASE? WITH A CANNON AIMED AT—
WD$
KA-CHOOM!
WD$
WITH THIS LASER CANNON, I CAN STOP OTHERS FROM CHALLENGING ME FOR MY BELT!

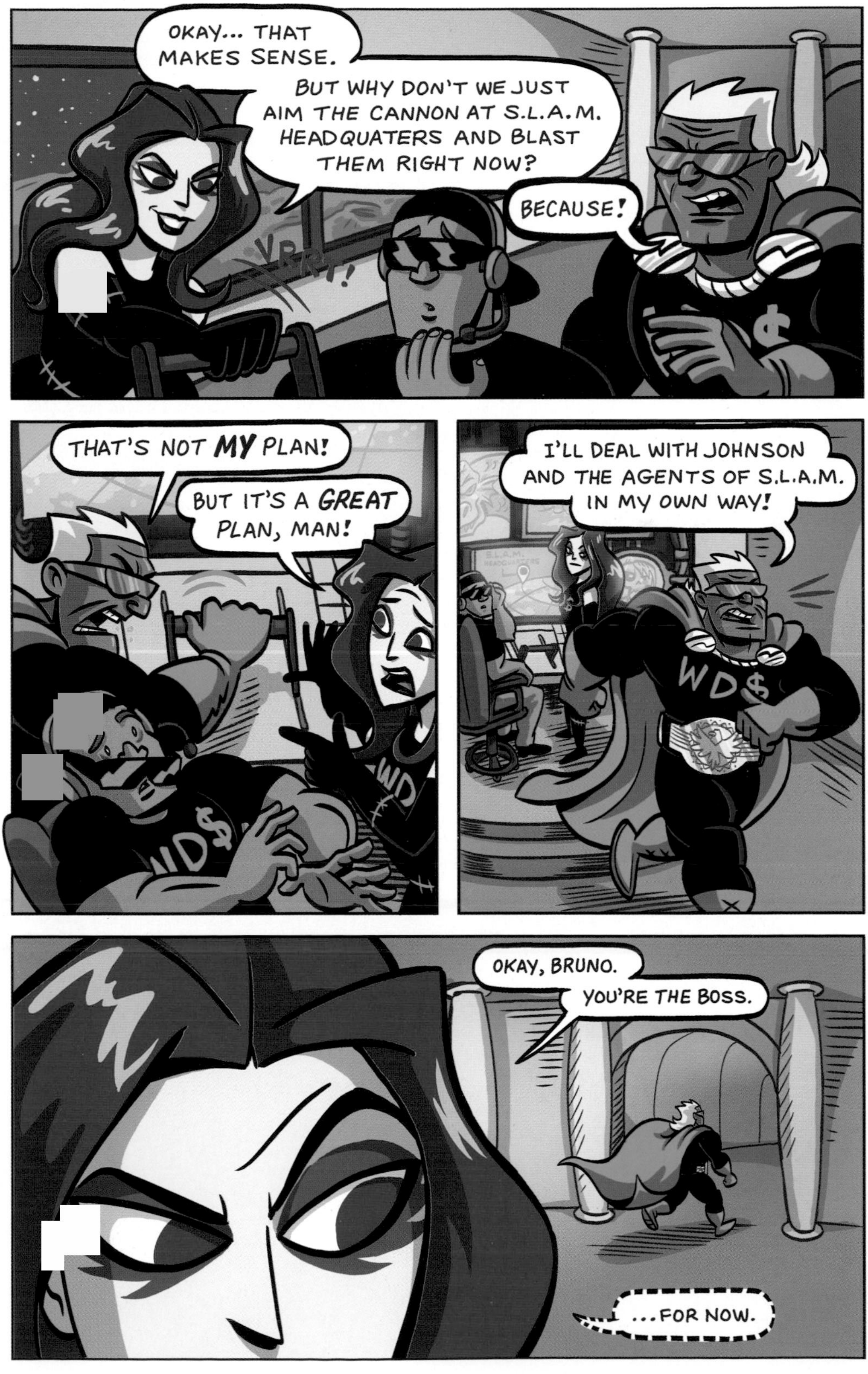
OKAY... THAT MAKES SENSE.
BUT WHY DON'T WE JUST AIM THE CANNON AT S.L.A.M. HEADQUATERS AND BLAST THEM RIGHT NOW?
VRRRT!
BECAUSE!
THAT'S NOT **MY** PLAN!
BUT IT'S A **GREAT** PLAN, MAN!
I'LL DEAL WITH JOHNSON AND THE AGENTS OF S.L.A.M. IN MY OWN WAY!
WD$
OKAY, BRUNO.
YOU'RE THE BOSS.
...FOR NOW.

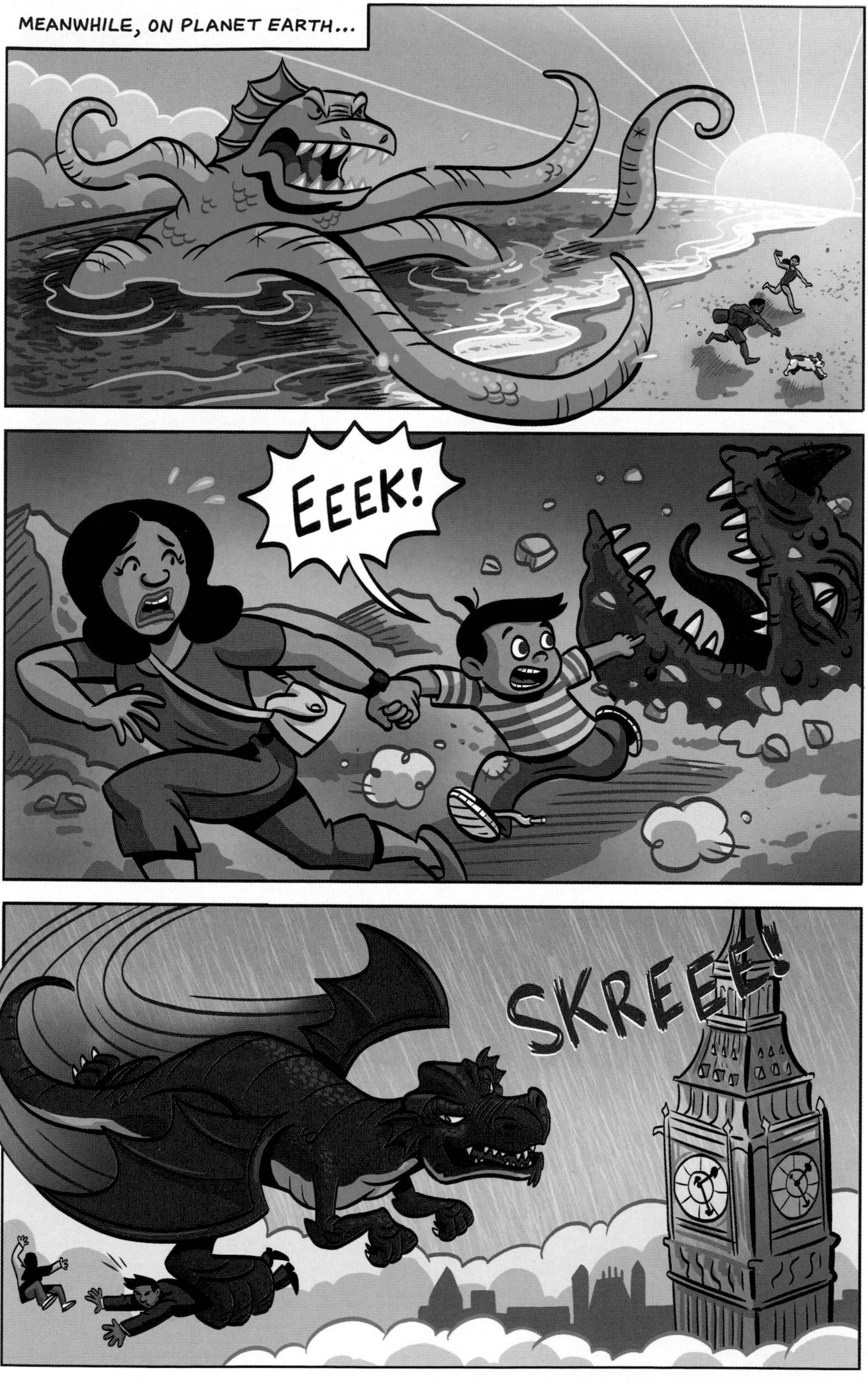
MEANWHILE, ON PLANET EARTH...
EEEK!
SKREEE!

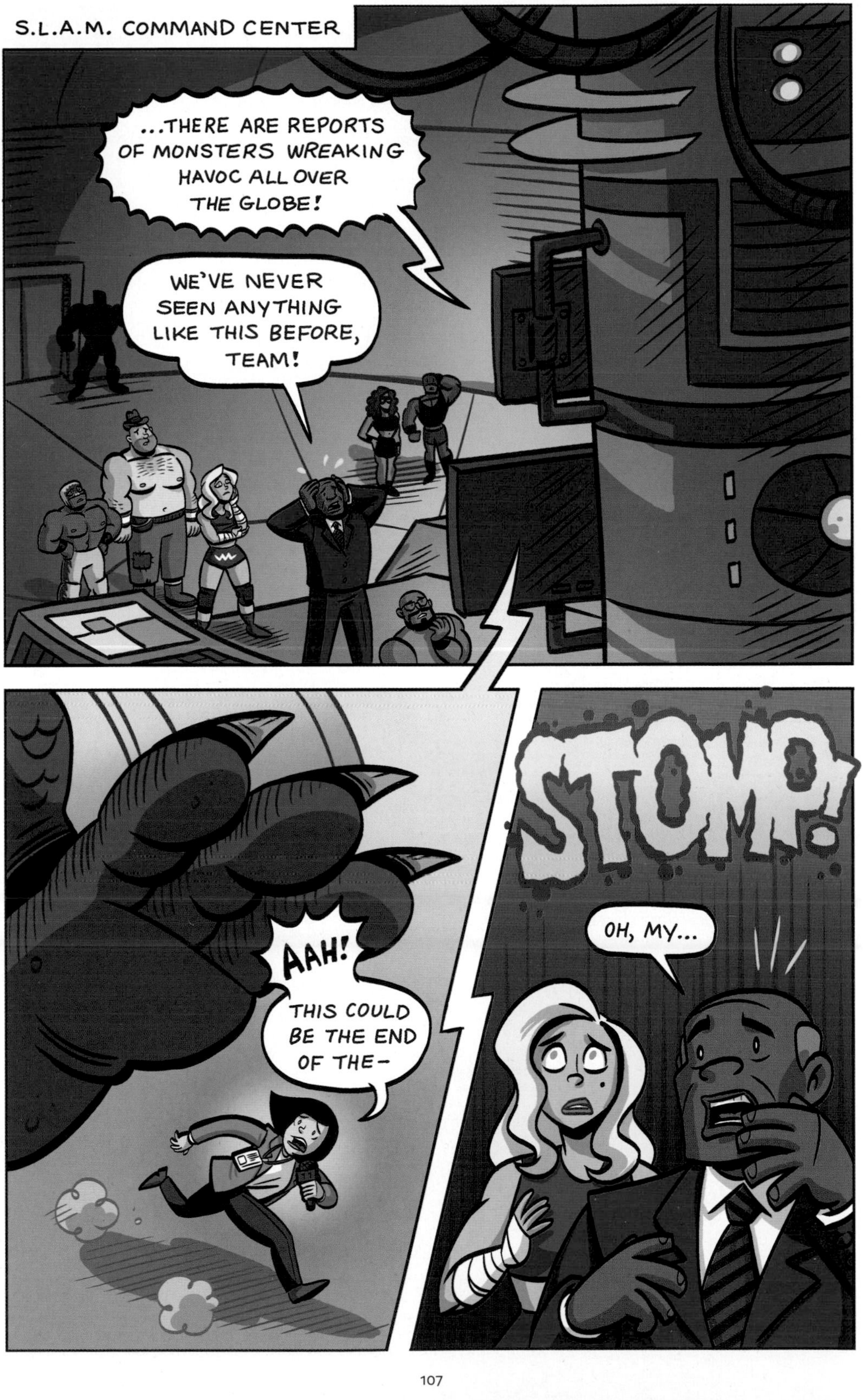
S.L.A.M. COMMAND CENTER
...THERE ARE REPORTS OF MONSTERS WREAKING HAVOC ALL OVER THE GLOBE!
WE'VE NEVER SEEN ANYTHING LIKE THIS BEFORE, TEAM!
AAH!
THIS COULD BE THE END OF THE-
STOMP!
OH, MY...

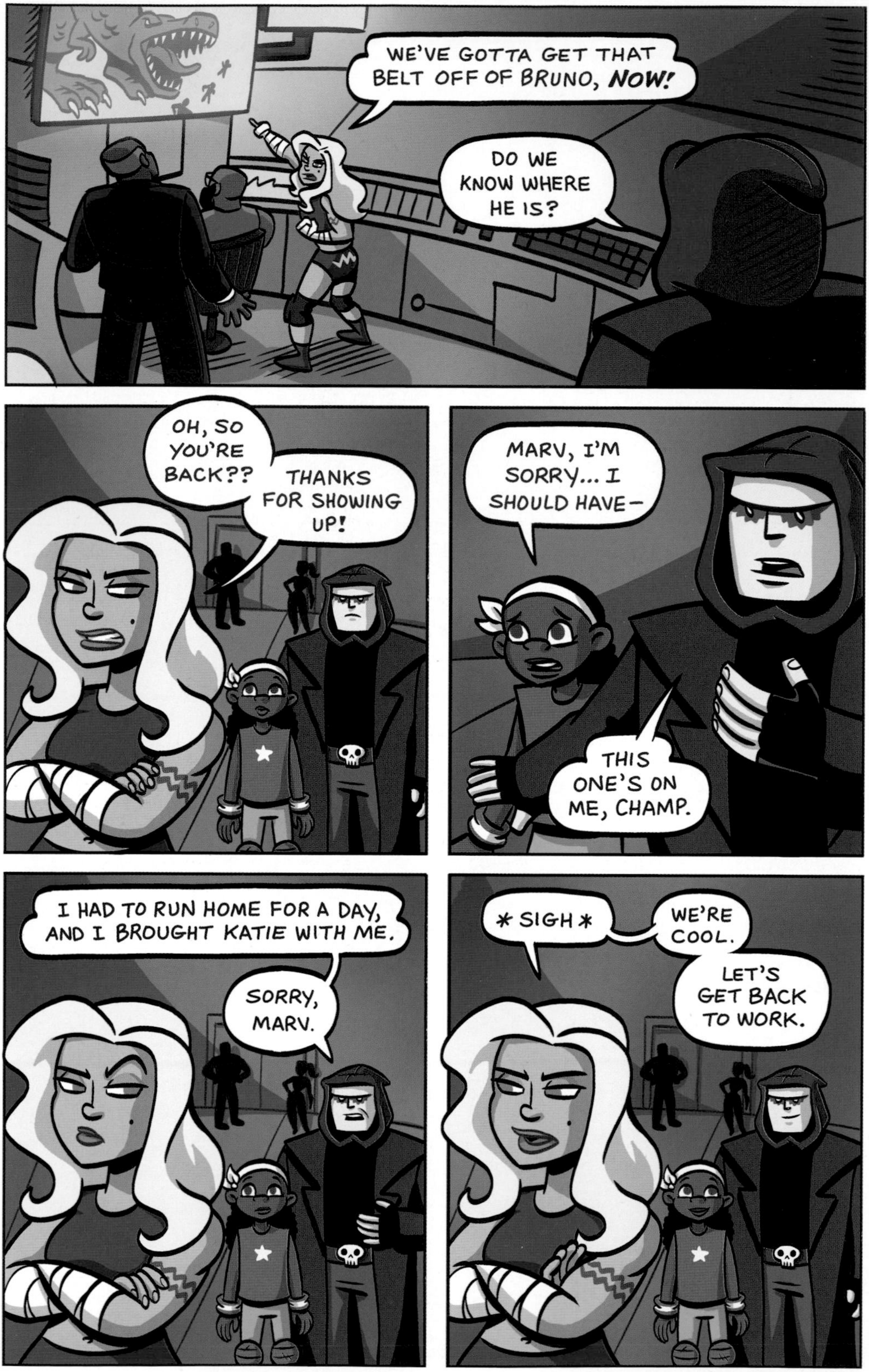
WE'VE GOTTA GET THAT BELT OFF OF BRUNO, NOW!
DO WE KNOW WHERE HE IS?
OH, SO YOU'RE BACK??
THANKS FOR SHOWING UP!
MARV, I'M SORRY... I SHOULD HAVE—
THIS ONE'S ON ME, CHAMP.
I HAD TO RUN HOME FOR A DAY, AND I BROUGHT KATIE WITH ME.
SORRY, MARV.
SIGH
WE'RE COOL.
LET'S GET BACK TO WORK.

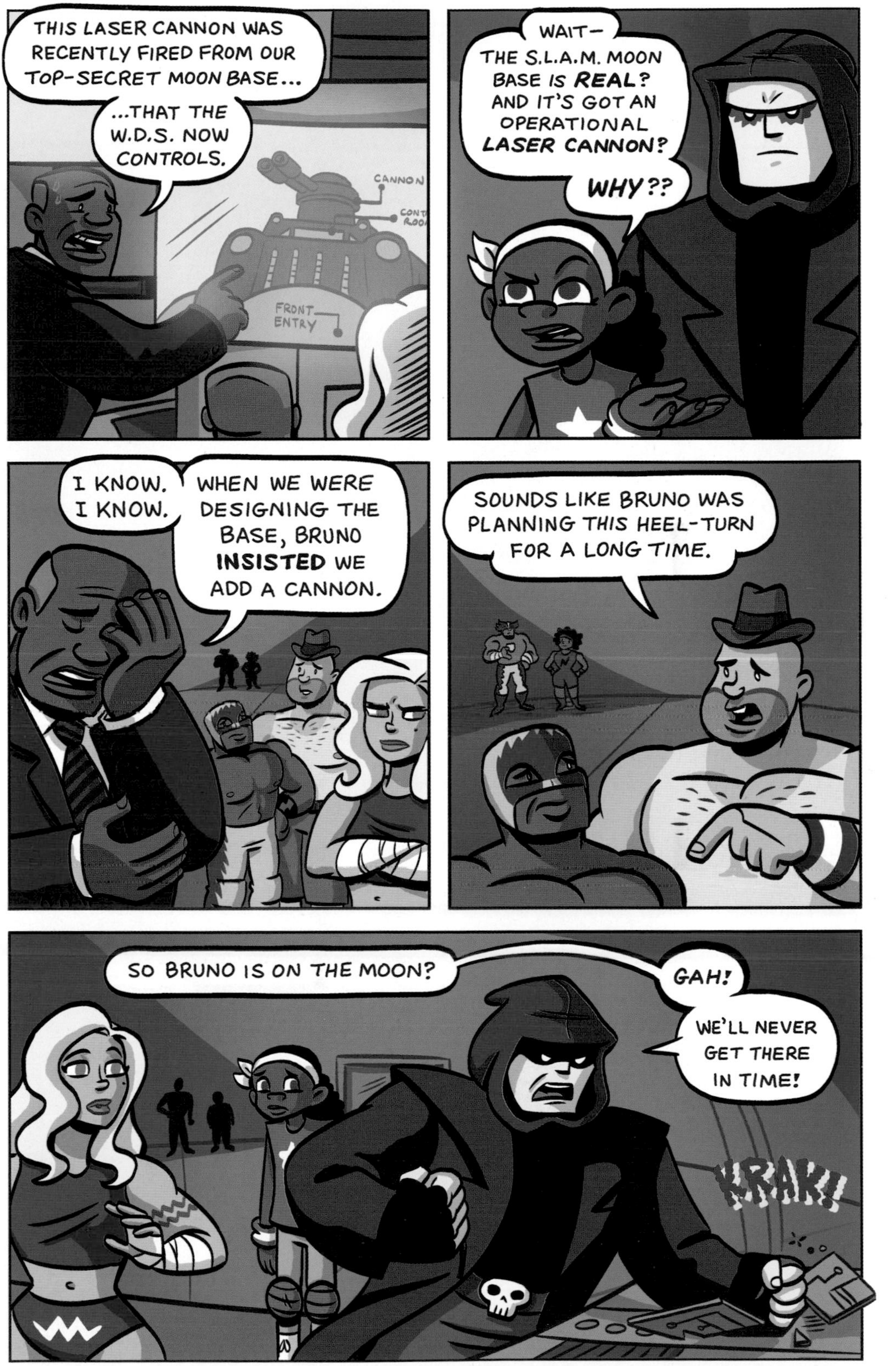
THIS LASER CANNON WAS RECENTLY FIRED FROM OUR TOP-SECRET MOON BASE...
...THAT THE W.D.S. NOW CONTROLS.
CANNON
FRONT ENTRY
WAIT—
THE S.L.A.M. MOON BASE IS REAL? AND IT'S GOT AN OPERATIONAL LASER CANNON?
WHY??
I KNOW. I KNOW.
WHEN WE WERE DESIGNING THE BASE, BRUNO INSISTED WE ADD A CANNON.
SOUNDS LIKE BRUNO WAS PLANNING THIS HEEL-TURN FOR A LONG TIME.
SO BRUNO IS ON THE MOON?
GAH!
WE'LL NEVER GET THERE IN TIME!
KRAK!

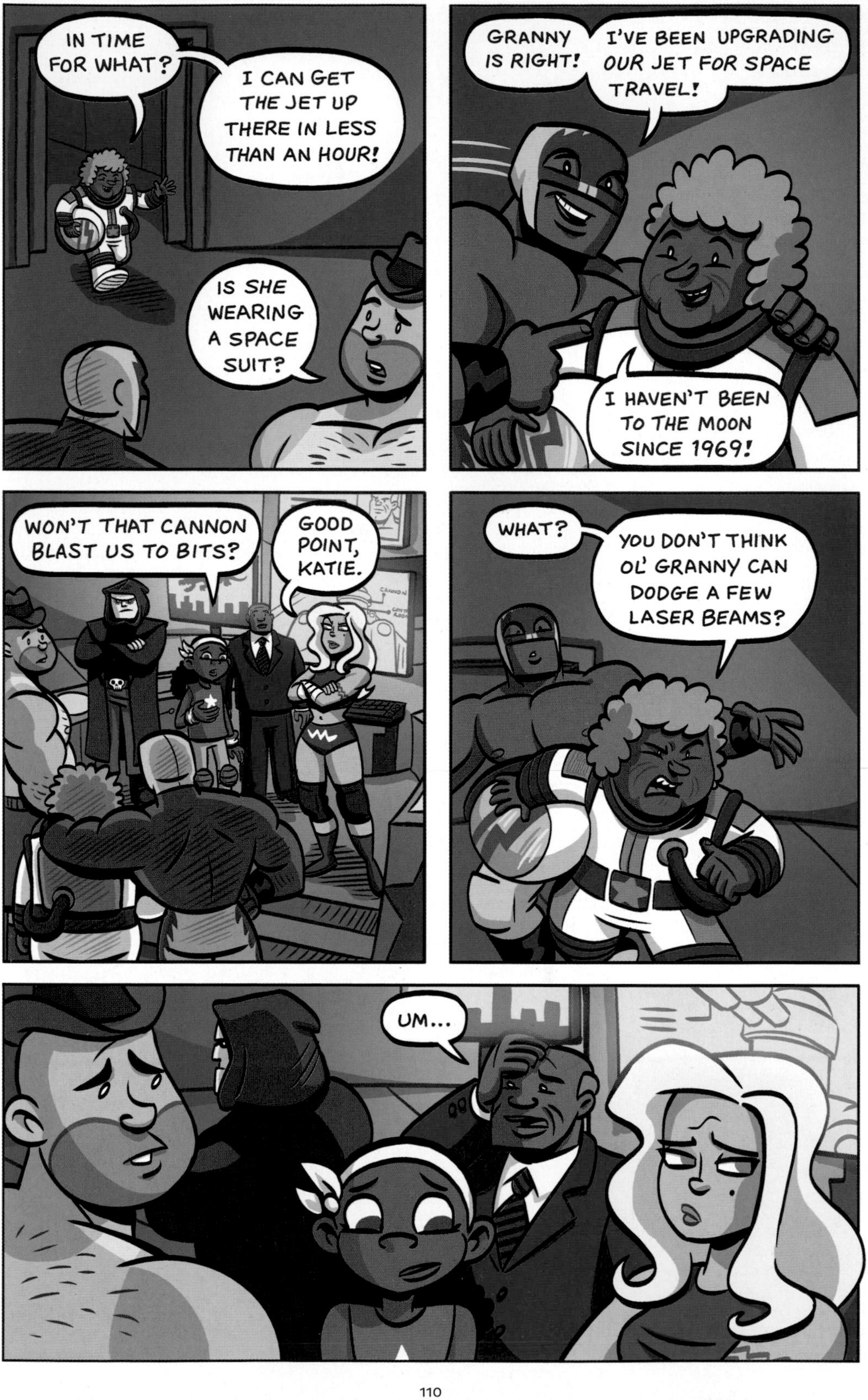
IN TIME FOR WHAT?
I CAN GET THE JET UP THERE IN LESS THAN AN HOUR!
IS SHE WEARING A SPACE SUIT?
GRANNY IS RIGHT!
I'VE BEEN UPGRADING OUR JET FOR SPACE TRAVEL!
I HAVEN'T BEEN TO THE MOON SINCE 1969!
WON'T THAT CANNON BLAST US TO BITS?
GOOD POINT, KATIE.
WHAT?
YOU DON'T THINK OL' GRANNY CAN DODGE A FEW LASER BEAMS?
UM...

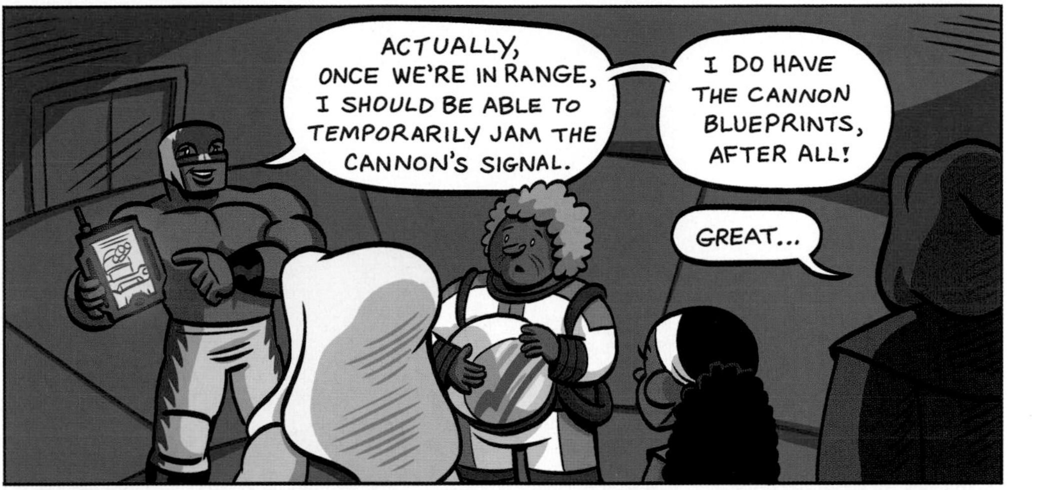
ACTUALLY, ONCE WE'RE IN RANGE, I SHOULD BE ABLE TO TEMPORARILY JAM THE CANNON'S SIGNAL.
I DO HAVE THE CANNON BLUEPRINTS, AFTER ALL!
GREAT...

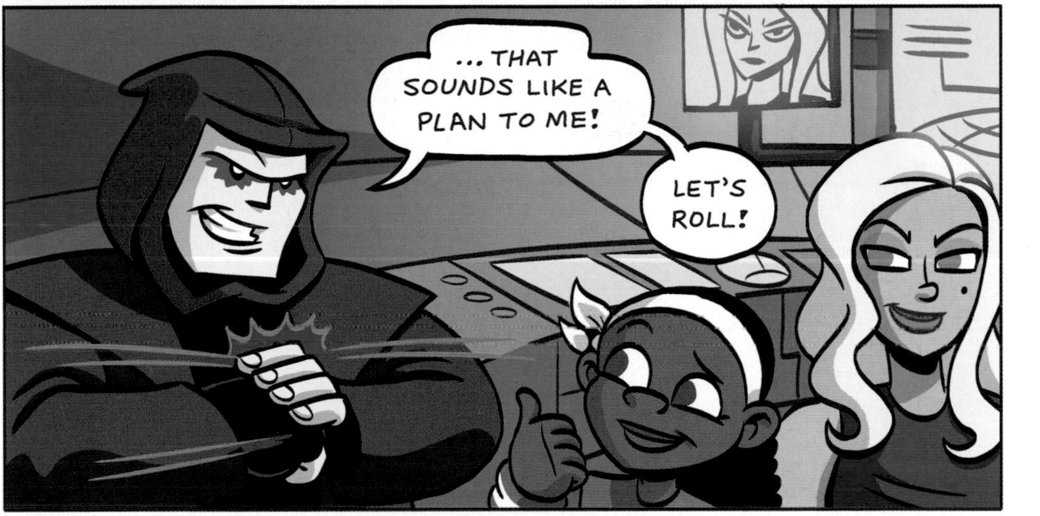
...THAT SOUNDS LIKE A PLAN TO ME!
LET'S ROLL!

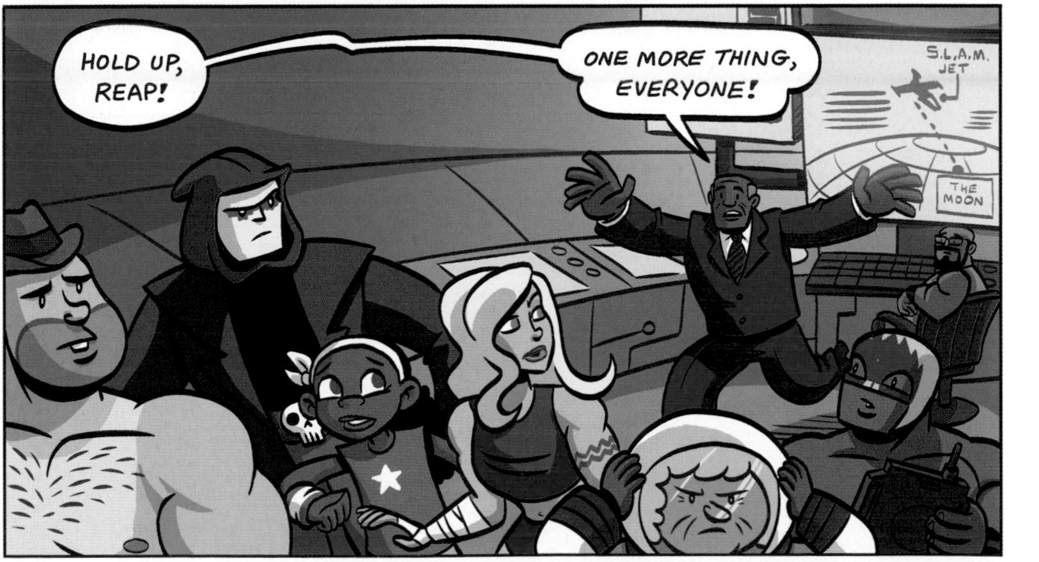
HOLD UP, REAP!
ONE MORE THING, EVERYONE!
S.L.A.M. JET
THE MOON

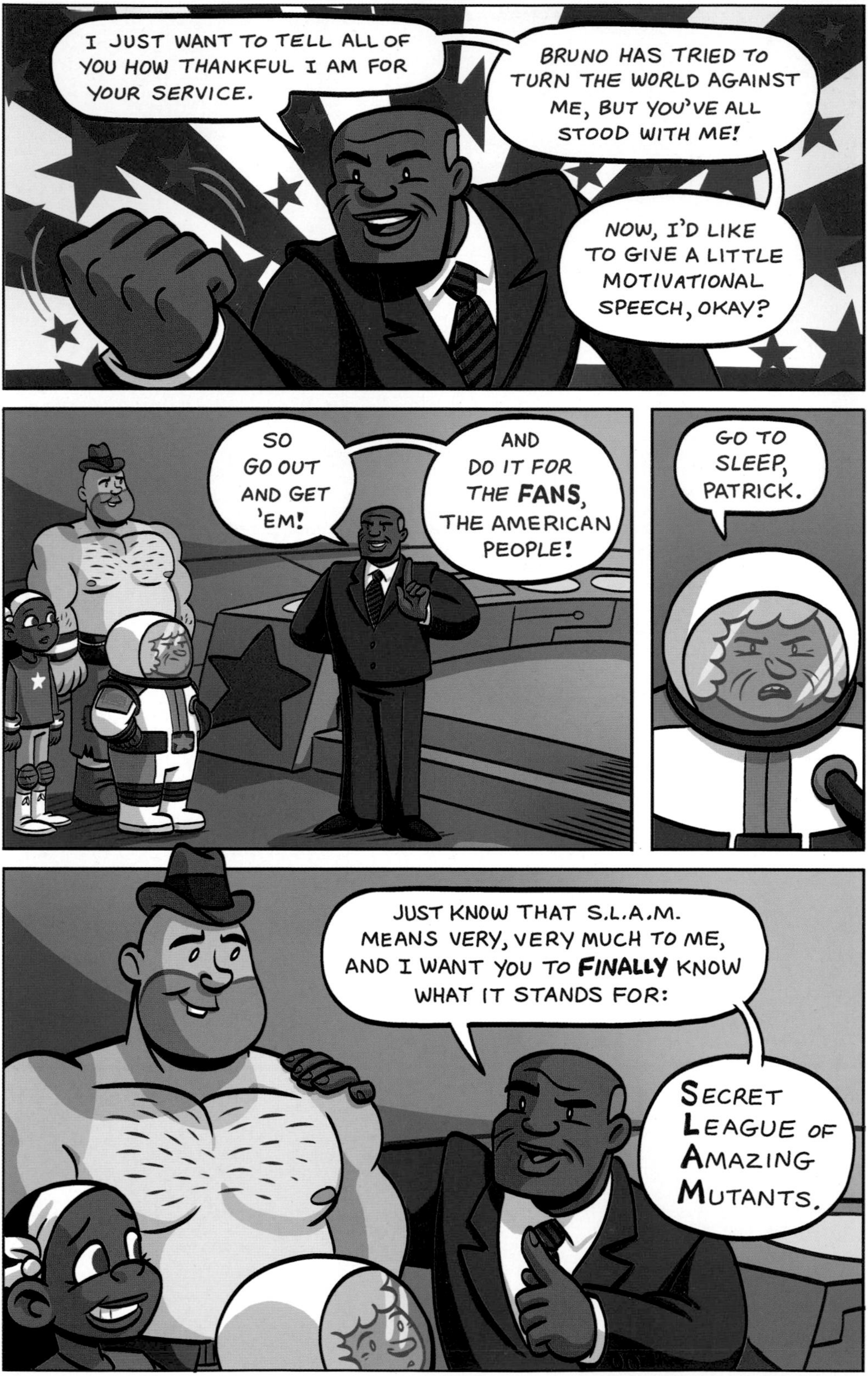
I JUST WANT TO TELL ALL OF YOU HOW THANKFUL I AM FOR YOUR SERVICE.
BRUNO HAS TRIED TO TURN THE WORLD AGAINST ME, BUT YOU'VE ALL STOOD WITH ME!
NOW, I'D LIKE TO GIVE A LITTLE MOTIVATIONAL SPEECH, OKAY?
SO GO OUT AND GET 'EM!
AND DO IT FOR THE **FANS**, THE AMERICAN PEOPLE!
GO TO SLEEP, PATRICK.
JUST KNOW THAT S.L.A.M. MEANS VERY, VERY MUCH TO ME, AND I WANT YOU TO **FINALLY** KNOW WHAT IT STANDS FOR:
SECRET LEAGUE OF AMAZING MUTANTS.

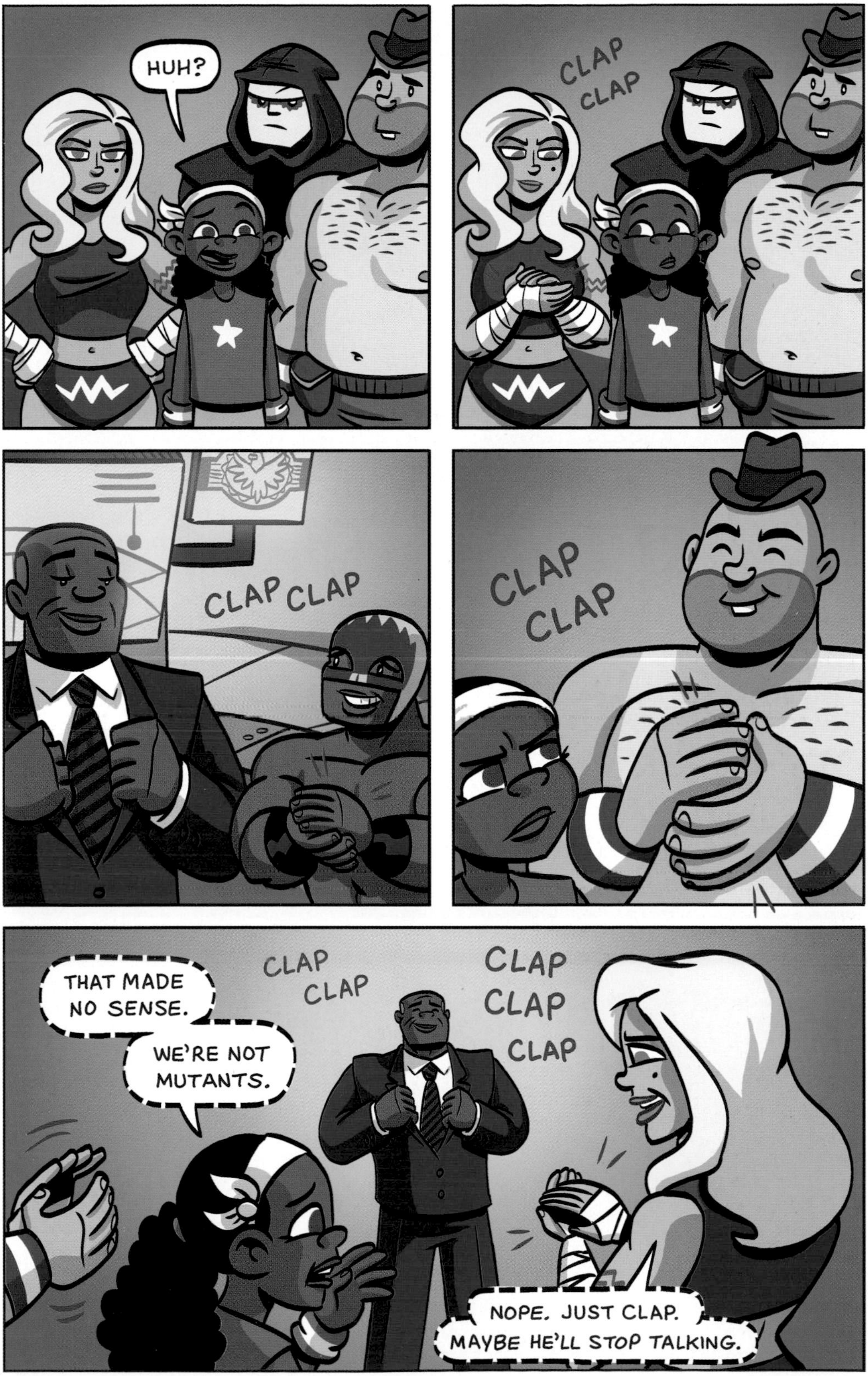
HUH?
CLAP
CLAP
CLAP CLAP
CLAP
CLAP
THAT MADE NO SENSE.
WE'RE NOT MUTANTS.
CLAP
CLAP
CLAP
CLAP
CLAP
NOPE. JUST CLAP. MAYBE HE'LL STOP TALKING.

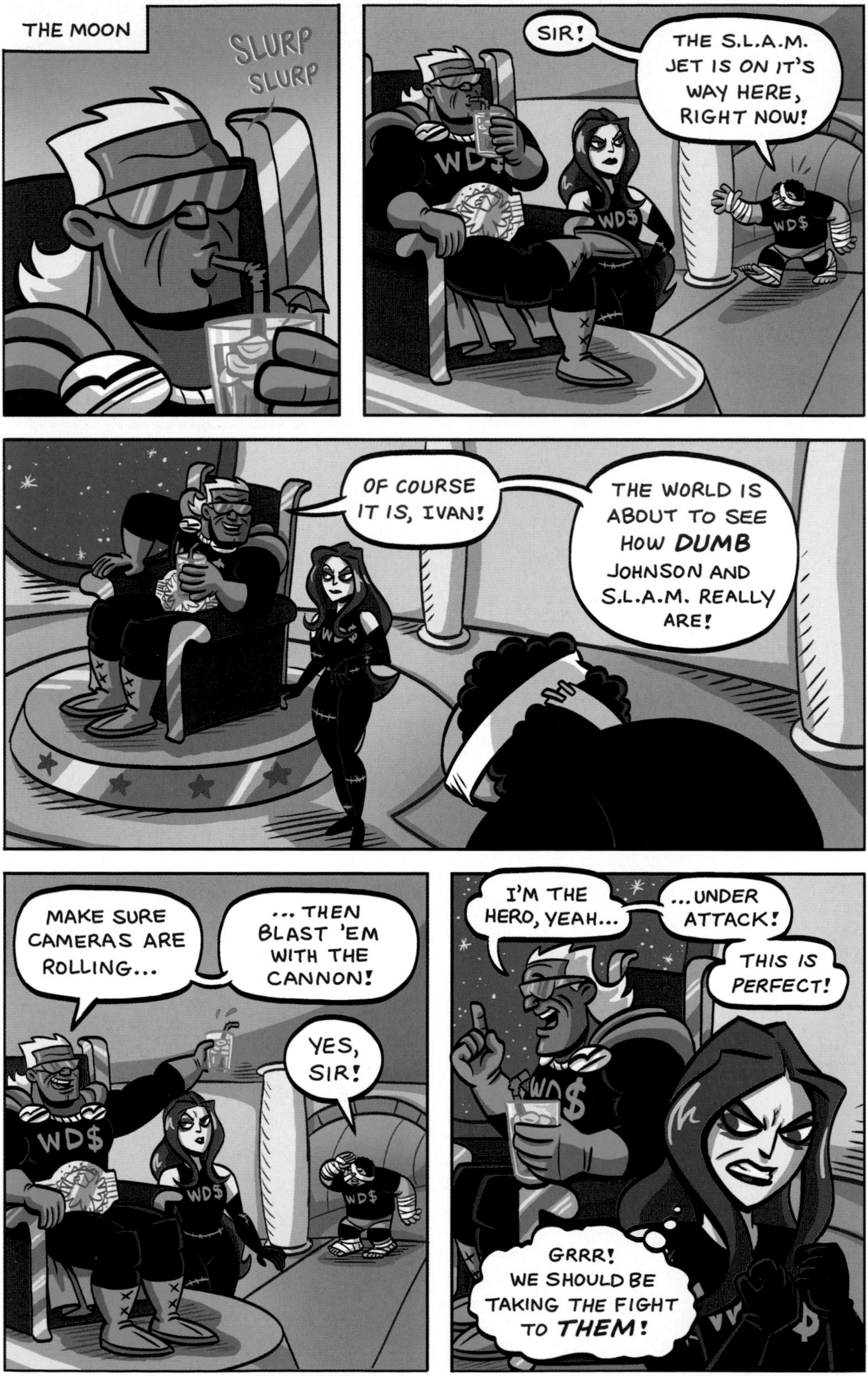
THE MOON
SLURP SLURP
SIR!
THE S.L.A.M. JET IS ON IT'S WAY HERE, RIGHT NOW!
OF COURSE IT IS, IVAN!
THE WORLD IS ABOUT TO SEE HOW DUMB JOHNSON AND S.L.A.M. REALLY ARE!
MAKE SURE CAMERAS ARE ROLLING...
...THEN BLAST 'EM WITH THE CANNON!
YES, SIR!
I'M THE HERO, YEAH...
...UNDER ATTACK!
THIS IS PERFECT!
GRRR! WE SHOULD BE TAKING THE FIGHT TO THEM!

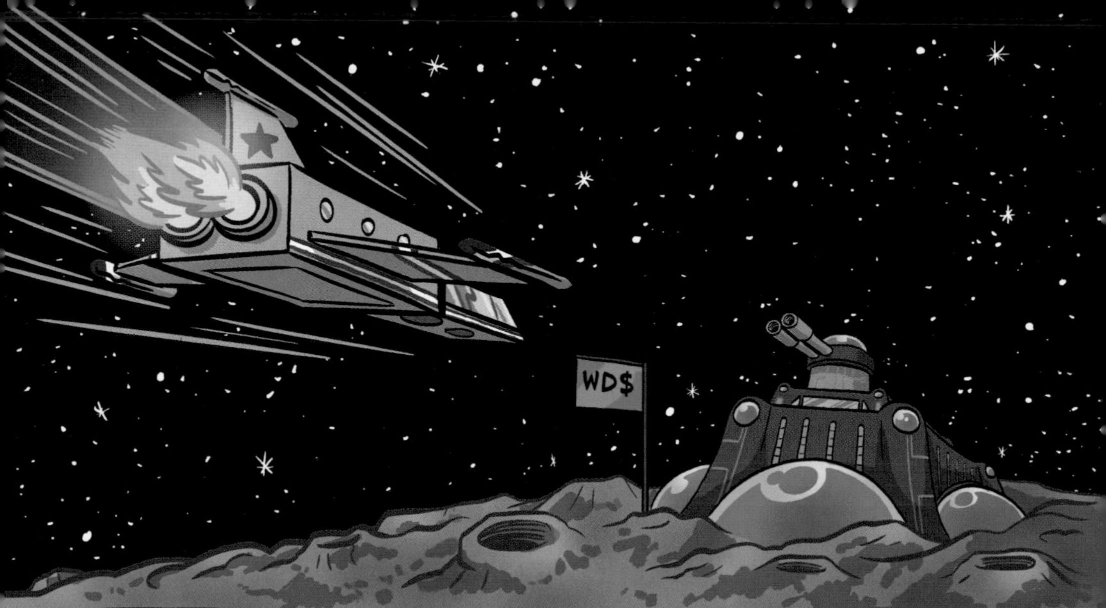
WD$

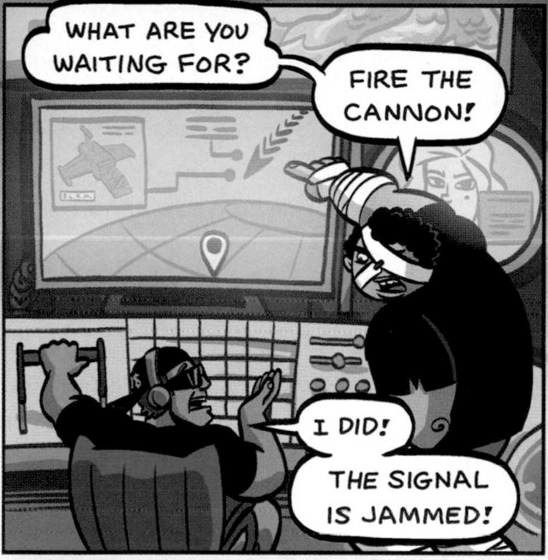
WHAT ARE YOU WAITING FOR?
FIRE THE CANNON!
I DID!
THE SIGNAL IS JAMMED!

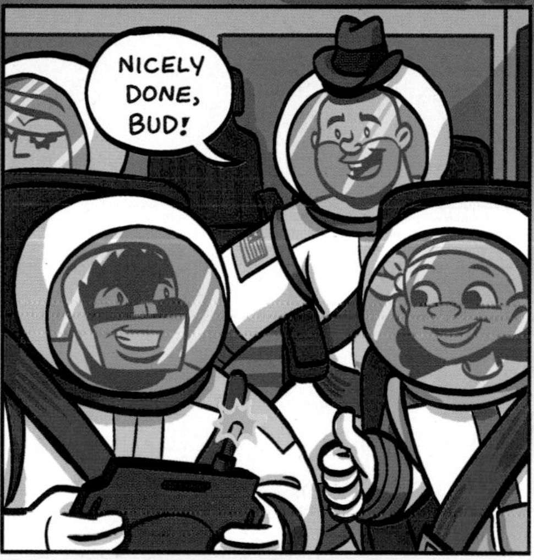
NICELY DONE, BUD!

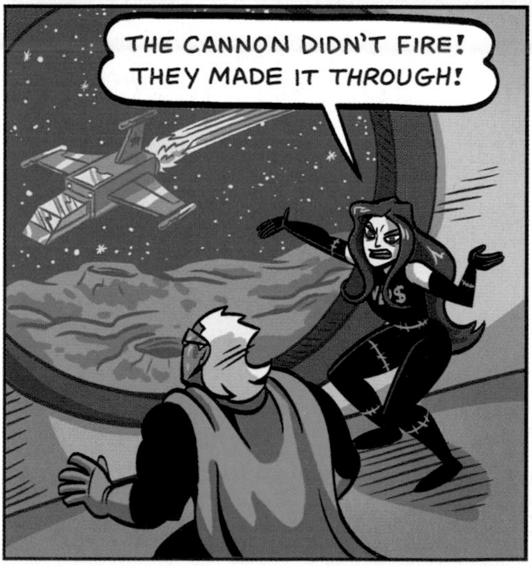
THE CANNON DIDN'T FIRE! THEY MADE IT THROUGH!

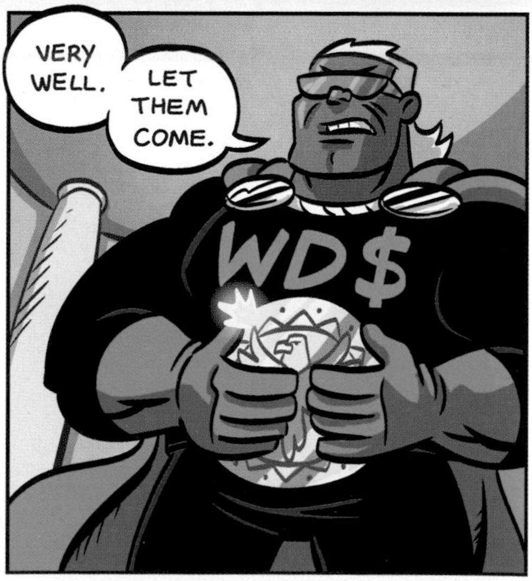
VERY WELL.
LET THEM COME.
WD$

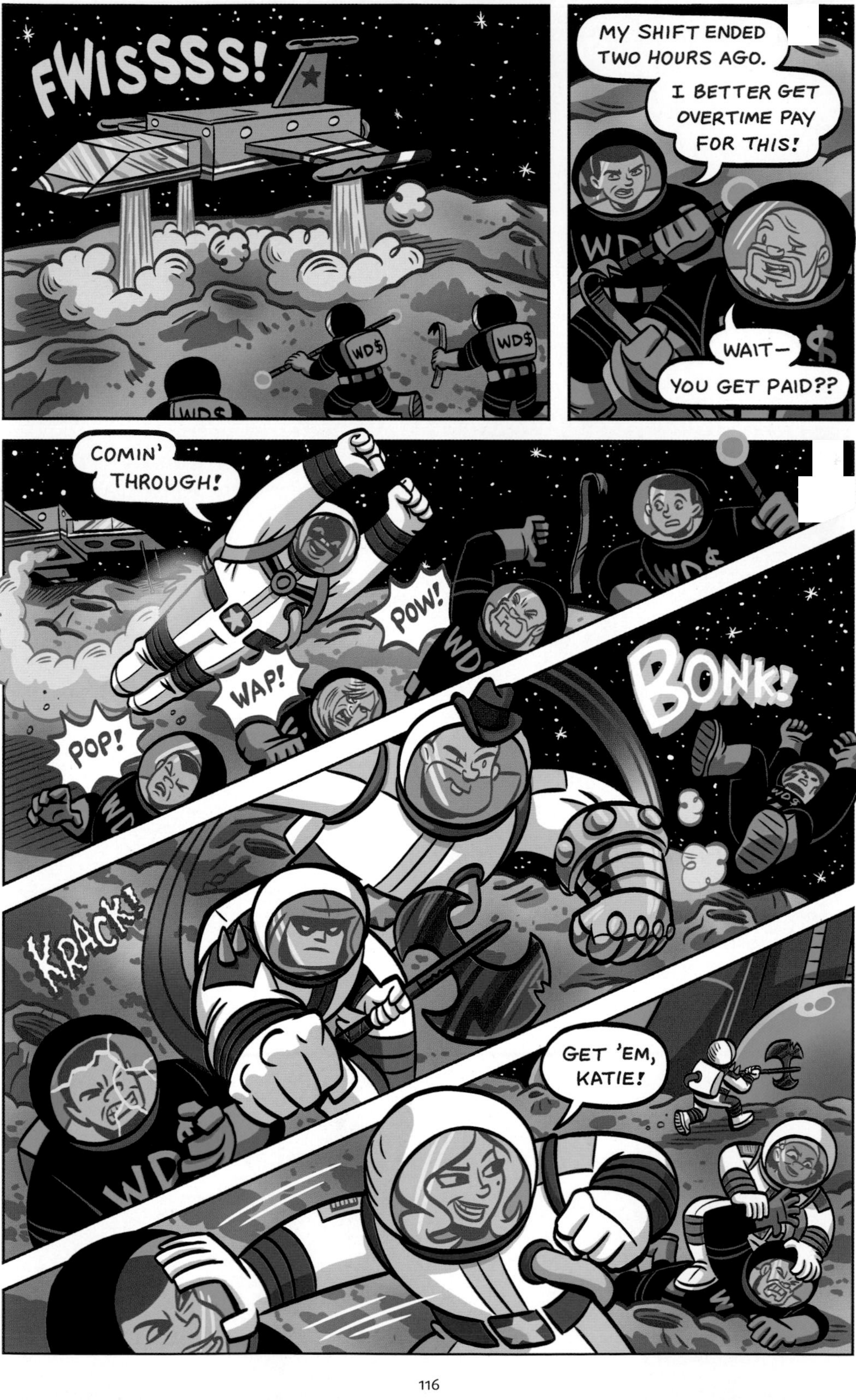
FWISSSS!
WD$
WD$
WD$
MY SHIFT ENDED TWO HOURS AGO.
I BETTER GET OVERTIME PAY FOR THIS!
WAIT— YOU GET PAID??
COMIN' THROUGH!
POW!
WAP!
POP!
BONK!
KRACK!
GET 'EM, KATIE!

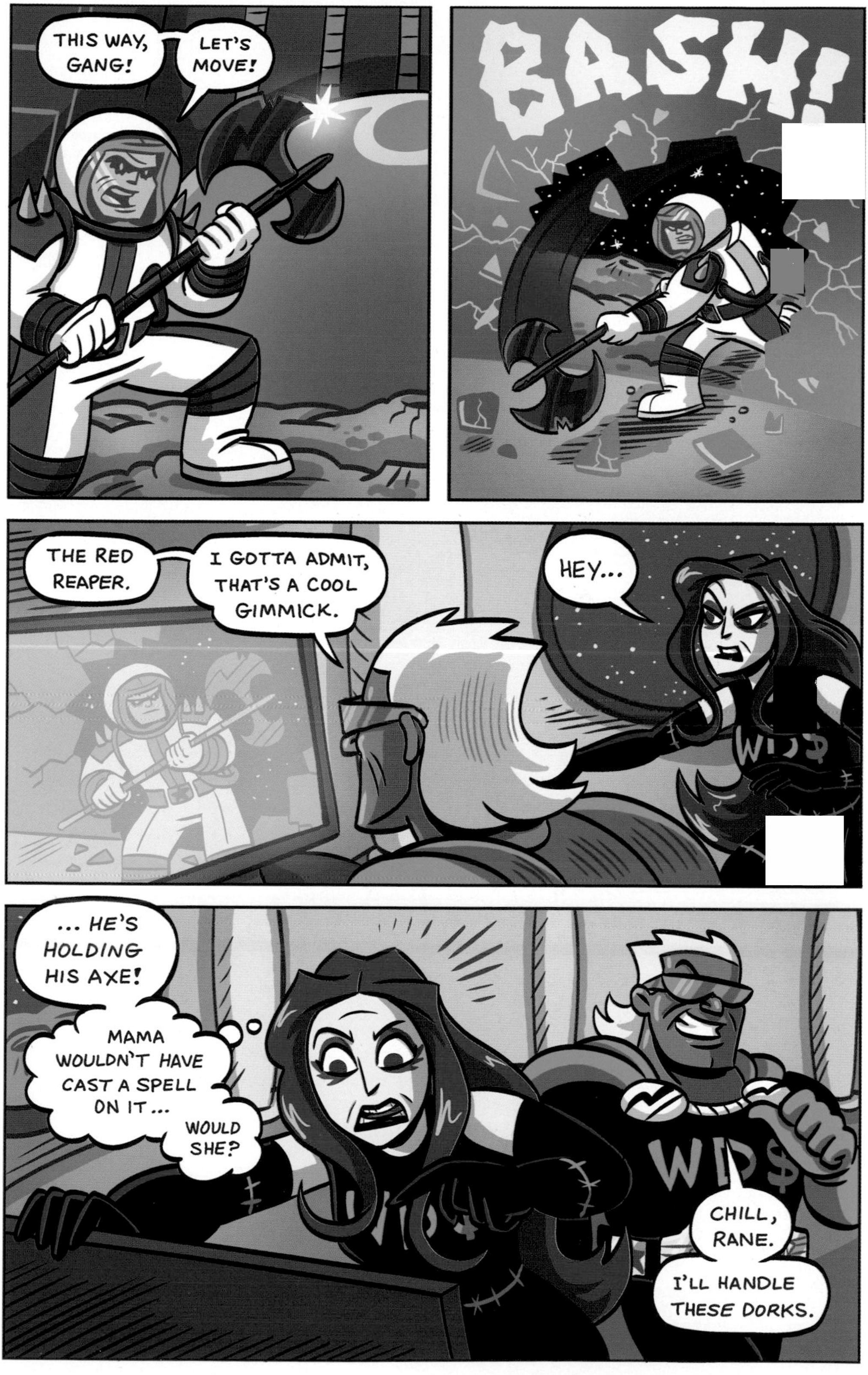
THIS WAY, GANG!
LET'S MOVE!
BASH!
THE RED REAPER.
I GOTTA ADMIT, THAT'S A COOL GIMMICK.
HEY...
... HE'S HOLDING HIS AXE!
MAMA WOULDN'T HAVE CAST A SPELL ON IT...
WOULD SHE?
CHILL, RANE.
I'LL HANDLE THESE DORKS.

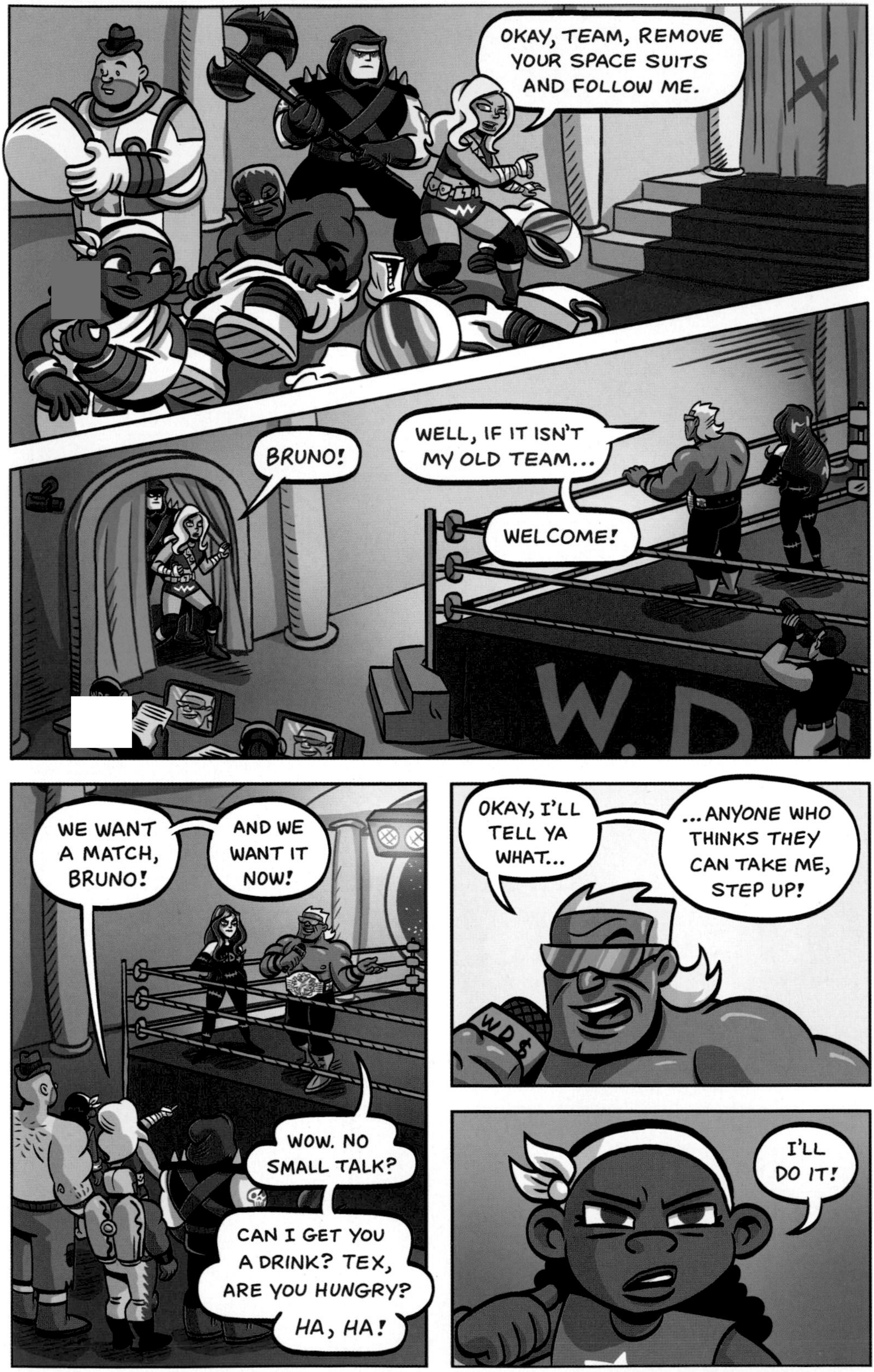
OKAY, TEAM, REMOVE YOUR SPACE SUITS AND FOLLOW ME.
BRUNO!
WELL, IF IT ISN'T MY OLD TEAM...
WELCOME!
W.D.
WE WANT A MATCH, BRUNO!
AND WE WANT IT NOW!
WOW. NO SMALL TALK?
CAN I GET YOU A DRINK? TEX, ARE YOU HUNGRY?
HA, HA!
OKAY, I'LL TELL YA WHAT...
...ANYONE WHO THINKS THEY CAN TAKE ME, STEP UP!
W.D.$
I'LL DO IT!

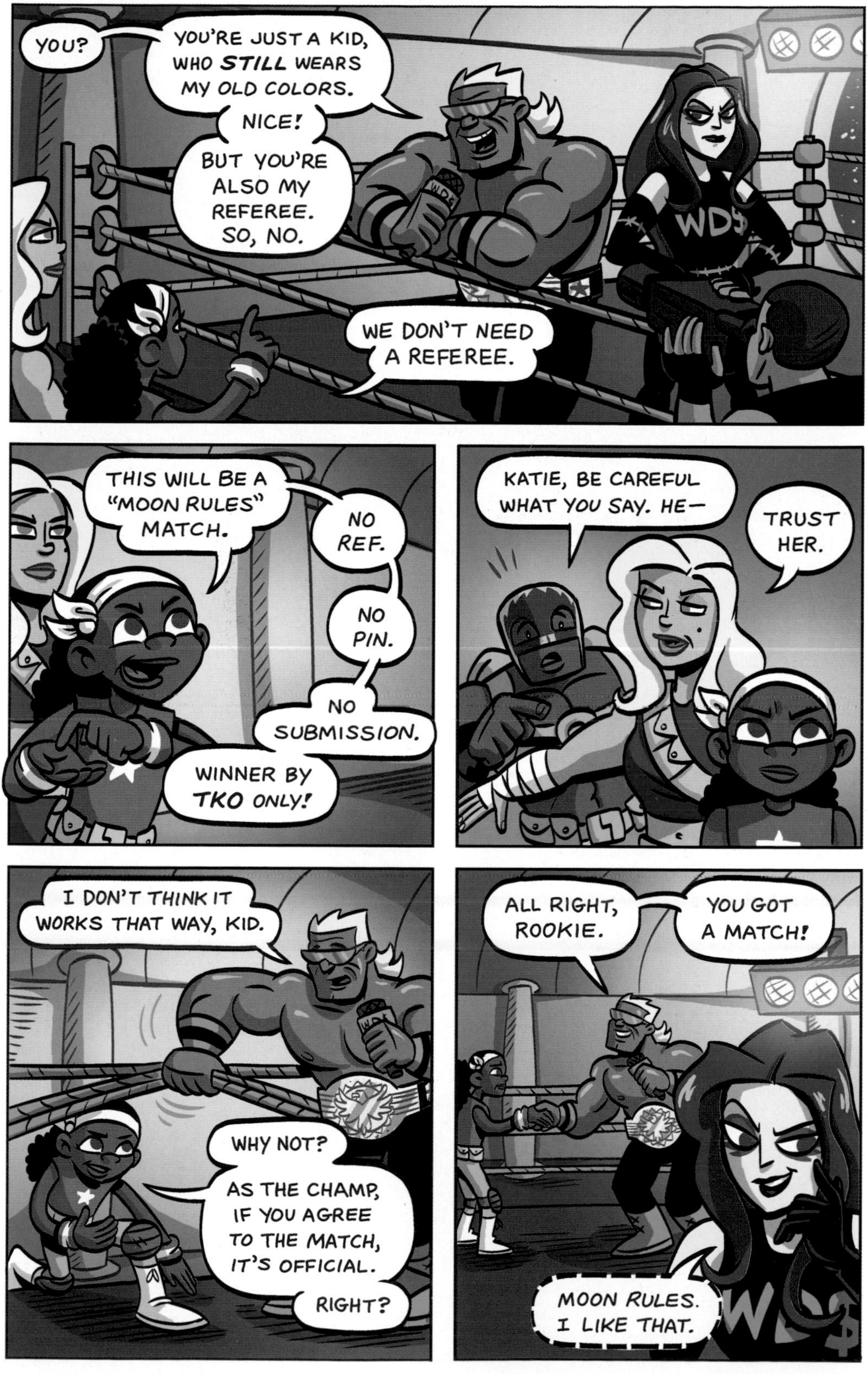
YOU?
YOU'RE JUST A KID, WHO STILL WEARS MY OLD COLORS.
NICE!
BUT YOU'RE ALSO MY REFEREE. SO, NO.
WE DON'T NEED A REFEREE.
THIS WILL BE A "MOON RULES" MATCH.
NO REF.
NO PIN.
NO SUBMISSION.
WINNER BY TKO ONLY!
KATIE, BE CAREFUL WHAT YOU SAY. HE—
TRUST HER.
I DON'T THINK IT WORKS THAT WAY, KID.
WHY NOT?
AS THE CHAMP, IF YOU AGREE TO THE MATCH, IT'S OFFICIAL.
RIGHT?
ALL RIGHT, ROOKIE.
YOU GOT A MATCH!
MOON RULES. I LIKE THAT.

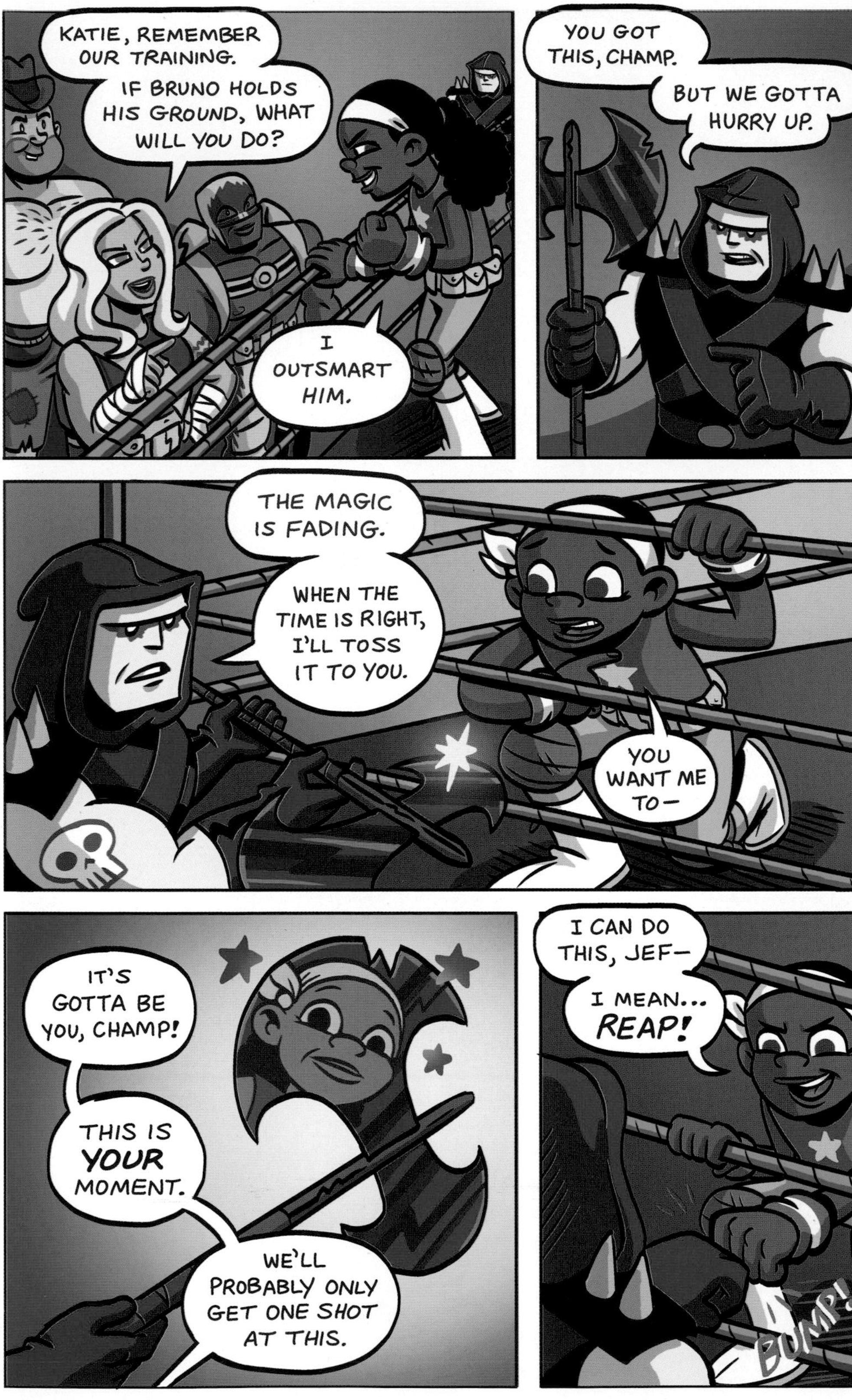
KATIE, REMEMBER OUR TRAINING.
IF BRUNO HOLDS HIS GROUND, WHAT WILL YOU DO?
I OUTSMART HIM.
YOU GOT THIS, CHAMP.
BUT WE GOTTA HURRY UP.
THE MAGIC IS FADING.
WHEN THE TIME IS RIGHT, I'LL TOSS IT TO YOU.
YOU WANT ME TO—
IT'S GOTTA BE YOU, CHAMP!
THIS IS **YOUR** MOMENT.
WE'LL PROBABLY ONLY GET ONE SHOT AT THIS.
I CAN DO THIS, JEF—
I MEAN... ***REAP!***
BUMP!

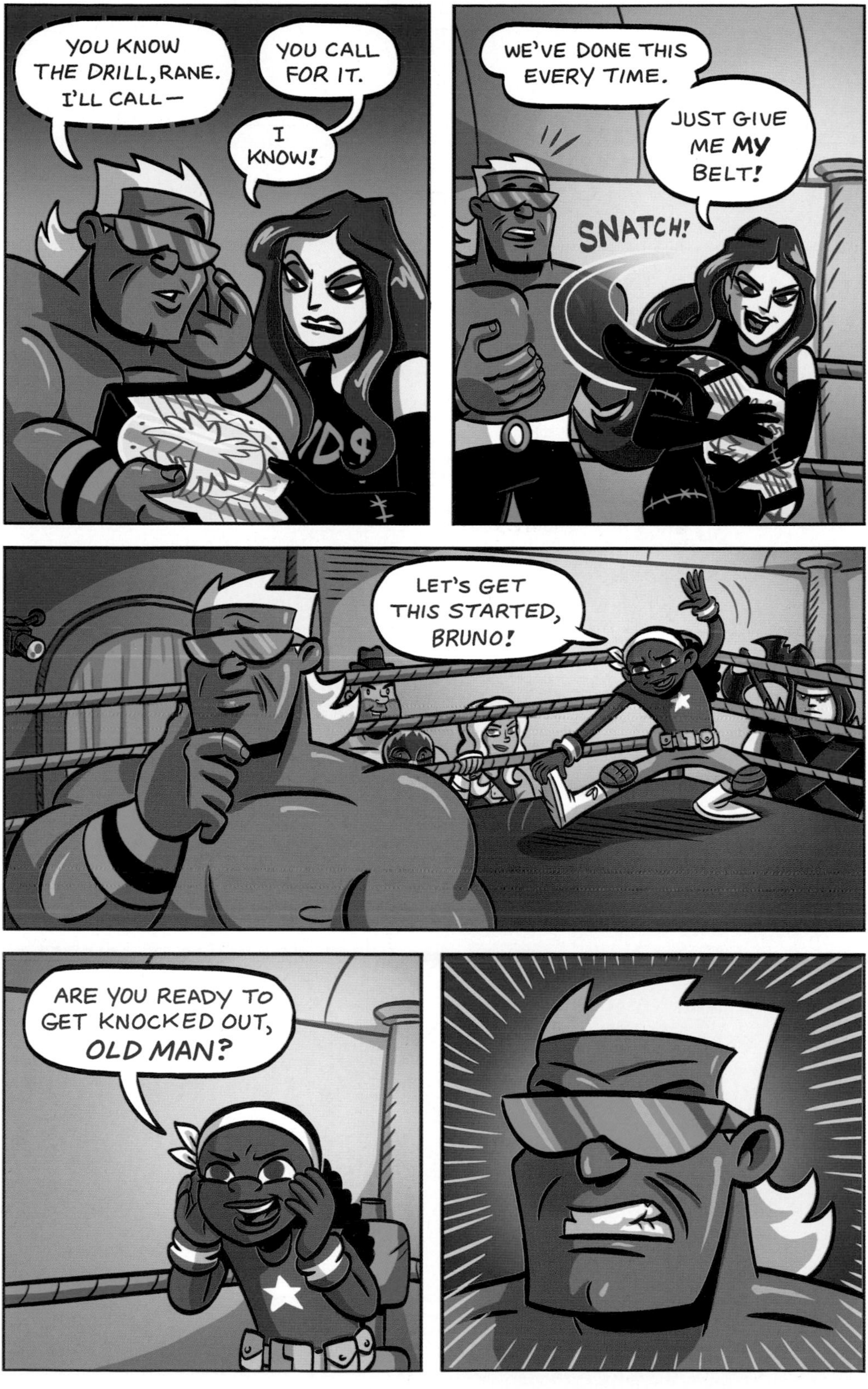

YOU KNOW THE DRILL, RANE. I'LL CALL—
YOU CALL FOR IT.
I KNOW!
WE'VE DONE THIS EVERY TIME.
JUST GIVE ME **MY** BELT!
SNATCH!
LET'S GET THIS STARTED, BRUNO!
ARE YOU READY TO GET KNOCKED OUT, **OLD MAN?**

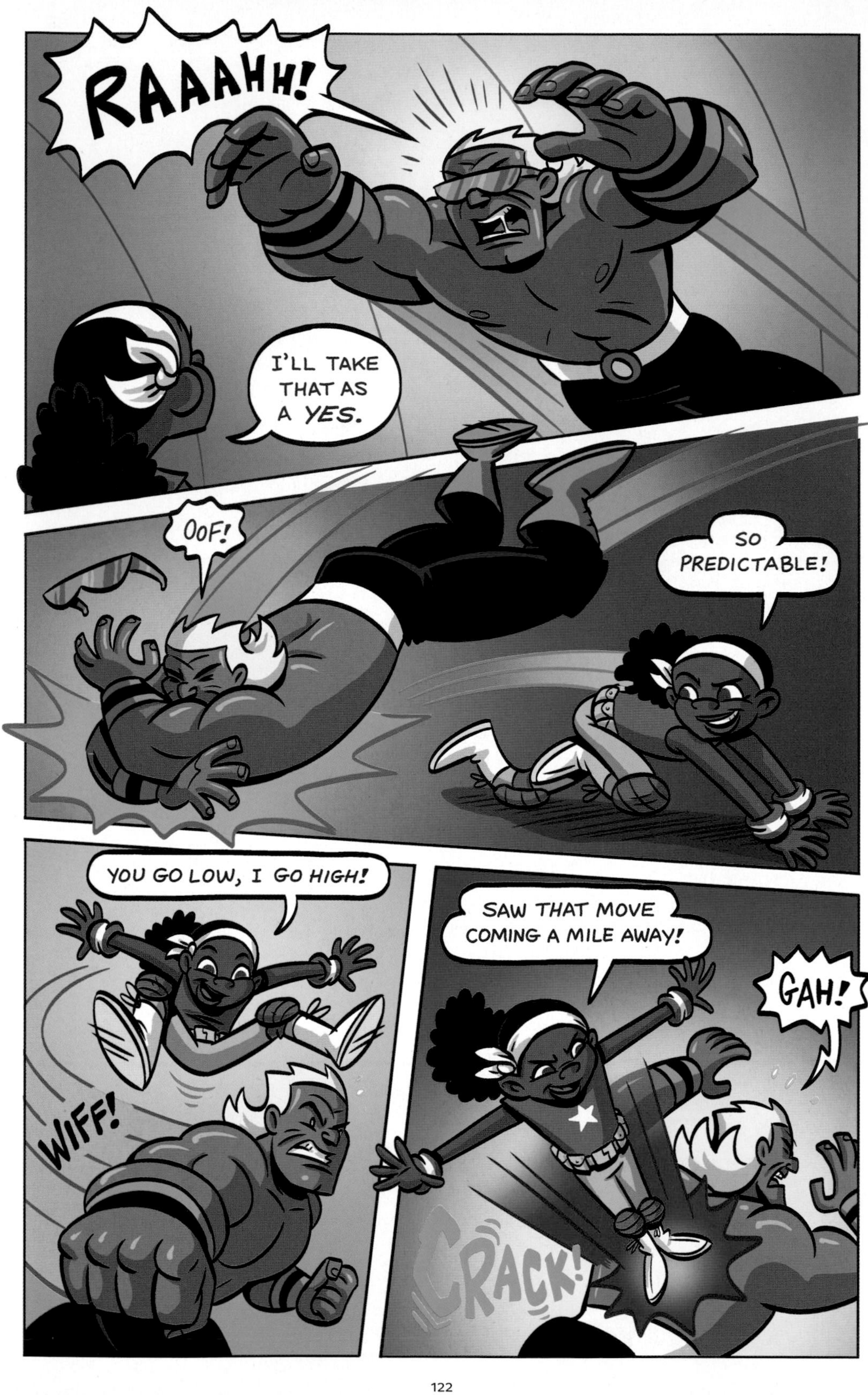
RAAAHH!
I'LL TAKE THAT AS A YES.
OOF!
SO PREDICTABLE!
YOU GO LOW, I GO HIGH!
WIFF!
SAW THAT MOVE COMING A MILE AWAY!
GAH!
CRACK!

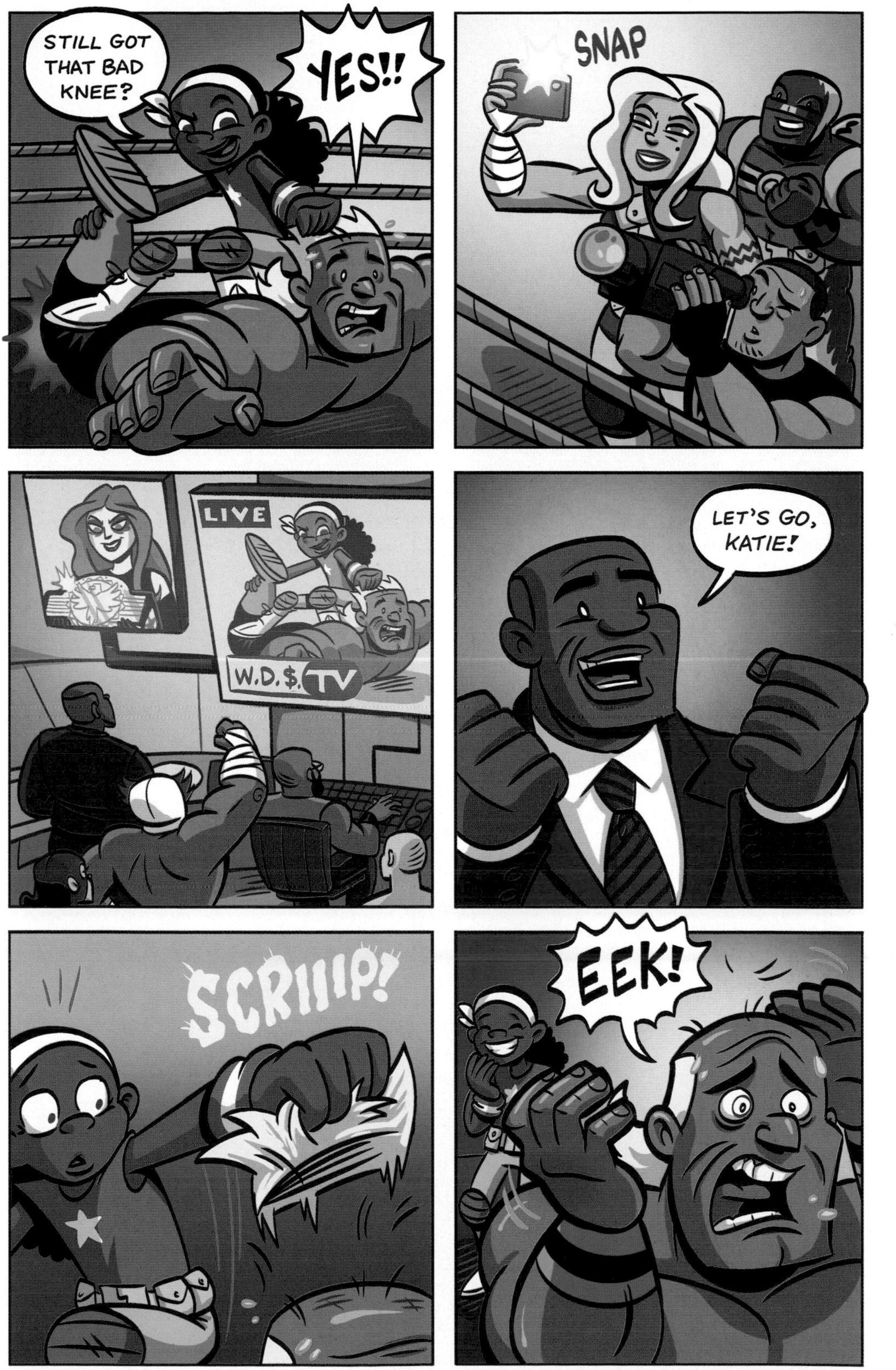
STILL GOT THAT BAD KNEE?
YES!!
SNAP
LIVE
W.D.$. TV
LET'S GO, KATIE!
SCRIIIP!
EEK!

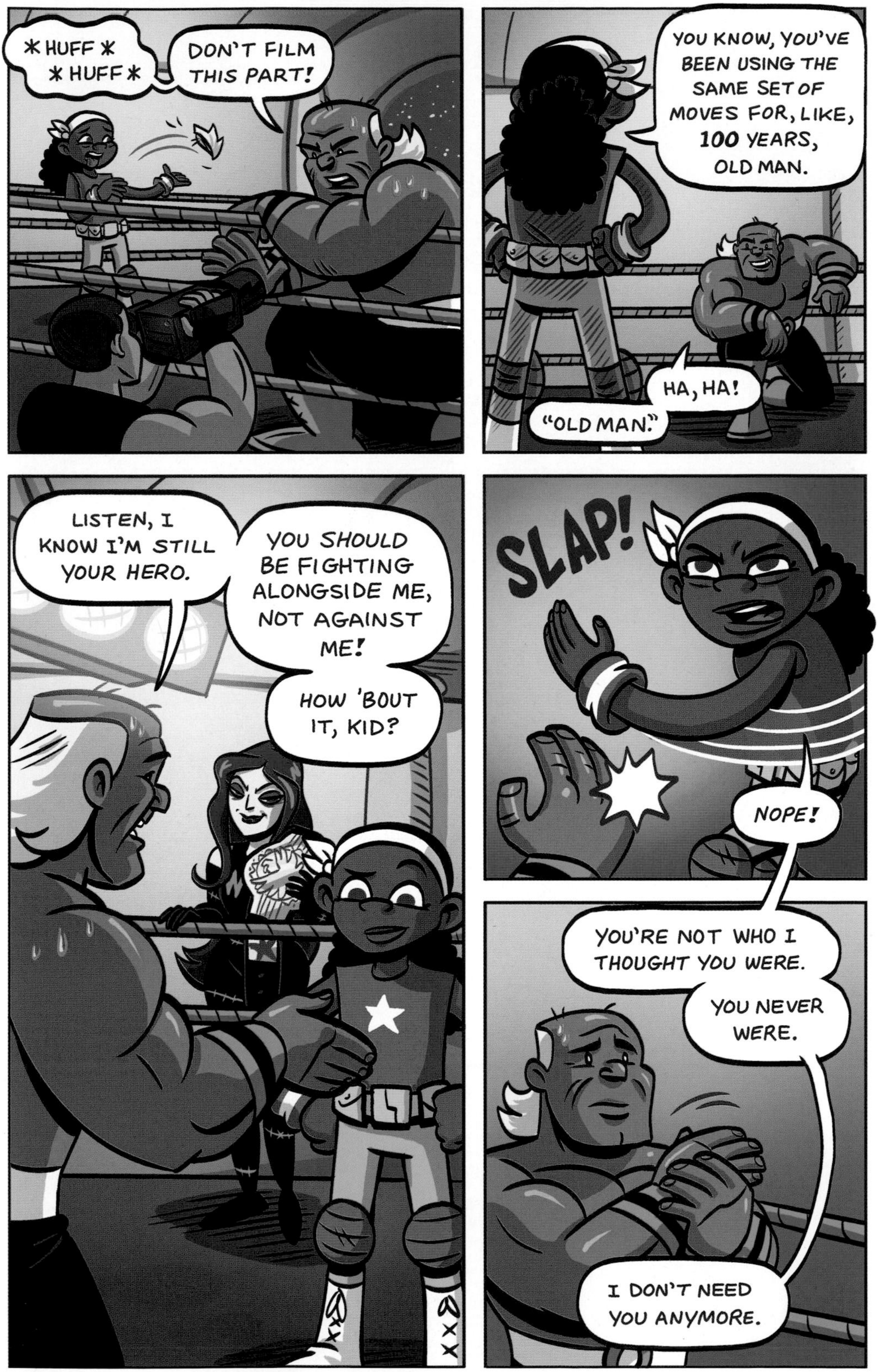
HUFF *HUFF*
DON'T FILM THIS PART!
YOU KNOW, YOU'VE BEEN USING THE SAME SET OF MOVES FOR, LIKE, 100 YEARS, OLD MAN.
HA, HA!
"OLD MAN."
LISTEN, I KNOW I'M STILL YOUR HERO.
YOU SHOULD BE FIGHTING ALONGSIDE ME, NOT AGAINST ME!
HOW 'BOUT IT, KID?
SLAP!
NOPE!
YOU'RE NOT WHO I THOUGHT YOU WERE.
YOU NEVER WERE.
I DON'T NEED YOU ANYMORE.

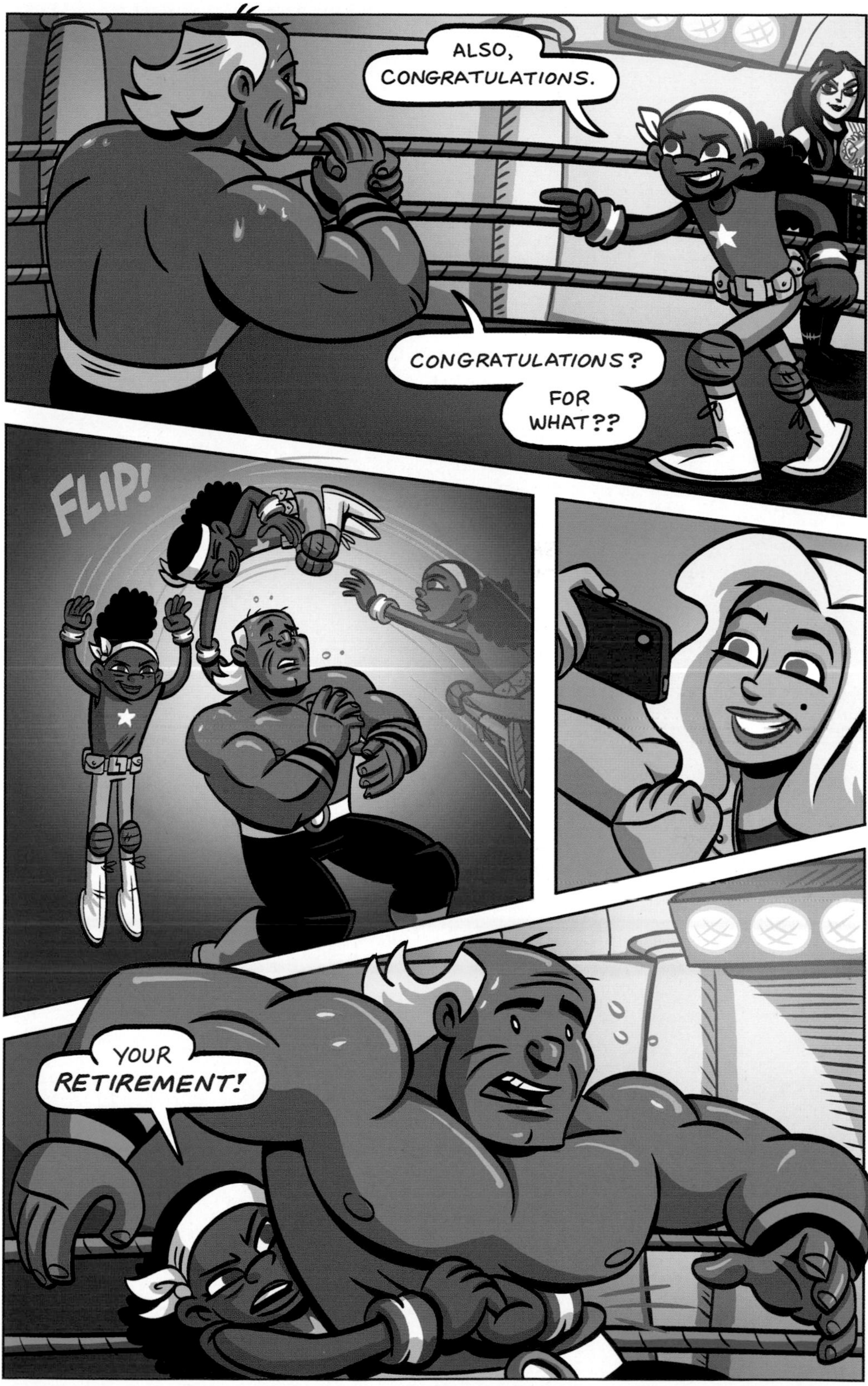
ALSO, CONGRATULATIONS.
CONGRATULATIONS?
FOR WHAT??
FLIP!
YOUR RETIREMENT!

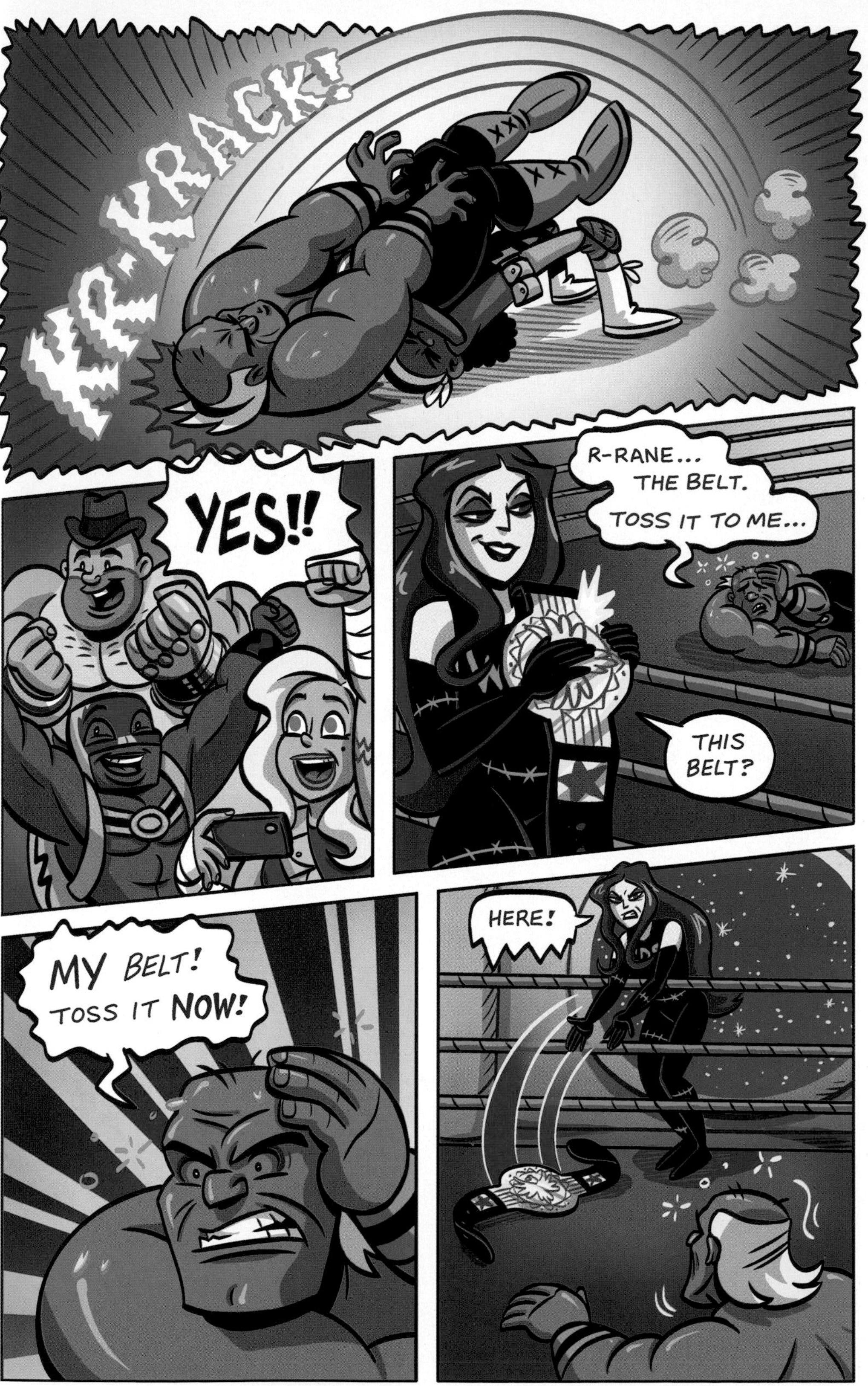
KR-KRACK!
YES!!
R-RANE... THE BELT. TOSS IT TO ME...
THIS BELT?
MY BELT! TOSS IT NOW!
HERE!

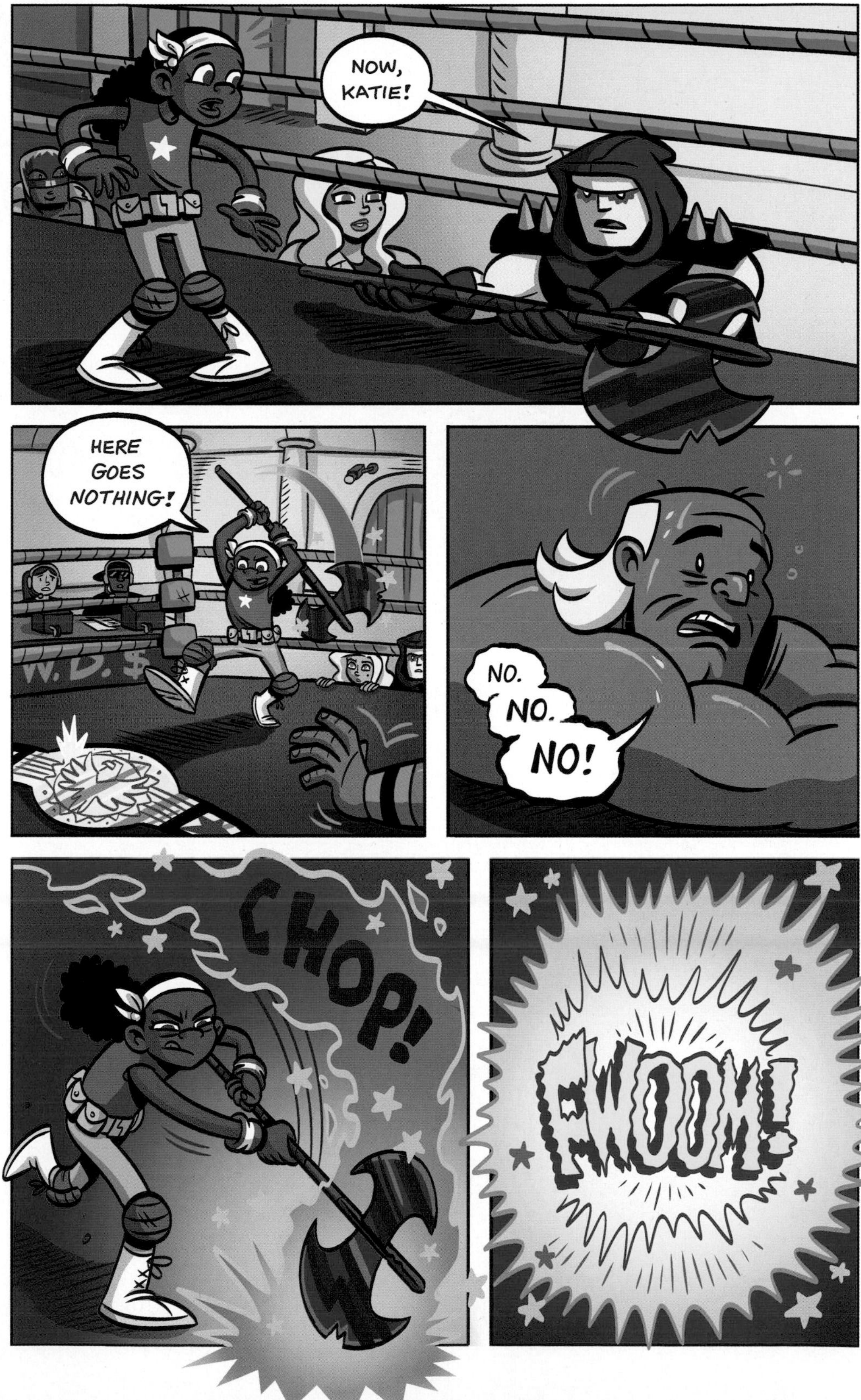
NOW, KATIE!
HERE GOES NOTHING!
W.D.$
NO.
NO.
NO!
CHOP!
FWOOM!

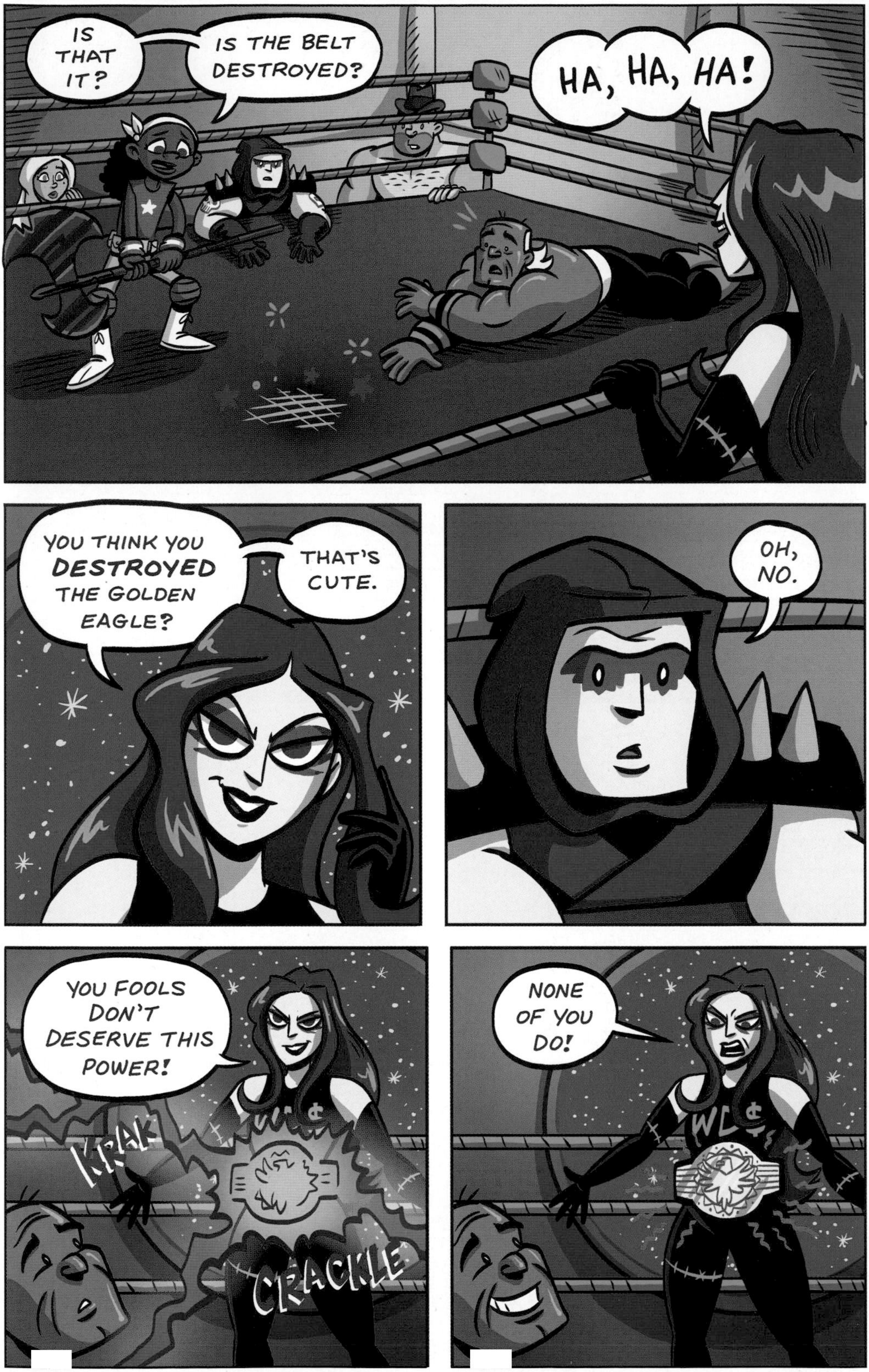
IS THAT IT?
IS THE BELT DESTROYED?
HA, HA, HA!
YOU THINK YOU **DESTROYED** THE GOLDEN EAGLE?
THAT'S CUTE.
OH, NO.
YOU FOOLS DON'T DESERVE THIS POWER!
KRAK
CRACKLE
NONE OF YOU DO!

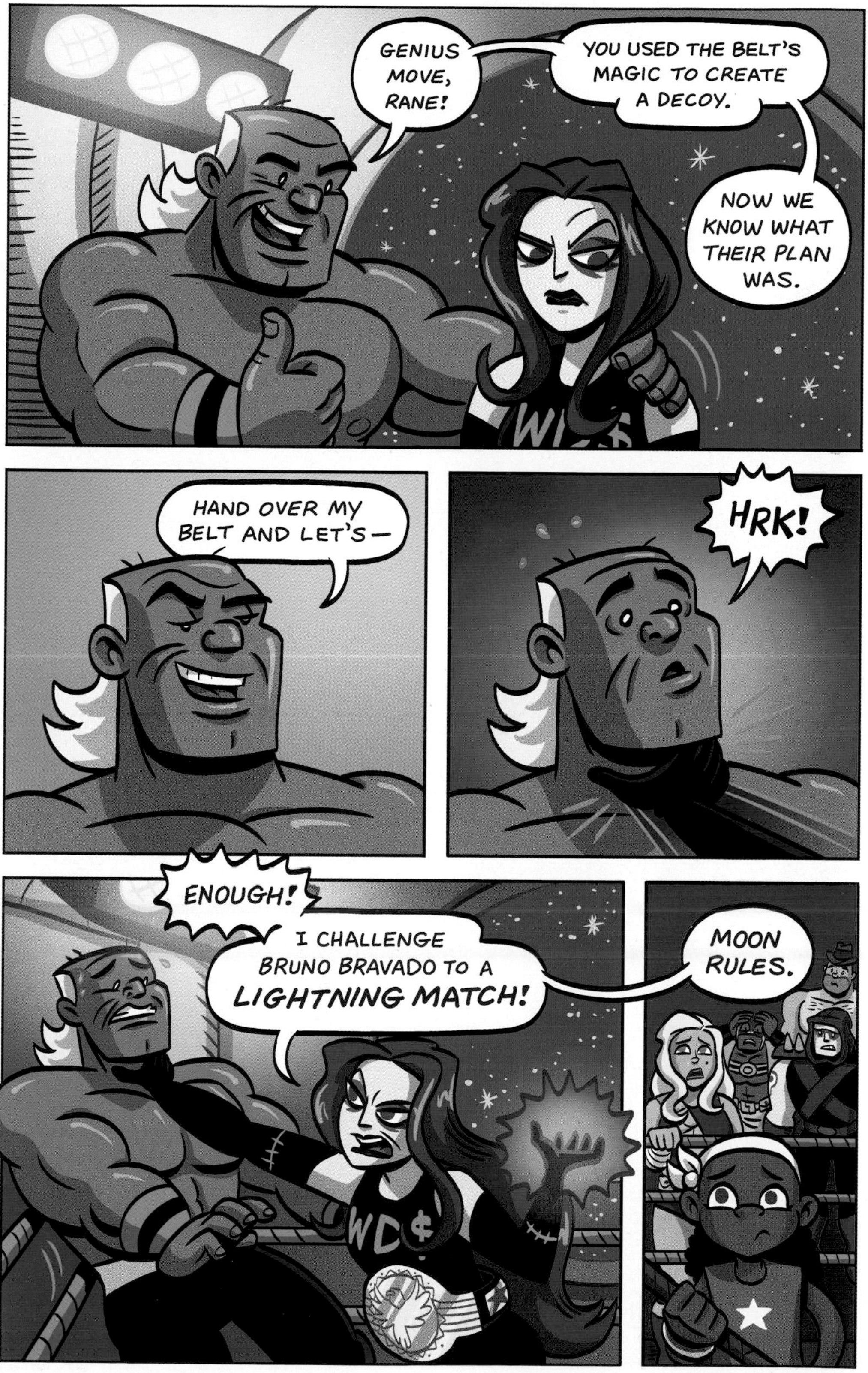
GENIUS MOVE, RANE!
YOU USED THE BELT'S MAGIC TO CREATE A DECOY.
NOW WE KNOW WHAT THEIR PLAN WAS.
HAND OVER MY BELT AND LET'S—
HRK!
ENOUGH!
I CHALLENGE BRUNO BRAVADO TO A LIGHTNING MATCH!
MOON RULES.

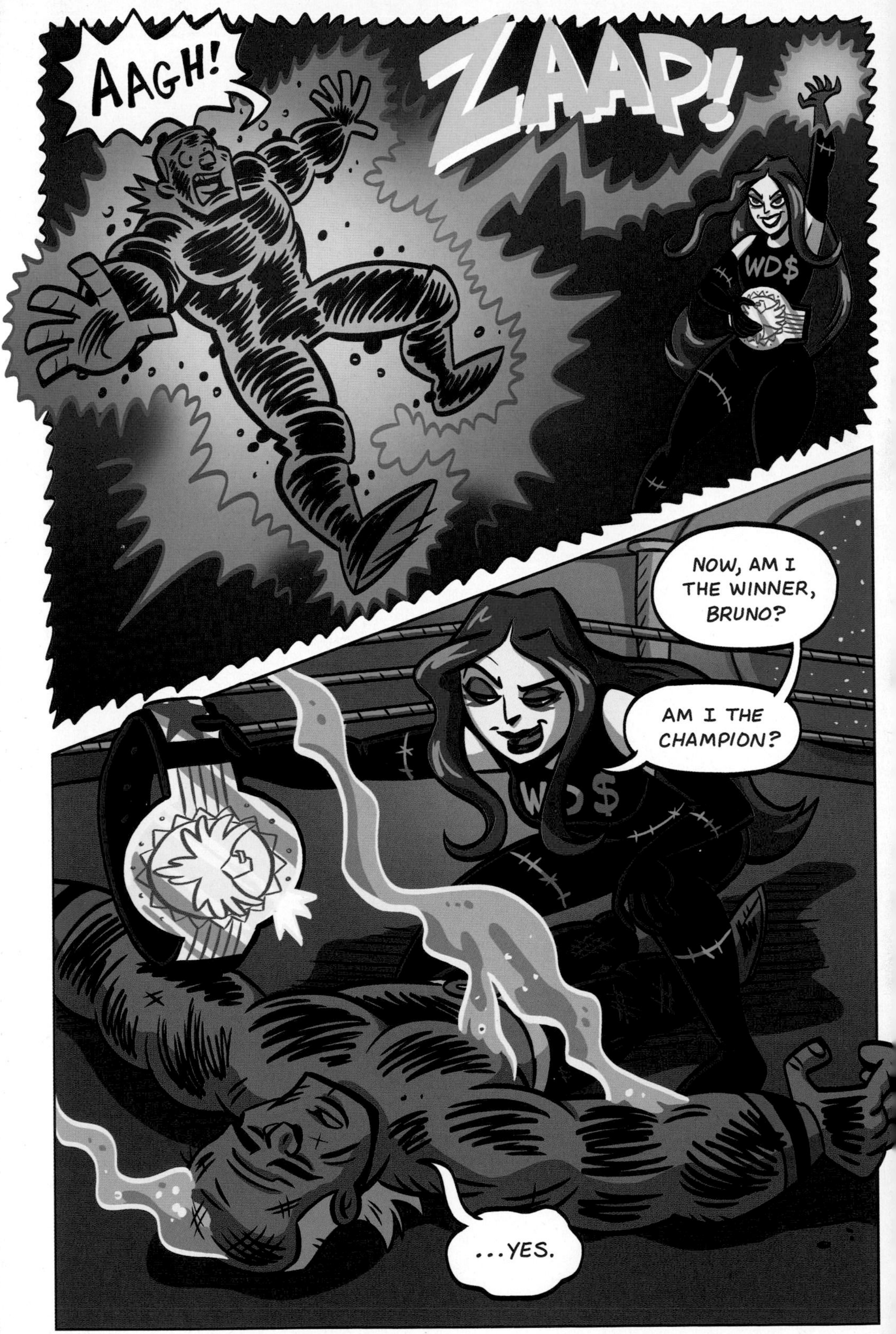
AAGH!
ZAAP!
WD$
NOW, AM I THE WINNER, BRUNO?
AM I THE CHAMPION?
WD$
...YES.

CHAPTER 5

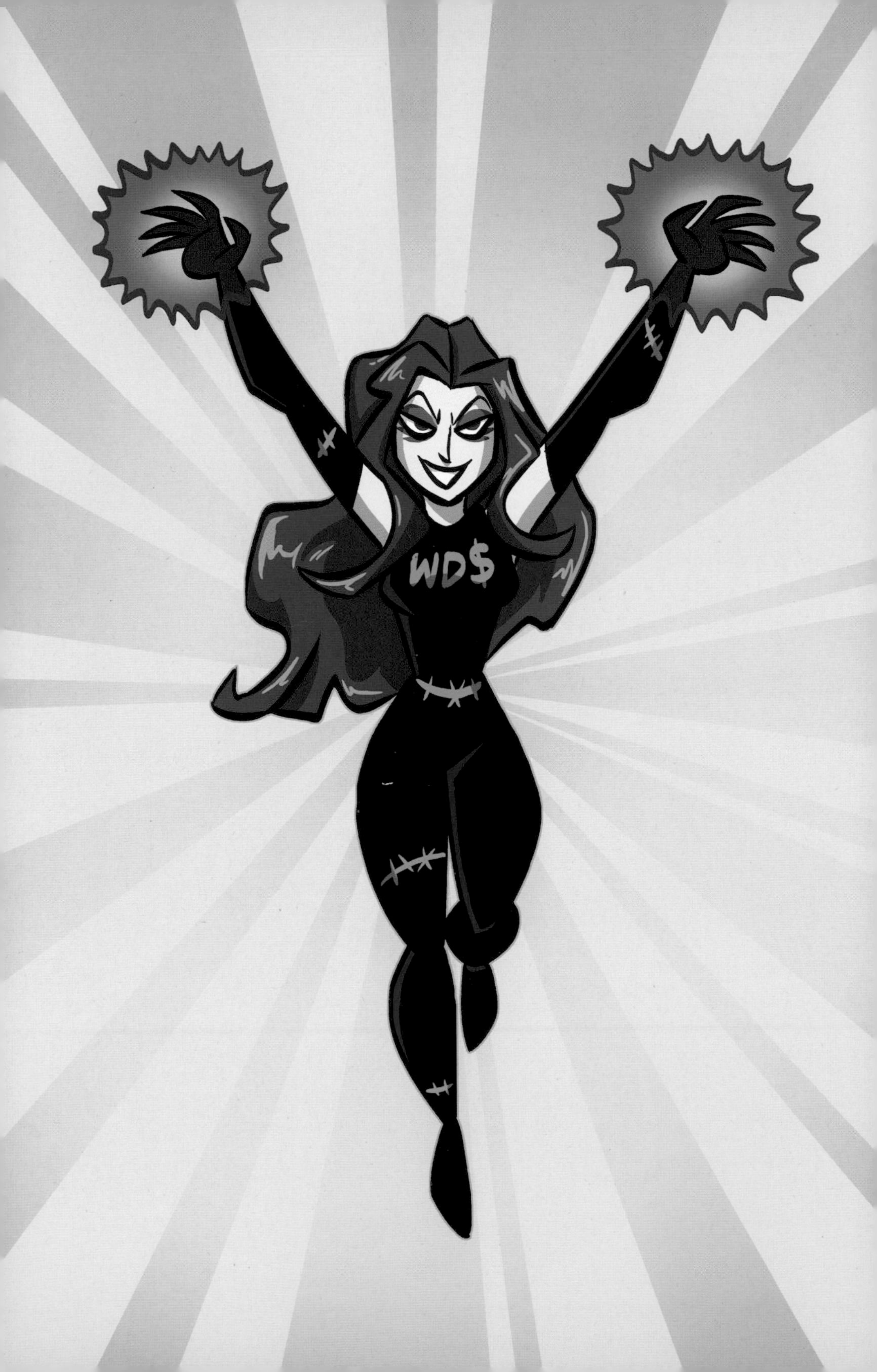
WD$

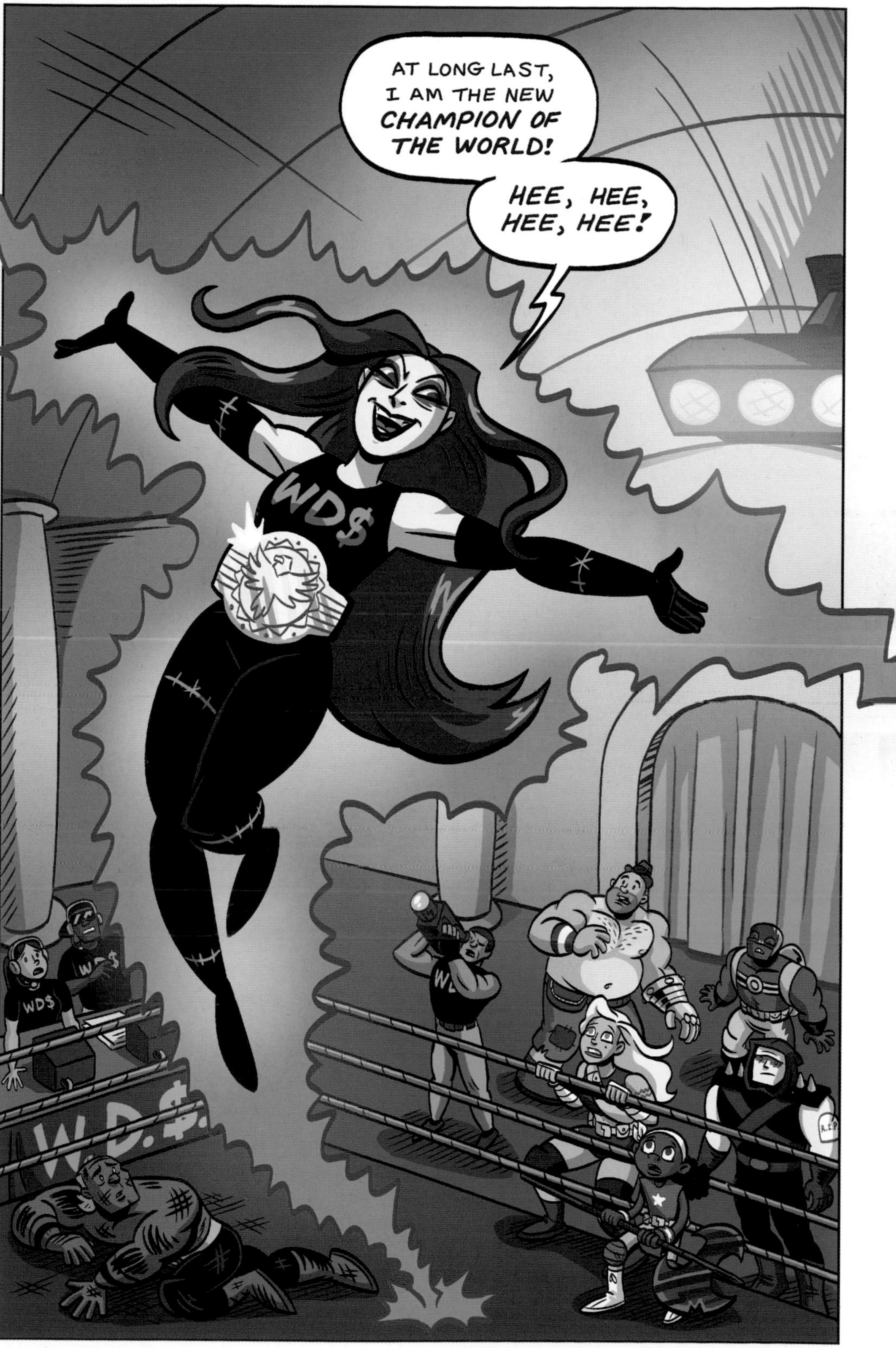
AT LONG LAST, I AM THE NEW CHAMPION OF THE WORLD!
HEE, HEE, HEE, HEE!
WD$
WD$
WD
W.D.$.

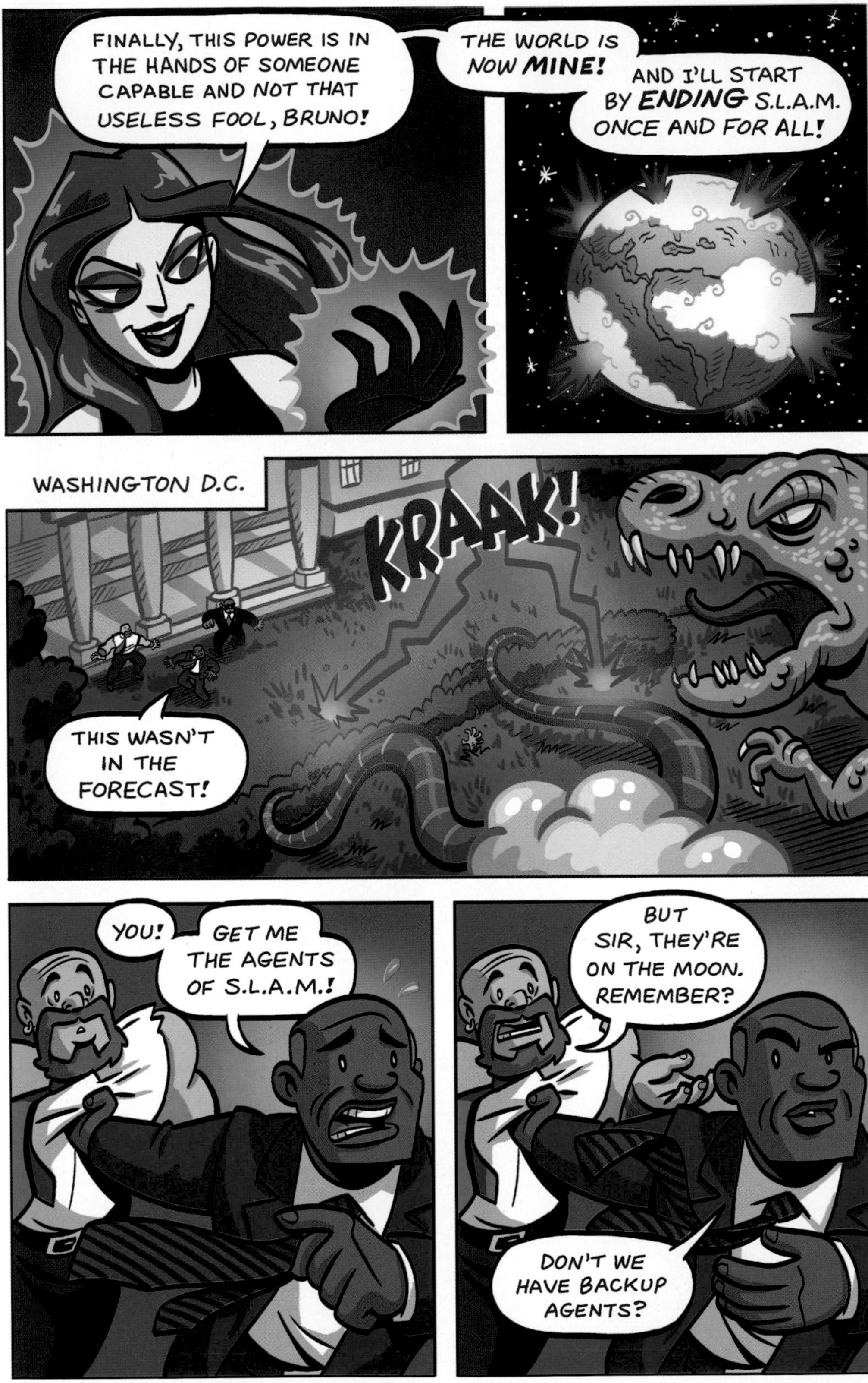
FINALLY, THIS POWER IS IN THE HANDS OF SOMEONE CAPABLE AND NOT THAT USELESS FOOL, BRUNO!
THE WORLD IS NOW MINE!
AND I'LL START BY ENDING S.L.A.M. ONCE AND FOR ALL!
WASHINGTON D.C.
KRAAK!
THIS WASN'T IN THE FORECAST!
YOU!
GET ME THE AGENTS OF S.L.A.M.!
BUT SIR, THEY'RE ON THE MOON. REMEMBER?
DON'T WE HAVE BACKUP AGENTS?

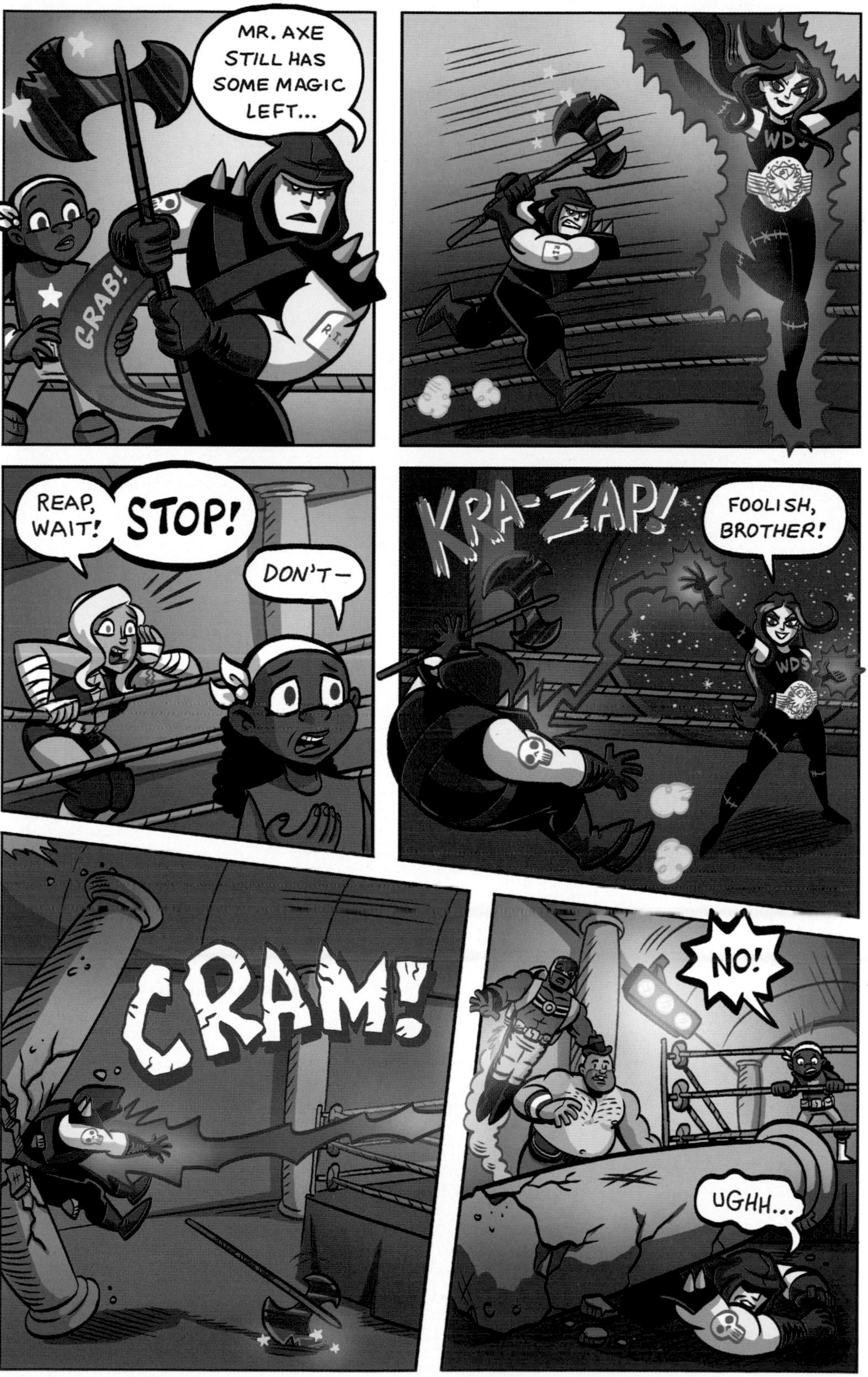
MR. AXE STILL HAS SOME MAGIC LEFT...
GRAB!
R.I.P.
WDS
RIP
REAP, WAIT!
STOP!
DON'T—
KRA-ZAP!
FOOLISH, BROTHER!
WDS
CRAM!
NO!
UGHH...

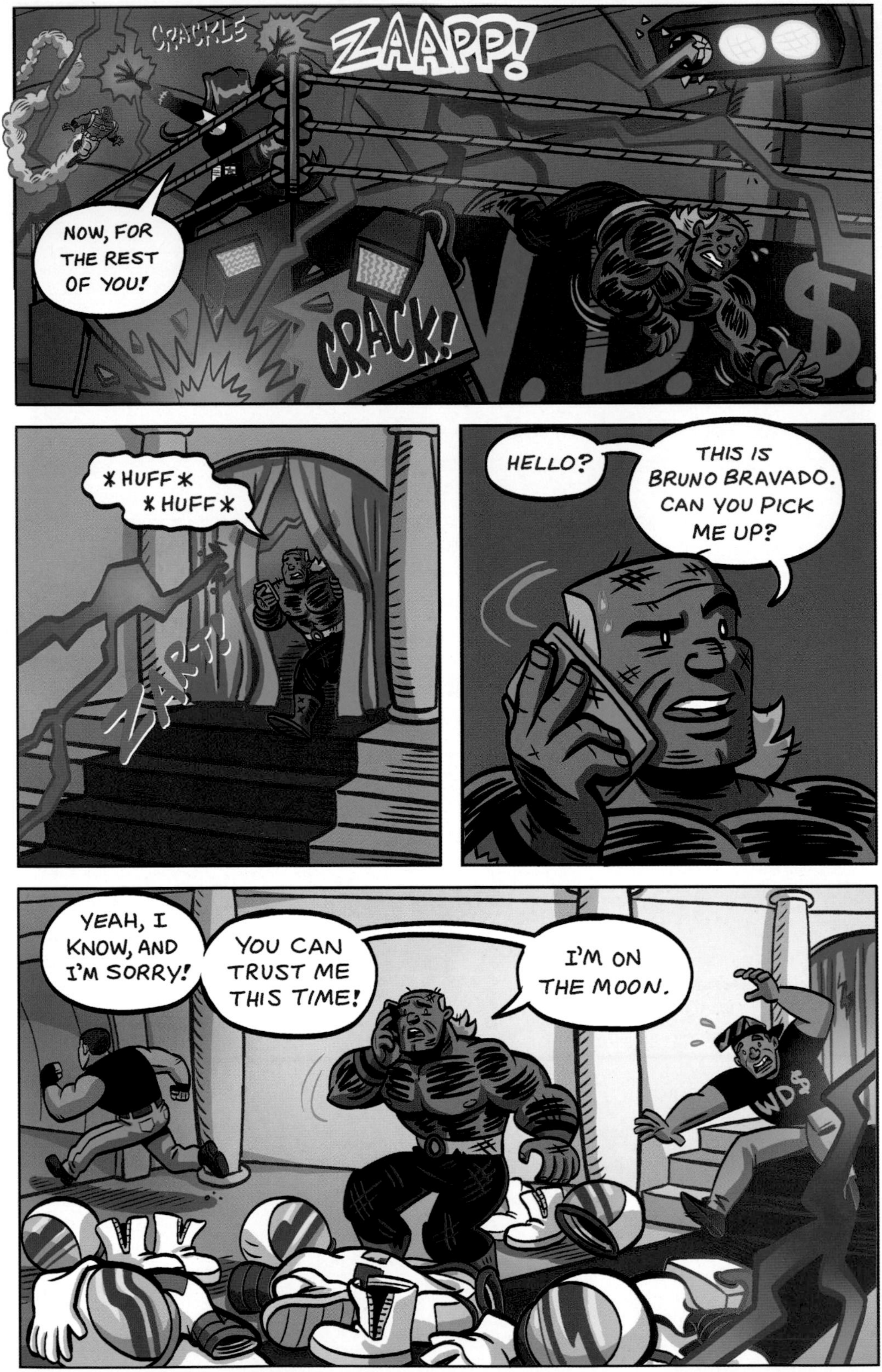
CRACKLE
ZAAPP!
NOW, FOR THE REST OF YOU!
CRACK!
HUFF *HUFF*
ZART!
HELLO?
THIS IS BRUNO BRAVADO. CAN YOU PICK ME UP?
YEAH, I KNOW, AND I'M SORRY!
YOU CAN TRUST ME THIS TIME!
I'M ON THE MOON.
WD$

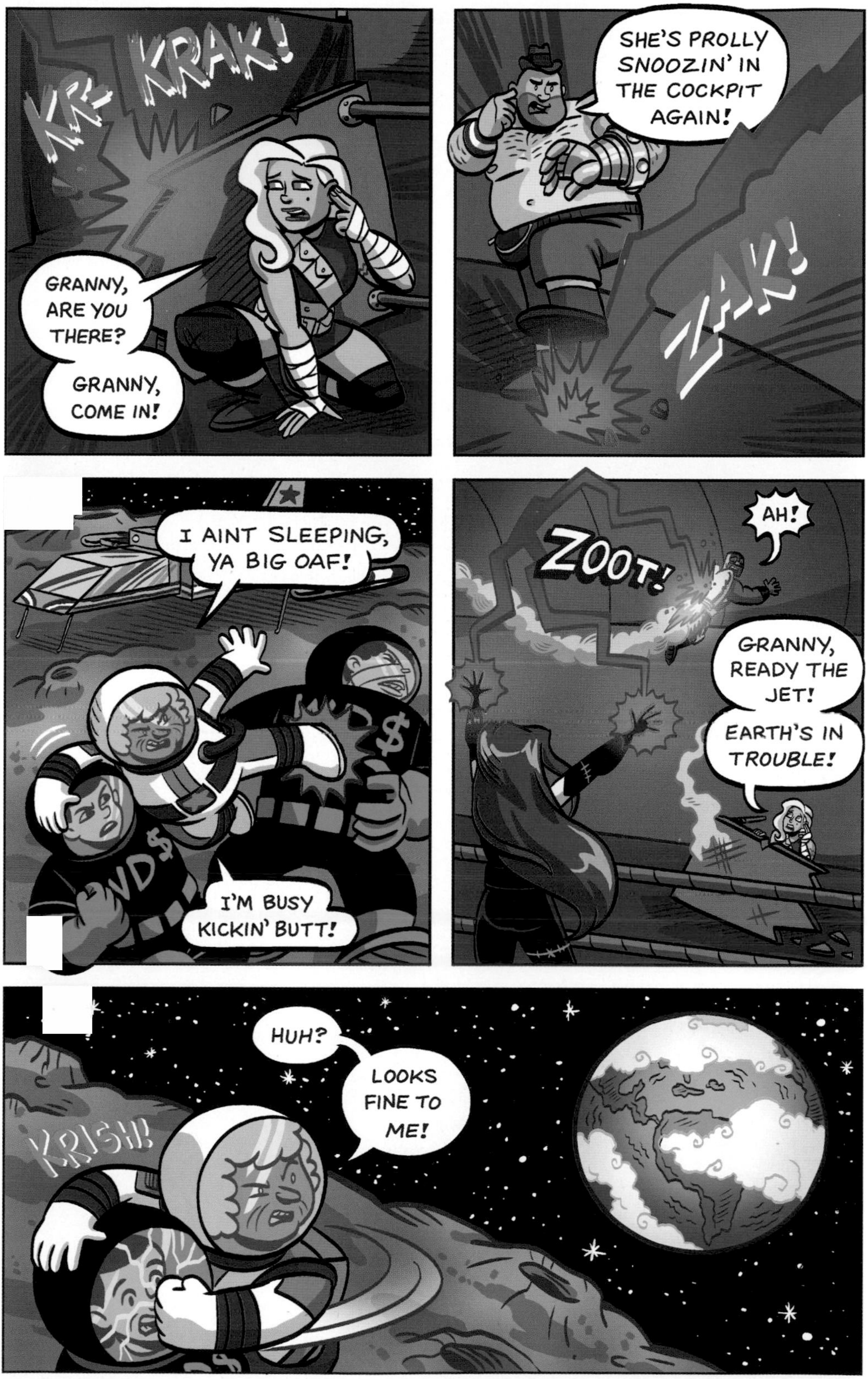
KR- KRAK!
GRANNY, ARE YOU THERE?
GRANNY, COME IN!
SHE'S PROLLY SNOOZIN' IN THE COCKPIT AGAIN!
ZAK!
I AINT SLEEPING, YA BIG OAF!
I'M BUSY KICKIN' BUTT!
ZOOT!
AH!
GRANNY, READY THE JET!
EARTH'S IN TROUBLE!
KRISH!
HUH?
LOOKS FINE TO ME!

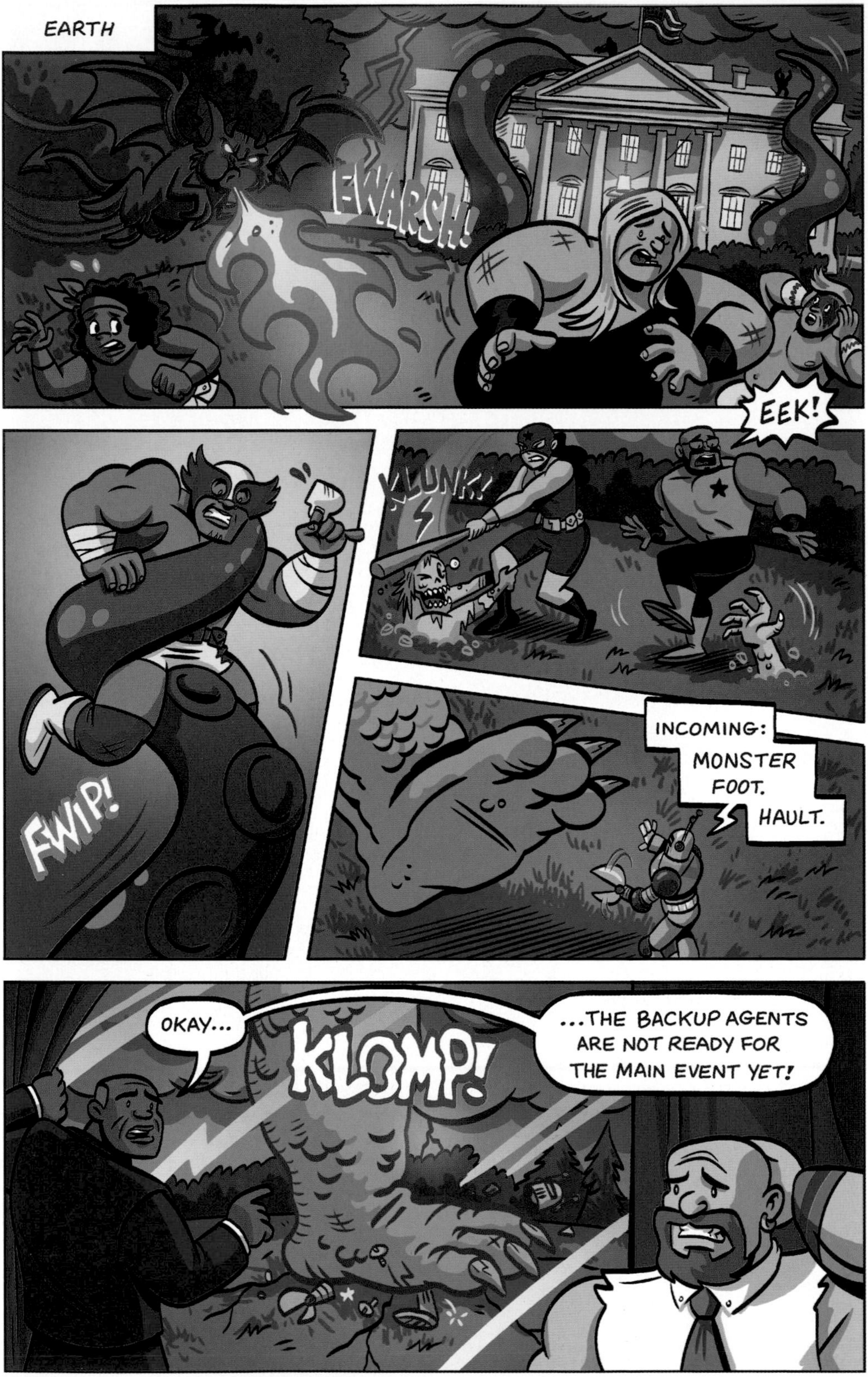
EARTH
F-WARSH!
EEK!
KLUNK!
FWIP!
INCOMING:
MONSTER
FOOT.
HAULT.
OKAY...
KLOMP!
...THE BACKUP AGENTS
ARE NOT READY FOR
THE MAIN EVENT YET!

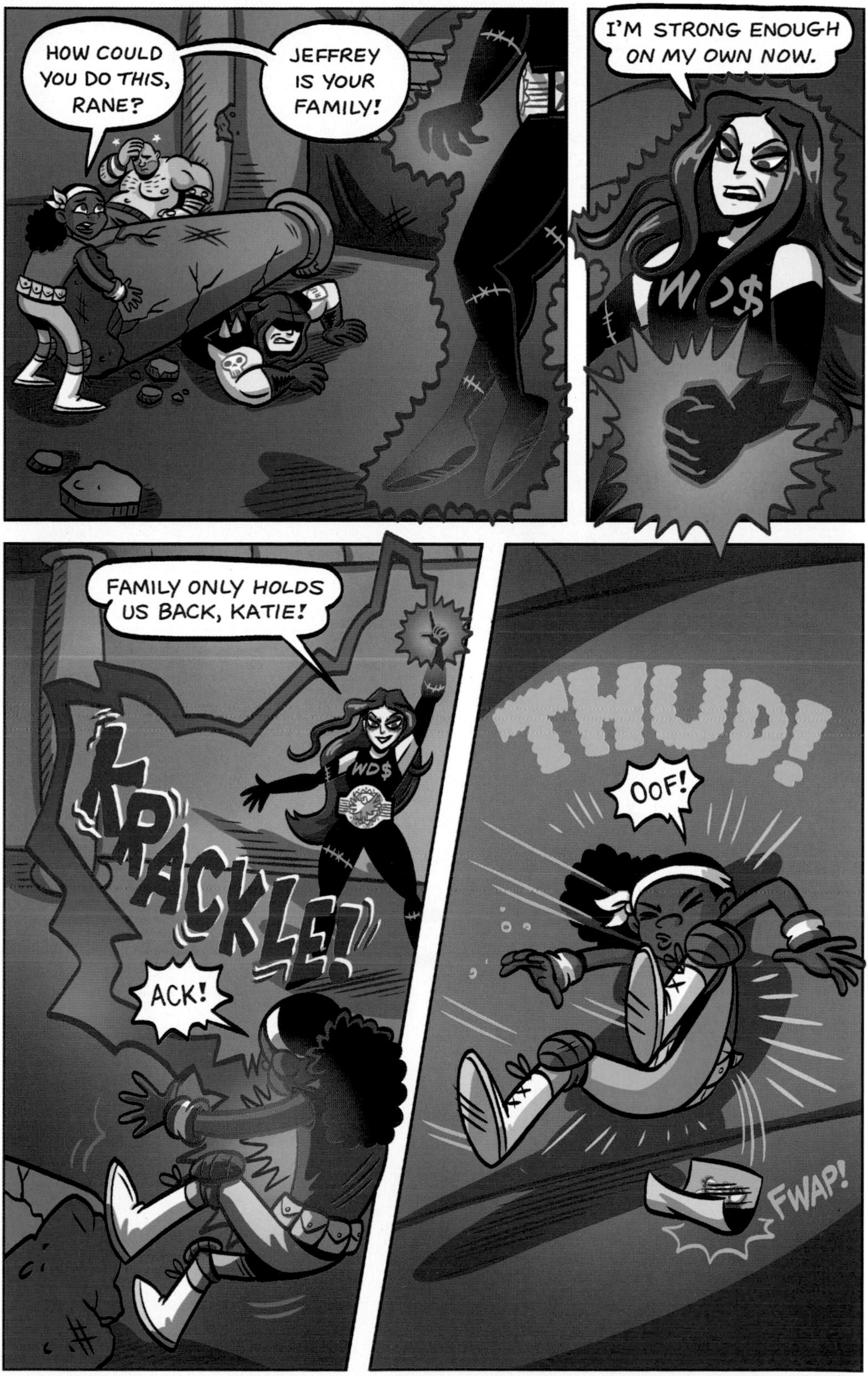
HOW COULD YOU DO THIS, RANE?
JEFFREY IS YOUR FAMILY!
I'M STRONG ENOUGH ON MY OWN NOW.
FAMILY ONLY HOLDS US BACK, KATIE!
KRACKLE!
ACK!
THUD!
OOF!
FWAP!

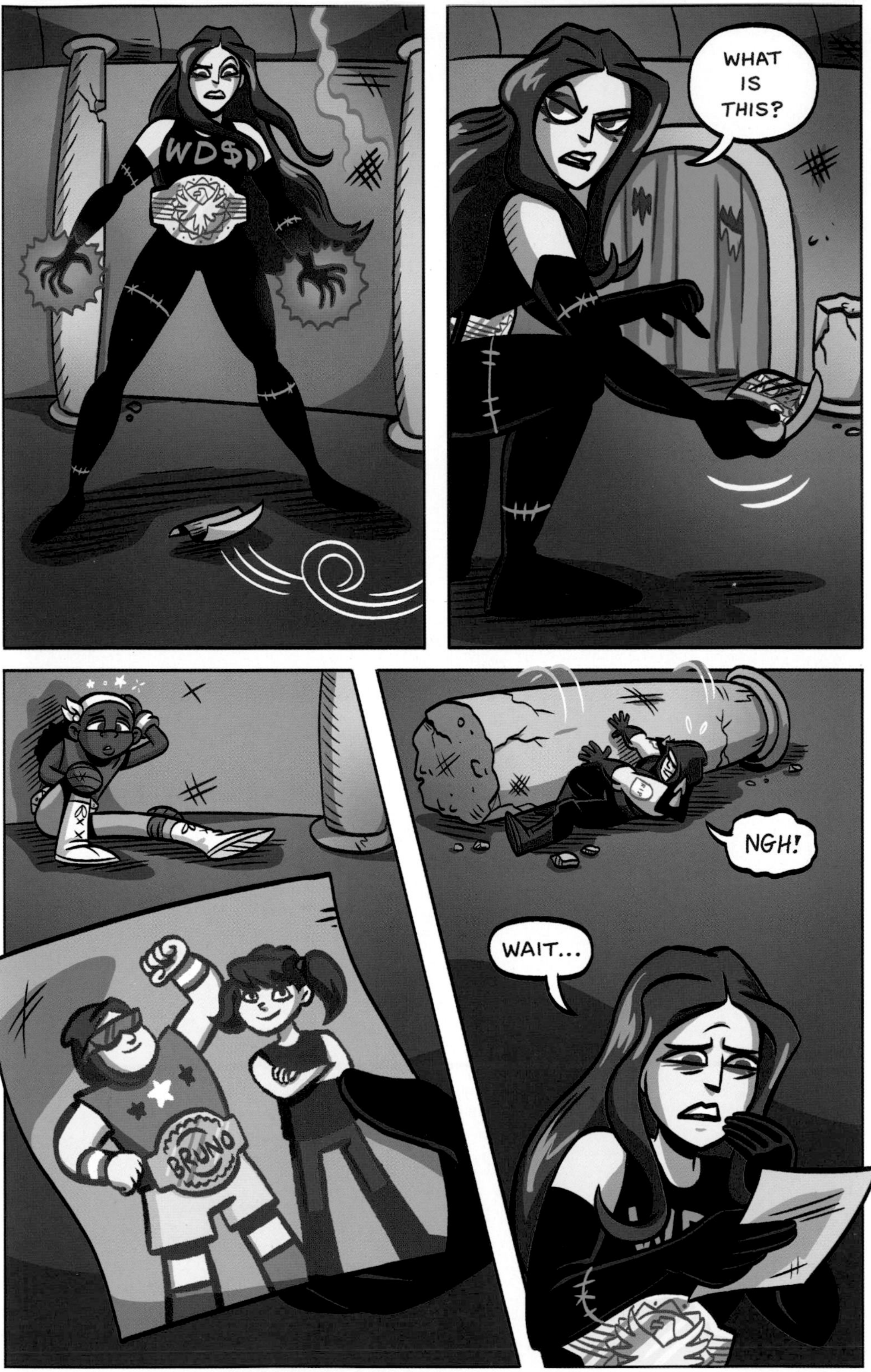
WD$
WHAT IS THIS?
NGH!
BRUNO
WAIT...

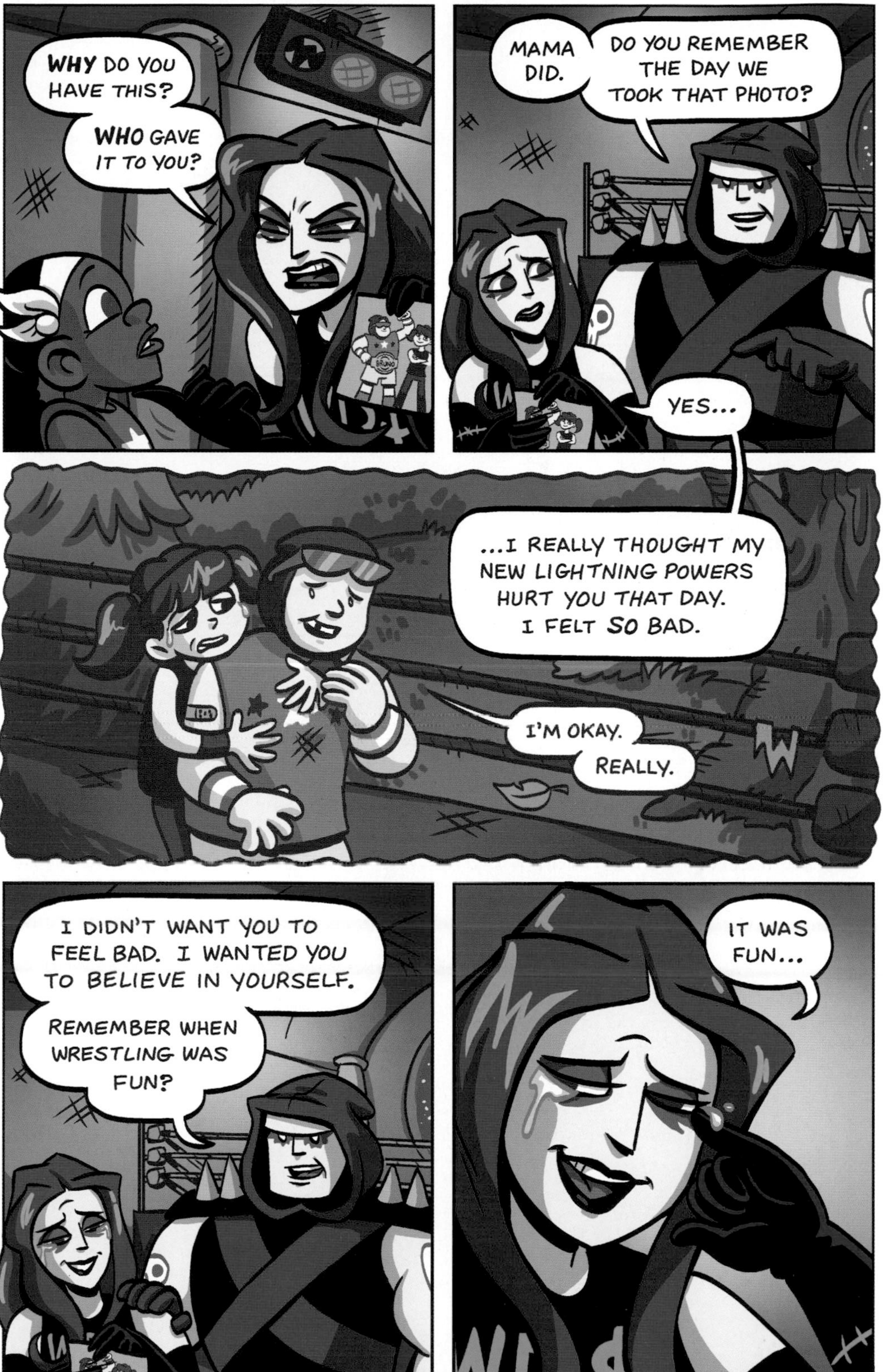
WHY DO YOU HAVE THIS?
WHO GAVE IT TO YOU?
MAMA DID.
DO YOU REMEMBER THE DAY WE TOOK THAT PHOTO?
YES...
...I REALLY THOUGHT MY NEW LIGHTNING POWERS HURT YOU THAT DAY. I FELT SO BAD.
I'M OKAY.
REALLY.
I DIDN'T WANT YOU TO FEEL BAD. I WANTED YOU TO BELIEVE IN YOURSELF.
REMEMBER WHEN WRESTLING WAS FUN?
IT WAS FUN...

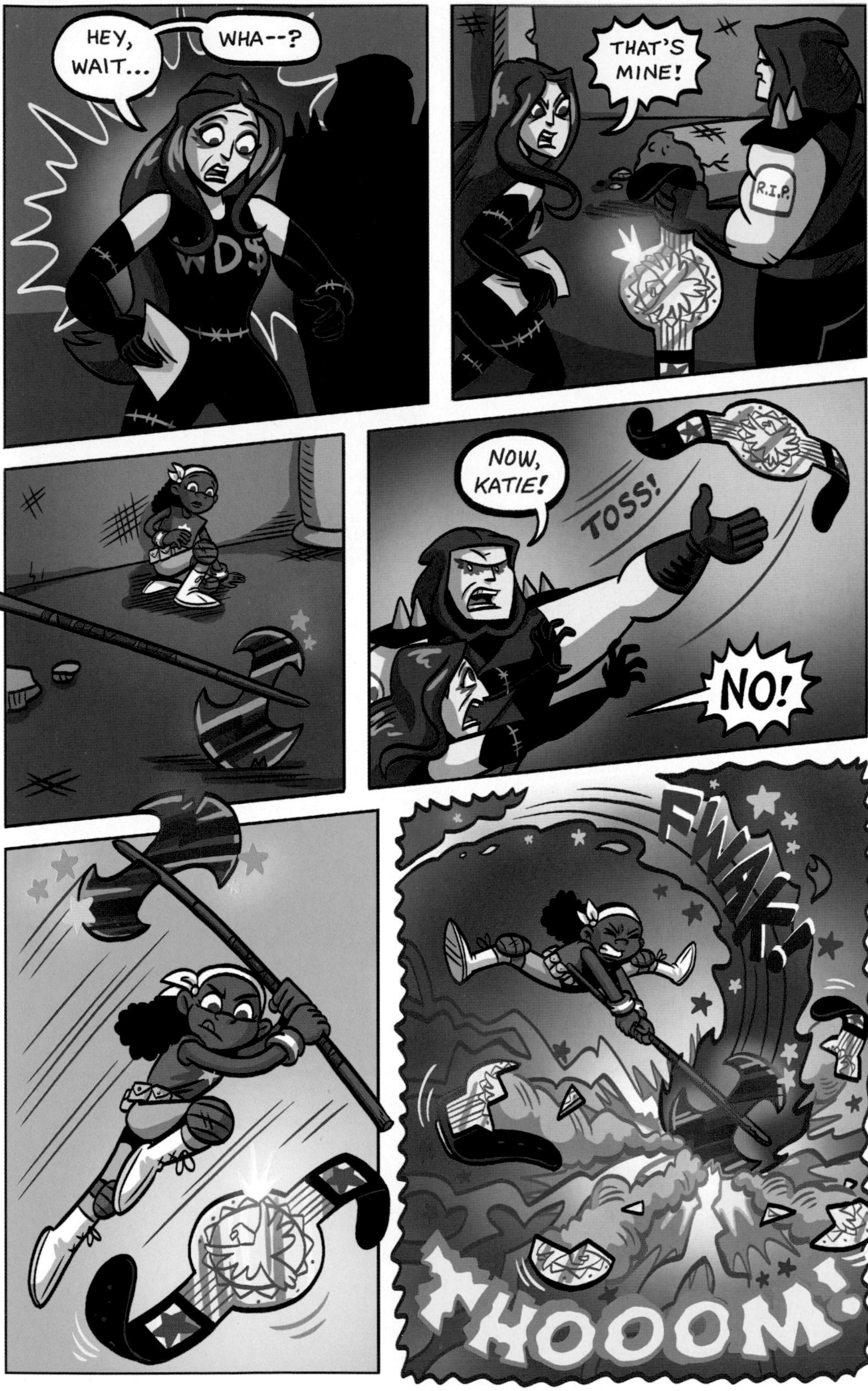
HEY, WAIT...
WHA--?
THAT'S MINE!
R.I.P.
NOW, KATIE!
TOSS!
NO!
FWAK!!
THOOOM!

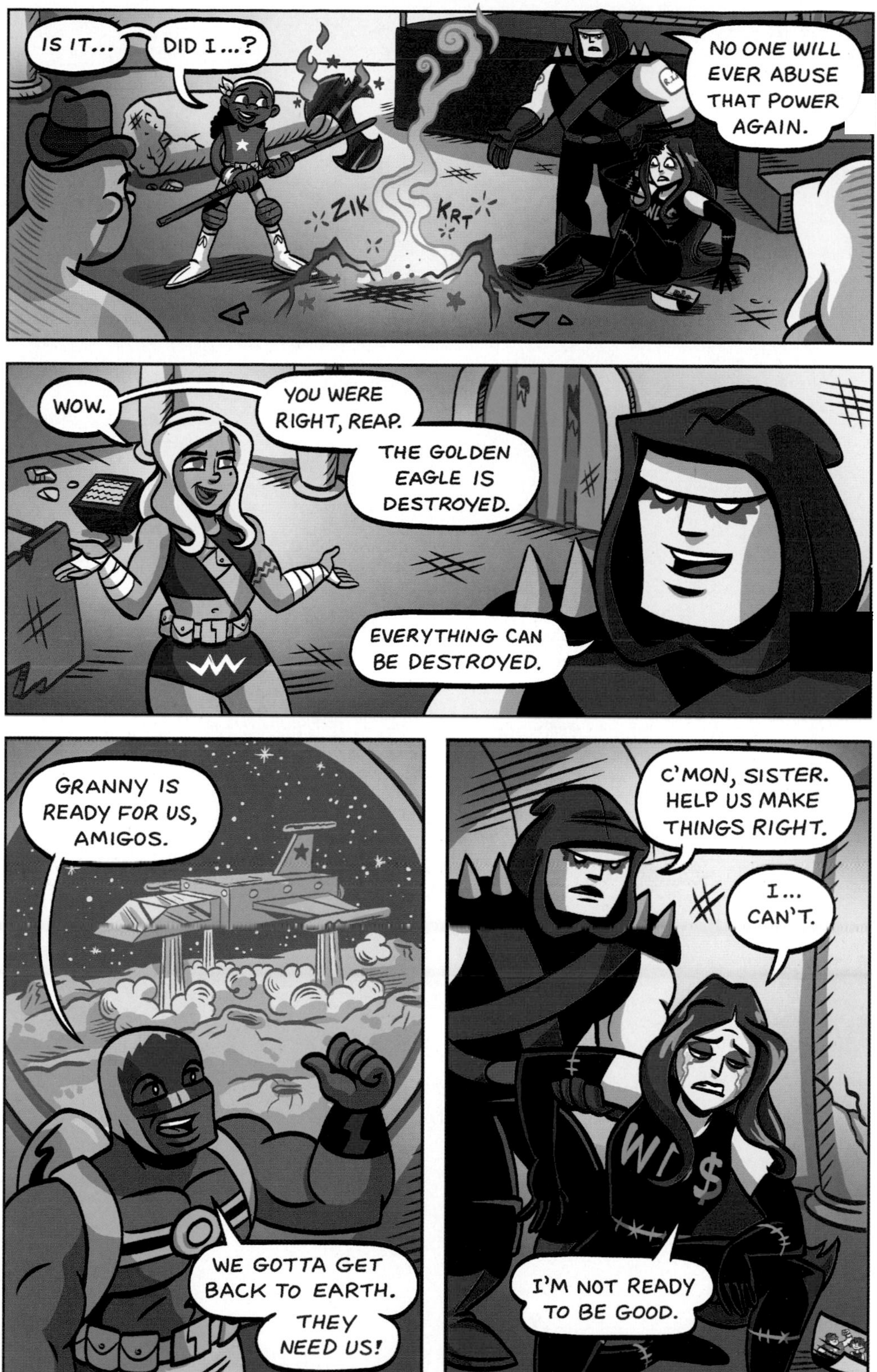

IS IT...
DID I...?
ZIK
KRT
NO ONE WILL EVER ABUSE THAT POWER AGAIN.
WOW.
YOU WERE RIGHT, REAP.
THE GOLDEN EAGLE IS DESTROYED.
EVERYTHING CAN BE DESTROYED.
GRANNY IS READY FOR US, AMIGOS.
WE GOTTA GET BACK TO EARTH.
THEY NEED US!
C'MON, SISTER. HELP US MAKE THINGS RIGHT.
I... CAN'T.
I'M NOT READY TO BE GOOD.

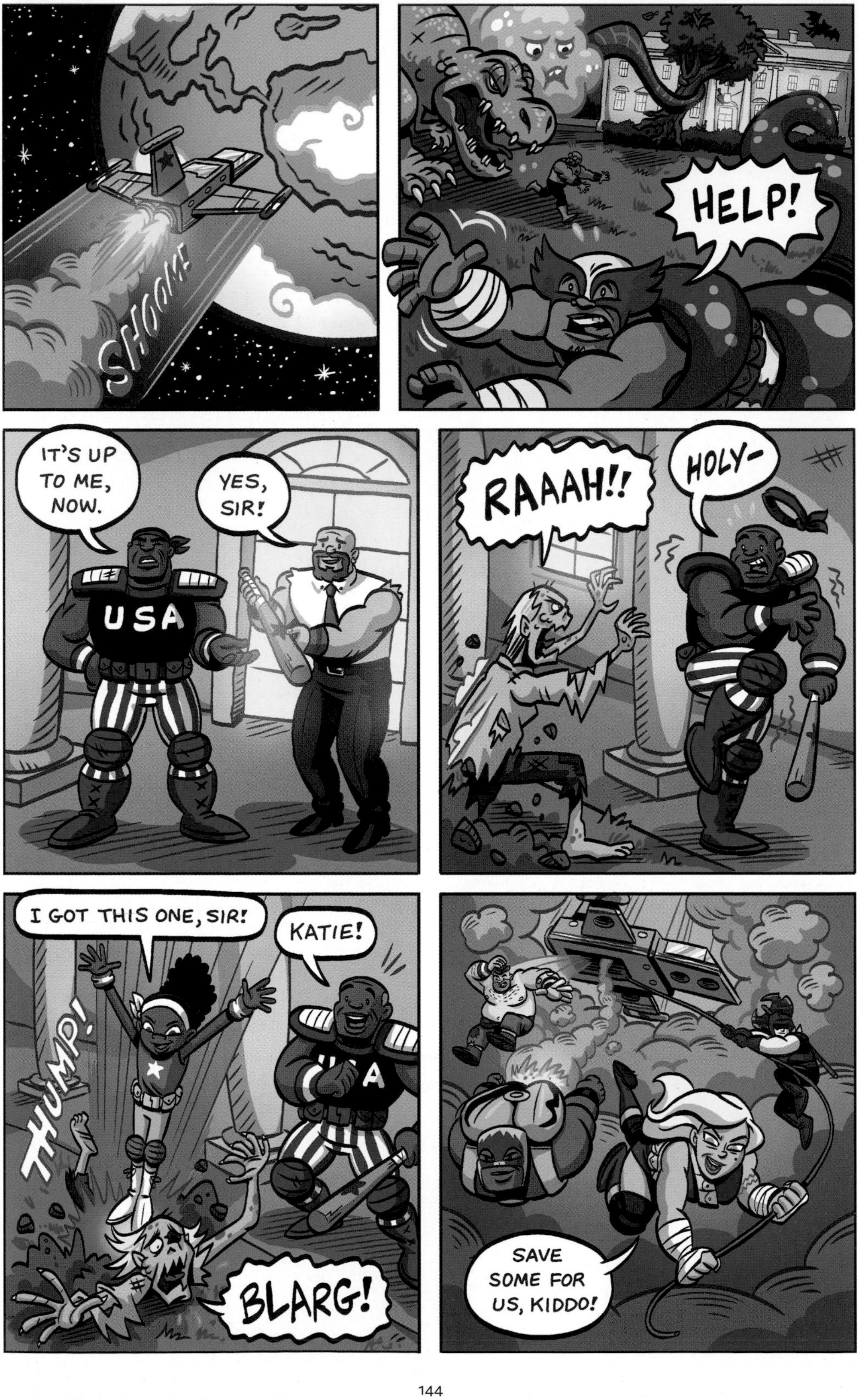
SHOOM!
HELP!
IT'S UP TO ME, NOW.
YES, SIR!
RAAAH!!
HOLY-
I GOT THIS ONE, SIR!
KATIE!
THUMP!
BLARG!
SAVE SOME FOR US, KIDDO!

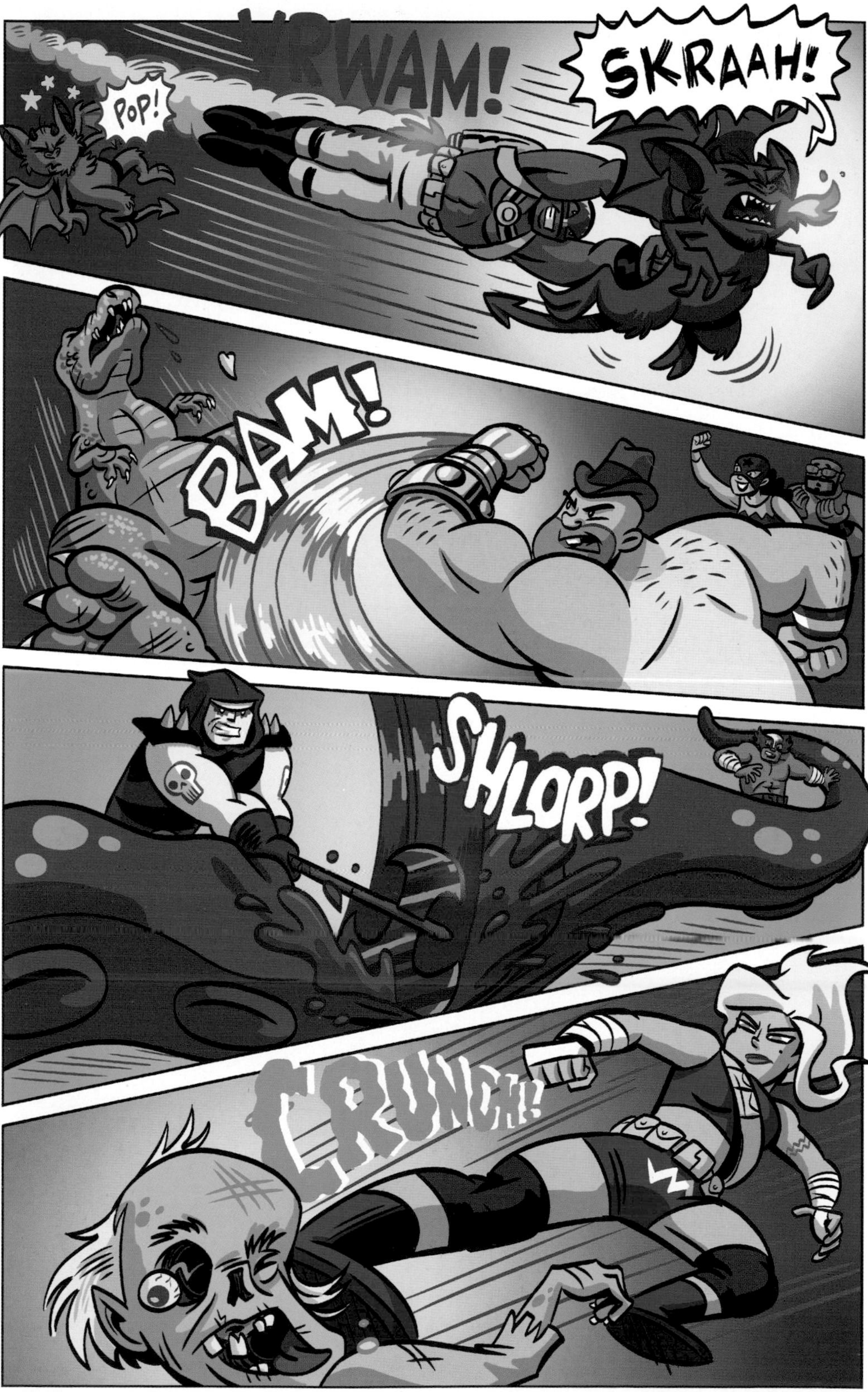
POP!
WRWAM!
SKRAAH!
BAM!
SHLORP!
CRUNCH!

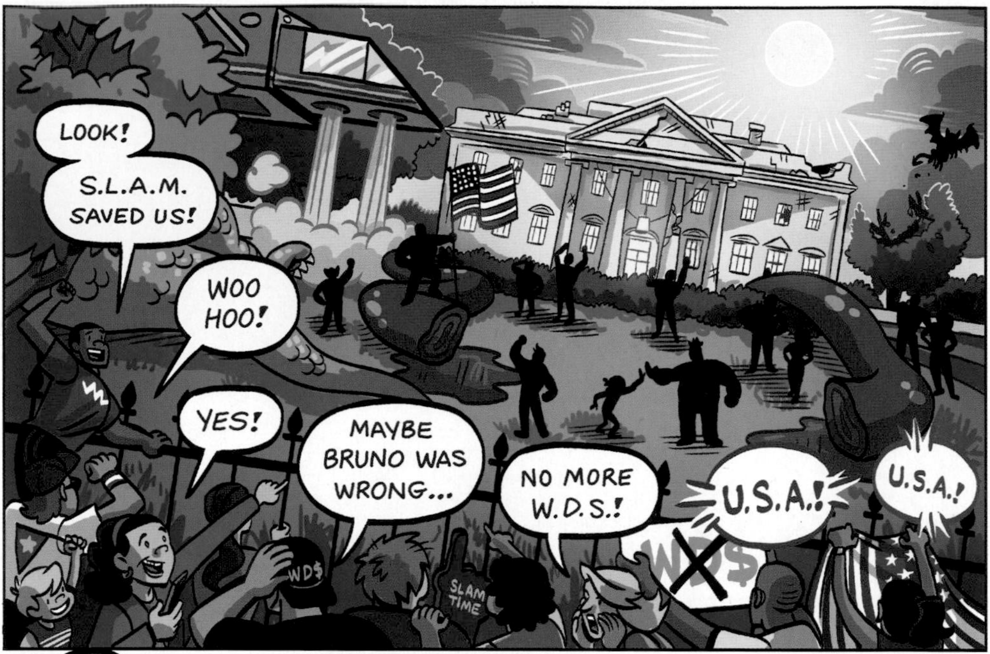
LOOK!
S.L.A.M. SAVED US!
WOO HOO!
YES!
MAYBE BRUNO WAS WRONG...
NO MORE W.D.S.!
U.S.A.!
U.S.A.!
WD$
SLAM TIME
WD$

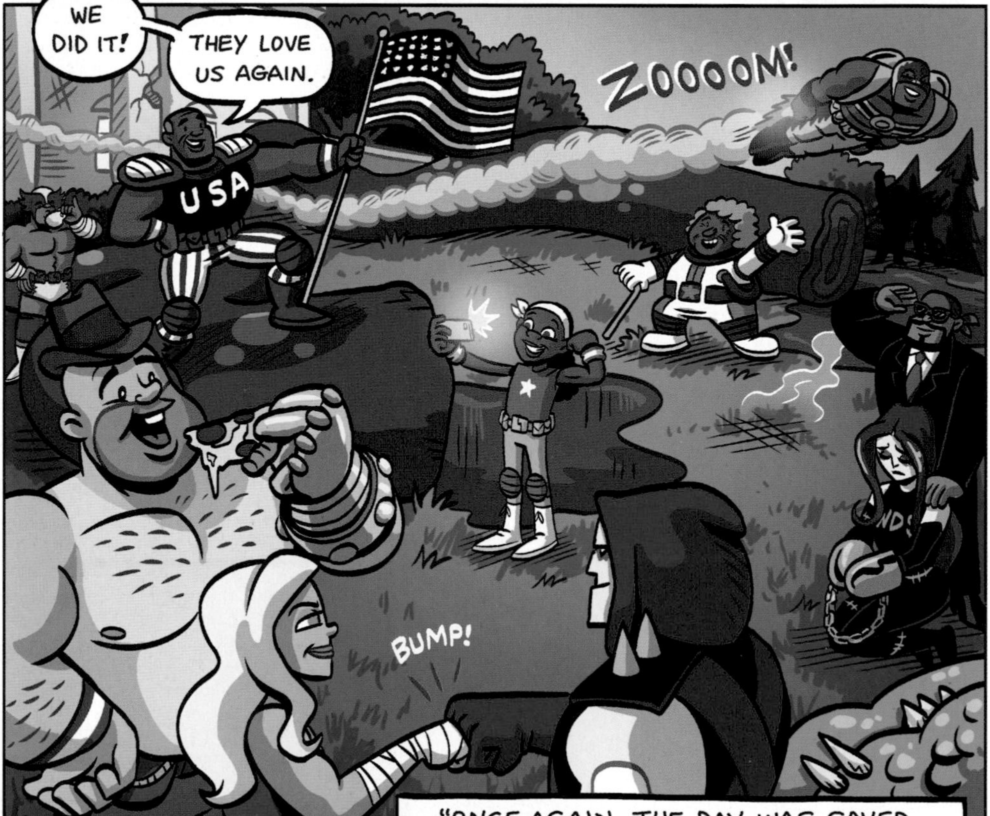
WE DID IT!
THEY LOVE US AGAIN.
ZOOOOM!
USA
BUMP!
"ONCE AGAIN, THE DAY WAS SAVED, THANKS TO THE AGENTS OF S.L.A.M..."

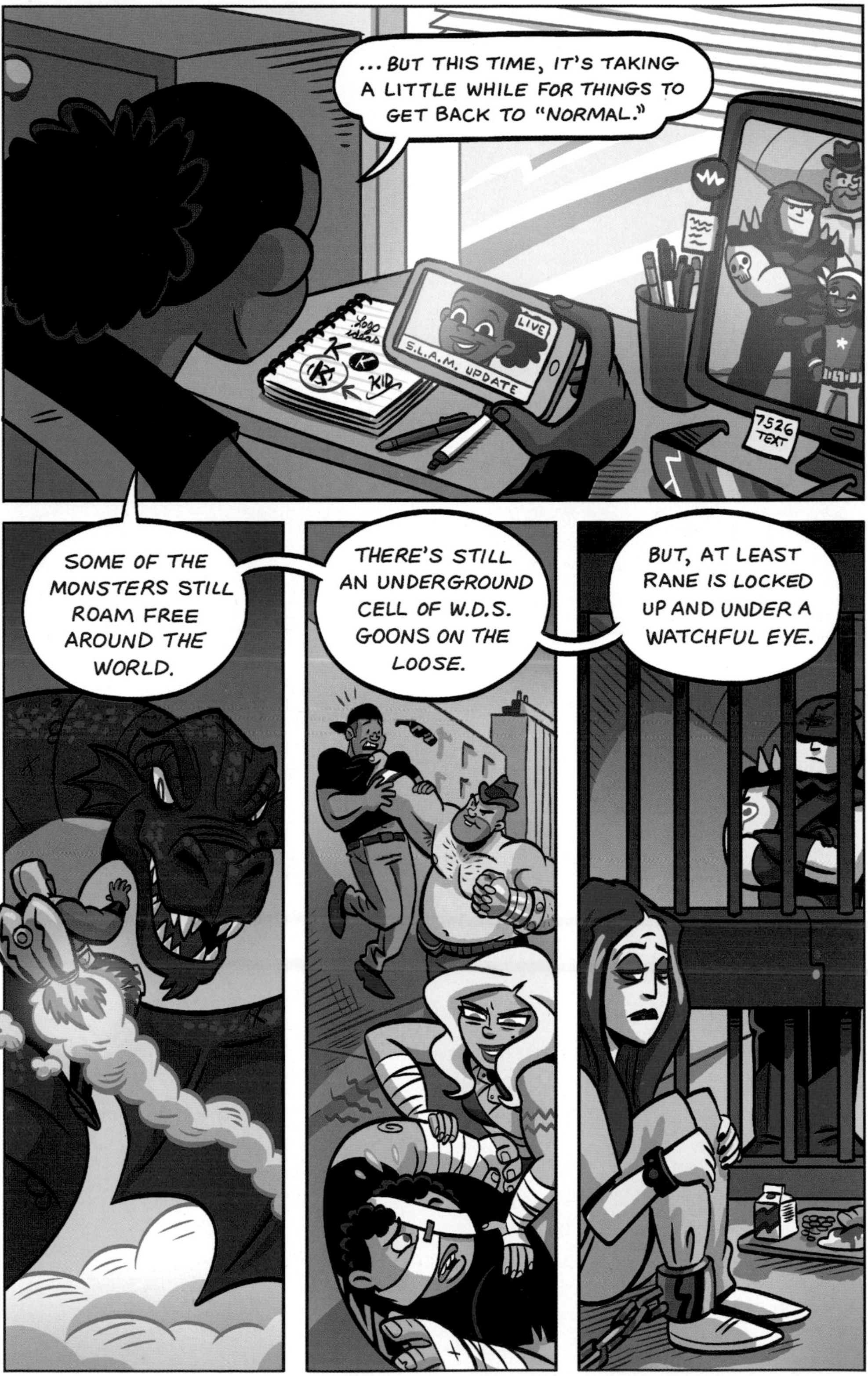
...BUT THIS TIME, IT'S TAKING A LITTLE WHILE FOR THINGS TO GET BACK TO "NORMAL."
LIVE
S.L.A.M. UPDATE
7526 TEXT
SOME OF THE MONSTERS STILL ROAM FREE AROUND THE WORLD.
THERE'S STILL AN UNDERGROUND CELL OF W.D.S. GOONS ON THE LOOSE.
BUT, AT LEAST RANE IS LOCKED UP AND UNDER A WATCHFUL EYE.

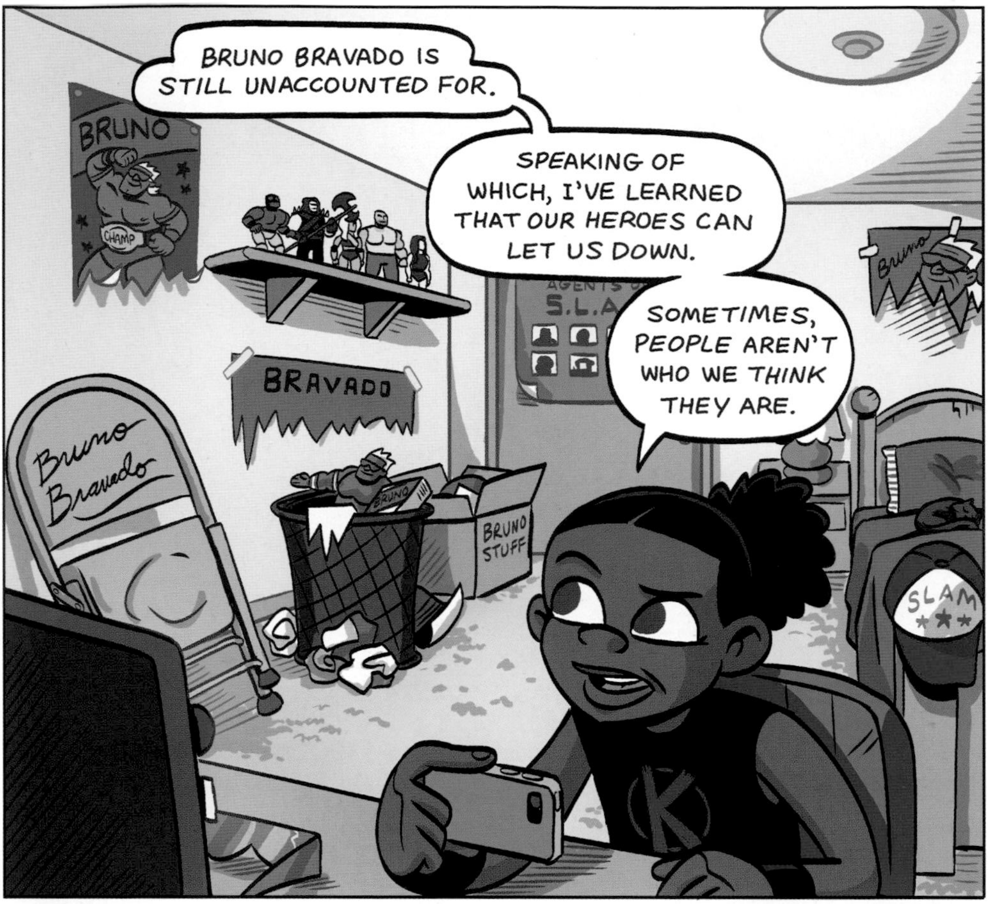
BRUNO BRAVADO IS STILL UNACCOUNTED FOR.
SPEAKING OF WHICH, I'VE LEARNED THAT OUR HEROES CAN LET US DOWN.
SOMETIMES, PEOPLE AREN'T WHO WE THINK THEY ARE.
BRUNO
CHAMP
BRAVADO
Bruno Bravado
BRUNO STUFF
AGENTS OF S.L.A.
Bruno
SLAM

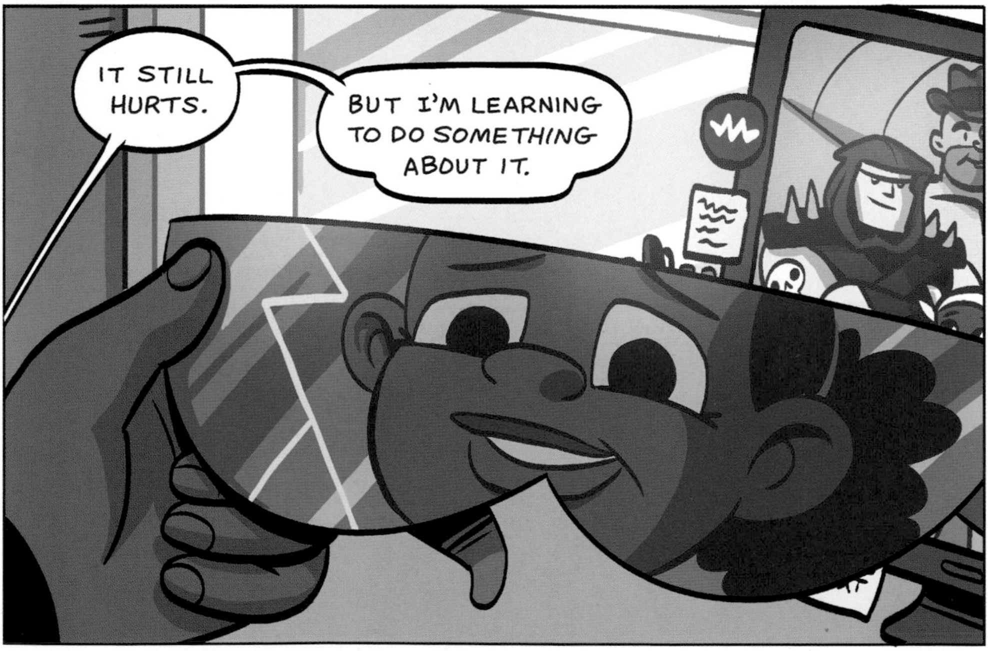
IT STILL HURTS.
BUT I'M LEARNING TO DO SOMETHING ABOUT IT.

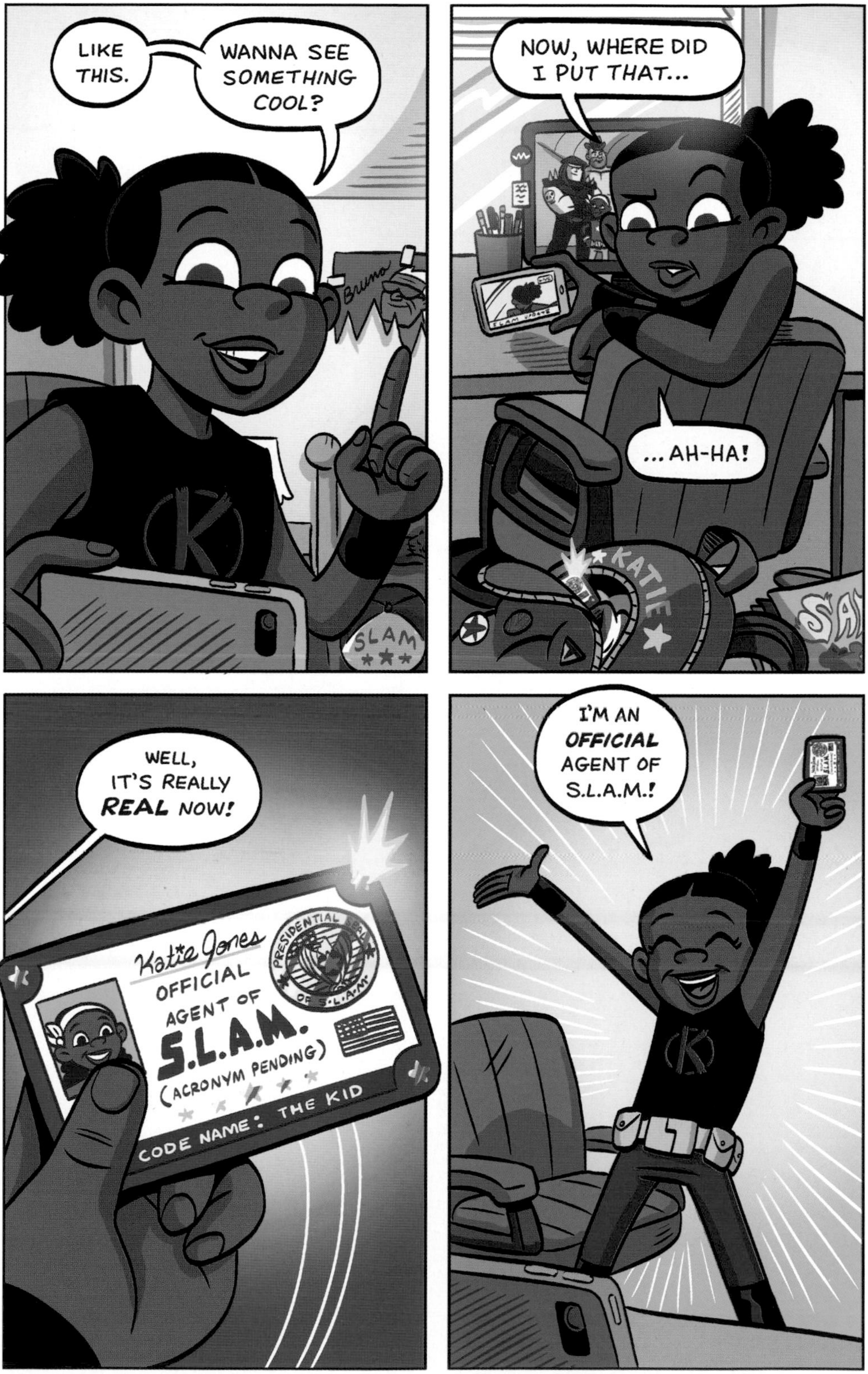
LIKE THIS.
WANNA SEE SOMETHING COOL?
Bruno
SLAM
NOW, WHERE DID I PUT THAT...
...AH-HA!
KATIE
WELL, IT'S REALLY REAL NOW!
Katie Jones
OFFICIAL AGENT OF S.L.A.M.
(ACRONYM PENDING)
PRESIDENTIAL SEAL OF S.L.A.M.
CODE NAME: THE KID
I'M AN OFFICIAL AGENT OF S.L.A.M.!

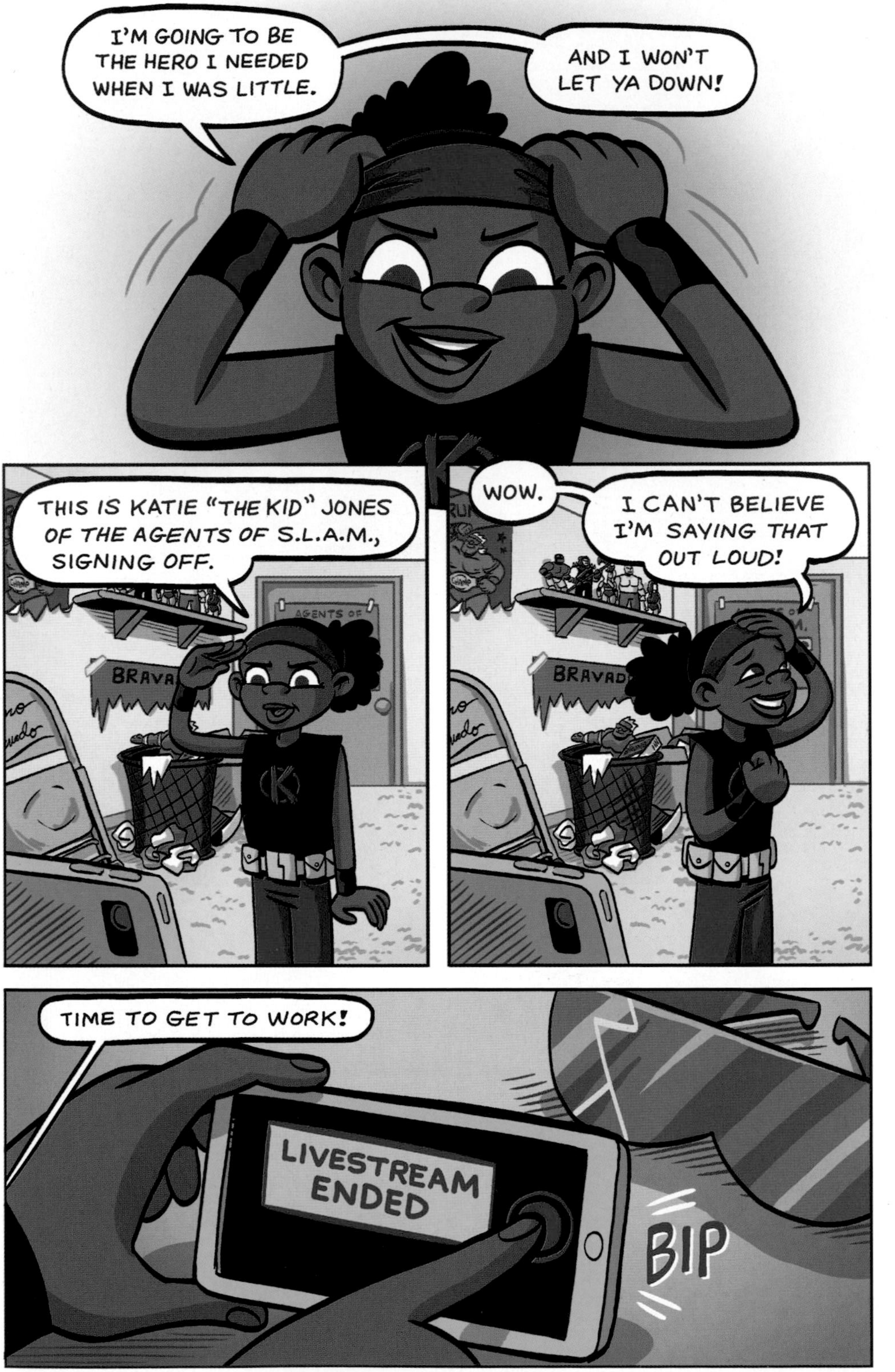
I'M GOING TO BE THE HERO I NEEDED WHEN I WAS LITTLE.
AND I WON'T LET YA DOWN!
THIS IS KATIE "THE KID" JONES OF THE AGENTS OF S.L.A.M., SIGNING OFF.
WOW.
I CAN'T BELIEVE I'M SAYING THAT OUT LOUD!
TIME TO GET TO WORK!
LIVESTREAM ENDED
BIP

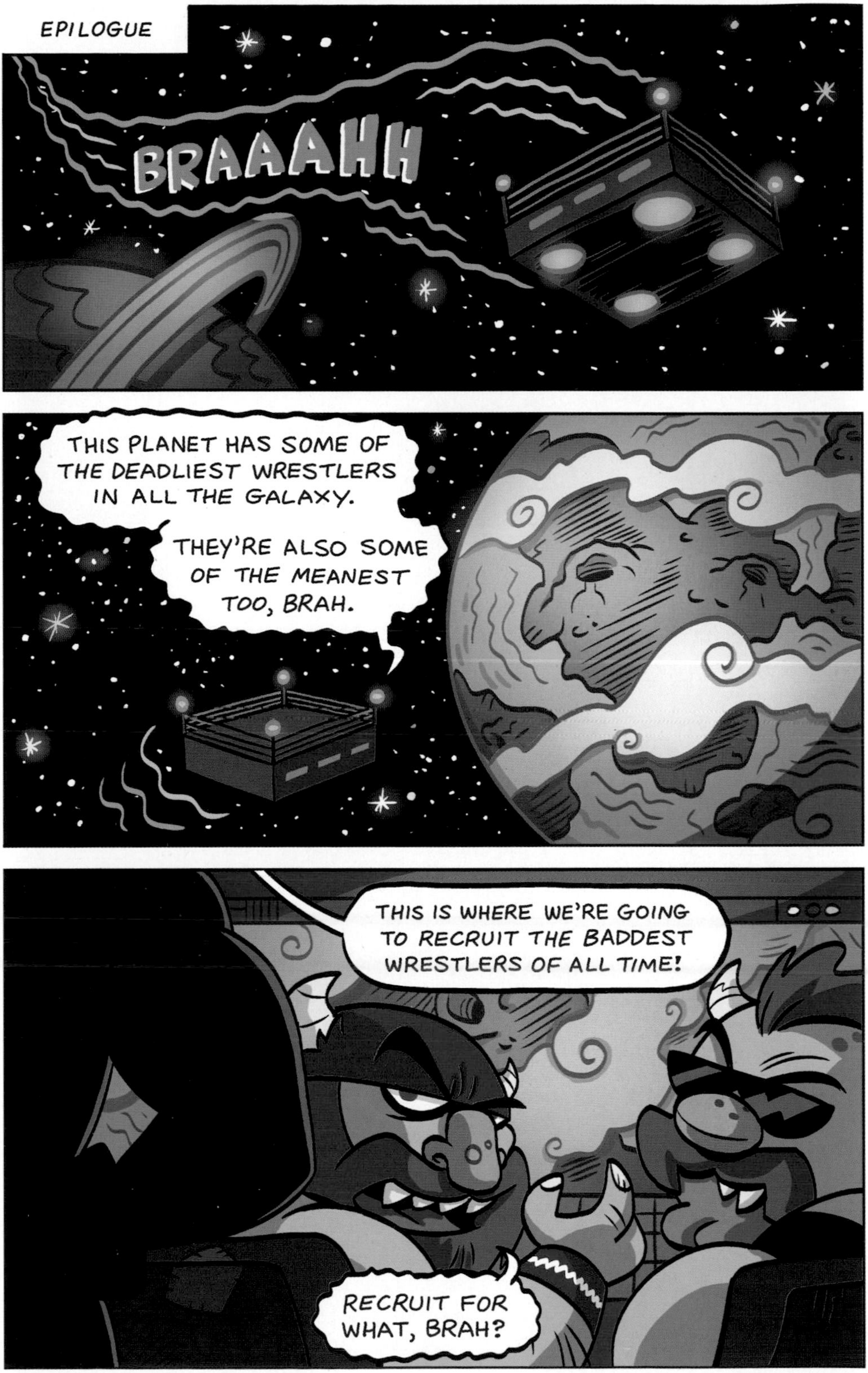
EPILOGUE
BRAAAHH
THIS PLANET HAS SOME OF THE DEADLIEST WRESTLERS IN ALL THE GALAXY.
THEY'RE ALSO SOME OF THE MEANEST TOO, BRAH.
THIS IS WHERE WE'RE GOING TO RECRUIT THE BADDEST WRESTLERS OF ALL TIME!
RECRUIT FOR WHAT, BRAH?

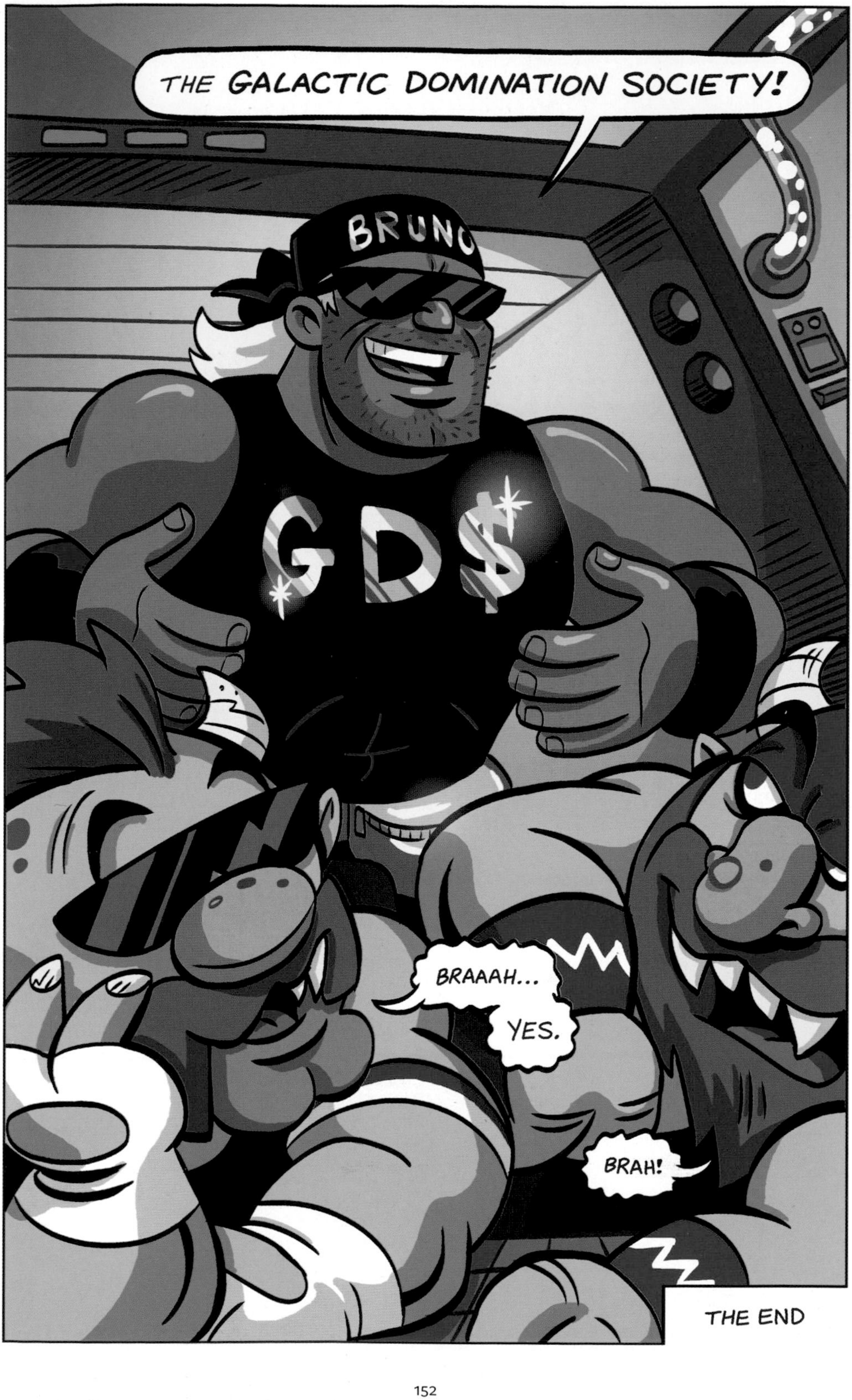
THE GALACTIC DOMINATION SOCIETY!
BRUNO
GD$
BRAAAH...
YES.
BRAH!
THE END

★★★ BONUS CONTENT

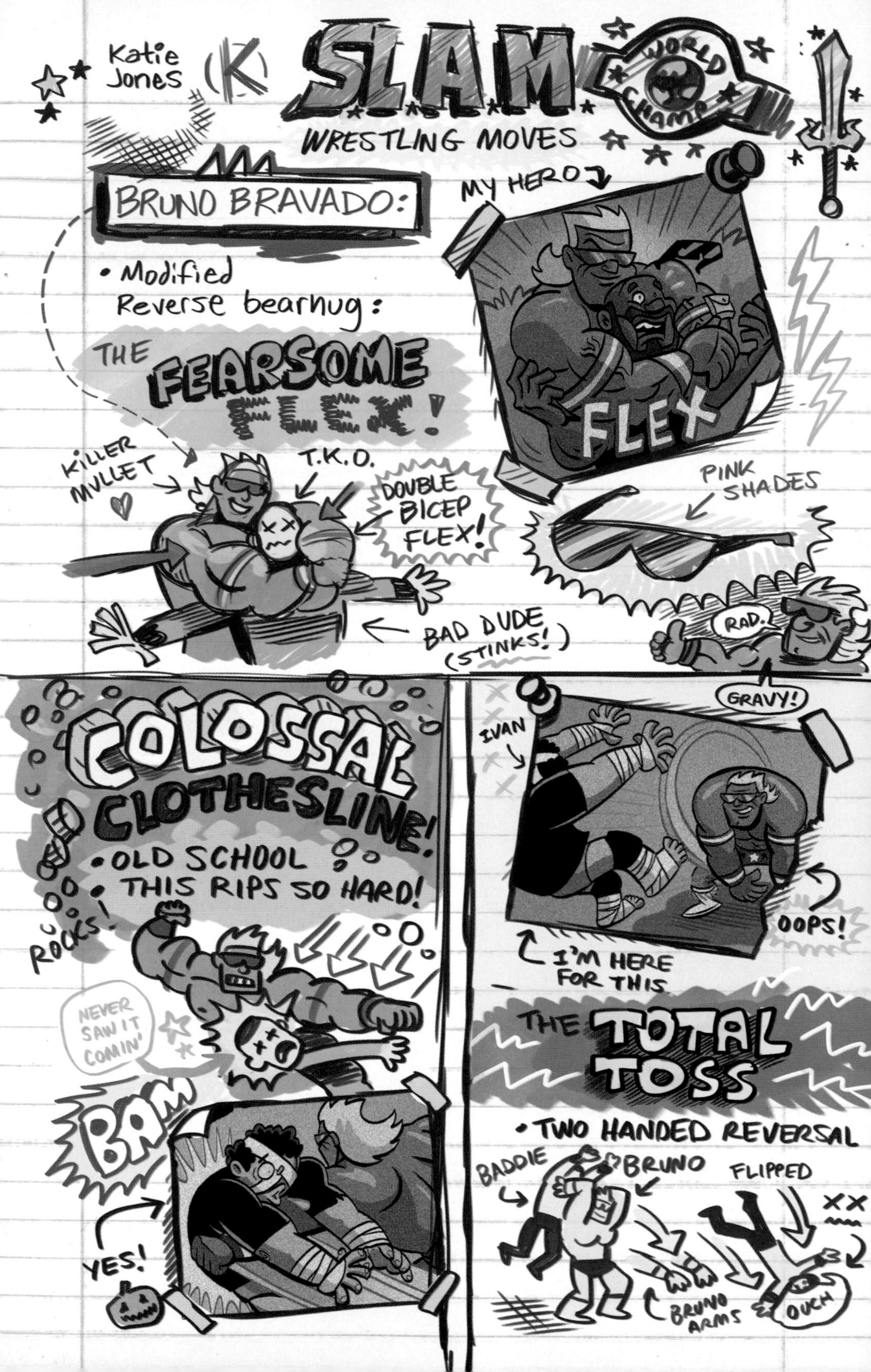
Katie Jones
SLAM
WORLD CHAMP
WRESTLING MOVES
BRUNO BRAVADO:
MY HERO
• Modified Reverse bearhug:
THE FEARSOME FLEX!
FLEX
KILLER MULLET
T.K.O.
DOUBLE BICEP FLEX!
PINK SHADES
BAD DUDE (STINKS!)
RAD.
GRAVY!
COLOSSAL CLOTHESLINE!
• OLD SCHOOL
• THIS RIPS SO HARD!
ROCKS!
NEVER SAW IT COMIN'
BAM
YES!
IVAN
OOPS!
I'M HERE FOR THIS
THE TOTAL TOSS
• TWO HANDED REVERSAL
BADDIE
BRUNO
FLIPPED
BRUNO ARMS
OUCH

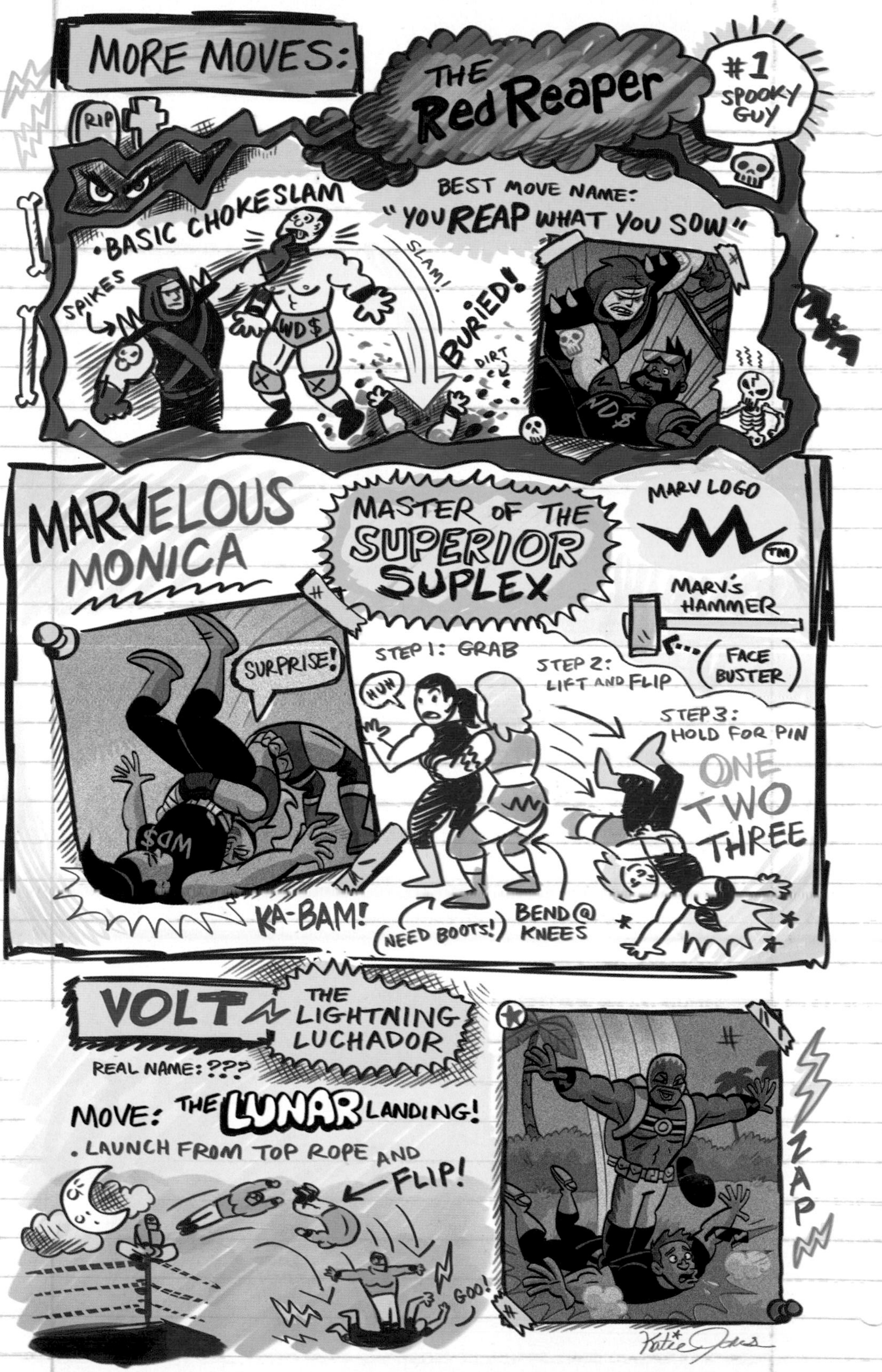
MORE MOVES:
THE Red Reaper
#1 SPOOKY GUY
RIP
BEST MOVE NAME:
"YOU REAP WHAT YOU SOW"
• BASIC CHOKESLAM
SPIKES
WD$
SLAM!
BURIED!
DIRT
MARVELOUS MONICA
MASTER OF THE SUPERIOR SUPLEX
MARV LOGO
TM
MARV'S HAMMER
(FACE BUSTER)
SURPRISE!
STEP 1: GRAB
HUH
STEP 2: LIFT AND FLIP
STEP 3: HOLD FOR PIN
ONE
TWO
THREE
WD$
KA-BAM!
(NEED BOOTS!)
BEND @ KNEES
VOLT THE LIGHTNING LUCHADOR
REAL NAME: ???
MOVE: THE LUNAR LANDING!
. LAUNCH FROM TOP ROPE AND FLIP!
GOO!
ZAP

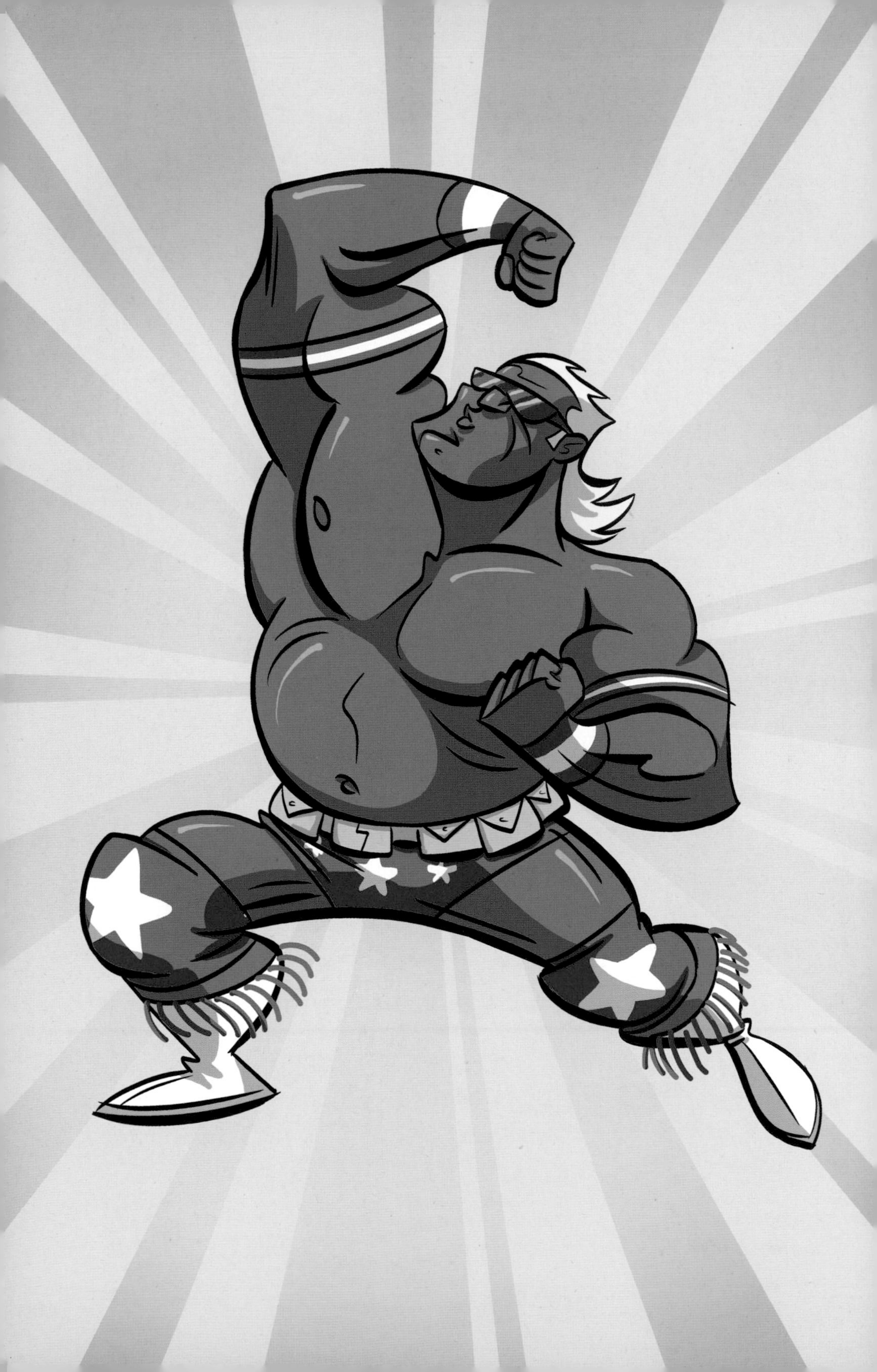

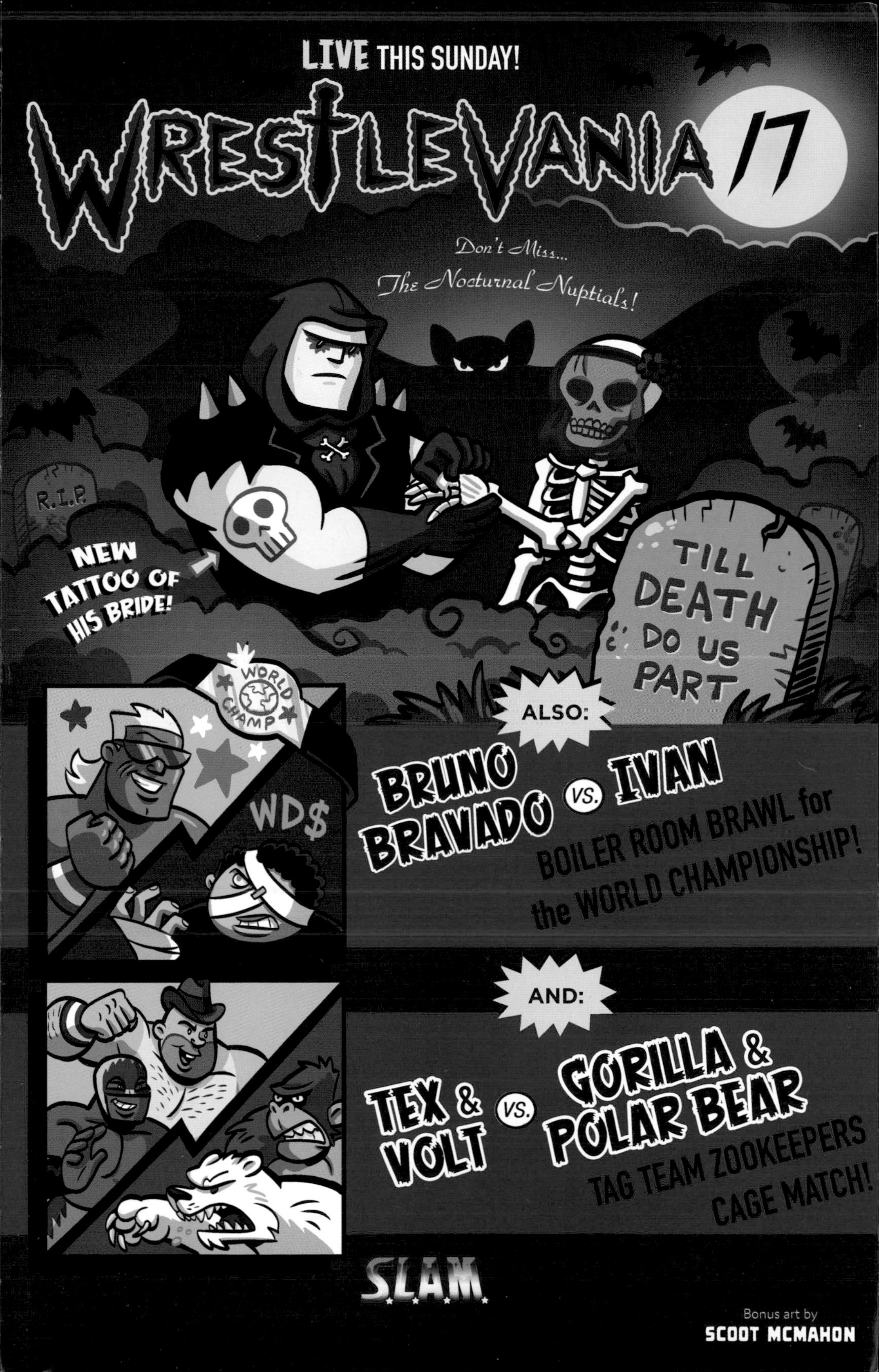
LIVE THIS SUNDAY!
WRESTLEVANIA 17
Don't Miss...
The Nocturnal Nuptials!
R.I.P.
NEW TATTOO OF HIS BRIDE!
TILL DEATH DO US PART
ALSO:
WORLD CHAMP
WD$
BRUNO BRAVADO VS. IVAN
BOILER ROOM BRAWL for the WORLD CHAMPIONSHIP!
AND:
TEX & VOLT VS. GORILLA & POLAR BEAR
TAG TEAM ZOOKEEPERS CAGE MATCH!
SLAM
Bonus art by
SCOOT MCMAHON

ACKNOWLEDGMENTS

To Dad, Sarah, and Eric, who have always been in my corner since day one.

To Scott "Scoot" McMahon, who is the best co-creator and friend anyone could ask for. Working with him is a dream, and I look forward to making more books with him. The world's greatest tag-team partner to have on your side.

To Heidi Black, who did an incredible job on the colors and helped really make this book pop.

To Natalie, for your endless support and advice and guidance and love. There's no one I'd rather eat snacks with than you.

To Andrea Colvin, who helped give this book life and kept it alive during some strange times.

To Grace Scheipeter, who understood our vision and guided us toward that goal and helped us create something special.

To all the behind-the-scenes folks at Oni Press, like Shawna Gore, Amanda Meadows, Holly Atchinson, Charlie Chu, James Lucas Jones, Desiree Rodriguez, Chris Cerasi, Alex Segura, and Henry Barajas. You do thankless work, and you all do great work, and it's a pleasure working with you.

Lots of love to all the local comic shops that have supported my work from the beginning, like Patrick and Dal at Challengers, Nick and Selene at Alleycat, Raphael at Chicago Comics, Aw Yeah Comics, and many more.

This one goes out to each and every wrestler out there, whether it's in the indie circuit or big leagues, who sacrifices everything to put on a good show. The amount of love and blood and tears and talent it takes to put on a match is a constant inspiration, and this book wouldn't be possible without you.

Lots of love to all the librarians and educators out there, too.

 -DAVE

To Kendra, for her love, support, and sacrifices, not only during the creation of this book, but always.

To Oliver and Felicity, for providing continuous inspiration and joy.

To Mom, Dad, Tim, Jeff, Amy, Alivia, Connor, Carole, Jim, Emily, Rick, Travis, Kayla, and Corinne, for your love, support, and words of encouragement.

To my co-creator and tag-team partner, Dave; thank you for being a good friend and eating all the pizza while I did all of the work. Let's do this again, BROTHER!

To Heidi Black, who's coloring and artistic feedback helped bring our book to life.

To our Aw Yeah Comics family: Art, Franco, Johnny, Brother Bear, Mike, the other Mike, Kurt, Alejandro, Christy, and Skoke, for being awesome friends. Without Aw Yeah Comics, there would be no Scoot and Dave!

To Andrea and Grace, who believed in our book and pulled us back into the fight when we were ready to tap out!

To Oni Press for being super easy to work with, especially Chris Cerasi and Desiree Rodriguez for helping us to the finish line!

To Rockwell, for assisting in bringing the S.L.A.M. name to life.

To the RHS Wolfpac (Kurt, Ian, Eric, and Luke) for never turning your back.

To the teachers who inspired, encouraged, and promoted storytelling and art.

To the pro wrestling community and the wrestlers who love comic books, like Christopher Daniels and Frankie Kazarian, for all of your kindness and support.

Finally, to family and friends living in or near the great city of Rossford, Ohio, for believing in a boy who loved drawing and cheered him on no matter what!

 -SCOOT

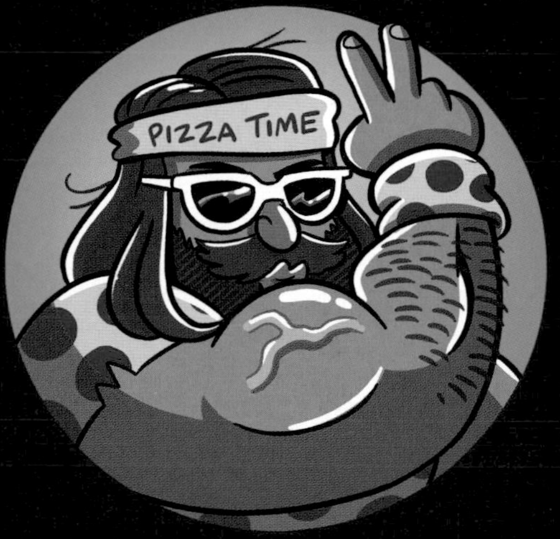
PIZZA TIME

DAVE SCHEIDT is a writer from Chicago, Illinois. When he's not making comic books, he enjoys eating pizza. He's the writer and co-creator of *Wrapped Up* with Scoot McMahon and *Mayor Good Boy* with Miranda Harmon.

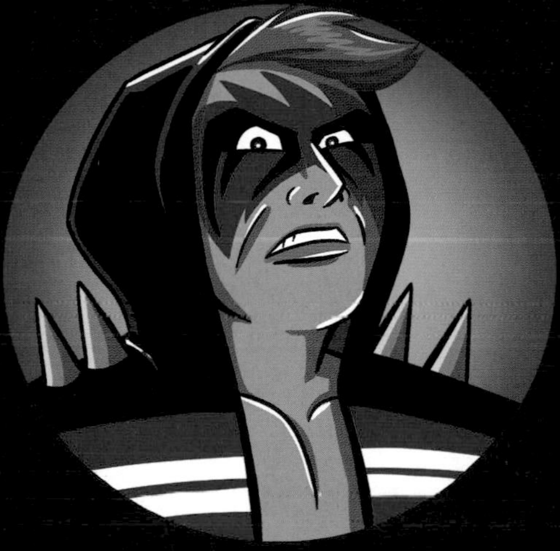

SCOOT MCMAHON is a versatile cartoonist based out of Rossford, Ohio. His catalogue of comics includes *Wrapped Up* (Oni/Lion Forge), *Tales from the Con* (Image), *Aw Yeah, Comics* (Dark Horse), *Sami the Samurai Squirrel,* and *Spot on Adventure* (Action Lab). Scoot is currently working on books for Source Point Press and DC Comics. When Scoot isn't cartooning, he enjoys dropping flying elbows from the top rope!

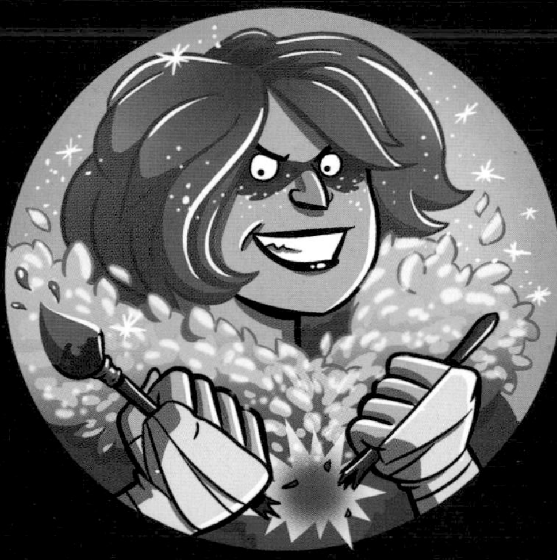

HEIDI BLACK makes art magic in their Cincinnati apartment. Their other works include a piece in the Eisner-winning anthology *Puerto Rico Strong,* and the graphic-novel series *Sons of Fire*, both written by Adam L. Garcia. Heidi also spends a good deal of time playing video games, and even more time keeping their cat off of their art (usually unsuccessfully).

"GREAT FUN!" -Dav Pilkey, creator of Captain Underpants and Dog Man
Dave Scheidt & Scoot McMahon
WRAPPED UP
#1 COOLEST DAD

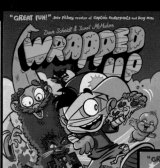

WRAPPED UP VOL. 1

By Dave Scheidt and Scoot McMahon

Milo is just your average twelve-year-old boy. His loving parents are mummies, his best friend is an old wizard, and his babysitters are witches. When Milo isn't busy at school or visiting the comic book store, he loves to hang out with cool teen vampires, play with magical kitties, feed a hungry kaiju, and avoid a love-crazed gorilla at all costs. You know, typical kid stuff.

"GREAT FUN!" -Dav Pilkey, creator of Captain Underpants and Dog Man
Dave Scheidt & Scoot McMahon
WRAPPED UP

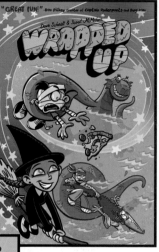

WRAPPED UP VOL. 2

By Dave Scheidt and Scoot McMahon

Your favorite mummy boy, Milo, just can't catch a break! No matter how much he tries to stay out of trouble, trouble finds him! Snacks go missing during a camping trip, his dad gets pulled into a dangerous martial arts tournament, and his best friend ends up in Wizard Prison! No matter how weird the circumstances, Milo will always come through to save the day!

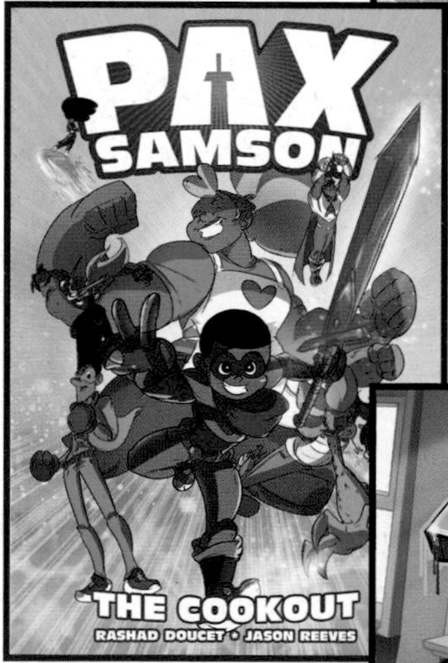

PAX SAMSON
THE COOKOUT
RASHAD DOUCET • JASON REEVES

PAX SAMSON: THE COOKOUT

By Rashad Doucet and Jason Reeves

When it comes to the kitchen, no one knows cooking better than twelve-year-old Pax Samson. He's a hero when it comes to testing recipes and supplying copious amounts of Dragon Noodle Soup at his family's cookouts. It's tough being a master chef, though, when the rest of your family are world-famous superheroes, and they expect Pax to take up the beacon to keep the world safe with his telekinetic powers.

SCI-FU
Book 1
KICK IT OFF
YEHUDI MERCADO

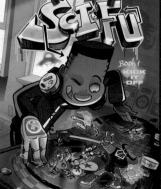

SCI-FU: KICK IT OFF

By Yehudi Mercado

Set in 1980s Brooklyn, a young DJ accidentally summons a UFO that transports his family, best friend, and current crush to the robot-dominated planet of Discopia. He'll have to drop the perfect beat to save his crew and get back to his block in Brooklyn.

ONI PRESS

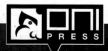

CHECK OUT THESE ONI TITLES!